"I'VE BEEN LOOKING FOR YOU . . .

. . . I believe you have something of mine."

When she tried to go the other way, Julian blocked her with his other arm. She did look at him then. His jaw was set, his brown eyes steely. Her heart beat like a fist against her ribs. "I have nothing of yours," she whispered. That, after all, was no lie.

He leaned toward her, bending near, close enough that she could hear the rain on his hat. "We both know you do. What game do you play?"

"It's no game. You aren't safe here," she warned him. But when his arm wrapped around her waist and pinned her between his body and the wall, she knew she wasn't safe either.

BOOK YOUR PLACE ON OUR WEBSITE AND MAKE THE READING CONNECTION!

We've created a customized website just for our very special readers, where you can get the inside scoop on everything that's going on with Zebra, Pinnacle and Kensington books.

When you come online, you'll have the exciting opportunity to:

- View covers of upcoming books

- Read sample chapters

- Learn about our future publishing schedule (listed by publication month *and author*)

- Find out when your favorite authors will be visiting a city near you

- Search for and order backlist books from our online catalog

- Check out author bios and background information

- Send e-mail to your favorite authors

- Meet the Kensington staff online

- Join us in weekly chats with authors, readers and other guests

- Get writing guidelines

- AND MUCH MORE!

**Visit our website at
http://www.kensingtonbooks.com**

AUDREY
and the
MAVERICK

ELAINE LEVINE

ZEBRA BOOKS
KENSINGTON PUBLISHING CORP.
http://www.kensingtonbooks.com

ZEBRA BOOKS are published by

Kensington Publishing Corp.
119 West 40th Street
New York, NY 10018

All Kensington titles, imprints, and distributed lines are available at special quantity discounts for bulk purchases for sales promotion, premiums, fund-raising, educational, or institutional use.

Special book excerpts or customized printings can also be created to fit specific needs. For details, write or phone the office of the Kensington Special Sales Manager: Attn. Special Sales Department. Kensington Publishing Corp., 119 West 40th Street, New York, NY 10018. Phone: 1-800-221-2647.

Zebra and the Z logo Reg. U.S. Pat. & TM Off.

ISBN-13: 978-1-4201-0552-0
ISBN-10: 1-4201-0552-3

First Printing: February 2010

10 9 8 7 6 5 4 3 2 1

Printed in the United States of America

*This book is dedicated to my brave,
extraordinary daughter,
who serves in the U.S. Coast Guard.
Fair winds and a following sea, Ryan.
Your father and I are very proud of you.*

And remember—never, ever, settle.

Chapter 1

Defiance, Dakota Territory, May 1868

Audrey Sheridan peeked around the corner of an abandoned store, watching her mark come closer. Her palms were damp and her hands shook. She'd practiced the maneuver she would use to steal his purse a hundred times in the last two days, but now that the time was here, she doubted her ability to see it through.

Julian McCaid was less than half a block away. He lifted his wide-brimmed Stetson and swept a hand through his thick dark hair. Resettling his hat, he scanned the street near where she stood. The energy of his gaze rolled in her direction like a hot desert wind.

Withdrawing into the cover of the alley, she listened to his boots crunch in the gravel of the dirt road. When he came even with her, she stepped in front of him and reached for his coin purse. Fast as a whip, he snatched her wrist. She gasped and looked up, in time to see shock and recognition register in his eyes.

The 5:00 p.m. Cheyenne stage had just arrived, and passengers had begun filing down the street toward them, heading for Maddie's Boardinghouse. She yanked at her wrist and he let her go. She quickly drifted into the small crowd and slipped away, her heartbeat overriding all other sound as she began to run. She didn't stop—didn't dare give her conscience time to catch up to her actions. The sheriff had been very clear in describing the consequences should she fail to engage McCaid's attention.

She took a circuitous route to the sheriff's, careful that she wasn't being followed. At the side stairs leading up to his apartment, one of his men stepped in front of her, blocking her. His gaze leisurely moved over her, a boldness he would never have attempted before she'd become the sheriff's flunky. She went around him and climbed to the second floor. Her fingers gripped the neck of the small pouch until her nails dug into the palm of her hand. She pounded on his door with her fisted hand.

One of the sheriff's men opened it. "It's Sheridan," he said, looking at her but speaking to someone behind him.

"Let her in."

Audrey moved stiffly into the room. She looked at each of the five men inside—Sheriff Kemp and four gunmen, two of whom she didn't recognize. Kemp always had new gunfighters loitering about town. It wasn't worth getting to know them; they never stayed around long.

The sheriff leaned against his scruffy wooden table and waited for her to speak. She tossed him the leather pouch and watched as he poured it out on his desk. Light from the window at the front of the room flashed off the metal star on his chest, brightening a spot on the gritty floor as he leaned forward to count her take.

"Ten dollars. Hardly worth the trouble." He frowned as he looked her over. "What are you dressed like that for?"

"I didn't want McCaid to recognize me."

A rattle of laughter started deep in his chest. He covered his mouth with his fist as if to stop himself, but by the time the sound hit the air, it was a high-pitched, dirty giggle that his fist did nothing to hide.

"Oh, he's gonna recognize you. By the time he's finished with you, he's gonna know you with your clothes, without your clothes, and in any stupid getup you want to wear." He looked at her as he fondled McCaid's purse. "You done good, Sheridan. He'll take the bait. I know it."

Audrey gritted her teeth and fought to suppress a shudder. She hated this town and the sheriff and his men. She would see this terrible thing to its end, then leave Defiance. There had to be work for an honest girl in Cheyenne or Denver. There had to be someplace where she, her brother, and her foster children would be safe from his manipulations.

Sensing her resistance, Kemp narrowed his eyes. He crossed the room to her. Yanking her hat off, he dug his hand in her hair and twisted hard. "You start chattering, girl, and them kids of yours will find you with your neck slit one fine morning," he hissed. "You're nothing. *Nothing*. You hear me?"

"I hear you," she bit out, only to have her head yanked once more.

"And if you think that half-breed sheep farmer's gonna help you, you better think it over. Every wrong step you make will cost you a kid." He grinned, baring yellowed teeth in a venomous smile. "I reckon you got eight chances to get it right. Then there's still your brother."

Audrey clamped her jaw shut both to stop its quivering

and to keep from telling Kemp what she thought of him. He tightened his grip. She tried to free herself, but his hand was fisted too deeply in her hair. "You keep the breed busy for a month. You hear me, girl? I need a month."

Trying to appear tougher than she felt, she gave him a bored glare. "I hear you."

"Get outta here." He flung her away, shoving her toward the door and tossing her hat after her. "Get the hell outta here."

Audrey picked up her hat and left Kemp's apartment. Walking down the steps to the street, she moved blindly. Woodenly. She looked toward the far end of town, her eyes seeking solace in the white and blue mountain ridges that ripped into the sky.

There had to be more—so much more than this. Why hadn't she seen this situation coming? She thought back over the past month, the past year. There had been plenty of signs—the drop in the number of customers who sent her their laundry, the school's closing, the abandoned businesses on Main Street. She'd been so preoccupied caring for the kids, she hadn't noticed the gradual shift in power from the town's law-abiding citizens to the sheriff's growing number of gang members.

And now it was too late.

Heavy clouds thickened across the sky, darkening the town as a spring storm quickly blew in. The air had a chill about it and a soothing damp smell she drew greedily into her lungs. It was going to pour. The street was emptying of people as the few who were about hurried out of the rain. Something across the way drew her attention. Frowning, she tried to see what it was, even as the hairs tingled at the back of her neck.

McCaid.

He stepped down from the boardwalk in front of the old hotel and stopped. He turned slowly and faced the alleyway. Four roughnecks gathered in a half circle around him. He stood there—stood still—and let them draw near.

Audrey felt sick to her stomach. The four of them would tear him apart. She looked away. It wasn't her business. *He* wasn't her business. She should keep on moving. If McCaid couldn't handle the trouble in Defiance, he shouldn't have come back. She looked his way again. Kemp's boys were almost within arm's reach of him. It wasn't fair. She'd already hit him—there couldn't be anything left for them to take. The wet wind brought a whisper of cruel laughter her way.

Four against one wasn't right.

She crossed the street, determination making her heart thunder, her pace quicken. They were closing in on him. She broke into a run and reached the pack of roughnecks in time to slip between them and McCaid. Backing up against him, she glared at the four facing him. "Not today, Paul, Hammer." She eyed the sheriff's men warily. She knew only the two, but she'd seen the others hanging around town lately.

"Get out of the way, girl." Hammer leaned toward her. Audrey spread her arms out at her sides, heedless of the ridiculous sight she made. The top of her head barely came to McCaid's chin. His shoulders were twice the width of hers. Her spread arms protected only the top of his thighs.

"It's no use," she growled, hoping they caught her meaning.

"Shit, Sheridan! He's only just come in."

"Maybe if you hadn't needed to round up a gang—" she suggested.

Anger flashed in Hammer's bleary eyes. He grabbed her collar, lifting her toward him only to have an equally large hand twist his collar and hold him at bay.

"Let her go," McCaid quietly ordered, "now." Never had a man's voice affected Audrey as his did. It was deep and resonated with quiet authority. Hammer's eyes widened as he looked over her head at McCaid. He set her free with a string of curses and stormed away. The others followed close behind.

Audrey drew a ragged breath, finally becoming aware she hadn't been breathing. Rain began to fall in earnest. For the length of a heartbeat, neither she nor McCaid moved. She listened to the rain plink against the adjacent building, acutely aware of him standing behind her. Slowly, careful to keep her face shadowed by her hat, she turned around. Her gaze collided with his chest, and her mind absorbed random images of him, like a patchwork. The heavy duster he wore over his gray wool suit. The coffee-colored splotches of rain spreading and connecting into ever-larger blotches at his shoulders. His hard jaw with its afternoon growth of dark beard. The water pooling on his hat brim and spilling off the back.

She felt the weight of his gaze but avoided looking at him as she glanced across the street toward the sheriff's office. Drat it all, they could see her from here. Audrey started to edge around him.

His arm shot up in front of her, his hand locking against the side of the building. "A moment, Miss Sheridan. I've been looking for you. I believe you have something of mine."

When she tried to go the other way, he blocked her with his other arm. She did look at him then. His jaw was set, his brown eyes steely. Her heart beat like a fist against her ribs. "I have nothing of yours," she whispered. That, after all, was no lie.

He leaned toward her, bending near, close enough that she could hear the rain on his hat. "We both know you do. What game do you play?"

"It's no game. You aren't safe here," she warned him. But when his arm wrapped around her waist and pinned her between his body and the wall, she knew she wasn't safe either.

Chapter 2

Julian leaned into Audrey. Her hat fell off, exposing her golden hair to the rain. Her pale eyes were huge, full of fear and lies. "In the last half hour, you've both robbed and protected me," he growled, his mouth near hers. "If you want to play games, we'll play—but by my rules."

Her hands pushed against his arms, a puny resistance in the presence of his crushing need to do what he'd wanted to since he met her last year.

Kiss her.

His mouth took hers. His hat shielded her face from the rain. He breathed her scent, a strange mixture of rain and dust and roses. Her lips trembled. From the cold, perhaps. Or maybe he was the one shaking. He moved his mouth against hers, feeling her warmth, waiting for her lips to part and give him access to her soft secrets. His arm curled tighter around her, drawing her against himself. He cupped her head with his other hand, holding her in position for his invasion. She drew a ragged breath, opening for him. His tongue entered her mouth, rolling along the pointy ridges of her teeth, seeking her tongue. He was vaguely aware of her hands moving up his arms, to his shoulders, tightening around his neck.

Her tongue pushed and played against his. His cock shot to life. He moved a leg between hers, easily separating her pant-clad legs, pressing his thigh to the cradle of her hips. She sucked in a breath against his mouth even as her hips bucked him. He rubbed against her and when her thighs clamped his leg, he silently cursed. She was all woman, more responsive than he'd dared dream, but they couldn't do this here, in the rain, in this alley where anyone could see them. He pulled back and stared at her. Her nose was pink, her cheeks flushed. They both breathed heavily under the brim of his hat.

Lightning flashed, followed almost instantly by a deafening clap of thunder. She pushed free and backed a few steps away, glaring at him while rain poured down her face, matting her hair to her cheeks and neck. He retrieved her hat and handed it to her. She pressed her lips together, her eyes condemning him as she gave a quick shake of her head; then she took the hat and turned away.

Julian watched her lope into the sheeting rain, quickly disappearing. He didn't chase her. He couldn't move. He sucked in a deep breath of cold air, forcing his body to simmer down. Unable to reconcile Audrey's actions today with his memory of her, he let his mind slip back to the night they'd first met, almost a year ago. That same sweet scent she wore tonight had risen from her heated skin then as well in the warm summer air. She had boldly watched him throughout their waltz, her gaze stirring things in him. He'd stared into her strange, sage-green eyes and had somehow kept himself from acting on the promise in them—she was, he'd thought, a respectable young woman.

How wrong he'd been.

What mischief was she involved in here? How long had she been picking pockets? Had she thought he wouldn't recognize her? Perhaps he hadn't made as memorable an impression on her as she had on him. He sighed and watched the cloud of his breath dissipate into the rain. Likely he'd made an impression now. He'd have to hunt her down tomorrow and get to the bottom of this.

Wind lashed the rain against him as he moved out of the alley, slapping his coat against his calf. Up the street, the large Homestead Savings and Loans sign hung askew over the bank's gaping doors, squeaking back and forth in the storm. Two saloons stood empty, one with rain pouring into its broken windows and missing door. Countless other businesses were boarded up. Most of the residences at the north end of town were abandoned.

What the hell had happened here? Just last year, Defiance had been a thriving outpost. Now it was all but a ghost town. A movement inside one of the empty buildings caught his attention. He frowned, trying to peer through the downpour, certain he'd seen a man inside. A surreptitious glance around the street revealed someone in the upper window of another abandoned building. Yet another stood on a corner in the shadows and protection of the covered boardwalk. The town was lousy with sentries.

Defiance was ready for Jace.

Julian crossed the street and stepped onto the boardwalk in front of Sam's Saloon and Restaurant, the one remaining watering hole in town. He sent another look around the street, noting the men's positions before he stepped inside. He shrugged out of his coat and hung it and his hat on a peg by the door, then took a seat at a table near the front. Sam's was surprisingly busy, though most tables were filled with cards, not food.

The waiter came by, and Julian ordered the house special—the only meal being cooked that day. Fortunately, it was a thick sirloin and a baked potato. The man returned with the bottle of whiskey and a shot glass he'd ordered. Julian poured a full measure and downed it. Then, leaning back in his seat, he refilled his glass and glared at the amber liquid.

He'd wired Sheriff Kemp with a complaint when his fences had been cut and several of his sheep slaughtered out at Hell's Gulch earlier this spring. When one of his supply wagons had been ambushed and his cook murdered, Julian had wired the deputy U.S. marshal in Cheyenne. Apparently the marshal had received several complaints from the stage line and its passengers about holdups in the area. With so many outposts like Defiance, too many for the government to deal with, Julian had been surprised when he received a response from the marshal letting him know they had hired a resource to clear the sheriff and his gang out of town.

He was even more surprised when that resource turned out to be his old friend, Jace Gage, a man who had made his living since the war as a vigilante for hire, earning himself the nickname "Avenger."

Julian thought back a few years ago when he, Jace, and their friend Sager had fought bushwhackers along the Kansas-Missouri border. Even then, fresh off the farm, Jace had been a phenomenal sharpshooter.

Julian threw back the whiskey and studied the empty glass as two of the hoodlums he'd met in the alley came into Sam's. "Paul" and "Hammer,"Audrey had called them. A couple of rougher-looking cowpunchers Julian had never seen.

Making a cut in the steak the waiter had just brought him, he observed them—not with his eyes, but with his senses in a game his grandfather taught him, a game he'd practiced since childhood. He drew their smell into his nostrils. He listened to the sound—the rhythm— of their footsteps. He heard their low, almost furtive, laughter. He felt their eyes on him, felt the tension in the room shift.

They went to the bar. Julian heard the barkeep slide a couple of full glasses their way. He took another bite of meat.

"Hey, Sam—don't that sign out front say 'No Injuns'?" The barkeep didn't answer. The cowpoke narrowed his eyes.

"Sam, I'm talking to you."

"Forget it, Paul. I just got my front window fixed from the last fellow you thought shouldn't be in here."

"Sam," Hammer chimed in, "there's a reason you put that sign up."

"I didn't put it up."

"Don't matter." He shrugged. "You got a reputation to uphold. You can't let just anyone come in and mix with upstandin' folk." He leaned over the bar. "It could get real expensive for you."

"Hey, breed!" Paul turned to the man in question. "Didn't you see that sign out front?"

Julian swallowed a grim smile with the meat he was chewing, waiting for the violence to come his way. He cut into his potato, ignoring the two at the bar.

"Think he's deaf, Hammer? He wouldn't be ignorin' us, now, would he?"

"Maybe he don't speak English. Maybe we should explain things to him," Hammer suggested.

Paul swallowed the last of his beer and swaggered up

on one side of Julian, Hammer on the other. "You talk English, breed?" Hammer leaned two hands on the other side of the table and bent close to Julian's face.

Julian sat back in his seat and spread his hands out before him. "Gentlemen, I'd appreciate it if you'd back away from my supper. Your smell makes this fine steak taste rancid."

Hammer gathered spit in his mouth and sent it splattering into the plate before him.

Julian's bland expression never faltered, and seeing that, an edge entered Paul's eyes. He looked Julian over, noticing his fine gray city suit, the crisp whiteness of his shirt. Paul grinned and swiped at some dust on Julian's shoulder.

"He dresses fussy like a girl, Hammer. Think he likes petticoats too?"

"I like petticoats one hell of a lot more than I do the two of you!" Julian growled. His foot snaked out to his side and hooked around Paul's ankle, jerking his leg out from beneath him.

Hammer reached for Julian's throat, but the cowpuncher wasn't fast enough. Julian wrapped his hand behind Hammer's neck and shoved his face into the steak he had spit on. The blow shattered the plate. Hammer screamed, recoiling instantly with a hand over his bloodied, broken nose. Paul made as if to stand, but Julian jammed his elbow into his jaw, laying him out once more on the floor.

Julian rose out of his chair to meet three more men who crossed the room toward him, but before more blows could be exchanged, a burly man entered the saloon and stepped into the fray. He faced the three men.

"That's enough." He held up a hand. "This ain't any way to welcome Mr. McCaid back to Defiance."

The three newcomers moved away, eyes narrowed, bodies still tense. "Get these two outta here." He waved irritably in the direction of Paul and Hammer. "They're stinking things up."

Sheriff Kemp turned to face him. "I'm sorry, Mr. McCaid—"

Julian extended his hand to the local dignitary. "Forget it, Sheriff."

"I'd heard you were back in town, but I hoped it wasn't true. Seems there's always a mess to clean up when you're around."

Julian grinned. "I got a feeling that's only beginning."

The sheriff leveled a hard look on him. "I don't want you stirring up trouble. There's enough to deal with in this town as it is."

"That's a true statement, what with the Avenger on his way. You've riled some powerful people, Sheriff."

Kemp's face went still. A hush fell over the room. "What do you know about the Avenger, McCaid?"

"I know he leaves few men standing—few criminals, that is. If I were you, I'd close up shop and search out a more hospitable place to run your little gang."

Kemp shook his head. "Can't oblige you there. I got a fondness for Defiance. Besides, the Avenger's just one man. I got two dozen and more on the way."

Julian met his look. "That a fact? Then while we're drawing battle lines, Sheriff, you best tell your men anyone visiting Hell's Gulch without the decency to use the front drive will be shot on sight as a trespasser."

The sheriff's mouth thinned slightly. "You ain't very smart, are you, boy? Settin' yourself up against me."

"I guess that will be decided by whichever of us survives. You should know the odds are in my favor."

The sheriff's eyes narrowed. He made a sucking noise out of the side of his mouth, then nodded. "Sam!" he barked, his narrowed eyes still on Julian. "Give Mr. McCaid here another steak. His has gotten cold." He touched the edge of his hat, then slammed out of the saloon.

As sudden as its onset, the chaos was over. Julian rolled his shoulders to loosen the tension lodged there. He looked at Sam standing behind the bar.

The barkeep grinned and held his hand out to Julian. "Glad you're back, Mr. McCaid."

Chapter 3

Audrey stepped into the road early the next morning. Her boots caught in the mud as she crossed the street between two blocks. She'd spent another sleepless night, worrying about what the day would bring. She could no more outrun what was coming than she could a tornado. Her best option was to keep busy until it hit.

She'd just finished delivering yesterday's laundry to the last of her remaining clients. The sun was still low enough that shadows from the buildings stretched the width of the road. In a couple of hours, the air would be dry and hot, soaking up the moisture from last night's rain. The roads would crack, and dust would once again blow through Defiance.

Her month with McCaid would have started by then.

She passed the alleyway where he'd cornered her yesterday, manhandling her as if she were one of Sam's girls. Her eyes fixed on the wall where he'd pinned her, her pace slowed and blood warmed her face as she remembered the feel of his body pressed against hers, the way his mouth moved over hers.

She forced herself to look away and encountered the

devil himself. A peculiar weakness stole through her limbs as she met his dark-eyed gaze. What was he doing up and about so early? Good heavens, now what? She wasn't ready! Not yet! Should she brave it out or run? But where was there to run in this stupid town?

She climbed the steps, feeling as if she were walking into the jaws of a prowling mountain lion. "Mr. McCaid," she greeted him with icy reserve.

"Miss Sheridan." He nodded at her.

She passed him, her stride purposeful. He fell into step behind her. She quickened her pace, as did he. Cool fingers of dread swept down her spine, warning her, hurrying her along.

She neared Jim's place and slipped down the alley on this side of the store. Dropping her empty laundry basket, she lifted her skirts and ran. If she could just make it to the back of the building, she could lose him. Her boots crunched in the gravel. Her heart was pounding with the beat of a war drum. The prickly weeds growing between the buildings grabbed at her skirt and scraped her legs.

Still he was gaining on her.

She reached the far corner of the building just as McCaid's black-clad arm snatched her about the waist and reeled her back against him. She breathed in harsh, rasping gasps, but he was barely winded—she'd never had a chance of eluding him.

He bent and whispered in her ear, "Why did you run?"

Shivers of warning rippled through her flesh. "Why did you chase me?"

"You have something of mine."

Audrey tried to hold herself erect, but his arms were crossed over hers, immobilizing her. "I told you last night—I have nothing of yours. Let me go."

His arms curled tighter about her, his hold viselike. She was unable to keep the fear from her voice. "Let me go!" she demanded. She wiggled and writhed, but to no avail. If his grip tightened any farther, she would not be able to breathe. She stomped on his boot, but other than winning a grunt from him, her struggles had no effect. "I don't want this!"

Julian looked down and realized she was gripping his arm as tightly as he held her. "Don't want what?" He felt a splash of warm liquid on his hand. "What is it that you don't want?"

Jim came around the corner, his storekeeper's apron blazing white in the shadowy alleyway. "Audrey! McCaid!" His gaze swept over them. Audrey stiffened in his arms. "What's going on here?" Jim shouted at them.

Julian felt like a boy caught with a mouthful of cookie before supper, standing as he was with his arms wrapped around Audrey's lush, sweet-smelling body. "Answer him, Miss Sheridan."

"Let me go."

"No. You run like a goddamned rabbit. Tell Jim what's going on." He felt the breath she drew as she straightened in his arms. She dashed the moisture from her face with the tips of her fingers.

"This sheep keeper thinks I stole money from him."

"You did steal my money. I watched you take it."

"Let her go, McCaid." Jim's voice was less confrontational, modulated by what sounded like regret. Or disappointment. "How much did she take? I will pay you back."

"No, you won't, Jim! If he thinks I took it, let him take me to the sheriff. Don't get involved," Audrey warned.

"Twenty dollars," Julian answered, though his mind

had snagged on the fact that the sheriff had entered the equation.

Audrey gasped, flashing an angry look up at him. "There was only ten dollars!"

He grinned. "So you admit to taking it."

"No."

He studied her. Her mouth and her eyes lied, pleading an innocence that conflicted with the truth, an innocence that was long gone. Instinct whispered this situation wasn't as simple as it seemed, but the feel of her slim body in his arms and her curvy backside against his thighs deafened him to its warning.

He turned her to face him. She was as beautiful as he remembered, medium in height, lithe and willowy. Her eyes were still a haunting green, pale like wild sage, wrapped in mystery by the fringe of her thick, dusky eyelashes. Her face was smooth and cream-colored. Little freckles speckled her nose and cheeks. Twin indentations in her cheeks hinted at dimples that would appear when she smiled, which she wasn't doing now.

Why was she so eager to get the sheriff involved? He'd not be the one to dispense justice. Perhaps she and Kemp were in this together. Julian was curious to see how the two of them got along. "Let's go visit the sheriff. I'm sure he'll unravel this mess."

Julian guided Audrey out of the alley and back into the street. The storekeeper stayed close on their heels. Julian looked at Audrey as they walked. Her golden brown hair hung in waves off to one side in a collapsed bun, yet she moved beside him with calm resignation like a goddamned queen heading for the chopping block. No remorse. No shame. No hint she regretted stealing from him.

What had he expected? With few exceptions, the remaining townsfolk of Defiance had to be as rotten and corrupt as their sheriff.

As if aware of his perusal, she looked up at him. He stared into her odd, pale eyes, trying to find what it was about her that so unsettled him. She lowered her gaze and faced forward again. Julian, too, looked ahead, closing his mind to the sweep of her dark lashes and the creamy smoothness of her skin. She made him feel as if she, not he, were the victim of this crime.

A lanky yellow sign blew in the morning breeze, marking a low, two-story building as the sheriff's office. He tightened his hold on Audrey as the storekeeper opened the door. Julian exchanged a look with the older fellow, wondering what the man's connection to her was—why was he so willing to concern himself with her business? And why was she so comfortable letting him?

He ducked as he crossed the low threshold into the dark space of the sheriff's office. The smell of sweat and unemptied spittoons was cloying in the small room. A deputy dozed in a chair, his boots propped on the desk, his chin against his chest. The storekeeper closed the door with a loud bang. The deputy lurched to his feet, then crouched as he faced the door to the cells, his gun at the ready. Julian cleared his throat.

The deputy spun around and leveled his gun on them.

Jim sighed. "Put it away, Fred, an' get the sheriff."

"Sure. What's goin' on, Jim?" The deputy's gaze moved to Julian, then crawled over Audrey.

"Just get the sheriff."

A moment later, Sheriff Kemp came down the hallway, hitching up his pants. He set his hands on his hips and glared at the three of them. "A little early for so much commotion, don't you think?"

"Morning, Kemp. I guess that's what happens when thieves run rampant in your streets. This girl stole ten dollars from me yesterday. I'd like to press charges."

"Miss Sheridan? Stole from you?" He looked from Julian to Audrey, one brow arched. "Ten dollars, you say?" He glanced at Julian. His face showed amusement, but his eyes were angry. "You seem to be runnin' into one trouble after another in this town. It pains me to see that, friend." He sighed. "And, Audrey, reckon you can figure how bad you've disappointed me. How many times have I told you where your behavior was leadin' you? I've warned you and worried about you, and now my patience is at an end."

He picked up a large ring of jail keys from the desk behind him. "Let's go, girl. After a week in here with me," he said to Julian, "I doubt she'll steal from you again. She'll learn a lesson about being trustworthy, about paying for her actions."

Watching the proceedings, Julian had a sour feeling in the pit of his stomach. He knew, perhaps better than most, everyone must face the consequences of his—or her—actions. But he didn't care for the way Kemp or his deputy eyed Audrey, or the fact that she had moved fractionally closer to him.

"Don't do this, Sheriff," Jim spoke up. "Don't do this to her."

"I don't think you got a say in the running of this town, Jim." He gave Audrey a penetrating stare as he came forward to get her, and Julian found himself pulling her against his side.

"Forget it," he said.

"What?" Jim and Kemp both blurted.

Julian exchanged a look with Jim over Audrey's head. He didn't like this. The whole damned thing felt like a setup, and even knowing that, he just kept going in. "Forget the whole thing. I've changed my mind." He could feel the rope settling around his neck—this was going to come back to haunt him. "I won't press charges if Miss Sheridan agrees to work off the money she took from me."

She closed her eyes, then released a little huff of breath and looked at him with wary eyes. "How?"

Her voice was a whisper, nothing more. It put him in mind of other whispers, secret ones between lovers. His body tightened. He looked into her eyes, studying her. Clearly, she'd gone bad. Perhaps she'd always been bad; growing up in a town like Defiance would leave its mark on anyone. Nonetheless, he couldn't just hand her over to the sheriff. Tough though she was, she would never survive the bastard.

He steeled himself to his body's reaction, forcing himself to remember she, at some level, was friendly with his friends the Taggerts and wasn't open to a dalliance. "We're in need of a cook out at Hell's Gulch. I'd rather not bring a woman out to the camp, but I will if it lets you repay your debt to me—for a couple of weeks."

He didn't even ask her if she could cook. He didn't want to know. It was the only solution he could find. And no matter what her culinary skill was, it couldn't be worse than the poison the current cook served. Plus, it would get her out of the sphere of Kemp's influence and give Julian time to figure out what to do with her.

"Nope." The sheriff shook his head. "That ain't right. She stole a half month's wages. She should have to work it off for twice the time it would take to earn it. A month." He looked at Audrey. "At least."

Jim frowned. "You can't do that, Audrey. You can't go out there."

"I have no choice."

Jim sent Julian and the sheriff a pained look. He took Audrey aside and spoke to her in hushed tones. "Don't do this. Refuse. How can you leave? You're needed here."

"I don't want to stay with the sheriff," she said through clenched teeth. "Malcolm is almost eighteen. He's old enough to deal with things. He'll do okay."

Who was Malcolm? And deal with what things? Julian wondered. Their voices lowered a fraction, making it impossible for him to hear them. Audrey looked at him, then at the sheriff. Julian followed her gaze, his mood darkening to see the sheriff gloating like a ravenous dog with his paw on a new kill. No way in hell was he leaving her here.

"I accept, Mr. McCaid, but there is a condition," she said as they rejoined the group.

"And it is—?"

"I don't know if you remember, but I have a little girl. She would have to come with me."

Julian was taken aback. He'd completely forgotten about her little girl. And it confirmed his new belief that she'd lost her innocence a long time ago. He nodded his acceptance of her terms, then looked at the sheriff, wondering at his part in this skit. What did he gain by having Audrey at Hell's Gulch?

Jim and Audrey were heading outside, and Julian followed them. He wondered what the obligations were that kept her in town. Children? A husband? Maybe a lover? Maybe Jim was her lover. He certainly seemed protective of her. Was this little girl of hers their daughter?

"You have a day to prepare yourself, Miss Sheridan. I will be at your house tomorrow at dawn. Then we'll head out."

Audrey went straight to the general store. Jim followed her, but neither of them spoke. Since she was leaving town and wasn't sure if she would be able to return before the next month was up, she had better stock her pantry. Sally, Jim's wife, came to the door of the back storeroom and paused, studying her. Audrey tried to keep her face blank, but the older woman began wringing her hands as she hurried around the counter toward her.

"Oh, good Lord. You did it. You did it, didn't you?"

"I had no choice."

"There's always a choice, Audrey Sheridan. You go to Mr. McCaid. You tell him, warn him. He'll help you. He's a good man."

Audrey looked away from Sally, studying the shadowy patterns of the tin ceiling. She had no doubt about McCaid's moral rectitude; it was her own that was in question. The sheriff had left her no options. She knew he would make good on his threats against her family. He'd killed many a man—taking a child's life would be nothing to him. Besides, the less McCaid knew, the safer he would be.

The safer they would all be.

"I'm not going to say anything to him. And you and Jim need to keep silent too. Kemp will turn on you. You've seen his men. They are all over town, watching us. He's into something bad, and we're all in his way."

"Mr. McCaid's no fool. He'll know you're no Jezebel," Sally persisted.

Audrey straightened her back. She couldn't ask these people for help. To do so would just give the sheriff more fuel. "Then I will just have to convince him otherwise." Picking his pocket had to be a good start.

Sally shook her head and turned to her husband. "Jim—"

"Fetch her groceries, Sally," Jim quietly ordered, stopping her complaint.

Sally didn't immediately comply. She smoothed her apron, the corners of her mouth turned downward as she fought to suppress more comments. Drawing a deep breath, she composed herself enough to fill Audrey's order and pack it into a brown-wrapped package.

Jim said nothing as he tallied her purchases; the quiet was oppressive. How could she leave the children? How could she give herself to McCaid?

"That's eleven dollars, Audrey," Jim said quietly.

She counted the money in her reticule. It wasn't enough. It never was enough. "I only have four dollars and fifty cents."

"That'll do."

Audrey handed him the money. "No, it won't, but it's all I have now. I'll pay you the rest, I swear it."

"Audrey—" Jim began.

She shook her head, still unable to look at him. "I have to go. Thanks, as always." Tears burned her eyes, but she refused to shed them.

"Audrey!"

"What?" she asked, dragging her head up.

Jim took his apron off and slapped it on the counter. He exchanged looks with Sally. "We've been thinking— for some time now—that Malcolm is of an age where we could move him up to apprentice. I'd pay him a good wage. A dollar a day. Or he can take his pay in trade."

"You'd do that?"

He nodded. "Malcolm's been working for me a long time, doing odd jobs. He's honest and dependable."

The burning in her eyes was becoming intolerable. She sniffled, then nodded. "Thank you. I'm not sure what I did to earn friends like you and Sally, but I am grateful. I'll send Malcolm to talk to you this afternoon."

"You be careful. You'll be alone out there." Jim opened the door for her. "It can get mighty messy in those working camps." He stopped her on the threshold of his store. "You know what the boys around here have done before and are likely to do again to McCaid and his flock. I expect it'll get real ugly."

Audrey nodded, but his warning had little impact; first she had to find the strength to leave her family. Then she would worry about McCaid's range wars.

Chapter 4

Audrey took a steaming pot from the oven and set it on the stovetop. The children moved into a circle about her, hunger causing them to hover near at hand. She looked at the face of each child. This was their last dinner together for a very long time. What would they do without her? What would she do without them? She gave herself a mental shake and shoved those thoughts aside. There was nothing anyone could do about her situation, and if she broke down in front of the kids, it would only make their parting harder.

She sent the children outside to wash up at the water pump the houses on this end of the street shared. Her neighbor, Leah Morgan, leaned a hip against the counter and glared at her. Leah was the most beautiful girl Audrey had ever seen, with her rich mahogany hair and eyes that were sometimes dark blue, sometimes, as they were now, violet with anger.

"You don't have to do this," Leah quietly declared.

A sharp puff of laughter broke from Audrey's mouth. "What are my choices? He's threatening the children. You know what he's capable of—he shot your father,

Leah. Murdering a child would be nothing to him. I do have to do this."

"I could kill him for you," Leah quietly offered.

A chill rolled down Audrey's spine as she held her friend's unwavering gaze. This was what Kemp had brought them to—pickpocketing and murder. "No, you won't, Leah Morgan. Don't get involved in this. Promise me."

Leah crossed her arms and stayed silent.

"Kemp has half a dozen men around him at all times. They are everywhere—on the corners, in the alleys, on the roofs. As good a hunter as you are, Leah, you would be killed. But even if you were successful, without Kemp, who would keep his men in line? As bad as it is, it could quickly become worse. I have to do what he says."

"But you don't have to give yourself to McCaid. You can find another way of distracting him."

"How?" Audrey's knowledge of men was sadly lacking. She had no idea how she was going to keep him busy for a month, whether she seduced him or not. The children grew noisier outside as they returned from the pump, preventing Leah from answering. Her friend gave her one last glare, then started to put out a stack of plates. Audrey focused on setting out the food—more than any of them had seen in the last month. It was a feast, indeed, with the bread and the big pot of braised rabbit in gravy Leah provided and the mashed potatoes, carrots, peas, and apple pie Audrey made.

She dished out the food, watching the children's anxious, lean faces as they took their plates and waited for her to say grace. The table was too small and there were too few chairs to seat everyone, so they scattered about the room, some sitting on the floor, others on her bed.

The room was silent as Audrey blessed the meal and her growing family. Afterward, the clatter of silverware against plates was the only sound to be heard as everyone concentrated on eating. Audrey's throat was strangely constricted, making it hard to swallow. She moved the food from one side of the plate to the other, hoping her lack of appetite would not be noticed.

Fortunately the silence didn't last. As the meal began to warm their stomachs, the children's chatter began to fill the room. Two of the older ones, Luc and Kurt, regaled the others with a story about McCaid.

"He marched into Sam's," Kurt said. His hazel eyes animated, a lock of blond hair falling into his face, he captured the children's attention like a pied piper. "Bold as you please, he was, and ordered up a big steak. Hammer and Paul tried to scare him off, but he weren't having none of that. When they tried to rough him up—pow!" Kurt slammed his fist into his palm for effect, nearly overturning his plate. "He took care of 'em. He tripped Paul, making him fall so hard his skull cracked open. And he smashed Hammer's nose." Silence engulfed the room as the children listened with rapt attention.

Luc watched the other kids, his dark brown eyes missing nothing. "And he never even got up out of his chair," he added. "He was sitting the whole while!"

"That's enough of such talk, Kurt, Luc," Audrey warned the boys. The reproachful glare Leah gave her did little to alleviate her tension.

"It's true. It happened just like that," Kurt responded. "That's one mean Cherokee. He's come for Kemp. Tired of being stoled blind, they say. Tired of having his sheep slaughtered, his men killed."

"Who says?" she asked, trying to find out who they'd been talking to.

Kurt's gaze shot to Luc. "Folks," he said with a shrug, not looking at her.

Audrey set her plate down. If it was true, if McCaid had come back because of Kemp, things in this town would get mighty bloody. Maybe that was why the sheriff wanted him distracted—he needed a chance to bring in more men. It was doubtful whether anyone involved in the coming trouble would care if children got caught in the crossfire, especially if they were her odd collection of orphans.

"What's wrong, Audrey?" Malcolm asked.

She looked about the room, meeting the eyes of each child. "I'll be leaving tomorrow." The room fell silent. They all knew the sheriff had forced her into an arrangement with McCaid, just not when it was going to start—and hopefully not its true nature. Little Mabel started crying. Colleen patted her shoulder. Luc and Kurt swapped looks, and their conspiratorial exchange was not lost on Audrey.

"Are you coming back?" Joey and Colleen both asked. Leah crossed her arms and frowned at her.

Audrey held up her hands to quiet the room so she could explain. "Of course I'll be back. Mr. McCaid has offered me a job as camp cook. It's only for a month—until he can find a permanent one." The children silently accepted her announcement, and seeing their stoic reaction, she wished for the thousandth time she had gotten them out of Defiance long before this.

"Everything will continue around here as usual. Each of you will still be responsible for the chores assigned to you. Maddie will continue seeing to your lessons. We won't be taking in any washing while I'm away, so there won't be that work to do. Leah will oversee planting the vegetable garden. Jim will buy whatever extras come from the garden—we could put away a little money for the winter, so be sure to give her all the help she needs. I'll be home in a month to help maintain it. Nothing will be ripe by then anyhow."

"Can we come with you? We could help you at Hell's Gulch like we do here," Mabel said.

Audrey shook her head. "Mr. McCaid's ranch is no place for children. I've heard he's paying fighting wages. You know how folks around here feel about sheep—he's expecting trouble. I want you all to stay here, away from the worst of it." Audrey sighed. "I will be taking Amy Lynn with me, however. The rest of you are old enough to look after each other, and you're needed here. She's barely three years old and will just be more work for you."

Audrey ventured a look at Malcolm and winced at the glare he gave her. Choking out an oath, he lurched to his feet and went outside. She was torn between following him and letting him be alone to work through the shock of her news.

Leah got up and took her plate. "Go. Talk to him."

Outside, Audrey saw her brother head down the street toward the empty prairie that surrounded the eastern side of town. "Malcolm! Wait." She ran after him. He neither slowed his pace nor acknowledged her presence. His hands were shoved into the front pockets of his trousers. He was breathing hard through flared nostrils, his lips curled against his teeth.

The night air was cool, and Audrey had run out without a wrap. She crossed her arms and walked quietly beside him. The tall prairie grass hissed and crunched beneath their feet. Grasshoppers jumped out of her way. They walked until they reached a dry creek bed.

Audrey loved her brother more than anyone in the world. She'd been seventeen and he fourteen when they lost their parents almost four years ago. Their father had come back from the war, wounded and ill. He never recovered. And her mother had died later that year—of a broken heart, Audrey was convinced. They were orphaned in Defiance, just the two of them to raise each other, along with Dulcie, Luc, and Mabel.

"McCaid's going to make a whore out of you."

Audrey swallowed hard. "Listen to me very carefully, Malcolm. This isn't McCaid's fault."

"Why did he have to come back anyway?" He glared at her. "Why now, Audrey?"

"I don't know. Something is going on, something bad. You've got to watch the kids, keep them out of trouble." She looked into his eyes, a darker, stormier green than her own. When had he gotten so tall? "When I get back, we're leaving Defiance. We'll go to Cheyenne or Denver. Or even to the States somewhere. Anywhere. We can't stay here. It gets worse every day."

"We'll be ready." He made a face as he fought back a mouthful of words better left unspoken. "I don't want you to go with McCaid. You won't be safe. And it's not right, you out there alone. I should have done something. I should have protected you better."

Audrey closed her eyes. She struggled to find the words to help him accept this situation, but there were none. Her shoulders dropped beneath the weight they carried. Nothing good was going to come of what she would be doing when she left town tomorrow.

"There's nothing you could have done. Nothing

anyone could do. Please, promise me you won't confront the sheriff. He's meaner than I've ever seen him."

He drew her into a tight hug. "Promise me," she insisted, clinging to him.

"I promise I won't do something stupid."

"Malcolm—"

"I promise, Audrey."

She pulled away and looked up at him. "You'll have to hold the children to task for their chores, keep discipline among them. Keep things as normal as possible. I hope I'll be able to come into town occasionally. Leah said she would help with the kids in the afternoons and on Saturdays, while you work. And you know Jim and Sally will do what they can. And Maddie too."

He smiled, acknowledging her with a nod, but even dusk's fading light couldn't hide the heartache in his eyes.

The children were asleep. It had been easier than usual to get them to settle down since their stomachs were full. She prepared her bag for the trip and was just starting to set the tiny house to rights when she heard Leah's pet wolf howl next door. The ethereal sound changed to a bark, then a growl. Her whole body tensed when her front gate opened and booted footsteps climbed to her porch. She stepped outside, closing the door behind her, hoping the children had not heard the men—or the wolf.

"Hello, Sheriff." She looked beyond Kemp to a couple of his newer henchmen, taking stock of the situation.

"Hello, Audrey," Kemp answered, keeping his voice

as low as hers. "Didn't wake you, did I? Surely, you were expecting me?"

"What do you want?"

He smiled with false joviality. "I want to set some rules for your upcoming job." He took hold of her throat and shoved her against the doorjamb.

"See these two boys behind me? They're going to hire on with the breed. And you're not going to tell a soul about it. 'Cause if anything happens to either of them, stuff will start happening to those snot-nosed orphans you care so much about. Bad stuff. What I do to them will make you think long and hard about cheatin' me next time." He grinned. "Long and hard."

The sound of a rifle being cocked broke into the tension. "Get your hands off her, Sheriff," Leah calmly ordered as she stared down the rifle barrel toward him. Her enormous wolf stood next to her, his teeth bared.

The sheriff straightened and pulled away. "Put that down, Leah, and call off your mangy dog. We were just leaving anyhow." Kemp and his boys moved down the steps and exited Audrey's yard. He waggled a finger at her. "Remember what I said, girl, or it'll go bad for you and them kids!"

Leah kept her rifle trained on the men until they turned the corner; then she jumped the low fence between their yards and ran up the steps to check on her friend. "Are you hurt? What did they want?"

Audrey swiped the tears from her face. Her hands shook. She hated her own weakness. "When I come back, we're leaving this town, Leah," she vowed in a quiet whisper. "Anywhere's got to be better than here."

Chapter 5

Julian spotted Audrey's house as soon as he turned down her street. The houses at this end of the small town could generously be called shanties—such a contrast to the buildings only a block away. Audrey's house, though just as tumbledown as its neighbors, had a pretty yard. A few late daffodils peeked bright yellow heads out between the weathered slats of the picket fence. She had tamed some wild blue flax for her garden bed. Chickens roamed freely, pecking and scratching at the soil. Though the yard was fine, her house was ragged. Julian wondered why she'd been so hesitant to leave it.

Before he had even set the brake, Audrey stepped outside with a little girl in tow. The child was a fetching imp, bundled as she was in a dress that went past her knees and a heavy woolen coat. She wore a yellow bonnet whose bow consumed the entire space of her neck.

Julian's gaze moved to Audrey. A large, worn bonnet masked her face. She held on to the little girl with one hand, and in the other she carried an old carpetbag stuffed near to popping. She went down the steps and set her bag down, then turned to help the little girl down the steps, sending a harried look toward the house. Julian wondered if a man was going to come charging out of the door, brandishing a rifle.

"Come on, sweetie," she said to the toddler as they hurried to the gate.

Julian leapt down to help them up into the wagon. He set her carpetbag in the back of the loaded wagon, then lifted the toddler up onto the middle of the bench seat.

"Hello, mister," the little girl greeted him, cocking her head and giving him a cherubic grin of petite, white teeth.

This close to her, he could see the riot of blond curls her bonnet half hid. He would never have recognized her as the baby he'd seen last year.

"Good morning, miss." Julian found himself grinning at the little girl in a way he'd seen his father do a thousand times and instantly pulled the foolish expression from his face. His father loved children—he had a gift with them. Julian made a policy of avoiding them as he would a contagious disease. "What's your name?" he asked, surprised he wanted to win another smile from this baby angel.

"Amy Lynn," she said, her pronunciation shockingly perfect. "What's yours?"

"Julian."

She nodded, her face serious. "Juli," she announced, unknowingly using the nickname his siblings had given him years ago.

"He's Mr. McCaid to us, Amy," Audrey corrected.

Julian turned to her to assist her up to the bench, but halted as his hand wrapped around her elbow. She had tried unsuccessfully to hide vivid bruises on her neck with her bonnet's ribbon. The marks dotted her neck in a pattern suspiciously resembling a handprint. "What happened? Who did that to you?"

"I fell." She wouldn't meet his eyes.

"You fell with a man's hand at your throat?" Julian eyed her another moment, neither getting, nor expecting, an answer. He looked back at the house. His hand strayed to the rifle lying under the wagon bench. "Who's in the house, Miss Sheridan?"

Her gaze shot to the gun beneath his hand, and the terror that struck her face was like water bursting through a wall. "No one."

He looked from her to the house behind her. "No one," he repeated. "Then who's going to take care of your chickens?"

"I have a brother, but he's at work this morning. There is no one in the house, Mr. McCaid."

"Did your brother do this to you?"

"No. I told you. I fell."

Not satisfied with her answer, Julian accepted that she wouldn't be forthcoming. "We'd best be off." He helped her into the wagon, wondering at her bruises, wondering if there were others he couldn't see. He looked from Audrey to the skinny cherub next to her. She tucked her hands between her knees and hunched her shoulders as she stared back at him with big brown eyes, her expression a little anxious, a little hopeful.

Whatever the cause of Audrey's desperate actions, Julian doubted she would allow Amy Lynn to get caught in the crossfire. He climbed up into the wagon, ignoring the sudden itching between his shoulder blades. When he bent over to take up the reins, his gaze caught on Amy Lynn's odd shoes. The leather had been cut out of the tips of her boots to give her feet growing room. Her little toes hugged the edge of the thick leather soles. The black stockings covering her legs were worn thin and scarred with a multitude of mendings. Julian's gaze shot to Audrey, and he instantly wished he'd never looked at her. Her chin lifted. She offered him defiance in the face of his discovery.

Defiance.

Swallowing an oath, he slapped the reins and the horses pulled out.

Amy turned around on the wagon bench, kneeling to watch behind them. Audrey looked back toward the house. All the children had come outside, standing stoically, watching the wagon roll away. None of them waved. Audrey felt as if an invisible hand reached into her chest and squeezed her lungs like the folds of an accordion. She couldn't breathe. This was wrong. She couldn't leave the children. She looked at the hard profile of the man driving them away, farther every second from the seven little souls standing in her yard, desperately in need of her.

"McCaid." His name came out as a whisper. He didn't hear her. She couldn't speak with the vise clamping her chest. She reached over and gripped his sleeve. "Stop. Please," she managed to rasp.

"Whoaaa—" he called to the team of horses, pulling them to a stop as they rounded the bend in the road. Ahead of them was the open prairie, miles and miles of empty rangeland.

"What is it?" he asked, his brow knitted with concern.

"I can't do this. I can't leave."

"Why?"

"I just can't, that's all. I can't do this."

"I see. Then how are you going to repay the debt you owe me?"

Audrey studied his face. His lips were thinned, his

dark eyes unreadable. "I—I take in laundry. I could do your laundry."

"Hell's Gulch is a helluva long way from town, so that's not exactly a convenient option. Besides, the sum you took would cover my laundry for a year," he scoffed. "I'll only be here the summer."

Audrey looked behind the wagon. She was grateful her house was out of sight—she didn't want to run the risk that McCaid would see the children. "I share a vegetable garden with a friend. I could give you my portion of its harvest."

McCaid shook his head. "Your little garden looked scarce big enough to support you and Amy Lynn. How would you make it provide for a camp full of hungry men?"

Tears stung Audrey's eyes, but she refused to shed them. If she could get him to change his mind about taking her out to his ranch, surely the sheriff would relent? Her gaze lifted to his face. "You could forgive the debt."

He studied her a long moment. "I could, but then how would you learn there are repercussions for your actions?"

Audrey met his gaze unflinchingly. He wasn't going to give an inch. She watched as his gaze lowered to her lips, pausing there before slowly meeting her eyes again. She was no fool. She knew what men wanted from women, what he wanted from her. Perhaps it would make what she had to do easier.

"What else have you to bargain with?" he asked.

Her eyes traveled across the hard planes of his face, seeing his high cheekbones, his square jaw, the faint cleft in his chin. His mouth was wide, his lips molded by strong curves. A heat crept up her neck and into her face.

She couldn't do this. Not yet. Not like this. "I have nothing." Her voice was a whisper.

"So then, camp cook or town jail? Which is it, Miss Sheridan?"

Audrey shut her eyes. God help her. "Camp cook."

McCaid lifted the reins and called to the horses. Amy Lynn climbed onto Audrey's lap as the wagon lurched forward. Audrey hugged her foster daughter tightly.

The children would be okay, she told herself. Malcolm would be there. And Leah and Wolf. And Jim and Sally and Maddie would help out too. It was only a month. Only four weeks. Then she would be back to care for them.

And what then? an inner voice asked. How could she provide for her children any better than she had when she landed them all in this spot? She had no answer to that. Trying to calm her panic, she shut her eyes and focused on the cool morning air washing over her as the wagon rolled out of town.

"She ain't comin' back," Kurt whispered as he watched Mr. McCaid's wagon round the corner.

"Shut up, Kurt. She'll be back," Luc answered, shoving him off the last step.

"Oh yeah? Did your mom come back?" Kurt retorted, turning on Luc.

"My ma's dead, and you know that."

"My ma left, and she never came back," Mabel said. Colleen started crying. Tommy, the newest addition to the family, kept quiet.

"Now look what you've done!" Luc glared at Kurt.

"What'er we gonna do, Luc?" Joey asked.

"Audrey said she'd be back, and I believe her," Luc asserted. "I've been with her just about longer than any of you, 'cept Dulcie. She ain't never gone back on her word to us. Not ever. And we promised to do what we're supposed to do. Right now we're supposed to git over to Maddie's for school, so that's what I'm gonna do."

Chapter 6

Hell's Gulch was a welcome sight to Audrey after the long hours on the rough trail road. At contrast to its name, it looked like a paradise in the early afternoon sun. Situated in a lush, flat valley at the foot of the Medicine Bow Mountains, its prairie was awash with spring flowers, coloring the fields in wide swaths of white, purple, and yellow flowers.

A sprawling, three-wire fence demarcated McCaid's ranch. Judging by its length, they had to have been traveling along his property line for the last two hours of their trip. When they pulled onto the property at an open gate, Audrey felt her stomach tighten into a knot. What would the conditions be like out here? McCaid had a house under construction—she knew because of all the supply wagons that had rolled through town last year. Was the house finished yet? Where would she and Amy stay?

Coming over a slight hill, Audrey could see several corrals, a covered wagon, and a couple of buckboard wagons. Off to one side was a small white house. A large, open tent canopy covered the space between the house and a scattering of tables and benches. Farther out was a big fire pit with several wooden benches situated around it. Audrey looked across the encampment, seeing it was as she feared: not another woman was in sight.

There was a long low building, which Audrey assumed was the bunkhouse. Between it and the cookhouse were several white tents lined up in three neat rows. Would she and Amy have a tent of her own? Would they have to sleep among the men? Or would they be sleeping in the open air? She brought a coat for both of them, but hadn't any spare blankets to bring from home. She wasn't outfitted for a truly rustic existence.

Before McCaid could even draw the wagon to a stop, several of his men trotted over. Audrey helped herself off the wagon, not waiting for McCaid or any of the men to assist her. She lifted Amy down while McCaid walked around the wagon and unloaded her satchel. He seemed tense, which only increased her nervousness.

"Franklin, this is Miss Sheridan, from town, and her daughter, Amy Lynn. She's come out to cook for us," McCaid said to a balding, friendly faced man.

"Oh." Franklin looked from McCaid to Audrey and back again. "Oh, I understand. Cook for us, huh? We weren't expecting you to bring a woman back with you—I mean, a cook. Well, we expected a cook but not a woman." He drew a breath as color painted his face. "Have you told Jenkins?"

"It came up at the last moment. I don't think he'll be too upset—he never took to cooking anyway."

"True enough. Well, I guess they should take the cabin over by yer tent." Franklin pointed to a tiny struc-ture that Audrey had not yet noticed on the crest of a nearby hill. "What 'er you slack-witted hombres staring at? Come introduce yerselves to Miss Sheridan and her little girl," he barked to the crowd of men gathered behind him.

A half dozen men filed by, tipping their hats to her. Some looked happy to see a woman, some none too pleased. She recognized a few from town. Audrey's throat ached from Kemp's roughness. She tried to ignore the appraising gazes that strayed to her bruises, but couldn't help wondering if her whole neck was black and blue.

"Let's go see the cabin," McCaid said over his shoulder as he took off with her satchel in hand. His stride was too fast for her to match with Amy in tow. When she caught up with him at the doorway to the cabin, he pointed back toward the opposite end of the camp.

"That's the chuck tent and cookhouse. While you get settled, I'll let Jenkins know you're taking over the cooking. Check in with him when you're ready. Your duties will start with breakfast."

He entered the small cabin, and Audrey followed him. There was little room to spare inside the tiny space, especially with McCaid standing in the middle of it. A small bed was pushed against one wall, below the only window. There was a front door and a back door, a woodstove, and a small table with two chairs. A couple of shirts hung on pegs on the wall near the table. Here and there cracks in the wooden walls let in bright slivers of sunlight. The wood floor was dusty, the walls were cobwebby, and the window was opaque with grime.

"Whose cabin is this?" Audrey asked, wondering whom they were putting out.

"It's an old hunting shack that came with the land." He set her satchel down on the bed, stirring up a cloud of dust. "The boys are up before dawn each morning.

Jenkins, the current cook, feeds them at dawn, noon, and six, but you can learn more when you talk to him."

Audrey followed him to the door, none too anxious to be in the cabin. "How many men are there?"

"A dozen ranch hands, give or take a few. Depends on how many are in camp, not on watch or out with the herds. Add in the construction workers and you've another dozen or so."

At the doorstep, he turned around so abruptly she almost ran into him. He stared down at her, his expression uncomfortably intent. "Let me make one thing perfectly clear, Miss Sheridan. I don't want you stirring up trouble among the men. Now and then you may go back into town for a weekend. What you do with your free time when you're there is your business. When you're out here, you're on my time. I'm paying good wages to these men to build my house and keep my sheep alive, not to be fighting over you."

Audrey felt the sting of his assessment. It wasn't exactly accurate now, but it soon would be. She didn't try to defend herself. "Good day, Mr. McCaid."

McCaid's gaze dipped to Amy Lynn, who stood behind her, a hand fisted in Audrey's skirt, her enormous eyes watching him. His gaze slowly lifted to Audrey's face. He regarded her for a tense moment, a muscle bunching in his jaw. He lifted his hat and gave her a nod. "Good day, Miss Sheridan."

Amy Lynn pressed against her thigh as they watched McCaid's retreating back. Audrey touched her foster daughter's shoulder. "It's all right, baby." She looked down at Amy and smiled reassuringly though her hand shook as she smoothed a lock of hair from her daughter's pale face. "We'll be fine here."

It took several hours to clean the small cabin. Audrey

hauled the small mattress outside and beat the dust out of it. She retrieved a bucket under the table, then went in search of the river she heard nearby. She found some large, smooth rocks at its edge and managed a rough rinsing of the linens. She spread them out on bushes near the river to dry in the sunshine, then returned to the cabin with a fresh bucket of water. Taking one of the abandoned shirts to use as a washrag, she set about scrubbing the cabin's surfaces.

Soon the interior gleamed, and she turned her attention to the outhouse a dozen yards behind the cabin. She made sure it was cleared of cobwebs and spiders and clean enough for her and Amy to use. She brought the mattress back into the cabin only after a lengthy airing and a close inspection to be sure it was free of bedbugs and other critters left over from the cabin's last occupants. Once she had reassembled the bed and unpacked their few belongings, she was ready to face the rest of the camp.

The day had been warm, but evening was settling in, and the nights were still quite cool this time of year. She gathered up their coats, took Amy's hand, and headed off toward the cookhouse. Men had begun congregating around the fire pit as they awaited supper. She ignored their curious looks. Judging from Franklin's remarks earlier, she had no idea whether her meeting with Jenkins would be friendly or confrontational, but she hoped it would go well. Stepping into the warm interior of a large open room, she found an older man stirring a pot steaming on one of two enormous iron stoves.

"Mr. Jenkins?" Audrey addressed the man, pausing off to one side of him. He slowly, stiffly, turned to her. He looked her up and down once, his weathered face wrinkled into a frown, his bushy brows nearly meeting in the middle.

"I reckon you're the new cook."

"I am."

"You ever cook for a few dozen men?"

"No."

"You ever cook before?"

She smiled patiently, intent on overlooking his grouchy demeanor. "Of course. Could you show me around your setup here? I'd like to get my bearings before the morning meal."

He made a noise that sounded like a cross between a growl and a groan, then hung up the long metal spoon. Turning, he spotted Amy Lynn. He stood for a long moment, just staring at the little girl, who happened not to be hiding behind Audrey's skirts. Amy Lynn returned his frank perusal unflinchingly. Audrey smiled inwardly. If this crusty old man didn't frighten Amy, she couldn't let him frighten her either.

"This is my daughter, Amy Lynn."

Jenkins shook his head and stepped around the two females. "First a woman, then a kid. Next you know, we'll have a camp full of women and ankle biters running underfoot, confusing things. It ain't right. It just ain't right, if you ask me," he muttered under his breath. "Ain't nowheres a man can just be a man."

He walked over to a bank of cabinets and turned to her. "Ye're standin' in the chuck house. I got it all outfitted. Everything has a place and everything in its place." Jenkins quickly showed her around the room. "You got yer spices here, yer flour, oats, cornmeal, and such dry goods here. Yer pots are here. The boys' plates and cups and whatnot go here."

Audrey was impressed. Cabinets, drawers, and cubbyholes covered two full walls. Jenkins wasn't much taller than she was, so there were freestanding steps set by each wall so that the upper compartments could be reached. There was a long worktable in the middle of the room. And in the far corner was a narrow bed.

"Do you live here, Mr. Jenkins?"

"That I do. Besides the food supplies, we got a stack of rifles and ammunition. I stay here to keep an eye on things." He paused, giving her a narrow-eyed look. "You ain't takin' my bed, are ya?"

"No. We're staying at the cabin on the hill."

He nodded, relieved, and walked to the open door to point at some things that Audrey could not see. "There's a smokehouse over there by the bunkhouse, and a keeping house at the river. I'll show you those tomorrow. We got a chicken coop too. That corral over there has our milk cow. She'll be moving to the barn as soon as it's done."

Audrey was stunned. This was no temporary encampment, but a growing, functioning ranch. It was almost as if McCaid intended to live here throughout the year. That could only be trouble for Defiance, having a permanent sheep farm so close—especially with McCaid running it. He and Kemp would not get along. A part of her felt bad for McCaid. He was trying to build something nice here, but Kemp would never let him succeed. She wondered how long before McCaid folded the operation and went back East. She wondered if he would even survive his folly. A lot of men, less green than he, had ended up with a bullet in the back for daring to run sheep in the Territory, let alone take on a man like Sheriff Kemp.

"So, you got questions, girl?" Jenkins asked, drawing her out of her musings.

"Not yet. May I help with supper? Shall I put some coffee on?"

Jenkins made a face. "I guess you could do that. I woulda done it, but I been jawin' with you."

It took a bit of work to find the coffeepot, water, beans, and bean grinder, but she soon had a pot cooking on the stove. Outside, beneath the chow tent, she set out the tin plates, cups, and forks on one of the tables, then put some butter out for the biscuits Jenkins had in the oven. Soon an endless line of men filed by to have supper dished out for them. When they had all been fed, she filled her own plate. She frowned down at the meat and bean stew, wondering if it tasted as bad as it smelled. She took two biscuits, then chose a quiet spot for her and Amy to sit.

Sampling the stew, she knew it was as she feared. The beans were too hard to chew, and the meat was stringy and greasy. She mashed the beans as best she could and blew on a spoonful to cool it before feeding Amy. Amy made a face, her little nostrils flared, but she opened her mouth for more. Food was a scarce enough commodity that, even at three years old, Amy knew better than to turn away anything even slightly edible. Audrey and Amy both ate a few more bites, but only enough to dull their gnawing hunger. Audrey tried to butter one of the biscuits, but couldn't break it open. One bite proved it was tougher than hardtack.

For the first time since this whole fiasco began, Audrey began to feel hopeful. If this was the food these men were used to eating, her cooking would surely be a welcome change. After all, cooking had never been difficult for her—it was affording the ingredients that had limited her. In this rough camp kitchen, there was an abundance of foodstuffs for her to pick from. Tomorrow, she would start the day with flapjacks. Maybe there was some sausage or bacon in the smokehouse.

The only thing missing in the middle of all this abundance was the rest of her foster children. An ache settled in the middle of her chest. She would do what she had to do to protect them. If it meant seducing Mr. McCaid, then so be it. But if there was another way to occupy his time for a month, she would try to find it first.

Chapter 7

Julian lay atop his bedroll late that night, too restless to sleep. Crickets serenaded one another with their raw, relentless chirping. Stretched out on his back, his head resting on his knitted hands, he listened to the quieting camp. The fires were banked, but he could hear them crackling, hissing. Those of his men still awake talked in lowered voices. An occasional rumble of laughter rippled into the cool night. The air smelled of wood smoke and melting snow from the nearby mountains. It was fresh, virgin air, air unbreathed by a thousand other people.

A stiff breeze rustled the canvas of his tent. Julian sighed and gave up the wait for sleep. He tossed his tent flap open and went outside. Bare-chested, he felt the night air slip around his skin like a cool silk robe. He shoved his hands in the pockets of his pants, rocking back on his heels to gaze up at the stars. There were millions of them, almost too many to distinguish constellations. He looked at his camp, where his permanent crew slept in the bunkhouse, now completely dark. The construction workers were in a dozen or so tents organized in neat rows like a garrison of soldiers, which wasn't

surprising. The tents were army surplus—as were many
of his men, veterans from both sides of the war.

He looked at Audrey's cabin as eyes the color of the
wild sage drifted to his mind. Frightened, angry, sad, re-
signed, she seemed incapable of hiding her thoughts. A
heat spread through him, raising gooseflesh where his
warmed skin met cool night air. His body tightened as
he remembered kissing her in the rain, holding her
against him when he'd caught her in the alley, remembered their dance a year ago when his friend Sager was
courting Rachel. Why hadn't he been able to get her
out of his mind? Who was she, really? Why had leaving
Defiance caused her such angst?

Audrey rolled to her side on the narrow bunk, trying
not to awaken Amy. She missed her bed. She and Amy
slept together at home too, but her bed was much
larger, meant for two adults. It had been her parents'
bed. As children, she and Malcolm had slept in bunk
beds in the small back room. Dulcie was the first to join
their family. It took her years to recover from the
wholesale slaughter of her family. She'd been found,
more dead than alive, under her family's overturned
wagon where she'd hidden for three long days. Then
came Luc, then Mabel the year Audrey's parents died.
Then Kurt showed up. Shortly after that, Sam, the
saloon proprietor, had begged her to take Amy Lynn,
who was the daughter of one of his working women.

Malcolm had to build a second set of bunks when
Colleen showed up. Last year, Joey arrived. And Tommy
was their latest addition. Malcolm still slept alone
in his upper bunk, but all the other kids doubled or
tripled up in theirs, Luc and Kurt in one, Dulcie, Mabel,

and Colleen in another, and Joey and Tommy in the last. Every one of the children had come with a sad story—death of a parent, neglect, and for some of them, abuse.

Audrey sighed and rolled over once again to lie on her back, nudging Amy aside. Her little family was popping at the seams. Something would have to change. But what? And how? Her friend Logan Taggert had set up an account for her at the bank before he went East. But when the bank closed, that income was lost.

So many people had left town that her laundry business had all but dried up. With the increasing number of hoodlums the sheriff brought in, she would no longer be able to protect her family from the bad side of life. It would thread its way into their lives, into their home. She would lose them to the corruption that was the lifeblood of Defiance.

Audrey sighed. She was overtired and distraught about leaving her family, her mind too awake to settle into sleep. She got out of bed and found her shawl. It was late; she didn't think anyone would be about. Opening her front door, she peeked outside. Everything was silent, except the breeze. Drawing her shawl about her shoulders, she went outside.

Her cabin was on a slight rise outside the main encampment, affording her a bit of privacy. The cool evening air felt nice. Audrey lifted her face and shut her eyes, letting the breeze wash over her. Something would change in her life; she would find a way to support her family. She was stuck here for a month—enough time to make a plan.

The sound behind her of a man clearing his throat made her spin around.

McCaid.

His tent was only a dozen yards or so from her cabin. Off to the side as it was, she hadn't seen him when she looked out of her front door. She thought about a quick retreat; she wasn't decently attired. But then, nor was he. Good heavens, he was half naked. He faced the camp; the faint glow from the fires illuminated his bare, hairy chest. Audrey had seen Malcolm bare-chested before, but her brother's torso in no way resembled McCaid's. Her brother was lanky, still boyish, his arms more bone than muscle.

McCaid was enormous.

His shoulders were wide, his arms made of rippling layers of muscle on muscle. His nipples were small and dark and puckered in the cool night breeze. His ribs were covered with slabs of muscle that flowed, one ridge into another, down to a flat, narrow belly.

His suspenders hung limply by his thighs. His hands in his pockets drew his pants lower on his hips, revealing inches of his white linen undershorts below his navel. Audrey's heart started to beat hard, unnaturally.

Were all men made like this? Did Jim look like this beneath his apron and vest and shirt? She doubted it, because he was leaner in the arms and had a round paunch of a stomach. Perhaps Paul or Hammer, Kemp's thugs, looked like this, but they had short, squat necks making them appear as if their heads just sat on their shoulders, like boulders on a cliff.

Audrey's eyes moved up McCaid's chest, to his neck. It was a nice neck, strong and corded, his jaw well defined. There were twin hollows in his cheeks that gave him a hard-edged appearance. His lips were made with lush curves that, even as she looked, curled up at one end. Her eyes flew to his, and her mouth dropped in abject horror as she realized how boldly she had been examining him. His eyebrows were dark angles above his eyes, and as she watched, he drew one upward.

"Have you looked your fill? Shall I turn around now?" he asked, spreading his arms.

Speechless, mortified, Audrey could only shake her head. Vehemently. Then she turned her back to him, wishing she could die on the spot and vanish. Or that he would. Or that she simply had never come outside tonight. She couldn't just run inside her cabin; it would only make it worse when she faced him tomorrow. What to do now?

"What nefarious thoughts keep you wakeful tonight?"

Audrey wasn't certain what he meant by nefarious, but given the context, it couldn't be good. "What makes you think I think nefarious thoughts?"

"Besides the way you were just looking at me?"

"Oh, goodness. I'm so sorry." The wind further agitated her, expanding the voluminous folds of her nightgown like a bell, then sucking the air out and slapping the material about her legs, this way and that. There was a bench behind her, set against the wall of her cabin. She backed up to it, not willing to turn around and risk seeing McCaid again. She sat down and pulled her knees up, folding her legs and tucking the white linen of her nightgown under her feet. She wrapped her arms around her calves and rested her chin on her knees, making herself as small and covered as she could as she stared unseeingly at the encampment before her.

"Do you mind if I sit here as well?"

"It's your bench," she answered with a shrug, not looking at him. She wished he would go away, wished her body wasn't humming with a need to touch him—a need that had nothing to do with the sheriff's directive.

"So it is." He settled at the opposite end, no more than a foot from her.

Resting her cheek against her knees, she let her lashes mask her gaze as she looked at him. He was leaning back against the rough clapboards of her cabin. His hands were folded loosely in his lap, his long legs open and bent at the knees.

This would be a good time to start her seduction. How did one begin such a thing?

She would have to touch him. She could run her hands up his arms, feel his corded muscles. Or she could start at his chest, comb her fingers through the dark hairs there. She wondered what they felt like.

"If you keep looking at me like that, Miss Sheridan, I warn you I will take you up on what you're offering."

Quickly she turned away, pressing her forehead into her folded knees. It was bad enough to be forced to seduce him, but to discover she wanted to do it was indefensible. The moment stretched into an awkward silence. Audrey hoped he'd get bored and leave her alone.

"I'm a pretty good listener, Miss Sheridan, if there was something you wanted to say."

"I have nothing to say to you." It was true. And it was not. Logically she wanted him to leave, but her heart ached for her broken life and yearned for help resolving her situation. Through no volition of her own, words came tumbling out on a disgusted sigh. "I'm twenty, nearly twenty-one. I need to find something to do with my life." She looked at the camp in front of her, not daring to look at him again.

"Ah. The eternal, coming-of-age question. What are your options?"

"I'm not exactly marriage material."

"Because of Amy Lynn?"

Amy Lynn and the other children. These thoughts were raw inside her. It hurt to talk about her situation—to McCaid, of all people, who was wealthy and strong and could face the sheriff without fear. "Yes," she whispered.

"It seems that in a frontier town like Defiance, where women are not in plentiful supply, a man would overlook your past."

She knew he thought Amy Lynn was her own child—she hadn't corrected his misperception. There was no point in trying to convince him she lived a moral life; in a very short while, immorality would in fact be her reality.

"Perhaps, but I have yet to meet such a man. Defiance has a sad shortage of good men. No, I will need to find work."

McCaid reached over and took her hand. She tensed, watching him examine it in the shadowy darkness. He spread her fingers, rubbed the pad of his thumb across her skin to feel the texture of her palm. She was too stunned to pull away from him. Her hands were lye-burned from her laundry work, her skin red and chapped, her fingers as calloused as his.

"What of the laundry you take in? Is there enough business there?"

"No." Her voice was a whisper. "Not anymore. Defiance is dying." Her hand burned in his touch. She pulled away from him.

"I can see you aren't a stranger to hard work. You could take a position with a family, perhaps as a governess or house servant."

"There aren't any families who can afford to hire help in town. And with Amy, I can't take a live-in position." Not to mention her seven other foster children.

"Tell me you can cook," he said, his hard mouth lifting in a lopsided grin.

"I can cook."

"Better than Jenkins?"

"I would have to try pretty hard to cook as bad as Jenkins."

"Well, there's one thing you can do."

"A lone woman cooking for a bunch of men is just not done."

He sighed. "Each of us has to do what has to be done to survive. Your parents are gone, I take it?"

She nodded. "Since I was seventeen." She looked at him, then looked away. He was watching her, his eyes dark in the murky light. "I thought about becoming a seamstress."

"That's something. Do you like sewing?"

"I do. I made the dress I was wearing earlier. And all of Amy Lynn's clothes. And this nightgown." And all the clothes Malcolm and the kids wore.

"Well, now we are getting somewhere. What stops you from becoming a seamstress?"

"I'm only one person. I don't have a staff. I can't turn work out fast enough. Maybe if I had one of those newfangled sewing machines, I could go it alone. But I don't have references or a history of work a customer would find reliable."

"As it happens, I'm in need of a seamstress for my house here. Could you sew curtains and drapes?"

Audrey straightened, facing him. "I could."

"If I bought you a sewing machine, you could take the material I've ordered and get my windows covered?"

"I could. Of course. It would be easy." Hope leaked into her soul. Maybe this was the way she could distract him for a month—involve him in the preparation of drapes for his new home. Maybe she didn't have to surrender her body to him at all. "But I can't cook for your men and sew for you, both."

"Then I will hire another cook. I have to anyway, since you won't be staying beyond a month."

Audrey studied his face. Knowing what she did of men, she couldn't help being suspicious. "Why? Why would you help me? What do you get out of such an arrangement?"

"I get to know that there's one less criminal prowling the streets of Defiance."

That had a ring of truth to it. And it was an option that was sustainable, one that didn't involve selling her body or her soul. With McCaid as a backer, she could find enough work to sustain her. Laughing, she threw her arms around his neck, hugging him tightly as she thanked him. Gradually, she became aware of her body touching his, his warmth enveloping her, his thick, muscled arms wrapped around her. Her legs on the bench, her hip touching his, her chest to his, he held her as tightly as she held him. She belatedly remembered wearing only her nightgown and he only his skin.

This was a mistake. Breathing became difficult, not because he held her too tightly, but because she didn't want him to let go. A heat took flame in her body, a yearning long ignored at last feeling itself heard. She'd wanted to be in his arms, to be held like this, to feel his heart hammering against hers ever since their dance last summer. She'd wondered what it would be like to feel his face buried in the bend between her shoulder and neck, to feel him breathe the scent of her skin, as he was doing. She spread her fingers and dug them into the thick, silky hair at the back of his head.

His sideburn and then the rough stubble on his

cheek rasped along her skin as he lifted his head. His lips brushed her chin. Audrey gave in to the urge to arch against him and pressed her breasts against him. He gazed down into her eyes. Never had she been looked at so by such a man. She could see, even in the darkness, faint lines feathering the outer corners of his eyes. He smelled of horse and wool, leather and soap, an intoxicating mixture that Audrey knew she would never forget.

When his lips slanted across hers, she welcomed the touch, unable to help the shiver that rippled through her. His hard mouth was forceful on hers, opening her to his tongue. She felt him enter her mouth, his tongue searching for hers, dancing against her teeth. The heat in her body leapt to life. She uttered a moaning sound she'd never before heard herself make. Her tongue rose to meet his, following his into his mouth, pressing and moving against his.

He broke the kiss, his lips touching her upper lip, then her lower lip, then the space between her lip and her chin. She was bent back over his arm. His free hand came up, his thumb feeling the skin of her cheek, the line of her jaw. She looked at him, watched him as he watched his thumb move across her skin, over her lips. She touched her tongue to the pad of his thumb. His eyes flared. He crushed her to him, his lips moving fiercely against hers, his tongue thrusting into her mouth. His hand moved lower, over her collarbone, lower to cover her breast.

Audrey was unprepared for the desire that knifed through her at his caress. She sucked a sharp breath of air against his lips as she gasped. Slowly, it dawned on her that she lay sprawled against his lap as he arched over her, playing her body like a musician strums his instrument. Reality threaded itself into the heated length of her body, cooling her melting flesh.

She pushed away from him, then jumped off the bench and faced him in horrified mortification. Rage and embarrassment warred within her. He'd just offered her a viable alternative, and still she threw herself at him. She was a Jezebel. She should never have been out here with him, undressed as they were. She should never have sat with him, alone in the night, on the bench. What now? His offer of help was not innocent, as he proclaimed. It had its price. No man gave without taking, she realized, watching him slowly stand and face her.

"Forget it. Forget it all. I don't want your help. I won't pay that price."

"There is no price for my help," he rasped, taking a step toward her. She took two steps back. He stopped, his hands held up before him. "That was just a kiss— nothing more."

Audrey covered her mouth with a trembling hand. Even now, her faithless body craved his, craved being in his arms, craved his hot mouth on hers. She shook her head. She couldn't do what the sheriff wanted. She couldn't.

McCaid stood still. His voice was low and soothing. "I'm sorry I frightened you."

Audrey felt tears rise in her eyes, tears of frustration that she now stood several feet from him, tears that a man such as he would never be hers, tears that she was weak and needy and fallible. She spun on her heel and fled into her cabin. At best, she could only be his whore.

And it might be enough.

Julian watched Audrey's closed door and slowly, raggedly, released the air in his lungs. She'd come alive in his arms in a way that left him stunned and hungering for more. *Shit.* He had practically mauled her, with her still bearing the bruises of another man's rough handling. He started toward the river. The ice-cold water would be his body's only relief tonight.

Ignoring the pain of the rocks and stickers underneath his bare feet, he felt again the heat in Audrey's eyes when she'd looked him over so boldly a moment ago. He lifted his hands to his nose, breathing deeply of the faint rose scent that lingered on his skin. He could still feel her hard nipples pressed against his chest, her strong, slim arms wrapped around his neck in what he knew she meant as a chaste and fervent thank-you. And yet he'd taken her gratitude and filled it with his own dark longing and need.

He was glad she hadn't asked him to turn around; he wouldn't have liked seeing her reaction to his scars. He was as lost in his own way as she was. He wished she was still here, with him. He wished he could make her trust him, tell him what the hell was really going on. He wished he could have brushed away her tears. She was twenty. A baby. A baby with a baby. Jesus, he was a bastard. Tomorrow he would do what he could to make it right. He'd meant what he said about having one less criminal in Defiance.

Chapter 8

The noise in Sam's Saloon slowly settled down as Sheriff Kemp stood up by the bar and waved the men to silence. Sam's had been closed for this meeting. The women who usually worked the room were absent. In fact, so were most of the patrons. The men gathered were hand-selected by the sheriff. Their land bordered Hell's Gulch or they had formerly used Hell's Gulch for summer grazing. Some of them owned land that was downstream from Hell's Gulch. Some, perhaps most, were just plain sheep-hating cattlemen.

The sheriff wasn't a man who trusted in Fate. He wanted McCaid out of the area, come hell or high water. McCaid was either stupid or stubborn—if he and his men couldn't bully him out, the sheriff had begun a backup plan. He'd get the area ranchers to run him out. Hence the purpose of this evening's meeting.

"Gentlemen." The sheriff held up his hands, bringing the assembly to order. "I called this meeting to give you a forum to discuss your concerns regarding the invasion of sheep ranching in our area. We don't have a mayor in this town, so this task falls to me. I've been hearing grumbling, and I don't want any of you takin' the law into your own hands. I think it's time we confront this issue and decide as a group how we're gonna deal with it."

"It's illegal, is what it is, him buying public grazing land. Weren't no hearing, no announcement—he just up and buys thousands of prime acres from the government."

"It's legal all right. I looked his deed over a year ago," the sheriff countered.

"That don't make it right, Sheriff," another rancher spoke up. "We're dependent on the water that comes down to us through McCaid's property, which he's fouling up with sheep waste. I had to dig wells to water my herd 'cause I didn't want to lose 'em to poisoned water."

"And he's got too many sheep grazing that land. There won't be nothing left for us once he folds up and runs back East."

"He's paying unfair wages. I can't get any of the help I need—I can't compete with him."

"I heard he's planning on bringing a railroad spur here so he can get his sheep and wool to Cheyenne and Denver."

"Well, hell, that's something that could help us all."

"You think he's gonna let us use it to run our cattle down to Cheyenne? Hell no. Leastwise, not without gouging us for the service." The speaker spit a stream of tobacco juice in the general direction of a nearby spittoon. "Any way you look at it, McCaid's trouble."

"There's the other matter too, Sheriff," Deputy Fred added to the conversation, right on cue. "He took one of our town's good women with him. God knows what he's doing to her out there." He looked at the sheriff. "She's alone and depended on us to protect her. We let her down." The men's voices fired up in angry conversations at that news.

Malcolm watched the proceedings from his position at the back of the room. He'd like to see McCaid run out of town, for a fact. But he had mixed feelings about sending trouble out to Hell's Gulch where Audrey could get tangled up in it. He crossed his arms and held his silence, ignoring the sheriff's look as he indicated Malcolm should join the discussion.

"So, gentlemen, what are we going to do about him?" the sheriff asked.

The bunkroom was dark, and the night was cold. Mabel couldn't sleep. She tried to think of all the things that she liked, as Audrey had taught her to do when she was edgy and restless, but tonight that didn't work very well. Mostly she thought about all the things she missed, like her mother, of whom she had only vague, shadowy memories. Or Audrey's mother, who was, for a short while, a true mother to her. Sometimes she couldn't picture Mrs. Sheridan's face anymore. Sometimes it was hard to remember what her voice sounded like. She was gone now, longer than the time they'd had together. But Audrey had always been there. When Mabel couldn't sleep, Audrey let her sleep in bed with her and Amy. Sometimes she would tell them a story. Sometimes she would just hold Mabel, and then the shadows didn't seem so scary.

Mabel sniffled. When people left, they didn't come back. She'd learned that, first with her mother, then with Mrs. Sheridan. And now Audrey. She missed Audrey. She looked over at Dulcie, who was sleeping soundly. She thought about waking her up to see if she missed Audrey too, but Dulcie usually saw scary things in the dark, and Mabel didn't want to know about them right then. She looked down at the foot of the bed, where Colleen lay. She slept as well, her legs snuggled against Dulcie. With Malcolm using Audrey's bed, Luc had taken his bunk. There was room for the three girls to spread out, but none of them had wanted to sleep with any of the boys. So they stayed together, crowded and comfortable.

Until tonight, when Mabel was sad and no one was awake to comfort her.

Today, she'd done some mending on her pinafore. Audrey had only recently begun to show her and Dulcie how to mend things. Mabel's stitches were chunky. Tommy and Kurt had teased her about them. She had ripped the stitches out three times and tried over and again to do it as Audrey had shown her. Now her fingertips hurt from being stuck by the needle, and her pinafore had a big ugly knotted scar where the small tear had been.

Mabel tried to sniffle quietly, afraid of waking her foster sisters. She got out of bed and went inside the main room where Audrey's bed was. If she was quiet, she could get into bed without waking Malcolm, and then she would feel better. She wiped her nose on her sleeve and crept cautiously toward the big bed.

The big empty bed.

"Malcolm?" she whispered, but got no response. She looked around the room, trying to see if he was sitting in one of the kitchen chairs. Maybe he was outside. She opened the heavy, creaky door but didn't see him on the front steps. "Malcolm?" she called again, a little louder this time.

A cool breeze blew around her, wrapping about her

feet, slipping through the thin material of her worn cotton nightgown. Malcolm was gone too. She started trembling. What would happen to them now? How would they eat? She wiped her tears on the back of her hand and went inside, shutting the door behind her. She returned to the bunkroom.

"Luc," she whispered, hoping she would wake only him, not the whole bunch of them. She wiggled his shoulder. "Luc! Malcolm's gone."

"Mabel! It's the middle of the night," he growled. "Go back to sleep."

"Luc, wake up. Malcolm's gone."

Luc braced himself on his elbows and looked at Mabel as her words slowly sank in. He ripped off his blanket and went into the main room. He looked on the other side of the bed. He looked under the kitchen table. He opened the front door and looked outside. Mabel followed him. The breeze made strange moaning sounds as it blew around their little house. Mabel put her hand in Luc's.

"What're we gonna do?" she whispered, gazing up at him.

Luc's hand tightened around hers as he looked at her, his lips pressed thin. "He'll be back, you'll see."

"People don't come back."

"Sometimes they do. Audrey will. She said she would."

"Who will feed us tomorrow, Luc?"

"If Malcolm isn't back in the morning, I'll feed you. And if he's not here tomorrow night, we'll make a plan. Maybe he just went for a walk." He turned her back to the house. "You better get to bed. You don't want the others to wake up and see you missing. I'll wait up a while for Malcolm."

"Luc?"

"What?"

"I love you." He didn't answer her. The look he gave her made her feel sadder.

"Everything's gonna be okay, Mabel. I ain't gonna let nothing happen to you. Or the others."

Chapter 9

Audrey was up early the next morning, even before the camp roosters. She dressed quietly and left the small cabin, leaving Amy Lynn still soundly asleep. She met Jenkins at the cookhouse. He had the stove stoked already.

"Get the fry pan, girl. We're going to make refried beans this morning."

"No. Show me where the smokehouse is. I want some bacon. And I need to see the chicken coop to get eggs. And the keeping house for some milk and butter."

"There's no need for that. I made plenty enough beans last night to refry for this morning. Do as I say, girl."

Audrey set her hands on her hips and switched to the voice she used for recalcitrant children. "Mr. Jenkins, this is my kitchen now. If you won't show me the smokehouse, I will find it myself. I have a lot to do before being able to serve breakfast and no time to spend arguing with you about this."

"So that's how it is, is it? Well then, it's your hide if there's trouble to be had for wasting food. Smokehouse is this way." He walked through camp, cutting through the neat rows of white tents, grousing all the while about women and their notions. The sun hadn't risen yet, but there was enough light to see without a lantern. Audrey set her shoulders and followed him, ignoring the men who angrily poked their heads outside their tents to see what the commotion was about.

The smokehouse was a treasure trove. There were several ham haunches hanging, strips of beef drying, a barrel of curing beef briskets. For a moment, she couldn't collect her thoughts. Her family had been starving while this little smokehouse was filled to the gills with foodstuffs. It didn't seem fair. She took a slab of bacon, wrapped it in a bit of burlap she found nearby, and handed it to Jenkins.

Next was the chicken coop. She woke the sleeping fowl, causing them to raise a ruckus as she dug for fresh eggs. She took down a wire basket hanging on a peg and easily filled it with a dozen eggs, which she handed to Jenkins. Next was the keeping house. Set deeply into the north side of a hill near the river, it was dark and cold inside. Jenkins set the eggs down and lit a small lamp near the door. Audrey walked down the steps into the dim interior. She found a can of yesterday's milk and a crock of butter. Taking the butter, she handed the milk to Jenkins, climbed back up the steps, put the lamp out, and stepped outside.

"What now, missy? Don't think I can hold much more," Jenkins muttered, adjusting the bacon, eggs, and milk in his arms.

"Now we cook." They walked back through the sea of tents, Audrey in the lead. Awakened earlier, some of the men watched them go by, a few of them grinning as they saw how burdened Jenkins was.

Audrey mixed up a huge batch of pancakes, then

sliced the bacon. She set a pot of coffee to boil on the stove, put milk, sugar, butter, syrup, plates, cups, and flatware outside on the main serving table beneath the cook tent. Jenkins sat on a stool and watched her, his arms crossed in front of him, brows lowered. Soon she had bacon frying and pancakes cooking, enough to fill several large platters. The smells filled the camp, rousing those who still slept. By the time she was ready to feed the men, they were standing anxiously at the serving table with their plates and forks at the ready in a neat line. Audrey smiled at the exuberance with which they watched her fill their plates.

She wished her children were there, lined up for the breakfast feast. She hoped Malcolm knew what to feed them to stretch their meager rations. She turned her attention to pouring out more pancakes and putting fresh strips of bacon out to fry. For the next hour, she filled and refilled the platters and plates and brewed two more pots of coffee.

When she could take a break, she filled a plate that she set aside to share with Amy, and took another to Jenkins, who still sat and stewed on his stool near the outdoor serving table.

"Mr. Jenkins, please eat. We have a lot of work to do today—you'll need your strength."

"Good morning."

Audrey jumped as McCaid's deep voice sounded behind her. She had tried all morning to keep her emotions controlled, to not think of last night, of what it felt like to be in his arms. All her best intentions shattered at his greeting. She remembered the feel of his embrace, the rippling muscles of his flat belly. She turned to face him, consciously regulating her breathing. His hair was damp, his jaw clean-shaven. He wore a blue chambray shirt and buff vest and pants.

It didn't matter that he was fully clothed. Her mind knew what was under them, how he smelled, how he tasted.

Resolutely, her gaze rose to his face. She wasn't sure what to expect from him this morning. Would he think her a wanton for throwing herself at him last night? Would he fire her now and demand she face her sentence in jail? He looked forbidding, his jaw set in a hard line, his eyes shuttered.

"Good morning," she answered, braced for the worst, hating the blood warming her cheeks.

"You wanted to see me, Mr. McCaid?" Franklin asked as he joined them.

"I did. Miss Sheridan and I have come to a different work agreement. As fine a cook as she appears to be, she is also an accomplished seamstress, which I need up at my house. I would like you to hire a replacement cook."

"No." The word popped out of Audrey's mouth, startling her as well as the men. Her mind was racing, following the paths of several courses of action. She was shocked that he still wanted to help her, despite the fact that she had stolen money from him and thrown herself at him so provocatively. The practical side of her shouted for her to take the sewing machine and any help he'd give her. The decent side of her warned the cost would be too high. The survivor in her said it was a cost she was bound to pay anyway, if it was the only way to keep McCaid away from town.

"No?" McCaid asked, a note of warning in his voice.

Audrey looked at Jenkins and Franklin, wishing she didn't have to have this conversation in front of them. "I will cook for you and that's it."

McCaid eyed her with all the irritation he would a stiff-legged mule. The silence stretched awkwardly into a minute. Jenkins buried his attention in his breakfast plate, noisily shoving food into his mouth. Franklin looked as if he wished to be anywhere but there.

"I can help you, Miss Sheridan," McCaid quietly offered. "Let me. Take the sewing machine. Learn a trade"—his gaze dipped to her chest—"a new trade."

"Boss, I just remembered a horse I gotta check on. Come see me when you're done here." Franklin said this last even as he hurried away.

Jenkins followed his example. "I got work to do in the cookhouse. Can't sit here all day watching you two moon over each other."

Audrey shut her eyes in shame. "Men like you don't help women like me," she whispered.

"I'm not most men." He reached over and lifted her chin, forcing her to meet his gaze. His hair was rapidly drying. A heavy lock had fallen free and curved down to his dark brow. "The sewing machine has nothing to do with what's between us. Take it." The corners of his jaw flexed as he glared down at her, but his voice was quiet.

"There's nothing between us."

He arched a brow. "There will be."

Chapter 10

The door slammed behind one of Bill Kemp's men. He was breathless and looked as if he hadn't slept in the last ten days, but his eyes were alight with excitement. Kemp hoped he brought good news.

"Get out," he ordered the rest of his men loitering in the jail lobby. When the room emptied, he faced Ike. "So let's have it. What did you find out?"

"It's no rumor, Sheriff. Dillard and Fiske opened a couple dozen logging camps in the mountains to cut railroad ties. They're gonna be sending ten thousand dollars in silver up to the main camp to cover payroll and operating expenses." He looked at the sheriff. "Every month."

Kemp eyed his hired gun, trying to see if he was lying or had been duped. This news was a helluva break. "You sure about this? Who did you talk to?"

"Word's out all over Cheyenne. They're hiring every man, Chinkie, and Mick they can. Paying three times what a cowboy makes, more if their camps meet quotas. They're flush, and it's coming our way."

"When's the first shipment?"

"Next week. Just like we heard."

"All right. Go get a beer. Tell Sam it's on me. I got some planning to do." Kemp mulled this over in the silence of his empty office. He was glad he got rid of McCaid, at least for this first shipment. But it was just plain bad luck the Avenger had Defiance in his sights. Something would have to be done about both men if he was to take full advantage of this windfall.

Chapter 11

For supper on her first night as camp cook, Audrey made a hash from a couple of the corned beef briskets in the smokehouse and some potatoes stored in the keeping house. The hash, along with large, fluffy sourdough biscuits, was an enormous hit with the men. Any worries she'd entertained about their accepting a woman in camp were rapidly vanishing. It was good McCaid had feed for the pigs; the scrap bucket had been empty after both breakfast and lunch. And given the way the men were silently, rapidly making her hash disappear this evening, she thought there would be little waste after this meal.

She had just set a plate down for Amy when one of the boys came around the serving table. She looked up, nervously expecting McCaid. He'd told her he would collect her after supper to go to his new house and assess his curtain situation—he wanted her to draft a list of notions and other things she would need to create his window coverings

The man standing there wasn't McCaid but a childhood friend she hadn't seen in years. She broke into a grin. "Hadley Baker!" Laughing, she ran to give him a hug. He picked her up and swung her around. "Just look at you." She smiled, leaning back to look at him. "How you've grown!" And he had too, perhaps a half foot since she last saw him three years before.

"Look at how I've grown—look at you!" Still holding her, he let his eyes take in her curves. She wasn't insulted by his audaciousness. Hadley was one of the first friends she had made when her family moved to Defiance. For several summers, they, along with Leah, Malcolm, and Logan Taggert—when he came to town—had romped, carefree and ignored by adults, through the long summer weeks. Hadley taught her and Leah how to ride. Logan taught them to swim. Leah taught them all how to hunt. The boys did not mind that she and Leah were girls; they climbed trees, swam, fished, and did everything together.

That changed the year she turned seventeen, when her parents had died. The next summer, Hadley worked on his father's ranch. And the following year, he had graduated. She had run into him once in town, but not since.

"What are you, a cowpuncher, doing on a sheep spread?" she asked.

He grinned and leaned forward conspiratorially. "Keep this to yourself, but my father's thinking of diversifying our holdings. Thought it would be smart for me to work here for the summer to see if it's what we want to do. Some of the boys were talking about you today when they came out to take the watch. I couldn't believe it when I heard your name." He frowned at her, his hand gently touching her bruised neck. "Who did this to you?"

"Kemp."

"Audrey, you shouldn't be here." He shook his head. "It's no place for a gal like you. What about the ch—"

Audrey made a face, silencing him. Leaning toward him, her voice lowered, she whispered, "McCaid doesn't know about the kids."

"Why? Why keep them a secret?"

She shrugged, not wanting to tell him the whole sordid tale. "I don't know him. I don't trust him yet. It felt safer to keep them a secret."

"Who's caring for them?"

"Malcolm. He's working at the general store. And Jim and Sally are helping as they can. And Leah and Maddie too."

They regarded each other for a long moment. Then Hadley pulled her hand through his arm and turned her away from the boys. "Audrey, what I asked you that second summer . . . I meant it. I wasn't just playing around. I want you to marry me."

Audrey remembered that exact moment. They were at their swimming hole. Malcolm had just jumped into the water, soaking them with a big splash. Hadley had jumped in after him. Ducking Malcolm under the water, Hadley had looked up at Audrey and told her they should get married later, when they were older. She of course had thought he was teasing and jumped in to save Malcolm. She had never thought of that moment again.

Until now.

She gradually returned to the present. Her gaze came to rest on a pair of large, dusty cowboy boots crossed at the ankles. Involuntarily, she followed the long line of buff pants upward, seeing where they tightened over strong thighs, narrow hips, thin waist, and up farther to tensely folded arms.

McCaid.

Her eyes flew to his face as one dark brow arched upward beneath that wayward lock of hair. "I think Miss Sheridan has work to see to."

"Yes, sir," Hadley answered, his voice respectful, his grin unsuppressed. He bent and gave Audrey a quick kiss on the cheek, then stepped away. "Bake something special for me," he called over his shoulder.

"Bake—what?"

He shrugged, disappearing into the other side of the table. "You pick!"

Audrey smiled, but her humor quickly dissipated as she faced the black look McCaid sent her. Determined not to let him see how unsettling he was to her, she forced a polite smile and greeted him. "Good evening, Mr. McCaid."

Julian returned her greeting as his mind replayed the little vignette he'd just witnessed, seeing the boy twirling Audrey, leaning back and leering at her, his hands on her waist. The joy on her face as she greeted him was genuine and stunning. And when they had leaned together and whispered, it was all Julian could do to keep himself from ripping the boy off her. He couldn't explain his reaction. He'd never felt such a feeling.

"That was touching," he commented. Instantly, he wished he could pull the words back. Audrey smiled up at him, pushing him further into an ill humor.

"Hadley's an old friend of mine. Is there something I can do for you, Mr. McCaid?"

Heat shot through a part of him that had no business in this conversation. He knew she didn't mean those words the way his body heard them. He couldn't remember why he had come over here. He straightened stiffly, his mind scrambling for something that made sense.

Kemp.

He reached out and touched the bruises on her neck, bruises he had kissed last night. "So Kemp did this. Why?" The fear that shot through her pale green eyes shot through his gut as well. He stood before her, studying her, curious to see if she would lie to him.

"Because he can. Who will stop him?" Her words were breathy. He brushed the pads of his fingers against her throat, wondering if it was fear making her voice rasp, or if she felt what he was feeling.

His body tightened. He looked above her head and caught a dozen men watching them, ogling her as Deputy Fred had done in town. She was not a toy for them, or him, or any man. But how to protect her?

"Let's go up to the house while the light's still good. I think Jenkins will have a pencil and some paper for you to make notes on."

A few minutes later, Audrey, Amy Lynn, and Julian headed away from camp toward his new house. Amy scampered ahead, curious about everything. She picked little wildflowers, collecting a motley bunch of weeds with stems that were too long or too short. As they walked down a dirt road, which the wheels of the supply wagons had rubbed bare, Amy ran up to Julian and handed him a fistful of flowers.

"Here, Juli. These are for you."

Audrey watched McCaid look at Amy and the weeds she offered, her fist crushing some of the delicate flowers. She braced a hand against his knee and reached up as high as she could to give them to him. He looked confused, uncertain what he was to do with them. He bent over to unstick the motley collection from her sweaty palm, then straightened and frowned at them a moment. When he caught Audrey watching him, he glared at her and shoved the weeds in his vest pocket.

"Pretty, Juli." Amy smiled up at him, withstanding his frown with unflappable cheer as she slipped her hand in his. She took Audrey's hand, and they continued on.

When they topped the next hill, his house came into sight. Audrey stopped walking, making the other two halt with her. His home was a sprawling, two-story dwelling built in red brick. The right side of the house boasted an octagonal turret two stories high. The house had a wraparound porch on the lower level and a white ginger-bread balcony that ran two-thirds of the upper floor.

"Do you like it?" McCaid's deep voice interrupted her inspection.

"It's huge." She looked at him. "Are you moving here permanently?"

"No." He looked at his house with a satisfied expression. "I hope to be out for the next several summers, however. And with the train running to Cheyenne now, I'll have easy access to this as a home base for a mountain hunting lodge."

They started down the hill. Posts had been set for a picket fence that would enclose the front yard. Off to one side, a carriage house was being built in a matching red brick. Audrey picked Amy Lynn up, worried she might step on a nail or any of the other sharp items tossed haphazardly about. The wood decking of the deep porch had been painted a crisp white. Audrey could picture rocking chairs in one corner and a small dining area in another. It would be a lovely place to sit and drink coffee after dinner or bundle up with a blanket and watch a summer thunderstorm roll through.

She yanked herself abruptly from that reverie. This was McCaid's house, not hers. She would never do those things on this porch. Never with him. Possibly never in her life.

McCaid walked to the large double front doors. Opening the right side, he stood back to let them enter. The interior was not quite finished. The sweet, acrid scent of fresh plaster and paint filled her senses. Several walls had bare wood slats exposed, waiting their turn for the plasterer's attention. The wood staircase was a raw, unstained oak. The entrance hall was wide, a gracious space dominated by the broad staircase on one side that turned once before reaching the upper floor. From where they stood just inside the door, Audrey could see two rooms, two to her left and one to her right, and a couple more off a hallway that led back beyond the stairs.

McCaid gave them a tour of the downstairs, and she discovered that in addition to a sprawling kitchen and suite of service rooms, there was a dining room, a den, a parlor, and a library on the lower floor. Amy wiggled to be put down. A pile of small wood blocks had been left at the base of the stairs, which she immediately started to organize. Audrey turned her attention to the work at hand—getting McCaid set up with the things he needed to have window coverings made.

"Do you have something to take measurements with, Mr. McCaid?"

"I have the measurements on the building plans in the library."

Audrey followed him across the hallway. The library was a spacious room. The walls not lined with shelves were covered with raw paneling in varying stages of completion. She crossed the room to one of the two large windows, thinking of the effort Maddie had put into decorating her boardinghouse years ago. It had caused much excitement among the women in town as they helped her select colors, fabrics, wall coverings, and furniture from catalogues and samples sent up from Denver.

Creating curtains was the least of the tasks needed to complete a room.

"How were you planning to decorate the house?" she asked, turning to look at McCaid.

"I don't know." He shrugged.

"What colors do you favor? Will you be using any wallpaper?"

"Pick something. What colors do you like? What do you think would suit a hunting lodge?"

Audrey frowned. "I think such decisions should be made by your wife, not by me."

"I'm not married." She watched McCaid glance around them at the half-done shelves. "When I do marry, I don't expect to bring my wife out here. It is too far to travel and still too dangerous a place."

Audrey felt a strange tightening in her gut, seized by an unwelcome jealousy for the faceless woman who would be his wife. What would it be like to marry a man such as McCaid? To be cosseted and protected by someone so powerful?

McCaid looked at her again. "So you see, I need your help. I don't know how to finish the inside."

"I think you should go to Cheyenne and hire someone to help you. Your drapes must match your furniture and your wall colors and your rugs. It's not something I know how to do."

"I've had no luck getting a decorator to come to Defiance. They are too afraid of the town's reputation. Besides, with all the construction under way in Cheyenne, there's no one available, even if I found one brave enough to come."

"Then take your plans to them."

He nodded and gazed out the window behind her before looking at her again. "I sent them in when I ordered the furniture. The fabric—whatever the shopkeeper has on hand—will be shipped with the household goods. I doubt it will match anything, but it will at least protect the woodwork from the sun. I just have no one to make the drapes." His gaze turned probing. "Why did you steal from me, Miss Sheridan?"

Audrey was taken aback by his change of topics. This was not a subject she could discuss with him. Ever. Too much was at risk, far more than he knew. But she was trapped—he stood between her and the door.

"Tell me, do Sager and Rachel know what you do for a living? Does Logan?" he prodded when she remained silent.

"You know nothing about me."

"Did no one teach you right from wrong?"

She couldn't keep the stunned look from her face. She straightened her shoulders and decided she'd best quit the room. "Good night, Mr. McCaid." She started to walk away from him, but he snagged her wrist, twisting her arm behind her as he pulled her to him. "I asked you a question."

"You have no right to pry into my life." She tried to yank free, but his grip was relentless.

"Except your actions have now made you my dependent. Why did you steal from me?"

Audrey stared into his endless brown eyes, then let her eyes drift across the granite planes of his face. Tension deepened the lines bracketing his mouth. He was beautiful and alive. And in danger—as were her children. His grip tightened on her wrist. She met his eyes.

"You are not safe here, McCaid."

"Am I not?" Humor whispered across his face. "Have you come to harm me?" Fear for her loved ones fused her teeth. She would not be drawn further into this discussion. The humor vanished from his expression. "What trouble are you mixed up with, Miss Sheridan? And, more importantly, have you brought it to my ranch?"

He was close—too close. She couldn't focus on his eyes. She looked at his mouth instead. That was a mistake, for she remembered it against hers, warm and masterful. "Let me go," she whispered, and though he released her, neither of them moved or spoke. They stood as if poised on a precipice, breathing each other's breath, like lovers. Then Audrey retreated a step, breaking the spell.

She moved back two more steps, then pivoted and retrieved Amy. Julian went to one of the library windows and watched her leave, Amy in her arms. He leaned his forehead against the cool glass of the windowpane. He'd had no idea, when he met her last summer, how perilous her situation was. Her eyes were filled with secrets and desperation. Yet he still couldn't tell what was an act and what was real.

He knew only two things: he didn't like being played, and he was finding it hard to care that he shouldn't take her to his bed.

Chapter 12

He left his house and slowly moved back toward camp, so preoccupied that he'd left the front yard before he smelled the cigar smoke. It was a distinctive tobacco blend he associated with only one man: Jace Gage. A quick scan of the area showed his friend leaning negligently against the shadowy wall of the half-constructed carriage house. An orange glow briefly lit his face as he drew air through the cigar.

Julian went to greet his friend. Seeing him, Jace grinned, his cigar clamped in one corner of his mouth. They shook hands rigorously. "Jace Gage. Damn, it's good to see you!"

Jace's grin widened. "Been a while, McCaid," he said in that strange, raw voice of his.

Julian passed a critical eye over his friend. His blond hair was overlong and ragged. He hadn't shaved in a fair number of days. His beard was thickening and growing into his mustache. He wore a double bandolier crossed over his chest, strapped into a double holster sporting twin Colts. A Bowie knife was sheathed near the buckle of his gun belt. He coat was torn and stained, and over one shoulder he wore a rifle. Julian could see how he'd earned his nickname "Avenger."

"You look like hell, Jace."

"And you've gone soft, McCaid." Jace shook his head. "Living on three squares and a bit of candy in your bed."

"I'll admit to three squares, but I sure as hell am not getting any candy."

"Then you're losing your touch, my friend." He blew out a puff of smoke and squinted through the haze. "Who's the girl?"

"She's a friend of Sager's brother." He made a face. "She pickpocketed me and is out here working off her debt."

Jace couldn't keep a straight face. "So the score's pickpocket one, industrialist zero."

Julian crossed his arms and braced his legs. Disliking the course their conversation was taking, he changed the subject. "How about you tell me why the deputy marshal's so interested in Defiance?"

"Railroad ties. The government has millions of dollars tied up in loan guarantees to railroad developers—it wants those lines built and needs railroad ties to do it. The marshal wants a safe route to transport money and supplies up to those logging camps. That route happens to come straight through Defiance." He blew out another cloud of smoke. "So here I am."

"Kemp's got Defiance crawling with his men."

"I know. I've been watching them."

"He's bringing in more."

"Won't matter."

Julian wasn't one to shy away from a fair fight. Hell, even an unfair fight. But the odds facing Jace were untenable. "What can I do?"

"Guard your perimeter. I'm gonna be raising all

kinds of trouble, which'll make the sheriff do the same. I wanted you here so that I don't have to worry about your ranch. Other than that, just stay out of my way."

"I don't like this, Jace. Not one bit. Even in the war, we didn't take on shit like this alone."

"I've been going it alone for three years, McCaid. I damn sure don't need a keeper now." ·

Julian stared at his friend. He thought back to the failed lynching that Jace's own wife participated in. He and Sager had gotten to Jace in time to save his life, but not before the rope—and the whole cursed event— had changed his life forever. "You're never going to kill all the bad guys, Jace."

Jace dropped his cigar butt and crushed it beneath his heel. "That's a true fact, Julian. But I can keep at it · till they kill me."

Chapter 13

Kemp eyed the man standing in front of his desk. "I'm not asking you to kill anyone. Just play it rough out at Hell's Gulch. I need McCaid focused on his ranch."

"Ain't that what you sent the girl out for?"

Kemp felt his temper ratchet up a notch. He didn't like being questioned. He slowly came to his feet. "I'm paying you good money to do what you're told and not ask questions. I thought you wanted a place of your own, thought you were ready to be your own boss. But if you don't need the money, or you're too squeamish to do the job, just tell me. I'll get someone else to take your spot."

The man sighed and lowered his gaze. "I could use the money, Sheriff. I just don't like doing it this way."

"Keep him busy. Keep him out there. That's all you gotta do."

Chapter 14

Audrey and Jenkins settled into a workable routine over the next couple of days. He took on the job of tending the farm animals and never seemed to mind Amy Lynn tagging after him to feed the animals or milk the cow or collect the eggs. Once, when Amy was distracted, he even fetched her for his round of chores. And he taught Audrey how to tend the smokehouse fire, maintaining a consistent amount of heat and smoke on the curing meat.

Though she and Jenkins had found a comfortable working relationship, she and McCaid had not. She was ever aware of him. When he wasn't watching her at mealtimes, he was glaring at his men, curtailing their interactions with her. And it didn't help her nerves that he was readying his ranch for an attack.

He armed his men with Colts and Winchesters, and as they rotated in from the flocks and outer pastures, they had target practice. For an hour each afternoon, gunfire shattered the tranquility of the ranch. Every night, after supper had been cleared, they took over the long serving table under the cook tent to clean and oil their weapons. She was glad she'd decided to keep her children away.

Something was coming.

Tonight she was serving shredded barbecue beef, rolls, and beans. The men were hungry. She looked down the line of men waiting to be served, wondering if she'd made enough. Her gaze caught on the leering face of one of Kemp's men. Her heart started a staccato beat. After the first few days, without seeing them, she had begun to foster a hope they wouldn't come out after all, or that Franklin would find them lacking and refuse to hire them. But here they were, standing a couple of men away from her in the food line.

She tried to maintain her composure as she served the men, but one by one, Kemp's men came closer until finally they were in front of her. Her hands shook as she scooped beans onto the first one's plate. He grabbed her wrist, squeezing her in a painful grip. The spoon she held clattered to the table, spreading brown sauce and bean residue in a wide circle.

He leaned forward and whispered, "Honey, you know I want more than that. I'm hungry. Fill it up," he growled.

This was unspeakably rude. The ranch hands, by an unwritten agreement, always allowed everyone to go through the food line once for a single serving before coming back for seconds. Kemp's man was insisting on extra food in the beginning, while there were still so many others to feed. Audrey was afraid of him. Afraid for her children whom she left unguarded at home. Afraid for Amy Lynn who was here, but sometimes out of her sight. It would be easy to make an accident happen.

She didn't look down the line at the other ranch hands, didn't seek help. She couldn't risk causing problems that would backfire for her and the children. She dipped the spoon back in the bean bowl and gave him an extra serving, then quickly went on to his sneering friend, hoping no one noticed her reaction to either of the men.

That night, after she had put Amy Lynn to bed, she came back to the cookhouse, watching for Kemp's men. Jenkins had a handle on the evening's dishes, but she had to prepare for the morning. Again there was little food left in the slop pot, but what there was, she fed to the pigs. She added a few items to a list of supplies she needed to have refilled when someone next went to Defiance. Then she went inside the cookhouse and filled the coffee grinder with beans for the morning's first pot of coffee.

As she worked the grinder box a man came up behind her, planting his hands on either side of her on the counter and rubbing his body against hers. Audrey went stiff. She knew without looking he was one of Kemp's men. She could smell him. His body pressed her stomach painfully against the edge of the counter. He nuzzled against her neck, his fetid breath as rank as the slop bucket she'd just emptied.

"I've been looking for you all night, darlin'."

Audrey shoved her elbow into his side and pushed to be free of him, but he didn't release her. "Leave me alone!" She looked hopefully at the door, but realized how isolated they were in the cookhouse, away from the protection of the other hands.

His wiry arms folded around her, locking her in place. "Aw, now, honey, that ain't no way to be. Zeke and me, we drew straws to see who would get to do you first, and I'm the lucky winner."

"Let go of me!"

"I ain't gonna do that." His hand squeezed her

breast. "And I don't think you really want me to. 'Cause you know where Zeke is? He's up at your cabin, keepin' that little brat of yours company."

Audrey stopped resisting, but her heart still pounded, filling her body with the need to fight or run, anything but stand still. The man lifted her skirt, raising the material slowly in fistfuls. His legs moved between hers, spreading hers on either side of him. No. No. This couldn't be happening.

Suddenly, he was gone, along with the sour cloud of his breath. Audrey spun around in time to see McCaid launch his fist into the man's face. The sheriff's man got one good hit in, striking McCaid's mouth. But in short succession, McCaid got the upper hand, landing powerful blows to the man's face and torso before shoving him outside, where he sprawled in the dirt.

McCaid wiped the back of his fist against his torn lip as he stepped outside. "What the hell do you think you're doing touching my woman?"

"Your woman?" The man came to his feet. "She ain't your woman. We been real friendly a long time. I think I'd know if you was doin' her." Those were the last words he spoke before McCaid's fist laid him out cold. By then, several men had gathered around, including Jenkins and Franklin.

"Throw him in a wagon and get him out of here," he told his foreman. "We don't need his like stirring up trouble."

Audrey, watching from the doorway, wrung her hands. This was exactly what Kemp had warned her against. Oh God, what now? How could she protect her kids if she didn't stop this? How could she protect herself and Amy if she did?

"Please don't send him away," she pleaded.

"You know that bastard?" McCaid turned his rage on her, his face folded in disgust.

She nodded. "He's a h-hard worker." She stumbled on the lie. "He only gets like this when he's been drinking. Please, please give him another chance. You need all the hands you can get, and he needs the work."

McCaid's brows lowered. "I don't want troublemakers in my camp. That goes for him. And you."

Audrey nodded rapidly, grateful he seemed to be entertaining her request. McCaid cursed and turned to Franklin. "Take him out to the southeast pasture. He can work that corner until he cools off. He is not to speak to or be near Miss Sheridan, is that clear?"

Franklin nodded, then hurried to carry out those orders. Audrey stepped outside and started for her cabin. McCaid followed her, but she didn't slow her pace.

"Where are you running off to?"

"I have to check on Amy."

McCaid kept stride with her. "Do you want to explain what just happened back there? Where do you know him from? Who is he to you?"

"You ask too many questions."

"And I'm not getting any answers."

"You won't like the answers." They reached Audrey's small cabin. She glanced about the outside as she approached. No one was around. Of course, McCaid's yammering probably scared Zeke off. Audrey opened the door to her cabin as silently as possible. The sun had not quite set; there was still enough dusky light to tell that no one but the peacefully sleeping Amy was inside. Audrey hurried out the other side. No one standing about there either. She walked from side to side of her cabin. Nothing. Perhaps Kemp's man had been bluffing. Perhaps Zeke had never been up here, waiting to harm Amy.

Perhaps he'd heard their approach and got away.

Whatever the case, Amy was safe. And for the time being, so were her other children since Zeke's partner wasn't being sent back to town. Audrey crossed her arms and shut her eyes as she filled her lungs with a deep breath and slowly exhaled. All was well. Everyone was safe.

For now.

"Start talking, Sheridan." McCaid stood before her, hands on his hips.

"I've got nothing to say."

"You were looking for someone. That man threatened you, didn't he? Who is he to you?"

Audrey waved a hand in an irritated manner. "He's no one to me. Just someone I know from town."

"How many of my men do you know?"

Audrey put her hands on her hips, facing him. They stood in the last rays of the day's sun, orange light washing where shadows didn't yet reach. Audrey felt anger fill the void left by her fear. She was furious with McCaid and Kemp and his nasty hirelings. Most of all, she was angry with herself.

"I know lots of them. All of them." She waved her hand angrily. "Surprise! I'm Defiance's best-kept secret, the high-priced whore wh-who l-lives in a shack." Tears welled in her eyes, and yet her mouth kept spouting terrible words. "And now you've told them I'm your woman." She drew a ragged breath. "Wh-what were you thinking? How could you do something as thoughtless as that?"

And then she was in his arms, her face muffled against his chest. His shoulders curved around her, and he rested his chin on her head. Still the tears came, great big tears she'd been storing for years. Years of trying to be brave for her brother and the kids. Years of making ends meet and saving child after child with no resources or hope for their future. She gripped handfuls of his shirt as she wept against his chest while he silently absorbed her sorrow.

"I'm sorry," he murmured against the top of her head. "It was thoughtless of me. I only wanted to protect you."

Caught between his heartbeat and the gentling pressure of his hand rubbing her back, Audrey felt her tears ease. He kissed her hair. He lifted her face and pressed his lips against her forehead, then lower to the space between her eyebrows, then one side of her nose. He kissed her wet cheek, the corner of her mouth, before his mouth slanted across hers. He cupped the back of her head and wrapped an arm around her waist, pulling her up and against him.

His tongue slid against hers, pushing and tasting until she forgot all else. Her hands moved up his chest so she could wrap her arms around his neck. He broke the kiss, then started it again, his mouth moving over hers ravenously, a man starved for affection. When the kiss ended, he slowly set her feet back on the ground.

She moved back fractionally. "I'm not your woman, McCaid."

"You are. I've claimed you."

Audrey felt shock stiffen her limbs. "You can't do that."

"I've done it. Men are simple creatures. They want food. They want work. And they want sex. I'm giving them food and work. I just made it damn clear that they won't be getting sex from you. You're safer if they think you're my woman." McCaid grew still. For the space of a few heartbeats, he simply regarded her, the emotion in his brown eyes sizzling like a lit fuse. He touched her cheek, his fingers feathering across her skin. Never had she known a man's touch could be so gentle. Audrey wondered if her bruises on her neck were still visible. They didn't hurt anymore.

"Give me one night," he whispered as he brought his other hand up to her face. His touch was so distracting that it took her a full minute to understand the meaning of his words. "One night. Then I will take you back to Defiance, your debt forgiven. You can get away from this camp, from me, from the men here. You can be settled again in your own home."

Audrey didn't say no, but she couldn't say yes. It was too soon for her to return to Defiance. His mouth took hers in a gentle kiss. She opened her eyes, seeing half of his face washed in the golden light of the lowering sun, the other half darkened by his own silhouette. His arms went around her. He was hardness and muscle and bone where she was soft and round and thin. Her toes barely touched the ground. She didn't fight the kiss, but she didn't assist it either. She was too absorbed in cataloging what it felt like to have his arms around her.

Glorious.

It was glorious. And deadly.

If she surrendered, he would return her to town. "No." She pushed away from him. "No." He dropped his arms, giving no resistance as she backed away. "Good night, McCaid."

Julian said nothing; he just watched her pivot and enter her cabin. He headed back to camp, where he poured himself a cup of coffee and cast a jaundiced glance over the men. Who of them had been with Audrey? Which of them had she let near her, hold her. Fuck her? Some looked at him, some ignored him. Shit. He dumped his coffee and went to the corral to saddle his horse. Maybe a ride would help this rangy restlessness consuming him.

He was just tightening his horse's cinch when Franklin approached him. "Boss, I gotta talk to you."

"What is it, Franklin?"

"That man tonight—there were two of them that came in together. One of them was that Howie character you just dealt with, the other a mean hombre named Zeke. I think we oughtta get rid of them both."

Julian straightened. Had Audrey been looking for Howie's partner? Who the hell were they? "No. They're here for a reason. Might go better for us to know about them, know what they are up to, than to have them out of eyesight. Keep them separated. Work them like sons of bitches. I want them too tired to cause trouble. Don't issue them rifles. They won't be at the target practices."

"Yessir."

"And, Franklin—get a cot set up for Amy in the cookhouse. She shouldn't be so far from Miss Sheridan at night."

"Will do, boss."

Julian swung up onto his horse as Franklin held the gate for him. He moved at a sedate trot past camp, then squeezed his horse into a lope. He listened to the sound of the wind and the beat of his horse's hooves, but he couldn't outrun his thoughts. What the hell had possessed him tonight? Never in his life had he begged a woman to be with him, yet just now, with Audrey, he had done that very thing. He'd never lost control before. Not in the war, not in his postwar business dealings, not in his careful vetting of potential wife candidates. But every time he looked at Audrey, he wanted her.

Naked. Above him. Beneath him. Wrapped around him.

He pulled up on a slight rise as the pinks and oranges cast by the setting sun gave way to purples, then blues, then the thin, wispy clouds turned gray. What did his hankering for Audrey mean for the plans he'd made for his future? Maybe his reaction to her had nothing to do with the woman herself. Maybe she was just a conveniently available female, something to distract himself from the fact that when he returned to Virginia, he was going to choose a wife from among the half dozen women he'd carefully selected—none of whom did he have a passion for, some of whom he knew as acquaintances, all of whom could trace their bloodlines back to the country's founding fathers.

He turned his horse around. On that slight rise, he could see the mountains in the west, rimmed by the long-gone sun. He sighed. Setting his knees lightly to his mount, he slowly made his way back to camp. Marriage was the right next step for his life, for the children he would father. He was going to marry one of the women he'd short-listed. And if he needed a last romp, then so be it. He would do it now and get it out of his system. He would honor his vows once they were said. And he would play like the devil this one last summer.

Chapter 15

Audrey finally made good her promise to Hadley. She hadn't seen him for almost a week and had a sneaking suspicion McCaid was keeping him busy and away from her. Franklin had told her he was due back tonight, so she'd prepared several double-crusted apple crisps from slices of dried apples she found in the storeroom.

She dished the treat out to ranch hands who looked like boys about to taste their first candy stick. When there was a break in the line, Audrey glanced over and found McCaid leaning against one of the posts supporting the tent canopy. Hands in his pockets, his dark eyes on her, a lock of his straight brown hair curved down over his eyebrow—it was all Audrey could do not to suck in a sharp breath.

"Would you care for some crisp, Mr. McCaid?" He looked from her to the baking dish and back again, a dark brow raised, his unspoken question hanging in the air.

Audrey looked at the crisp and grinned. So he knew it was Hadley's requested treat. "You don't have a sweet tooth?"

He didn't answer right away. "Oh, I have a sweet tooth," he drawled.

"But you don't care for apple crisp?"

"I don't care for that apple crisp."

Audrey's smile widened. "I see."

McCaid was spared having to respond by a ruckus that kicked up as a rider came tearing through camp. Ordinarily, the hands were careful not to stir up dust so near the cook tent, but the rider only pulled up a dozen feet from McCaid.

"Franklin wanted me to get you, boss. The northwest fence has been cut. It's a bloody goddamned mess. Dead sheep everywhere. Some not quite dead."

McCaid hollered for a man to saddle his horse. He barked out orders in rapid succession, setting hands to double up at their watch posts, to pass out rifles, to bring lanterns. Jenkins ran inside the cookhouse and popped open a large cabinet. He pulled out rifle after rifle, tossing them to the men who came to retrieve them, throwing boxes of ammunition like candy at a parade.

McCaid caught a rifle, and a box too. "Stay here," he ordered Jenkins as he loaded rounds into his Winchester. "Keep Miss Sheridan and Amy safe."

"Yes, sir!"

McCaid swung up into his saddle. Audrey couldn't decipher the look he gave her as his horse danced restlessly beneath him. She watched him spin away and ride off. Men rushed about the camp, taking up their posts, grabbing their horses. Amy Lynn was hugging her leg. She picked her foster daughter up.

"It's all right, baby. Don't be afraid." It was hard not to be frightened, with men shouting and horses thundering by, when just moments before the camp had been settling into its evening routine. Audrey wondered if she had seen McCaid for the last time, if—somewhere out there—Kemp's men were lying in wait for him. The sick tension in her stomach deepened.

"Don't you be frightened either, Miss Audrey. Them that done this, they gotta know the camp's armed. They'd be fools to ride in here. Not a one of 'em would make it out alive," Jenkins said as he pushed several rounds into his rifle. "I'll keep you safe."

Audrey looked at him. She had experienced some frightening things in Defiance, but this was far worse. "So we just wait?"

Jenkins nodded. "We just wait."

Hours passed. Audrey went about cleaning up the supper dishes and prepared what she could for the morning meal, all while Jenkins stood nearby, his gun at the ready. The camp was dark and quiet, strangely so after the tumult resulting from the rider's announcement. Eventually, she and Amy retired to their cabin, with Jenkins posted outside the door and a chair propped under the other door.

Despite her anxiety, or perhaps because of it, Audrey was asleep as soon as her head touched the pillow. Sometime in the night, a fierce pounding at her door roused her. Sleepily, she went to the door and opened it. Jenkins stood there.

"Miss Audrey! Come quick! There's been an injury—"

Audrey stepped outside, barefoot and in her nightgown, and closed the door behind her. Jenkins stopped her, a hand on her shoulder. "Honey, you can't come out like that. But there's no time to dress. Put yer coat on and grab yer boots."

Audrey turned around woodenly, blinking the sleep from her eyes. The cold night air was rapidly rousing her. She turned back, awake now and frightened.

Torches and lamps were lit all around the camp. "Is it McCaid? Is McCaid hurt?"

"No, Mr. McCaid's fine. It's one of the boys. Hurry now."

Audrey quickly donned her coat and laced up her boots over her bare feet. She ran to catch up to Jenkins, grabbing his sleeve. "Is it over?"

He looked at her, his lips thinned. "For now. For this round, at least."

They came to the cook tent. A dozen men were crowded around a man who was sprawled and moaning on the ground. Audrey pushed her way through the men and knelt beside him.

Hadley.

"What is it? What's happened?" she asked those standing around him as she began running her hands over her friend, starting at the top of his head, his shoulders, his arms, his chest. She saw no blood. Pulling his coat aside, she found a jagged slice across his upper thigh. It was fairly deep and long, but thankfully was on the outside of his leg, else he'd be long gone. She started to stand, intending to organize the men to gather what she would need to see to his injury, but Hadley pulled her back down. His hand bunched in her coat lapel as he drew her close to his face.

"You stitch this," he ordered from clenched teeth. "You do it, Audrey. I don't want to wait for that barber-butcher. I don't want him near my leg."

Audrey smiled, trying to reassure him. She was no doctor. She could stitch simple cuts, but she couldn't mend ligaments or stave off fever. And she didn't know yet how bad his injury was. "Easy now, Hadley." She brushed his hair from his face, feeling his forehead as she did so to make sure a fever hadn't set in. His skin was still cool. "That's far too much bellyaching for a little scratch. I'll stitch you up—we won't get the barber. Give me a minute to get my supplies." She pulled herself free of his grip and sat back on her haunches, looking at the men circled around her friend. She didn't know their names.

"You." She pointed to one. "Get some whiskey. You, bring some blankets and get him situated on the table over there. You, take his pants off and cover him with a blanket so he doesn't catch a chill—careful of that wound. You, start some water heating." She went into the cookhouse, opening drawers and cabinets, looking for the needles and thread she had seen earlier, as well as the bandages.

"Miss Sheridan—Audrey," McCaid said, coming over to her. Had he been in the circle? She hadn't seen him. She sent a quick look over him, glad he was in one piece. He took her arms, his face bleak. "You don't have to do this. I'll send for the doctor."

A harsh laugh broke from Audrey. "There's no doctor in Defiance, McCaid. The nearest one is a two-day ride from here. This man needs to be stitched now."

"Then a barber, someone in Defiance."

"The barber is heavier handed than a blacksmith. Would you want him to work on your leg?"

McCaid's brows lowered as he searched her face. "Are you up to this?"

"This isn't the first wound I've stitched, and it won't be the last."

"Here you go, missy," Jenkins asked, handing her the needle and thread. "I think you were lookin' fer these?"

"Bandages and a couple towels—where are they?" she asked.

"I'll get 'em," Jenkins said as he shuffled over to one of his cabinets.

Audrey rolled up her coat and nightgown sleeves, donned an apron, then scrubbed her hands. Drying her hands on a fresh towel, she went outside to Hadley. His friends had him laid out on a blanket on the serving table with another blanket rolled up under his head and two more covering him. The whiskey bottle was on the table, near his shoulder.

"Are you ready, Hadley?"

"Can I have some of that whiskey first?"

She nodded to one of the men standing near him. He braced an arm under Hadley so that he could lift the bottle to his mouth. While he drank, Audrey pushed the blanket aside to get a good look at his wound. "Can you tell me what happened?" she asked him.

"Dunno. Something spooked my horse. She shied away, catching my leg on a nail in a fence post."

One of the boys brought over the heated water she had asked for, and Audrey set to work. She cleaned the wound first, then drizzled whiskey on the jagged opening. She dragged the needle and thread through the whiskey to sanitize them. Pulling the edges of the wound together, she had him stitched up in short order. She washed the fresh blood away, then dribbled a bit more whiskey over the wound. Finally, she wrapped his leg in a clean bandage and covered him again with the blanket.

"All done." She took his hand in one of hers and gave it a squeeze. "It was a flesh wound. The nail didn't cut any ligaments or bone. You're lucky, because I couldn't have fixed those. It should knit up just fine."

Audrey sent one of the men to fetch Hadley's bedroll, which she had him set out by the large fire pit. She wanted Hadley close by so that she could keep her eye on him during the day tomorrow. While a couple of the men helped Hadley get settled for the night, she washed her hands and turned her attention to cleaning up the worktable so that it would be ready for the morning. When next she looked around, most of the men had retired. Only McCaid remained.

"Finished?" he asked as she hung up her bloodied apron.

She nodded. "How did it go tonight?"

"I lost about fifty head. And one man. His throat was cut like the goddamned sheep."

Audrey gasped. That had Kemp's signature all over it. How often had he threatened that very fate to her? she thought, unable to suppress a violent shiver.

"Come on," McCaid said, turning her toward her cabin. "Let's get you back to bed. Morning's but a few hours away. I've got the men on double shifts. The only good thing in their days for a long while will be your cooking, so you'd better get some sleep. You're going to need your strength."

Audrey folded her arms and tucked her hands beneath their warmth. Perhaps it was her fatigue making her so chilled. Or perhaps it was the reality of her situation sinking in. She was glad her children weren't with her here. It was far too dangerous a place for them to be.

At the doorstep to her cabin, she paused, turning to face McCaid. He watched her, quietly, his dark eyes tired and angry. Audrey wished he would hold her, tell her this would all work out right, that she and Amy Lynn—her whole family—would be safe. But that was false thinking. She knew, better than she wished to know, such assurances could not be kept. She had best look to herself for her own safety. It was foolish to rely on anyone else. And it was dangerous to want to.

Audrey started to fuss with one of her coat buttons. Looking down, she was disconcerted to see she'd put her coat on so hastily that big tufts of her linen nightgown escaped above and below the few buttons she had fastened. She touched her long braid, wondering if it was coming undone. Long tendrils of her hair probably stood at odd angles about her like a horse shedding its woolly winter hair. She was a dreadful sight. She gazed at McCaid, in some distress, wishing he would look away. Instead, a rueful smile lifted one corner of his mouth.

"Good night, Miss Sheridan," he said. "Thank you for what you did tonight. I wouldn't have asked it of you—I wouldn't have thought you equal to the task. You always seem to surprise me." He touched his thumb to her chin, feathering it gently across her skin as his eyes watched hers. "I'm going to Defiance tomorrow. Sheriff Kemp's got some explaining to do."

Fear stabbed Audrey's gut. "No!" She grabbed hold of his arms. "You can't go to town!"

McCaid frowned. "Why?"

"It isn't safe for you to go there. Please, McCaid. Please don't go."

"I'm not afraid of the sheriff."

"You should be."

"I have no doubt he's behind the attack tonight. I can't let it go unpunished. I'll be back tomorrow night."

"Then take me with you. Please." She had to check on her family—had to be sure they were safe.

"No. I haven't forgotten the bruises you came here with—have you?"

"I'm not safe here either. Look what happened tonight. Please, McCaid."

His intense expression was clearly visible by the light

of the moon. Her stomach knotted as her fear grew that he would not bring her with him.

"Fine. We'll leave after breakfast tomorrow and stay a night in town. Jenkins can tend things while you have a short break. You'd best get some rest—morning comes early after a night like this one."

Chapter 16

The wagon lurched as McCaid drew to a stop in front of the general store. Amy wiggled restlessly, anxious to get down. Audrey helped her off and she ran inside. McCaid stepped off the wagon and reached up for Audrey. She took hold of his shoulders as he swung her down. His hands were warm and large at her waist. He didn't release her right away, and she didn't entirely mind being held so close to him. She wanted to warn him again, but she knew he wouldn't listen. There certainly was no way to hide him, pretend he hadn't come to town. The best she could do was warn Malcolm and Leah to be extra vigilant with the kids.

"Will Kemp cause you problems?" McCaid asked. "I swear I will kill him if you're bruised when I see you tomorrow. Perhaps you should stay with me. I could take a second room for you and Amy at Maddie's."

"McCaid, this is my town, my home. I will be fine."

He made a face. "You will be here tomorrow. . . ."

"I'll be here. Thank you for bringing us to town." Worried their private conversation would be noted, she reluctantly pulled away from him.

"Audrey!" Malcolm called to her as Amy drew him by the hand out to the boardwalk in front of the store. Audrey started up the steps, hoping he hadn't seen her standing with McCaid. She gave her brother a quick embrace, then introduced him to McCaid. Both men shook hands and sized each other up.

Jim's wife, Sally, heard the commotion and came running out from the storeroom to greet them. She gave Audrey a big hug, then leaned back to give her a once-over. She sent McCaid a dark look as she asked Audrey, "Are you well, dear? Has it been terrible?"

"I'm fine. Mr. McCaid's ranch is beautiful, though there has been some trouble out there. Someone cut his fences and killed the sheep that got loose. One of his men was killed, another injured. You remember Hadley Baker."

"I do. Tell me he wasn't the one killed!"

"No, no! But he was injured. His leg was pinned between his horse and the wire fence. He has a nasty cut."

Sally gasped. "I wish you weren't out there, dear. It's no place for a woman, with all that trouble going on."

"My men and I watch out for her, Mrs. Kessler," McCaid reassured her. "We won't let anything happen to her. By the way, Amy Lynn is in need of some new shoes. She could use some new stockings as well, and anything else that Miss Sheridan requires. Please put it on my tab."

Malcolm's face tightened as his gaze shifted from McCaid to Audrey. "What about the others?"

Audrey gave a warning shake of her head.

"What others?" McCaid asked her.

"There are other children in town, besides Amy, in need of shoes as well, that's all." Audrey spoke before her brother could. McCaid gave her one of his disturbingly penetrating looks. She carefully kept her face blank.

"Well, boy," he said to Malcolm, "go get them. If the Kesslers don't have enough shoes, they can order more."

Audrey caught the look Sally sent her; it was not a pleasant one. "Why are you doing this?" Audrey confronted McCaid.

McCaid crossed his arms and stared down at her. "Doing what?"

Audrey leaned forward and spoke in a lowered tone. "Helping us. We don't need your help."

"Will you excuse us a minute, Mrs. Kessler?" He took hold of Audrey's arm, forcibly escorting her outside, away from where their conversation could be overheard or observed. "Don't be a stubborn idiot, Sheridan." He turned to her. "Your daughter needs shoes and stockings. Apparently, other children do as well."

"I don't want gifts from you. I won't be indebted to you."

"Trust me, my motivation is purely selfish. I'm outfitting your daughter so that you can focus on the work I need you to focus on instead of worrying whether you need to trim off more of her shoes to accommodate her growing feet."

Audrey gasped. She was saved from answering, however, by the arrival of her other children. Seven wiggling bodies mobbed her, pressing in to greet her. They jumped and spoke excitedly, all hurrying to tell their news since she had left. Nervously, she looked at McCaid over their heads. He was studying them curiously. Malcolm held the door for them, and they all filed inside.

"Who are all these children?" McCaid asked as they followed the kids inside.

"They come from different families. Times have

been hard in town," Audrey answered, being purposefully vague.

"Mrs. Kessler, please do what you can for them," McCaid directed her. "If you must order some things, do so and put it on my bill." Just then, Jim entered the store. He looked disconcerted to see all the children; then his face brightened when he saw Audrey. He greeted McCaid. Audrey absently heard him ask how things were going on the ranch. She became absorbed in the work at hand, fitting all the children for socks or stockings and new shoes.

It made sense to buy a pair for all the children, even if theirs were yet fine. She and Sally went up to the next size for the kids who didn't need new ones. Despite her concern at the hidden cost of McCaid's help, Audrey was greatly relieved. The kids usually went barefoot in the summer and in the autumn she faced the burden of buying new shoes. Now they would have plenty of pairs for the younger ones to grow into. Hopefully they could get through the next year without having to buy more than a couple of pairs. This was very generous of McCaid.

Once finished with the shopping, Audrey had each of the children thank McCaid. Luc and Kurt exchanged quick handshakes with him, giving him as dark a look as Malcolm had. McCaid appeared a little bemused, but said nothing.

Audrey left the store with the kids in tow. She was anxious to visit with them and see what had happened in the time she'd been gone. She listened as one and then another talked over each other, in a hurry to tell all their news. They had kept to their studies. Leah and Malcolm checked their schoolwork. And they had been good about their chores. They wanted to know all that had happened out at Hell's Gulch.

Audrey had just started to tell them about the cow and chickens and pigs that McCaid had out at his spread when Leah and Wolf came charging toward them. The two women hugged each other tightly. When they pulled apart, Audrey's eyes were watering. She missed being home, missed her children and her friend. The kids chattered all the way to their front yard, then dispersed, returning to their game of chase. Audrey called to Colleen and Mabel to watch Amy.

Leah smiled at Audrey and looped her arm through hers as they went up her front steps. "We'll have some coffee, and you can tell me all about Hell's Gulch."

A quick look around the small interior of her home set Audrey's worries at ease. The house was neat. Malcolm and the kids were keeping up with everything nicely. If they could do that for this long, they could do it for the remaining weeks of her sentence.

"Is it bad, at the camp? How is Amy holding up without the other kids?"

"Actually, the men are nice—they like my cooking. Jenkins, the previous cook, is a big help. He's taken Amy under his wing. They tend the animals together. She loves helping him milk the cow. I think the chickens help her to be less homesick."

Audrey looked at Leah and drew a deep breath. "Kemp sent a couple of his men out to the camp, said if I say anything about them to McCaid, he'll hurt the children. And I was supposed to keep McCaid away, but I couldn't. I don't know what the sheriff will do. I'm afraid, Leah." She crossed her arms, feeling a chill despite the room's warm temperature. "I meant what I said; when I come back, I'm taking the kids away from Defiance."

"Where would we go?"

We. The relief that Leah would come with her was overwhelming. She took hold of her friend's hands. "Cheyenne. Or Denver. I don't know. Anywhere. I could be a seamstress. I could take in laundry and start my business by doing small repairs and such. You could be a baker there. We would make ends meet."

Leah pulled her hands free and took a few steps into the room. "I like Defiance, Audrey. I still have enough customers to make a decent living. I can hunt and fish. I don't know if I could do that if we moved to a bigger town. And we have our vegetable garden. We just need Defiance to turn around."

"But what if it doesn't? What if everyone goes, and we're left with only Kemp and his men?"

"I'll think about it, Audrey. I promise."

Knowing she couldn't press further, Audrey caught her up on everything that had happened at the ranch, and Leah did the same for the news from town. As they talked, Audrey gathered bed linens and soiled clothes, taking care of the wash that hadn't been done since she left.

A few hours later, the laundry lines out back were full. She'd seen to baths for all the children and had a pot of stew on for supper. It felt good to be home. She missed the children's noise, missed visiting with Leah. She was putting fresh linens on her bed when Kurt came running into the house.

"McCaid's coming!" he blurted out.

Audrey exchanged a look with Leah. "Kurt, you and Luc keep the kids away. I don't know what he wants, but I will get rid of him."

Leah and Kurt went out the back way as McCaid's boots sounded on the front steps. Leah pointed to Audrey's chest. When she looked down, she remembered she had opened the top several buttons of her dress, trying to let air cool her skin while she did the wash.

As she fastened the buttons, she looked around her small dwelling with a conflicting mixture of pride and embarrassment. This house belonged to her and Malcolm. They owned it and the tiny lot it was on. Though McCaid could fit her little home in his house at Hell's Gulch ten times over, she was proud of it. And doubtless that was only one of his many homes.

A knock sounded on her front door.

Audrey squared her shoulders and lifted her chin, determined to focus on the gulf that stood between her and McCaid. He was not a part of her world, and she would never be a part of his. It didn't help that she hungered for the sight of him. It didn't help that she woke every day at Hell's Gulch knowing she would see him, perhaps speak to him. Even now her heart was hammering, her breathing shallow. Why was he here? She opened the door.

"Mr.—" she began, before getting a good look at him. "Oh! Good heavens!" He looked as if he'd been run over by a wagon. One cheek was red and swollen. The skin at his temple was scraped and bleeding. A corner of his mouth leaked a thin trickle of blood. She reached out and pulled him into her home, noticing his knuckles were in no better shape than his face.

"I'm fine." He resisted being drawn into the room. "I didn't come here for nursing. I just thought I'd check on you before I settle in at Maddie's for the evening."

She removed his hat and eased his hair away to examine the scrape on his forehead. "What happened?" she asked again, forcefully directing him over to the kitchen. She fetched a bowl of hot water and a clean cloth.

He leaned against the counter of the dry sink and crossed his arms. "The sheriff's not in town, but his men and I don't see eye-to-eye on the matter of his responsibilities to area ranchers—namely me. I guess they didn't like hearing his days as sheriff were numbered. When I left, two of his ramrods tried to rough me up."

Audrey dabbed at the cut by his lip, relieved at the news that Kemp was gone. McCaid winced and pulled away. She rinsed her cloth. "Be still. If I don't do this, Maddie will, and she hasn't the light touch I have." She risked a look at his eyes. "You should avoid the sheriff and his men. He'll be no help to you. Honestly, Mr. McCaid, as long as you run sheep, you won't have any peace."

"It's got nothing to do with the sheep, Audrey. It's me. Kemp doesn't like me."

That must have struck him as funny, for he flashed a grin at her. She quickly pressed the cloth to the injured corner of his mouth as she held her other hand against his cheek. "Don't smile. You'll open your cut again."

At her touch, his grin faded and his eyes darkened. He took hold of her wrist and moved her palm to his lips. Audrey couldn't breathe. No man other than McCaid had ever looked at her that way—not that she'd noticed anyway. She rinsed the cloth and started to work on his temple, hoping he wouldn't feel her hands shaking.

Julian watched her intent expression, felt the tremor in her touch. Her skin was dewy from the water steaming on the stove and the heat of the room. Little tendrils of hair curled about her face. She was close, not even a hand-span from his face. He could lean forward slightly—only a very little bit—and connect their lips.

His gaze dropped to her mouth, which was parted slightly as she worked on him. Inches. Scant inches separated them. He ached to have her in his arms, to taste the skin of her neck. Her breathing seemed irregular. The top few buttons of her blouse were haphazardly fastened, mismatched from her chest up. Blood throbbed in his groin. She pressed the cloth to his temple, hurting his bruised skin. "Ouch!"

"Sorry." She took hold of his chin. "Hold still. You wiggle like a twelve-year-old boy."

Julian clamped his jaw shut.

She switched from working on his face to his hands. "Tell me the others look as bad as you do," she said as she dipped his hands in a fresh bowl of water and rinsed the blood away.

He didn't answer her. He couldn't think; he could only feel as her hands slid over his, soothing, easing his pain even as she set him on fire.

"All done!" She took up a clean linen and gently dried his hands as she gave him an encouraging smile. He sucked in a long breath of air and looked around the interior of her home. Kitchen, parlor, and bedroom all shared the same cramped space. He started a slow circuit of the room, pacing like a caged animal, delaying his departure.

"Have dinner with me tonight, Audrey. I'll get Maddie to set a private table for us in her dining room."

"You forget I have Amy Lynn."

"I've forgotten nothing. Didn't you have a friend living next to you? Leah Morgan was her name, if I remember correctly. She could watch Amy Lynn tonight."

The back door opened and closed. Audrey tensed. McCaid's eyes widened. He went to open the door leading to the back room. Audrey quickly blocked him.

"Who are you protecting?" he asked

"No one."

"Let me pass. I'll see for myself."

"No."

"Why? Why, Audrey?" Hearing her given name in his deep voice, whispered so huskily, so near her ear, she couldn't suppress a shiver. He moved fractionally closer to her. She did not step away, fearful he would open the door and see the bunks, then know about her children. She gripped the edges of the doorjamb, blocking him as she stood her ground.

He bent to nuzzle her neck. "Why do you let other men near you but keep me at arm's length?"

Audrey's faithless body sizzled at the kisses he feathered against her neck. "What makes you think I let other men near me?"

He lifted his head to look at her. "Besides your rumpled bed and disarrayed clothing?"

She quickly looked down at her shirt and skirt, seeing the crooked closure of the top few buttons. There was nothing she could do about it without releasing the door. He touched his hands to hers where they clasped the doorjamb. His eyes holding hers, he drew his hands up her arms to her shoulders. He unfastened the first of the crooked buttons, then the next, then the last, baring a small expanse of skin at the top of her bodice. Gently, slowly, he drew his fingers down one side of the open material, stopping where the buttons were properly fastened.

"Give me one night, Audrey. One night. You won't have to return to Hell's Gulch. You could stay here." He gripped the back of her head, arching her throat for his kiss, his lips light, his breath hot. Audrey's breathing grew erratic. What was he doing to her? Why was he doing this? And worse, she didn't want him to stop.

"I will pay you, in addition to dropping your sentence. Tell me what your fee is."

Audrey shook her head, but his mouth came down on hers and rational thought took flight. He held her waist and drew her away from the door as he walked backward. Away from the door was good, Audrey reasoned with herself. At the table, he turned and lifted her to sit atop it, never breaking the kiss. She loved the way he smelled of leather and a faint spicy sweet scent, loved the way his mouth surged and retreated against her own.

Gradually, she became aware of sitting on the table in a very unladylike position. Her legs were splayed, and he stood between them. She thought she should close her knees but couldn't make her body comply with what she told it. She didn't want to push him away; she wanted him closer. She wrapped her arms around his shoulders, loving the feel of his hard chest against her breasts. One of his hands was around her back and one was on her thigh, pulling her to the edge of the table, bringing her against himself.

Through a haze of sensation, she felt him lift her skirt, exposing her bare knees and the ruffled ends of her drawers. "No," she whispered, but she must not have spoken aloud, for instead of stopping, he bent and licked the base of her throat. His hot tongue traced a path up the line of her throat to her chin, around her chin to her lips. A strange languor stole through her limbs. His hand was beneath her dress, stroking her thigh, moving slowly closer to her hip. And then he touched the most private part of her, a place no one had ever touched before.

She gasped.

"Easy, easy now," he whispered, his command hypnotic. His thumb caressed her through her cotton drawers, finding flesh so exquisitely sensitive that waves of sensation washed through her body, melting her, eroding her resistance.

She gripped his hand, but he didn't stop. "Let me do this. Let me give you pleasure. Let me show you what it will be like between us."

His able fingers found the slit in her drawers and touched her feminine core, skin to skin. Audrey threw her head back, bracing herself on the table with her hands. Suddenly, heat burst through her body in convulsions. Her legs gripped his hips as she bucked against his hand, wanting, needing more of him, more of— what? She didn't even know. He watched her as he did that thing with his thumb.

When the waves subsided, Audrey focused on McCaid. He grinned a self-satisfied male smile. "What was that? What did you just do to me?" she asked breathlessly.

Some of the humor left his face, to be replaced by an emotion she couldn't identify. "Have you never felt that before? Have you never climaxed?"

Embarrassed at her abandon now that the world was righting itself, she didn't trust her voice. She shook her head.

He took hold of her face, his eyes serious. "Come to me tonight. I will let you in—Maddie won't have to know. Let me love you. Please. It will be a night of this, a night like you've never felt before."

"No."

He leaned his forehead against hers. "Why?"

"I have plans for this evening."

He pulled back to look at her. "You're not going to be alone tonight, are you?"

Audrey knew she was misleading him. She pushed free of his arms and slipped off the table. It was better to face him standing on her own two feet. "No, I'm not."

"What is your fee? What does one night with you cost?" he rasped.

Audrey's mind scrambled for a coherent response, opening a fissure in her passion wide enough to let reality seep in. A night in his arms would be heaven. He raised feelings in her she'd never felt before, but even a single night could have disastrous effects. He would return to his normal life and she would be alone, possibly pregnant.

"I am not for sale, Mr. McCaid. Not for any price." She crossed the room on unsteady legs and opened her front door.

His face hardened as he silently regarded her. He set his hat on his head, gave her a brief nod, then left.

Chapter 17

The drive back to Hell's Gulch did little to soothe Audrey's raw nerves the next day. She was keenly aware of McCaid next to her. She found herself looking at his hands as he loosely held the reins, wondering what the leather of his gloves would feel like against her skin. She sat closer to him than perhaps she should, anticipating the small movements his leg made now and then as they rode the long way home. He caught her looking at him once. Her eyes rose to his. Blood heated her face.

To make matters worse, her body had gone strange. She had a constant moistness where he'd touched yesterday. Her skin was tingly, her breasts sensitized. Perhaps she was getting the flu.

Julian didn't know how much more he could take. He wondered if she was aware of the effect she was having on him, wondered if he'd broken through her resolve during their interlude yesterday. He checked over his shoulder. Amy was sound asleep in a little cocoon he'd made for her among the sacks of flour and sugar. That meant he and Audrey were virtually alone. With growing enthusiasm, he considered setting the brake and dragging her onto his lap, taking her right here on the bench, in broad daylight. Rough and hard. Without prelude. Burying himself in her warm, moist flesh.

He cursed silently and gritted his teeth. At this rate, his own thoughts would unman him. He should have left her in town. Keeping her near him was madness. He had a plan for his future, his children's future, and it couldn't be achieved through Audrey.

His prayers for a reprieve were answered when they reached the ranch: the shearing team had come in. Over the next few days, Julian joined the crews trimming sheep in the large barn built for that purpose. The work was backbreaking and left him little energy to pursue Audrey, which was as he intended.

The shearing team, along with some of his men, was organized into four crews of two to do the shearing, another small crew to do the tail docking, another for castration, a man who marked the newly sheared yearlings, and a couple more who gathered the wool and bagged it in large canvas bundles.

The days blurred, one into another, as Julian worked alongside his men, seeing to sheep after sheep. Each time the meal bell rang, he felt a rush of anticipation— he would see *her*. Unfortunately, it was a feeling shared by every other ranch hand he employed. She behaved no differently toward him than she did toward any of the boys, except perhaps Hadley, who was still recovering from his wound.

Audrey refused to let the boy be assigned any work that would disturb his mending leg. Franklin had set him to stationary tasks, such as mending leather halters and cleaning rifles. Julian asked himself a dozen times why the hell he didn't send the boy packing. Neither Hadley nor Audrey seemed to favor that option. Perhaps the boy had something to prove to his father. Perhaps he had something to prove to Audrey. Whatever the reason, having him around Audrey was about as much fun as chewing gravel.

It didn't help matters for Julian to realize what a clumsy crew of workers Franklin had hired. His men frequently had to stop work so that they could get patched up—minor things mostly. Ruptured blisters, gashes from careless handling of the sheep, digestive upsets, the list was endless. He mentioned his observation to Franklin as they made the rounds by the corrals after lunch.

His foreman burst out laughing. "Are you blind, boss?"

Julian gave him a warning face that would have frightened a man less familiar with him. "What's that supposed to mean?"

"They're hankering after Miss Audrey. Because you claimed her, they can't, in the normal course of things, speak to her. But if they get injured, she's the one who doctors them up. None of them are letting Jenkins near 'em."

Julian drew to a stop. "They're willfully injuring themselves?"

"I don't suppose it's willful. Hadley's injury wasn't."

Julian thought about that conversation that evening after the bell rang for super. His mood was foul. As he came around the corner, he caught sight of two of his men gleefully examining a fresh cut on a third friend's forehead. Julian glared at them. He had a cracked rib from a ram who didn't take to the idea of castration and hadn't been properly restrained, yet he wasn't running to Audrey for help.

He cleaned up for the meal, then went up to the cook tent where a makeshift medical area had been set up, intending to put a stop to this nonsense immediately. Besides Hadley, half a dozen hands were lounging around, some with bandages on their heads, another with an arm in a sling, another with his foot propped up, a few with bandaged hands. When they saw him, they all came to their feet. He looked from one to another, holding his silence long enough to make them nervous.

Julian put his hands behind his back, refusing to wince at the pain in his ribs, and considered the situation. Though it damned near killed him to reprieve Hadley, the boy's injury was still fresh. And if he were honest with himself, he couldn't bring himself to undermine any burgeoning passions between the boy and Audrey. Hadley would be here come autumn; Julian would not.

"Except for Hadley, anyone not healthy enough to work will collect his wages and head home. Is that understood?" The men muttered their agreement and took themselves off, limps spontaneously cured.

"Jenkins!" Julian bellowed.

"Right here, sir!" Jenkins hurried out of the cookhouse.

Julian frowned down at the older man. "Effective immediately, Miss Sheridan is out of the doctoring business, unless the injury is too severe for you to handle."

"Yessir!"

Audrey stood at the threshold of the cookhouse. "Those men were resting, Mr. McCaid, as I asked them to do." She faced Julian squarely, hands on her hips.

Julian turned his full attention on her. She was causing his men to act like idiots, exposing themselves and others to needless danger because of their lagging focus on their work. He had a cracked rib as proof. "They were taking advantage of you. And of me. I don't need anyone drawing pay who can't work, especially when the wound is self-inflicted just so they can get near you."

"No one would do such a thing!"

"If Hadley needs something, Jenkins will see to it."

"He's got a bad gash that clearly was not self-inflicted. I have to check his wound to be sure it is not getting infected. I will continue to do that a couple times a day. Other than that, Jenkins can see to his needs."

Julian glared at her, wondering why she couldn't simply follow his orders. He put his hand against his aching rib. He wished he had never brought her out here. Then he thought of what a day would be like if he didn't see her. He'd run his horses into the ground riding back and forth to Defiance every day just to hear her voice. He spun on his heel and went to take a plate, his ill humor closing in on him.

That evening Julian opened his shirt and examined his aching side. The area by his two lower ribs on his left side was sore as hell, and a black bruise in the shape of a cloven hoof stood in clear contrast to his skin. The mark was fitting; he felt as if he'd been kicked by the devil himself.

He drew a bar of soap out of his supplies and looped a towel about his shoulders. A long soak in the ice-cold water of the river might do him some good. Unfortunately, the source of most of what ailed him stood between his tent and the river. She was folding her dried laundry and putting it in a basket. The gold in her hair caught the evening's fading light. He ached to touch it, see if it was as soft as he remembered it. Why torment himself by keeping her here? He should pack her up and send her back to town.

His men would be better off, certainly. But would he?

"Hi," he said, coming even with her. He grasped the ends of the towel he'd draped about his neck, unsure what her reaction to him would be and wishing he'd buttoned his shirt.

She cast a quick look at him, then reached up to release another piece of laundry. "Evening."

"I was going to the river for a quick bath, but I could give you a hand with this, if you like," he offered.

"That's not necessary, thank you. I can manage." Just then she missed her grip on a shirt, and he reached up to steady it. His shirt gaped open, revealing the livid hoofprint on his side.

Audrey gasped. "McCaid! What happened?"

"I got in the way of an angry ram in the shed today." He shrugged his shirt back in place, but that didn't deter her. She brushed it aside and gently tested the area around the bruise.

She looked up at him, her hands cool on his raging skin. "This needs to be wrapped. These ribs are bruised, maybe broken. Why didn't you come to me?"

He gave her a self-deprecating grin as he tried to ignore the feel of her hands on him. "When should I have done that? When you had a line of my men waiting to see you? Or when I shut your infirmary down and chased them all away?"

She sighed and shook her head. "Sit on this log. I'll go fetch the bandages."

He didn't move. The breeze ruffled her hair. He caught the stray lock and smoothed it back behind her ear. Her hair was god-awful soft. She regarded him with a steady, worried frown. He pretended she was actually concerned about him. In truth, she had to be frustrated as hell. He was one of dozens of men trying to get into her bed. Still, he couldn't help but touch his fingertips to the downy skin of her cheek.

"Do you know how beautiful you are, Audrey? Sometimes, you honestly take my breath away."

She made a face. "That isn't me—it's the kick to your side making it painful to breathe. Wait here while I get the bandages."

"I'm headed to the river. I thought a good soak in the cold water would help the swelling." Hopefully it would clear up a couple of swellings.

"Yes, that's a good idea. Knock on the cabin door when you return. I'll patch you up then."

When the knock came, Audrey couldn't hide her smile. She was glad to see McCaid. He had been keeping his distance since she refused him in town. She was surprised to realize she missed him, missed the hungry way he looked at her. She quickly opened the door, but the man who stood on her threshold was not McCaid. It was the same man who had cornered her in the cookhouse. She tried to slam the door shut on him, but he pushed his way into the cabin.

"Did you forget about me? You put up enough walls. Made it hard to get to you. Was it your idea to get me and Zeke assigned to the back pastures? Not very nice of you. Not when we got unfinished business between us."

Audrey backed away, sending a quick glace to the bed where Amy slept. "McCaid's coming back. He'll see you," she whispered, worried about waking Amy.

"Sure he is."

"He'll kill you if he finds you here."

"You won't let that happen, now, will you? You ain't

gonna let nothing happen to me or Zeke, 'cause if something does happen, Kemp'll make your kids pay for it. Which one would you give up first? That little whore's daughter in your bed? Or maybe one of them boys who's growin' fast enough to be troublesome?"

Audrey was almost at the other door. If she made it, she could run to camp for help. But she couldn't leave without Amy. Several ideas careened through her head; each she dismissed out of fear. She backed up against the door, standing flush against it instead of opening it and running free. The man smiled, his whiskered cheeks parting to reveal tobacco-stained teeth. He stood against her. And then she heard it.

Whistling.

McCaid was returning from his bath. The man heard it too. He cursed and shoved her out of the way, making his escape through the door behind her. Neither door in her cabin had a lock. Audrey quickly propped one of the two chairs against the doorknob.

Shaking, she checked on Amy, gently drawing the sheet over her foster daughter's sleeping form. This was an unacceptable situation.

A knock sounded on the opposite door. Even knowing it was McCaid, Audrey felt her heart slamming against her ribs. She forced herself to look calm, but her composure was only skin deep; her insides were still knotted with panic. She straightened her hair and smoothed her apron, then opened the door. It was indeed McCaid standing there. His hair was wet and darker than usual. He wore his denims but had not buttoned his shirt. He gazed down at her with his warm brown eyes, looking more handsome than any man had a right to be.

Audrey fetched the basket she'd used to hold the

salve, bandages, and scissors. She handed that to him, then returned to light a kerosene lamp. The sun had set, and she would need light to tend his ribs. She struck the match against the wood table and set the flame to the wick. Light flared in the room. She picked up the lamp and turned to see McCaid frowning at the far door.

He'd seen the chair.

"What's that about, Audrey?"

"The doors have no locks."

"You don't need a lock against me. I won't come in unless invited. And the boys wouldn't dare."

Audrey stepped over the threshold and shut the door behind her. "A girl can't be too careful." She and McCaid would be within eyesight of this door—she felt safer knowing no one could get into her cabin without being seen. She had McCaid sit on one of the tree stumps that were set up as stools in the open space behind her cabin. Putting the lamp on the next stump over, she frowned down at him. "You look blue."

"I'm freezing. I stayed in that blasted river as long as I could."

"I'll do this quickly, then, so you won't get a worse chill." She set the basket with her supplies on the ground next to his feet and knelt between his legs so that she could get close enough to pass the binding around him. His thighs were long and thick. She thought about touching them, feeling his muscles beneath her hands. He watched her, his eyes warm despite his chill. She swallowed hard. Forcing herself to focus on the task at hand, she dipped a couple of fingers into the jar of salve.

Bracing her left hand against him, she felt his wiry dark chest hair beneath her palm and promptly lost her ability to think. A thin, faint scar crossed his chest. Surrendering to her curiosity, she moved her hand up and down in a slow path, following the scar, her fingers combing through his springy hair. He sucked in a sharp breath and held it. She glanced up in time to see his hooded eyes, dark and hungry, watching her.

Closing her mind to the feel of him against her hand, she eased the salve over his bruised flesh. His belly contracted. "You'll need to take your shirt off, McCaid."

He didn't immediately comply. "Call me 'Julian,'" he corrected her as he slipped out of his shirt.

She pressed her lips together and gave him a quelling look, pushing her own raging thoughts aside. "I don't think we should be on a first-name basis."

"Why?"

"Because you're my employer and I'm your dependent. We are not equals."

"We're friends."

"We'll never be friends." She shoved the end of the fabric strip into his hand and pressed it to his chest. "Hold this. Tell me if I hurt you." She passed the roll of fabric around his back, leaning forward as she did so. Her breasts touched his belly. He shivered reflexively, and Audrey felt his tremor ripple through her. She bit her lip. She'd never felt less like a friend to anyone.

She passed the binding around him again, this time drawing the whole thing tighter. Another pass. She smoothed the top layer with her hand. The bruise was now covered. Three more wraps would do it. When she finished, she cut the top layer and tied a flat knot just under his right breast. Then she took the end he'd been holding, split it, and made another flat knot at the bottom.

She smoothed her hands over the whole works, passing gently over the bruised area. "How does that feel? Any better?" she asked, looking up at him. His nostrils were flared, his breathing shallow.

Julian was afraid to move. Her warm body was pressed against his groin. Her clever hands were rubbing his chest. If she didn't step away very soon, she would find herself on her back beneath him. He took her hands and pressed his mouth to one palm, kissing it, learning the ridges of her work-roughened hands with his tongue. He lifted her other hand and repeated the gesture there. Audrey's eyes were wide, her lips parted.

"Don't." She pulled free. "My hands are not nice."

"Give me that salve."

He unscrewed the lid on the jar she handed him, then dipped two fingers into the salve and gave the jar back to her. He turned her free hand palm-up on his knee and rubbed the soothing cream into her skin, smoothing the cream from the base to the tip of each finger and into the calluses on her palm. She watched him worriedly. As he massaged her wrist and hand, working the cream into her skin, he saw her tension slowly abate. He switched hands and repeated his ministrations.

When he finished, he looked at her, her hand still firmly gripped in his. "These are hardworking hands. The hours you work put some of my men to shame. You have a surprising work ethic for a pickpocket."

She met his eyes. "Sometimes, people aren't what they seem."

"If you are not a thief, what are you, Audrey Sheridan?"

"I am a mother."

"Yes." He drew her forward, against him. "And a woman." He leaned down to kiss her, feeling her mouth part beneath his in surrender. Her hands gripped his thighs. He wanted her as he had never

before wanted another woman. He groaned and deepened the kiss, his mouth twisting against hers. He
broke the kiss and leaned his forehead against hers, his
breathing embarrassingly rapid.

"Audrey, this hurts my ribs. Come up here," he directed, not giving her time to pull away or rethink their
encounter. He helped situate her on his lap, her legs together across his, her arms wrapped about his shoulders.
Her breasts pushed against his chest. He held one arm
around her waist and tried not to think about the feel of
her bottom on his lap, the curve of her hip against his
hand. He wondered if she could feel his erection against
her thigh, through the layers of their clothes.

Such thinking was getting him nowhere fast. He
closed his mind to it. Kissing was nice. He'd scared her
off before by touching her too freely. He was perfectly
content to kiss her until she was mindless, until she
melted, until she hungered for more.

Audrey loved the feel of McCaid's arms around her.
Though he was freshly bathed, he had not shaved. She
ran her hand against the stubble at his jaw, feeling his
mouth work against hers. She pulled away just slightly,
enough to look into his dark eyes, eyes of warmed mo-
lasses. She stroked his cheeks, feeling his whiskers
against her palms. It tickled. She smiled.

"I should shave. I don't want to leave a rash on your
face."

Audrey said nothing. She could say nothing. She welcomed such a rash, welcomed being marked as his
woman. She looked into his eyes as she leaned forward
and gently kissed his closed mouth. He was not hers,
she reminded herself. Doubtless a woman somewhere
waited for him to return to her.

"Have you ever been faithful to a woman, McCaid?"

He looked at her a long minute, his expression revealing nothing of his thoughts. "I've never needed to."

"Have you no one waiting for you back home?" He did not answer her. The hard set of his face indicated this was not a welcome turn in the conversation. "I thought as much." She started to get off his lap, but he held her in place.

"I am not committed to anyone at the moment, though I intend to find a wife when I go back to Virginia."

A cold ache slipped around Audrey's heart.

"My marriage won't be based on love."

"You're choosing to live your life with someone you don't love?"

"There are other reasons for marriage."

"What other reason is there for tying your life to someone else's?"

"Business. One of the women I am considering courting is the daughter of a man whose bank I would like to form a partnership with."

"And so you are going to make a home and have children with a business partner. It sounds—cold."

McCaid shrugged. "It's how it's done." His face hardened. "I don't want to talk about my future fiancée. What about Hadley?"

"What about him?"

"Is he a contender for your marriage option?"

"Perhaps, though an unlikely one. I have known him since my family came to Defiance, but I don't think he is ready to stand on his own yet. When he's not here, he still works on his father's ranch. I doubt his mother would like him to bring me and Amy into her home." Not to mention all the other children who came with them.

McCaid touched his fingertips to the sensitive skin of

her throat, his eyes dark and intense. "I'll increase my offer to a thousand dollars."

Audrey gasped. A thousand dollars was a lot of money—three times what her brother would make in a year working for Jim. With that, she could fund the move to Cheyenne or Denver.

"But I want more than a night with you. I want the rest of the summer. We could move into the house. The furniture I've ordered should be here soon. We could camp out inside until it comes."

"And what if our time together leaves me with a baby?"

Emotion shot through his eyes. "If there's a child, you will tell me. I will not abandon you."

Audrey smiled though she felt sad inside. She wondered if the fathers of all her children had said something similar to their mothers. She wondered if all men said such things, said anything, just to be with a woman. Had the mothers of her children hungered for their man's touch, starved for the sound of his voice, beggared themselves for a glance from him? That was a chilling thought. Julian McCaid was not her man, and he'd just made it clear he never would be, at least, not for more than a summer.

"No, McCaid. I cannot do it." Her voice was a whisper. She almost hoped he didn't hear her.

"There are ways to prevent pregnancy, Audrey."

She squelched her curiosity; this was not a conversation she was going to have with him. She got off his lap and retrieved her basket of bandages. She shook her head as she studied him. Leaving him at this moment was the exact opposite of what she wanted to do. Like catching her clothes on a protruding nail and walking away anyway, she had snagged her heart on him and felt it rip as she retreated to her cabin. He followed slowly, bringing her lamp. At her door, she hesitated, staring down at the white rolls of fabric in the basket she held, which was all she could see in the night's darkness. Her heart was hammering, fighting her, like a bird caught beneath a cat's paw.

She looked over her shoulder at McCaid. "I have never sold my body for money, McCaid."

He held her gaze, his expression hard. "Were you in love with Amy's father, then?"

She winced. "I—I didn't know her father."

Julian shut his eyes, unable to look at her stricken face as the implications of her statement hit him. Rape, then, not love. She'd been how old—seventeen—when the bastard had attacked her. A child still. He remembered seeing her cornered by Howie in the cookhouse. She'd stood immobile, offering no resistance to the man's depraved advances. He saw again the bruises she had sported the morning he brought her out here. Had any man treated her with respect?

Certainly he hadn't.

Shit.

He looked at her, steeling himself to the pull she had on him. "Do you have a second chair in your cabin?"

"Yes."

"Prop it up against the door. I'll give it a test." Maybe those damned chairs weren't such a crazy idea. She did need some protection from him.

She nodded and entered her cabin. She set the basket down and took the lamp from him. He thrust his hands into his pockets and watched as she closed the door. Hope flamed briefly when she reopened the door, until he saw the look in her eyes.

"McCaid, I must ask you to please not kiss me again." Not waiting for his answer, she quickly shut the door.

Julian felt like a prisoner of war told there would be no food for him—cornered, defenseless, and now doomed to die. He heard the chair scrape against the door, heard the doorknob rattle as Audrey settled it in place. He couldn't breathe. Like a body dispossessed of its soul, an empty husk of a man, he went to her door and tested her barricade. It held. It wouldn't keep a determined man out, but it would slow him down.

"Audrey," he called against the door, careful to not be so loud that he woke Amy. "It will hold long enough for you to open your window and holler for me." He leaned his forehead against the splintery wood of the doorjamb. "I will help you," he whispered, knowing he would give her the thousand dollars anyway, recompense for his guilty soul.

Chapter 18

Julian spent a rough night, exhausted but unable to sleep. Images of Audrey as an adolescent, pregnant from a rape, young and alone, haunted him. Were her parents still alive then? Had she had anyone to help her other than Malcolm? How had she survived through those days? And here he'd come along, arrogant, spoiled, hungry for a tryst. He'd scolded her for stealing from him.

He swallowed an oath; his thoughts were brutal companions.

When the eastern sky whispered of the dawn to come, he was there, watching it, waiting for another miserable day to begin. He needed some space between himself and Audrey. Maybe he'd ride into Defiance and see what the sheriff was up to. And he'd wire his bank to send out the money he'd give to Audrey.

He'd have to leave word with Franklin, though, not to tell Audrey where he'd gone. She'd panicked the last time he'd told her he was going into Defiance. The last thing he wanted to do was upset her.

* * *

Julian sipped his whiskey as he surveyed the four women working the room at Sam's. Two seemed to have made connections; two were flirting with several different men, touching, leaning, whispering in their low, husky voices. He caught the eye of the prettier of the two. Tauntingly, she sauntered over, glad to have another man to play against the others. She set her hands on her hips and sashayed up to Julian's table. She was of an indeterminate age, neither young nor old but somehow ancient. Her dark, curly hair was drawn up to the top of her head, baring her neck for a black velvet choker from which a glass ruby heart dangled. Her face sported a heavy application of rouge on her cheeks as well as her lips. Her eyes had been darkened with some kind of cosmetic. Red earrings matching her choker's charm danced in the saloon's candlelight.

She wore little more than a fancy black corset with puckered strips of ribbons that emphasized her wide bosom and narrow waist. Her skirt was made of layers of black and red ruffles that fell to just below her knees. Scandalous indeed. He thought of seeing Audrey in such an audacious getup and grew hard instantly. That thinking was why he was here in the first place.

He swallowed a mouthful of whiskey and made himself focus on the woman before him. Leaning back in his seat, he gave her access to his lap. She giggled and sat on him without any hesitation. "I've been watching you, wondering when you was gonna need a little comfort." She moved ever so slightly against his groin, intensifying the pressure already built up there. She looped an arm around his neck, pressing her breasts against his chest.

Julian's mood darkened. He remembered what it felt like to have Audrey sit on his lap, Audrey's arms wrapped around his neck. He tried to envision any of the women he was considering courting sitting on his lap, rubbing against him, hungry for sex. Somehow the picture seemed unreal. His limited interactions with them had not lit a spark. He did not feel the all-consuming burning for any of them that he did for Audrey.

The woman on his lap had a strong scent. Julian drew it into his nostrils, testing it like one might taste an unfamiliar food. She smelled of sweat, woman, and sex all woven together with a soapy perfume. It wasn't exactly pleasing, but it wasn't entirely off-putting either. He reached up and drew her in for a kiss. Her mouth was open and wet and welcomed him. He closed his eyes and pretended she was Audrey. He twisted his face against hers and thrust his tongue deep into her mouth, hungry for possession, hungry for a connection, trying to shut his thoughts off.

When the kiss broke, she looked into his eyes, knowing she had won, knowing she would make her fee with him. Julian didn't care about the money. He didn't care about her triumph. He sipped his whiskey, washing the taste of her out of his mouth. She cupped his groin, felt the ridge of his erection, and made a purring sound low in her throat. Leaning into him, she whispered that they should go upstairs.

"Lead the way," he answered. Julian watched her hips as she moved across the saloon to the stairs, realizing the flounces and ruffles of her skirt emphasized each step she took. A bit of her scent lingered in the air behind her. He decided he didn't like it. He didn't care. He needed a woman, and he was going to have this one. He would take her until he was depleted, until he was too exhausted to move. And then he would go back to Hell's Gulch and not give Audrey another thought.

In her room, he closed and locked the door, then set

his hat down on an adjacent dresser. When he turned around, she was already on the bed, fully clothed. She lay with her knees open and her skirt drawn up around her waist, her legs still clad in dark stockings, still wearing her high heels. She had no drawers on. He watched as she touched herself, touched the dark, secret folds of her womanhood. Her other hand had freed a breast, and her fingers worked a nipple.

He looked at her and felt—nothing. He was hard. He could do her. But he didn't want to. He realized he was more than the sum of his urges and silently cursed. This was a helluva time to grow a conscience. He didn't move. He didn't know himself anymore. A cold sweat broke out all over him. Suddenly, this was not where he wanted to be. He turned stiffly, slapped some money on the dresser, took up his hat, and slammed out of the room.

He'd been wrong. Not just any goddamned woman would do. There was only one he wanted.

Chapter 19

Julian went back to the bar. He ordered a bottle of whiskey and took up his seat again in the far corner. What the hell was it about Audrey Sheridan that made him so crazy? Perhaps it was her persistent refusal of him. Perhaps it was that she represented all he was giving up in thinking to settle down with some woman who was little more than a bloodline to him. Whatever it was, he determined he would avoid her when he returned to the ranch. Hell, he might as well go back to Virginia, spare himself the frustration.

He didn't like that option either. A day wasn't complete if he didn't hear her laugh, see her smile, watch her hug little Amy, catch her blush when one of his men complimented her cooking.

Julian tossed back the whiskey in his glass. As he refilled his glass, a shadow crossed his table and another glass banged down next to his. He looked up to see the unwelcome face of Sheriff Kemp. Julian poured a measure of whiskey into the sheriff's glass, then leaned back in his seat. The next best thing to a good screwing was a bar fight. He slowly smiled. Maybe there was something yet to be redeemed from this wretched night.

"What can I do for you, Sheriff?"

The sheriff sat across the table. "Don't suppose you're inclined to sell the Gulch, are you?"

Julian shook his head. "Don't suppose I am."

"That's a shame. I wouldn't want things to get ugly around here. I'm doing what I can to keep folks calm, but they're not taking to having a sheep ranch fouling up their livelihoods."

"And how does that concern me?"

"I'm just passing along a warning, friend. Seems the ranchers hereabouts are forming an association. They're offering to buy you out. They want to pasture their cattle on Gulch land, like they used to. And they're afraid your sheep will strip it bare and foul the water with their urine."

"That so? Well, I'm not interested in selling. And it's no concern of theirs if my sheep strip my land. I'll do all the worrying about that that needs to be done. And to spare them a snit about fouled-up water, how about I dam it up? I could use a few reservoirs. Then they wouldn't need to worry about the quality of the water on the other side of the Gulch, because there won't be any."

"So your answer's no?"

Julian grinned and shook his head. "My answer's 'hell no.'"

Sheriff Kemp gave him a hard look as he came to his feet and shoved his chair back under the table more forcefully than was needed. "Well, boy, thank you for the whiskey. I'll pass your response along." He touched his hat. "It's been nice knowing you."

* * *

The next morning, Julian was awakened by the sound of Amy banging the breakfast bell. Instantly alert, Julian focused on the unfamiliar décor of his room at Maddie's Boardinghouse. He must have dreamt the chow bell. He sighed as he sat up and put his feet on the floor. He braced his elbows on his knees and dropped his face into his hands. He felt like hell. He had a two-day growth of beard on his face. He wasn't sleeping well anymore. He had an impending range war to deal with, yet all he could think about was one curvy, proud, audacious, golden-haired woman.

The breakfast bell sounded again. He hadn't dreamt it, then. Going over to the bowl and pitcher, he did a quick wash, then shaved and cleaned his teeth. He dressed, packed up his saddlebag, and went downstairs. He was completely unprepared for the wall of noise that hit him when he entered the kitchen.

Half a dozen loud, unwashed children were gathered around Maddie's kitchen table. They saw him and went quiet, the sudden silence as bruising as the noise had been a moment earlier. Seven children, he counted. Where were their parents? They must have come in during the night, though how they had done so without his being aware of it, he couldn't imagine.

Maddie was at the stove, frying chopped potatoes, sausages, and eggs. Julian went over to the coffeepot and poured himself a cup. He didn't want to talk to her, and he didn't want to be around the kids, but the smell of breakfast was too tantalizing for him to leave without eating. He snagged a biscuit and slathered it with butter, staying near Maddie at the stove. The biscuit was flakey and light and made him painfully aware of missing Audrey.

"Maddie, this is delicious. It tastes like Audrey's."

"Well, it ought to. I taught her how to make them. In fact, I taught her everything she knows about cooking, 'cept bread baking, I guess. I reckon she learned that from Leah. Leah's our town baker, like her mother before her. Never been a finer bread or pastry than what that gal can come up with."

Maddie filled platters of food and set them on the table for the kids to pass around. The two older boys helped the younger ones fill their plates from the heavy platters. As he watched, seven little heads bowed at once, and one of the older boys said a quick and heartfelt grace. It was humbling, and made Julian regret his harsh judgment of the kids. Noise descended on the table once again as they dug into their food.

"Where are their parents? Still upstairs?"

Maddie gave him a strange look. "These are the town's children, Mr. McCaid, the ones you bought shoes for. I've been teaching them since the school closed." She glanced at the table. "There's no sense me trying to teach them on empty stomachs. Even the brightest among us can't learn when he's hungry."

She handed him a plate, and they took their seats at one end of the table. "How are things at the ranch, Mr. McCaid?" she asked him conversationally. The dark-haired older boy looked up from his plate, his attention focused on Julian's answer. The intensity of his gaze was unnerving.

"Things are pretty busy right now. The shearer team's helping us collect the wool. The lambing is about finished."

"And how are Audrey and Amy doing?"

Julian wasn't comfortable having so many children focus on him. It felt predatory. He did not understand children, and he did not understand people who did. He looked around the table. Most of them dropped their gaze, except the two older boys, who watched him unblinkingly. He moved a piece of sausage around his plate with his fork. "She is well. Amy has taken to helping one of my men tend the animals. She's growing like a weed. I believe she eats more than two of my men put together."

Maddie smiled. "We miss them. It will be good to have them back."

"Mr. McCaid, I'm Luc," the dark-haired boy spoke up. "I'd like to come work for you. I'm stronger than I look. Kurt and me, we tend Maddie's stable when she's got guests and help out at the livery too." He jumped, then turned angrily to the towheaded boy next to him. "What'd you kick me for, Kurt?"

"I didn't kick you."

"You did."

Kurt turned his back to the table and leaned toward Luc. "You ain't supposed to be talking to *him*," he said in what was more stage whisper than true whisper.

Luc shoved him. Kurt shoved him back. And as fast as that, they came to blows, falling out of their chairs and pounding each other fiercely as they rolled around the floor. Julian hurried over to their end of the table and yanked them both up. Holding them by fistfuls of shirt and suspenders, Julian looked from one to the other with disgust.

"You boys are out of line. And you owe Miss Maddie an apology. She's brought you into her house to feed and educate you, and you repay her kindness with this nonsense."

Unable to set feet flat on the floor, their arms and legs dangling uncomfortably, the two boys glared at each other. They had no choice but to do as he bid in order to regain their freedom. Fortunately, their apologies sounded sincere. Julian set them on their feet, but did not dismiss them. Folding his arms, he stared down at them from his considerable height.

"You're too young to come out and work for me. Maybe if things were different, if my ranch were just a regular working ranch. But it's not. I'm raising sheep. We've already had our share of trouble, and there's more on the way. It's not a good place for children."

"Or for Audrey either," Kurt said.

"And Amy. What good are they gonna be when the trouble comes, mister?"

Julian made a face. Leave it to a kid to cut to the chase. "That's a true concern of mine. I haven't decided how to handle it. For now, you kids need to stick with your studies. In a couple years, if you're still wanting to work for me, and are willing to work hard, I'll give you summer jobs. But only if Miss Maddie says you're doing well with your schoolwork."

Luc glared at him and scrubbed the back of his wrist against his nose. Kurt answered for both of them. "Yessir. We'll take that offer. You'll see."

Julian was still thinking of that exchange a few minutes later when he went into the general store. He had Jim send a wire to his man of business to forward the money he would give to Audrey. It helped his conscience a little, but not nearly enough.

Outside again, he mounted up and went to the eastern edge of town where the road dead-ended into a larger dirt trail that ran north–south. He looked to the south, where Hell's Gulch was just a four-hour ride. And Audrey. Thoughts of her filled his gut and made his nerves edgy. He wasn't ready to face her yet, so he turned north. A few more days away from her wouldn't be a bad thing.

Chapter 20

Night came fast on the heels of the long spring evening. The cool breeze carried the sound of crickets and distant coyotes. Julian paused on a slight ridge overlooking the Crippled Horse Ranch, absorbing the peace of the night air. He would miss this when he left for home.

He turned his horse toward the stables, intending to put him up and then find a cozy patch of hay to bed down in. No need to wake the household this late at night. He turned up the lantern and was unsaddling his horse when a ranch hand came in to see who was in the barn.

"Mr. McCaid!" Digger, one of the younger cowboys on the ranch, came over and eagerly greeted Julian. "What're you doin' way up here? Got trouble at yer spread?"

Trouble in spades, Julian thought. "Thought it was time for a friendly visit. I wanted to meet Sager's son."

"Well, I'll just go let the boss know you're here. The missus will rustle you up some dinner."

"No, don't bother them. I'll see them in the morning. It's too late tonight."

"Can't do it, Mr. McCaid. The boss won't like you spending the night out here." Without another word, Digger hurried out of the barn.

Julian was finished rubbing down his horse and had just given him some oats and water when Sager came in. "Son of a bitch!" he exclaimed. "It is you!"

The two men shook hands. Sager's smile was genuine and made Julian glad he had come. "I told Digger not to wake you up."

"We weren't asleep." Sager put a hand on Julian's shoulder and led him out of the stable. "Rachel's putting a dinner plate together for you. Don't you offend her by turning it down." They paused outside the kitchen at a wash station where a fresh pitcher of water was set up. Julian rinsed the trail dust off his hands and face, and then they entered the kitchen. The room was a huge space with a long table where two dozen ranch hands could eat. The chairs and benches were tucked neatly against the table and a lone place was set at one end of it. A lamp burned cheerily toward that end of the table and another two were lit over by the stove. The scent of meat in the frying pan filled the room. Coffee brewed on the stove. Julian's stomach growled; he hadn't eaten since he left Maddie's.

Sager's wife, Rachel, set her spatula down and hurried over to give Julian a hug. She wore a light wrapper over her nightgown with a starched white apron on top. Her long blond hair was still tied in a braid for the night. He felt bad disturbing them this late, yet her welcome was as warm as Sager's had been.

"You look great, Rachel. I'm sorry to arrive so late and without your expecting me."

"Nonsense. You two sit down. I think the coffee's ready." She returned with a pitcher of milk and the coffeepot, then poured two cups and went back to the steak and potatoes she was frying.

Julian looked at Sager. Gone was the anger that had simmered just below the surface all the years they'd known each other. In its place was something resembling contentment. Julian sipped his coffee, hot as it was. "Nice to see you set roots down, Sager."

"There's something to be said for it, believe me. You should try it."

"I think I will."

"That's great news! I'm happy for you. Who's the lucky girl?"

Julian couldn't hide his grin. "I've narrowed the field down to six. Any one of them will do."

Sager leaned back in his seat as he regarded his friend. "Still looking for that pedigree, McCaid? Thought you would have grown out of that by now."

Rachel served Julian his fried steak and potatoes and a roll left over from supper, then refilled their coffees and sat at the table. "Julian, you deserve to be happy, to marry for love."

Sager exchanged a look with Rachel. Julian's parents did that, talked with a look, embraced with a glance. It was an intimate exchange he wished he hadn't seen. He changed the subject. "You heard Jace was in town? The marshal in Cheyenne sent him in."

"Why the sudden interest in Defiance?" Sager asked.

Julian explained what was happening. "Might be best to avoid the town for a while." Just then a strange sound entered the room, guttural like a howling cat. Julian frowned, but Rachel smiled.

"Jacob's up. I'll just go feed him, then bring him in to meet you!"

Julian dug into his meal, glad for the distraction eating gave him as he tried not to think of Rachel in the next room, breast-feeding her son. It was sexy, in a circle-of-life kind of way. He wondered if any of the women he was planning on pursuing would nurse their children, but quickly discarded that notion. They would have to hire a wet nurse for the babies.

He could, however, imagine Audrey nursing her children. She'd find quiet time in the mayhem of her life to sit with her babe and suckle him. But Julian would not be there to see them, would not be a part of her life after the next couple of weeks. He wished suddenly that he was at Hell's Gulch. He didn't want to waste a single day of their remaining time together.

Rachel returned carrying a small, blanket-wrapped bundle, which she was talking to as if it could understand her. "This is our good friend, Julian. He helped protect you before you were even born."

Julian leaned forward to get a look at the infant, half afraid he would hear it answer Rachel. She smiled at Julian and handed the baby to him. He lurched to his feet, not at all pleased to have to hold the thing. Babies leaked and made strange noises and invariably screamed once they got a look at him.

But not this one.

He looked solemnly up at Julian, his face the only part of him not covered by the blanket. He had intensely blue eyes and a thick covering of black hair that the blanket couldn't hide. His nose was tiny, his mouth just a small bow, his eyes bright and intelligent. Julian held him in two hands—one would have been enough, but two were safer. No one spoke in the room; no one broke the silence.

This infant, Julian realized, was what life was all about. He lifted the bundle to his face, breathing in his scent—a sweet mixture of milk and soft infant skin. He would have one of these. A son of his own. With sage-green eyes and golden curls. He could see Audrey smiling as she tended their baby. Julian's heart grew, swelling as it recognized what it most desired.

And then reality returned.

His son would have dark blue eyes and pale blond hair—a trait he was selecting in the women he had chosen to court. Through his mother, Julian's son would have ancestors who could be traced back to the country's founding fathers. No one would ever call him a mulatto and detain him as an escaped slave. No one would ever doubt his son's heritage with so much pure, white blood in him. It was the best he could do for his children. And if the woman he chose to be the mother of his children was not the warmest parent a child could have, well, Julian would take up the slack.

This was the answer he'd sought in coming out here. Julian handed Jacob back to Rachel. "He's beautiful, Rachel. Something to be proud of."

Chapter 21

Julian walked his horse down the narrow road to his ranch a few days later. Dusk was settling about the land, casting long shadows and tinting the light with a soft rose color. He unsaddled his horse, then rubbed him down before turning him out in the corral with some feed. It was past dinnertime. The camp was quieting down for the evening. Julian shoved his hands in his pockets. June was fast approaching—his time with Audrey almost at an end.

A couple of the boys were playing cards outside the bunkhouse. The shearers' tents were still in place. Julian approached the cookhouse, drawn to Audrey. Franklin saw him and came trotting over to give him a rundown of all that had happened while he had been gone.

Julian listened halfheartedly. Was Audrey still up?

The shearer team was almost finished.

Julian sent a look to the cookhouse, anxious to see her. Had she missed him?

Teams of riders had twice been spotted along the northern pastures.

Had she taken Amy to the cabin for the night?

Their supplies were holding up well, but Jenkins was missing some ammunition. And Zeke and Howie had taken off. That cut into Julian's distracted thoughts. "When did they leave? Before or after the ammunition went missing?"

"After."

"Jenkins keeps that locked up, doesn't he?"

"No. There's no lock."

"Get one installed with three keys to it, one for you, me, and Jenkins. Thanks, Franklin." Julian started toward the cookhouse.

"She's not there," Franklin called out.

Julian's mind spun through several unpleasant possibilities, the worst of which was that she was gone. "Where is she?" he asked, his voice quiet.

"At your house."

Julian frowned. "What's she doing there?"

"Putting your furniture away and getting the place ready for you. Eight wagonloads of household goods came in while you were gone. She's been working up there every spare minute."

Julian started for his house, but his foreman stopped him. "Boss—one more thing."

"What?"

"We got a lead on a cookie named Giles over at a ranch outside Laramie who might be interested in making a change of employers, but you'll have to pay a hefty fee to steal him from his current position."

That was good news. It would give Audrey a reprieve. "Pay it."

Julian looked his house over as he came down the hill in front of it. The picket fence had been finished while he was away and now glowed in the evening's dusky light in a fresh coat of whitewash. He opened the gate and crossed the raw dirt to his front porch. Inside, he closed the door loudly to announce his arrival—he didn't want to startle Audrey. A lamp glowed on a table next to the stairs. Another one cheerily brightened the front parlor.

"Jenkins? Is that you?" Audrey leaned over the upstairs railing and looked down, her heavy golden-brown braid falling over her shoulder.

"No." Julian looked up at her. Blood thrummed through his body, bringing him alive in places he'd taken the past few days to cool down. He watched Audrey come down the stairs. She seemed hesitant. He had not left under the best circumstances, and still she had done all this for him.

"You're back."

"I am."

They looked at each other, the silence stretching the moment thin.

Audrey put her hands behind her. "Your things came. I was afraid a rainstorm might ruin them. I had the deliverymen put them in the rooms I thought they were intended for. If I guessed wrong, you could have a couple men rearrange them for you." She turned and started up the stairs. Julian followed her.

"I thought you were Jenkins. He walks me to the cabin after finishing the dinner cleanup." At the landing, she faced him. He was two steps below her, yet they were eye-to-eye. "I'll just get Amy and leave you to your house."

"Don't go."

Her gaze dipped to his mouth. Julian's body tightened. "McCaid, I cannot stay in this house alone with you."

"I've already declared you to be my woman. The damage is done."

"But not in fact."

"No, not in fact." Julian couldn't help the timbre of his voice; it sounded raspy, even to his own ears. "I put my tent next to your cabin to protect you. Your safety is my responsibility while you're here. Even while I was gone, Jenkins and Franklin stayed near your cabin. I cannot live here and you there."

"I won't do it, McCaid."

"Julian," he corrected. "I am Julian to my friends."

"We're not friends. I'm not even an employee. I'm a thief, remember? I might steal things from you should I live under your roof."

He moved up a step, standing taller than her once again. Her eyes widened. "Take what you need. Hell, take what you want. I don't care. It would be worth it to see you happy."

She sighed and looked past him before meeting his gaze again. "I don't want things, McCaid."

"Julian."

"Julian."

"What do you want?"

"What every woman wants. A home. A husband. Family. A future. Security." She studied him a moment. "Most of all, I want to be cherished. I don't want a love-less marriage such as yours will be. I want a husband who adores me beyond reason. I don't suppose that's very realistic, though, do you? I think I will have to settle for anyone who would have me."

Julian sucked in a breath, envisioning her with some man who didn't see her as he did. "Don't settle. My mother and father are more in love today than when they first married. So are my grandparents, my brother and his wife, and my sisters with their husbands. Same with Sager and Rachel."

"And yet you choose business over love."

"I'm different from them."

"How?"

Julian shrugged and changed the subject. "Will you show me the house?"

They toured the downstairs. Each room on the ground floor had some furniture, but in total it was barely enough to call the house furnished. The parlor had a sofa, a couple of side chairs, and two end tables. In the dining room, a long table sat squarely in the middle, surrounded by chairs. There was no breakfront, no china hutch. The library had a sofa, an end table, and a long table with a few chairs. The furniture vendor in Cheyenne had sent what he had available, most of it mismatched. Pieces were made of oak and pine, and a couple were mahogany. The fabrics were mostly in hues of red, some already sun-bleached as if they'd sat too long in a storefront or worse—outdoors. He had sent rugs for the downstairs rooms; some matched the suites of furniture, and some did not. On the whole, it was a rather motley collection.

Of all the rooms, the library was the least settled. There were several crates of books waiting to be unpacked. Julian had a book vendor select volumes of interest to male readers—he'd thought, if he had any visitors here in the wilds of the Dakota Territory, they would be his friends coming out to hunt. Julian pried one open and lifted out a small leather-bound piece, almost afraid to read the title in front of Audrey. The book was innocuous enough—a travel piece on the territories west of the Mississippi. She looked at him expectantly.

"Do you like to read, Audrey?"

"I do."

He handed her the book and watched her reaction, curious to see if she really was literate. She ran her fingers over the gold-embossed words and images on the cover. "I've never been to the States." Her voice was quiet. "I've never been anywhere except within this Territory." She looked at him as she handed the book back. "Have you been to the Mississippi River?"

He nodded. "I've crossed it many times."

"I should like to go there someday."

Julian looked away. What was it like living in a world as small as Defiance? No past. No future. No change—except if the town you lived in died. How was she handling what was happening to Defiance? "Perhaps tomorrow you could help me put these away? When we're finished, you could pick something to read. Some of the titles might not be appropriate, but you can choose from any that are."

Audrey looked at the dozens of crates, shocked at his extravagance. Luc and Kurt would be in ecstasy to see so many books in one place. They saved their pennies to buy any dime novel that came to Jim's store. "We could start now, if you like."

"It's late. I think it best if we toured upstairs, then get you and Amy home—unless, of course, you wish to stay here?"

"No."

Julian picked up a lamp and headed toward the door, pausing to let her precede him. If the rooms downstairs were sparsely furnished, the ones upstairs were austere. Even the gloaming light couldn't soften the contrast made by the whitewashed walls against the stained pine doors and trim. The craftsmanship of this house was impeccable; it was just—bare. No rugs softened the hardwood floors. No textiles muted the hard corners of the windows. The six bedrooms each had a bed, a nightstand, an armoire, and a commode with a bowl and pitcher. Three of the rooms had a couple of beds. He'd ordered extra, thinking he would have the attic finished for staff. He would have the beds moved later, after that space was finished.

Audrey had made the bed in the master bedroom. The white linens looked crisp against the maple bed frame. Julian stared at the soft mattress longingly, regretting his inability to convince her to move into the house. He walked through the large dressing room separating the master bedroom from the adjoining bedroom and found Amy Lynn sleeping in the next room, a cherub on the large bed. It occurred to him what an enormous task Audrey had in raising a child by herself, one she took on cheerfully and competently.

He handed the lamp to Audrey and lifted the toddler into his arms. She nestled her head against his shoulder and leaned into him without fully waking. Julian led the way back downstairs, focused on the warm little person in his arms. She stirred, and he rubbed her back, hoping to settle her as they waited for Audrey to turn out the lamps on that floor.

They left the house and crossed the distance to Audrey's cabin in silence. Inside the tiny space, just as he was about set Amy on the narrow bed she shared with Audrey, her arms went about his neck.

"Juli?"

"I'm here, infant."

"We missed you, Mama and me." She kissed his cheek. Julian felt a twinge in the center of his chest. He didn't look at Audrey. He couldn't. He set Amy on the bed, then quickly left the little cabin.

The next day seemed a week long to Julian as he waited for evening and the time he would have with Audrey at his house. He was restless and at odds with himself. The shearer team packed their gear and headed out in the early afternoon. Julian oversaw the loading of the wool bales into wagons. He sent them to Cheyenne with a double crew of outriders for protection. He didn't like taking men off guard duty, but the wool was the ranch's purpose—he couldn't risk leaving it here to be destroyed in a raid when he had a mill in Virginia waiting for it.

At last the chow bell rang for supper. Julian waited off to one side and watched Audrey serve his men. She'd pinned her hair in a loose bun. The wind had teased strands loose, tossing them about her face as if by a restless caress. Hell's bells. Now he was jealous of the wind.

He shut his mind to the sight and sound of her and took his place in the chow line. By the time he was next to be served, she'd gone back inside the cookhouse to refill dishes. Jenkins dished out his serving of stew and corn bread. He ate quickly; then, as there was still time to burn before Audrey would be finished for the day, he sought out Franklin.

He and Franklin walked the perimeter of the corrals, reviewing ranch business. Julian asked him to modify the guard rotations used for the last week. With riders having been seen on the north perimeter, and given they were short a few men, he didn't want the enemy to catch a pattern in the watches they set.

He went to his tent to shave and don a fresh shirt. An hour passed. The sky was softening with the descending sun. At last it was time. His mouth felt dry and his hands felt damp. They had so few evenings left. He wanted this one to be special. He headed for the cook tent, wondering how he was going to let her go when her month was up.

* * *

Audrey's hands were shaking as she hung up her apron. Feeling as if she'd swallowed a crate full of butterflies, she stepped outside and watched Julian heading toward her. She couldn't help but smile as she looked at his anxious face.

"Hello, sweetheart!"

Audrey jumped as a man's voice sounded behind her. "Hadley!" She looked toward Julian, hoping he hadn't heard the endearment. "Was there something you needed? I'm about to quit for the night," she said as she drew on her shawl, realizing she'd been so focused on Julian she hadn't been aware of Hadley's approach.

He smiled at her. "I was wondering if you would like to take a stroll with me," he asked, as Julian entered the cook tent.

Audrey felt the clash of two realities—one a dream, one the truth. She was nothing to Julian. Nothing at all. He would leave at the end of the summer, but Hadley would be here. She'd known him since childhood. He'd said he wanted to marry her. He knew about the kids, and still he wanted her. Hadley was her future, not Julian.

Hadley's gaze moved between her and Julian. "Unless of course you had other plans?"

"Miss Sheridan's evenings are hers to spend as she likes," Julian said, his dark eyes on her.

Jenkins came to the threshold of the cookhouse. "You run along now and take some time for yerself, missy." He waved her off. "Amy's asleep already. I'll keep an eye on her till you get back."

Audrey sent Julian another quick glance. His face was shuttered, his eyes unreadable. She wondered if he was as disappointed as she was. "Very well, Hadley. I'll walk with you."

She stepped around the table and passed Julian,

feeling the invisible attraction between them as if it were a tangible thing. This was for the best, she told herself. She needed more than he was willing to give. She had to see to her future and the well-being of her family. She walked silently beside Hadley, absorbed by her thoughts. They'd passed her small cabin and were heading for the river before she took note of her surroundings.

Hadley held out his hand. "Will you hold hands with me, Audrey?" She took his hand, though she didn't want to. "You're thinking about him, aren't you?" Hadley stopped and faced her. The sun had set. Light was rapidly vanishing from the sky.

"Who?" She feigned ignorance.

"Have you let him kiss you?"

Disliking this turn in the conversation, she tried to pull her hand free. His grip tightened, and he watched her struggle long enough to alarm her. He took hold of her arms and drew her against his body. She noticed his eyes had gone dark, tense.

"I think about you all day, all night. I wonder what you're doing with him."

"No." Audrey tried in earnest to break free. His grip was unrelenting.

"The boys talk about you in the bunkhouse at night. McCaid's Woman, they call you. They expect you'll be increasing before the end of summer. They've put bets on it."

Audrey gasped, horrified to hear what McCaid's men thought of her. Of course, it wasn't surprising; he'd claimed her as his woman. Even if he hadn't, the sheriff had made it clear what she was supposed to be doing out here at Hell's Gulch.

Hadley smiled. "I just want what you've given him. I was going to ask you to marry me, after all." He hauled her against himself and tried to kiss her, but she turned away. He slapped her cheek, stunning her. Taking advantage of her momentary shock, he began yanking at her clothes, tearing her shirt free from her waistband.

Survival fired in Audrey's mind. She punched his still tender leg and wrenched free of his hold, running blindly for her cabin. She'd almost reached it when she thought of its isolation; and with doors that didn't lock, it would do little to deter Hadley's advances. She veered around it, running for McCaid's house. Twice she looked over her shoulder, surprised to see him fall back. His leg must not be as healed as she thought.

Her heart was thundering. She felt violently ill. She'd known Hadley for years. They'd played together as children. What had come over him?

She ran through the front gate at McCaid's house, relieved to see light inside. Her cheek stung. She swiped the tears from her face and straightened her hair as best she could. She'd lost her shawl somewhere. She'd have to look for it tomorrow. Tugging her sleeves in place and dusting her collar, she marched up the steps and into Julian's house.

She found him in the library, putting books on the higher shelves, his back to her. He did not turn to greet her. He'd been angry when she left with Hadley. She shouldn't have gone, not when this was where she wanted to be.

The crates were opened and scattered about the room. Picking a spot at the opposite end from where Julian worked, she took up a handful of books and set them on a nearby shelf. Again and again she did this, the action cathartic to her shattered mind. Hadley had been her friend; she'd helped him mend after his terrible accident. What had happened to him? When had he become a monster? Had he always been one? The thought of him anywhere near her kids made her shudder. She stared blindly at a set of books she had just placed on a shelf, trying to find some composure. Her mother had always told her to focus on the good, to think happy thoughts.

Tonight, there just were none.

She missed her children. She missed her brother. She missed Leah. She even missed Leah's half-blind wolf.

"Julian," she asked, hoping her voice didn't waver, "what makes you happy?"

Julian was not in a mood for polite conversation. He hadn't been since he'd come to his house alone. And he sure as hell didn't want to continue their conversation from last night about happiness.

"I don't know." He stared unseeingly at the spines of the books he'd just placed, trying to calm himself. She was here now. Now was all that mattered. It was all they had. He drew a breath. "I guess seeing a job to completion. Winning a difficult business negotiation." A good, fucking bar fight.

He turned and looked at her, glad she had come after all, until his eyes caught sight of her disheveled appearance. Her hair was mussed, and her shirt was pulled nearly free of her skirt. She hadn't been gone long, but long enough for a quick tumble apparently.

"Audrey, your shirt is untucked," he snapped. She turned abruptly and looked at him. The light from the single lamp glittered on the moisture in her eyes. The rough outline of a man's hand could still be seen on one cheek.

If Julian had been angry before, it was nothing compared to the rage that gutted him then. He threw the book he'd been about to shelve across the room with a vocal curse. Anger was all he knew, all he was. *Goddamn Hadley. Goddamn him to hell.* Julian tore his eyes away from Audrey as she hurriedly stuffed her shirttail back into her waistband. He drew a breath through clenched teeth.

This was not her fault.

He stared at the rows of empty bookshelves, trying not to hear her whispery voice as she'd asked, *"Julian, what makes you happy?"* How often did she have to re-place bad thoughts with good ones? Was that how she managed her life? *"I want to be cherished."* He looked back at her and could only get one word past the emo-tion choking his throat.

"Come." He opened his arms to her. Not a heartbeat later, she was clinging to him. He wrapped his arms around her. Tightly.

"I'm sorry," he whispered against the top of her head. "I'm so goddamned sorry. I shouldn't have let you go tonight."

"I didn't want to. All day I wanted to come here. With you." Her words were muffled, spoken against his chest.

"Me too." He rubbed her back. She wasn't crying, just quietly holding him. Her silence—her composure—was more unsettling than loud sobs would have been. He held her tighter, and tighter still, as if he could draw her inside himself. If they were one person, if she were part of him, she would be safe. He eased his hold, bending to capture her face with both hands.

"Audrey, give me the right to protect you. Please."

She regarded him intensely, her beautiful sage-green eyes pale in the dim light. "Why would you do that?"

"Because you should be able to live without any more of these," he said, softly brushing his thumb over her bruised cheek.

"You can't protect me. No one can."

"That's not true. No one would dare harm you if they knew they would have to contend with me."

"And what happens when you leave? I will be fair game for any man then, all the ones you held off. No, it is better this way. I don't want to become dependent on you. On anyone. It is a false security."

"When I leave, I can hire guards for you."

She smiled then. "And what will happen when I want the attentions of some man? Perhaps someone who wishes to court me?"

Julian felt his rage resurface. He wished he could lock her away, keep her safe here at his ranch, hide her so no other man could have her. But that was no life for her. She should be a wife and mother. And be cherished. He could not deny her her future. "You would only have to tell my men that he is acceptable."

She shook her head. "You see, that won't work. I would have let Hadley in. He was a friend. I've known him for years. I trusted him. And still he did this to me."

He led her over to the sofa and sat next to her, wrapping an arm about her shoulders. "Audrey, let me take you to Cheyenne or Denver or anywhere. I could set you up as a seamstress."

"Julian, the very fact that you set me up in business would make it impossible for me to live there. Men do not settle proper women in new towns."

"I could send you to the States. You said yesterday you wanted to go there. I could send you to my grandmother's plantation in Georgia. She never goes there. No one does. We could say you are a distant relative of my brother's wife."

"No."

Julian squeezed his eyes shut. There was one last option, one that left a bitter taste in his mouth. "Then let me find a husband for you. I know good men, men who would never lift a finger to harm you." *Men who would cherish you.*

Audrey looked up into Julian's eyes. He was the one she wanted. No other would do. And being near him, possibly in his social circle, seeing him with his wife— it would destroy her. Living at his family's estate would be agony too. She would always be watching for him, waiting for him, knowing all the while he would not come. She wanted the one thing he did not offer. She wanted him. Was he so blind?

"I am not your problem. I will see to my own life," she answered. His eyes hardened. Before he could argue further, she wrapped her arms around his shoulders and pressed her face into the crook of his neck. Her heart beat against his. She drew in the faint spicy-sweet smell of him. Cloves. He must use a clove-scented shaving cream. She lifted her face, distracting herself with the feel of his newly shaved skin against her lips as she moved her mouth up his neck, below his jaw.

His breathing was shallow and fast. He was waiting— she could feel his anticipation. She lifted her head infinitesimally more. Her lips encountered the hard line of his jaw. Her tongue touched the texture of his skin there, tasting him. She ran her lips along the line of his jaw to his ear. She drew his lobe into her mouth, nibbling gently. She felt his chest expand as he sucked in a sharp breath of air. He did not stop her. He did not take over the caress. He kept still, watching her as she gave her curiosity full rein.

Looking into his eyes, Audrey could not tell where his pupils ended and the brown of his eyes started. They looked dark, desperate. With her holding him, an arm around his neck, their faces were almost nose-to-nose.

She ran a hand up his cheek, across his sideburn, into his hair. It was warm and silky between her fingers. Audrey knew she played with fire, knew one—or both—of them would get burned, scorched by the desire they shared.

She had the uncanny sense that this encounter was hers to own, take it further or end it, the choice was hers. She drew his head against hers, bringing his lips to hers. Though he closed his eyes, his face remained taut, his nostrils flared. He followed her lead, opening his mouth when she opened hers, touching his tongue to hers when she put hers into his mouth, twisting to give her deeper access when she moved her head.

Audrey broke from the kiss. She licked his lips, using her tongue to trace the circumference of his mouth. She felt like a seductress, powerful enough to bend a man to her will, whole again after her frightening encounter with Hadley. Julian had given her herself back, she realized. She pushed his hair behind one ear and blinked the moisture from her eyes. He watched the path the tear made, watched and waited.

He was not smiling.

"I think I better leave now." She looked into his eyes. "Thank you for being here. Thank you for this." Still he did not speak, but that was all right with Audrey. There was nothing to say; she'd left him no options except to stoically accept her decisions. She pulled out of his arms and got to her feet, even as he came to his.

"I'll walk you and Amy home. While you're at my ranch, I can and will see to your safety, Audrey Sheridan."

She smiled at his authoritative tone. She would grant him that much and be grateful for it.

Chapter 22

Julian left Audrey's cabin and went straight to the bunkhouse. It wasn't late; light still shone in the windows of the long, low structure. Some of the boys were sitting around a table, playing cards. Others lay in their bunks in the double rows of beds. At the far end where Franklin had his own room, Julian could see him working at his desk.

Hadley was one of the boys playing cards. They were surprised to see him. A few put their cards down and stood up, seeing the look in his eyes.

"Hadley Baker, get your things, collect your pay, and get the hell off my ranch."

Hadley came to his feet, warily eyeing Julian. The boy wore no gun belt, but Julian wouldn't be surprised if he had a knife somewhere. The boys around the table looked confused.

"If that's what you want, Mr. McCaid. I'll go. Doesn't seem like the wisest choice. There's trouble brewing in town, and it's headed this way."

"You're right about that. And I need men I can trust when it gets here."

Franklin came forward, frowning. "Boss—what's going on?"

Julian never took his eyes from Hadley. "Hadley's leaving. Why don't you tell the boys why, Hadley?"

"I don't know why, Mr. McCaid," he answered evenly. Julian knew the others were surprised, especially given how often Julian deferred to Audrey's wishes when it came to maintaining Hadley's employment. The men who had remained seated now stood and quietly moved away so that they weren't standing between McCaid and Hadley.

"What went on between you and Audrey during your walk tonight?"

"That's a private matter. It's no concern of yours."

"It became my concern when you hit her. She's under my employ and my protection. You crossed the line, boy. You're done. Get the hell out of here. Franklin, get his pay." Julian turned to leave, regretting the matter was settled so peaceably. He wanted to make Hadley hurt. He wanted to tear the pretty bastard limb from limb and—

A faint sound, a hiss of movement, was all the warning he had as Hadley came at his back. Instinctively, Julian crouched and pivoted to face his attacker. Sure enough, he'd drawn a knife. Julian, the bigger of the two, grabbed Hadley's wrist to keep the knife away and pounded his other fist into Hadley's stomach. The boy doubled over, and Julian's next punch laid him out on his belly on the floor, coughing and spitting blood. Something small and white hit the plank floor.

"You broke my tooth!" He sat back on his haunches and held a hand over his mouth as blood and spittle drained down his chin. "You broke my goddamned tooth!"

"That was for Audrey." Julian glared down at him. "Maybe you'll think twice before laying a hand on another woman. Get him outta here, Franklin."

Julian stood on the ridge overlooking his camp, in almost the same place he'd been the night his month with Audrey had begun. They had only days left. Somehow, he had to convince her to stay. She wouldn't be safe in Defiance—not with Jace's war starting. As he considered his options, he became aware of a lone rider slowly coming up the front drive.

Jace.

Julian met him by the corrals. "I'm heading up to see Sager, but I wanted to swing by and tell you the chatter I'm hearing about your woman."

"What about her?"

"She's working for the sheriff."

"Damn it, Jace. She's doing no such thing."

Jace held up a hand. "He threatened her children. He forced her to come out and keep you distracted." He grinned at Julian. "Seems the sheriff doesn't like the idea of facing the two of us."

Julian ignored that. "What children? She only has the one daughter."

Jace shrugged. "I'm telling you what was told to me. She's an innocent, McCaid."

"I've already figured that out." Julian shoved a hand through his hair. "She's no different now than she was when she came out here, except she's one hell of a lot safer."

"You better keep her here, then, 'cause the men in town are waiting on their turn with her, now the sheriff's made her fair game."

* * *

Summer's heat had rolled in to the High Plains, sucking every living thing dry with its hot wind and blazing sun. The two stoves made the cookhouse feel like an oven. Audrey switched to cooking as much as she could over the open fire pit beneath the tent canopy, but sometimes the wind was relentless and forced her to work indoors.

She and Julian spent the next few evenings getting his library settled, after putting Amy to bed in one of the rooms upstairs. They brought in a side table and lamp from the parlor so that they could sit together on the sofa and read their respective books. He had put the books he considered inappropriate on the higher shelves—which left many of the lower ones bare.

They weren't alone as they worked in his library; her impending departure crowded them like a third companion. Sometimes she would look up and catch him watching her, his expression unreadable, his eyes dark. Other times, she found herself studying him, memorizing everything about him, burning his image into her mind so that she would never forget him.

Tonight was such a night. They sat in the library reading. In two days, her month would be up and she would leave. Audrey kept her eyes on the novel in front of her, but what she really wanted to do was focus on Julian. He sat at the other end of the sofa, wholly unaware of her discomfort. His long legs were sprawled open-legged in front of him. He had rolled up his shirt-sleeves, baring muscular, veined forearms. His large hand cradled the book he read.

Irritated with her wandering attention, Audrey turned on the sofa, leaning against the arm and curling her legs under her. She lifted her book so that it blocked him from her line of sight. Still, she reread the same page twice. None of it assembled itself into coherent words in her distracted mind. Sighing, she started at the top of the page and began again.

"What are you reading, Audrey?" Julian's deep voice imploded her weak attempts to ignore him.

"A fascinating story about a young girl, younger than I am, who must make her way in the world."

"What's the title?"

"*Fanny Hill.*"

A strange choking sound came from the opposite side of the sofa. Audrey lowered her book to look at him.

"That is not an appropriate piece for you to be reading." He set his book on the side table and reached for hers. "Hand it to me. We'll find something else for you."

Audrey pulled the book closer, confused by his reaction. "I'm enjoying the story so far, though it's very sad. Fanny and I have much in common."

"You have nothing in common with her. Nothing. Hand it to me."

Shocked at his vehemence, Audrey stood, putting the book behind her. "No."

He stood as well. "Yes." He came toward her, and she retreated around the sofa.

"Julian, what's come over you?"

He walked around the sofa, a murderous gleam in his eyes. She moved backward, circling around the sofa. Her heart beat with a violent hammering.

"That is not a good book for you. I don't want you to read it." He glared at her, the sofa between them.

"It was in the books I unpacked. I didn't take it from those on your shelves." She looked at the books he had declared off-limits to her. "Why, you have more books I can't read than those I can." She could have sworn a flush colored Julian's face, but in the dim light, it was impossible to be sure.

"I had not planned on having mixed genders here. I thought this would be a male domain." He started to walk around the sofa, but she moved in the opposite direction. Quickly he vaulted over the sofa, landing right where she was standing. She shrieked and ran away, only to be cornered against the wall with his arms braced on the shelves on either side of her shoulders, locking her in. She hid the book behind her protectively, laughing until she saw the blackness in his eyes. Slowly, so slowly, her laughter died.

"Give me the book."

"No. I want to learn what happens. Fanny is independent, as I am. Perhaps there is a lesson I can take away from the story and avoid in my own life. That is why we read fiction, isn't it?"

Julian could not explain his rage. Audrey—his Audrey—was no Fanny Hill. Her eyes dipped to his mouth, and his mind flashed back to their embrace in this room just days ago, an embrace he'd tried to put behind him ever since. But his faithless brain now trotted the memory out, reminding him what it felt like to have her gently explore his neck and face with her lover's mouth. His cock grew hard, his balls tightened, and he was damned near lost.

"Goddammit, Audrey. You are nothing like Fanny. Nor will you ever be, do you hear me?"

She looked up into his eyes, her gaze wide, still innocent. "But I am like her, Julian." Her voice was a throaty whisper, sad with the truth. "We both are alone in this world. We both must make our way by ourselves. Don't you see?"

"You aren't alone. You're a mother. You have a brother. You have me."

"I have no one to rely on, no one to share the burden of living with, no one for me to help, no one who will in turn help me. I am alone."

Julian squeezed his eyes closed, trying to calm his raging blood. God, it was no use. He looked into her pale green eyes. "Fanny Hill was a prostitute," he growled. "You are not."

Silence. Julian kept his gaze from wandering to her heaving chest, to time the rise and fall there against his beating heart.

"But you would make me one."

How quickly she caught on. "No." He shook his head. "Never."

"A thousand dollars for a summer with me. What was that, Julian?"

"I want to make love to you. I won't deny that. I've wanted you since we met last summer, since I first held you in my arms."

"It isn't love when you pay for it, though, is it?"

Her words hurt worse than the horsewhipping that had scarred his back. They laid his soul uncomfortably bare. If he did succeed in seducing her, what would happen to her after this summer, after he was gone? His eyes lowered to her mouth, her chin, the long column of her throat. The neckline of her blue gingham dress was cut below her collarbone, but the bodice molded the generous curves of her breasts and hugged the narrow core of her ribs.

He touched his fingers to the top of her neckline, where a ribbon of eyelet met sun-kissed skin. He lifted his hand upward, pressing his thumb against the heart-beat in her neck. Up and down, he slowly stroked her skin. He thought he would die if he didn't know her, didn't take her body, didn't have at least that memory to carry him through the cold, lifeless marriage he had consigned himself to.

And yet, if he gave in to his desires, if he seduced her, what would her life be like after him? As Fanny experienced, he would have opened a world of passion and desire to Audrey, a world she could all too easily satisfy, given the large supply of randy men in the area. Fanny Hill's story had a happy ending, but would Audrey's? Would he set her on a downward spiral that left her servicing men in a saloon like Sam's, carelessly spreading her beautiful legs for the money she needed to live, to support Amy?

He drew his hand away from her soft skin. "It isn't prostitution when a friend helps a friend with no expectation or understanding that sexual favors, or favors of any sort, are to be given in exchange."

"No one gives without taking. I'm no fool, Julian."

"*I* can give without taking. Please, may I have the book?" His voice was raspy, even to his own ears. He held his hand out, palm upward, and watched as she reluctantly placed the book in his hands.

He set it high on a shelf, out of her easy reach. His balls were so tight it hurt to move. He wished he had his coat to hide the bulge in the front of his pants that had become painfully commonplace when she was near. He stood immobile, letting his blood settle.

Audrey's head lowered. She looked at her hands, now clasped in front of her. "You fired Hadley."

"Yes."

"Thank you."

He looked at the wall of books in front of him, feeling grim. He wished he had some means of getting her to

trust him. There were no assurances he could offer her—
at least none she would accept. Their lives moved on sep-
arate tracks. He wished he never met her. She stirred
things up within him that he had not felt before, things
he wished he'd never known about himself, things
ripped from him that bloody summer, half a lifetime ago.

"You can't leave yet, Audrey."

"I have to."

"There's a war coming to Defiance."

Fear clouded her eyes. "What kind of war?"

"Big and bloody, like any war."

She grabbed his sleeve. "Julian, I have to get back
to town."

"Why?"

"I just have to go back. Please, can we leave tonight?"

Julian studied her, wondering at the secrets that
crowded her gaze. "Not tonight. Tomorrow, I'll take
you in. We'll pack up your household and move you
out here. I'm not leaving you there. I know that you
don't trust me, but I'm not giving you a choice in this."

Chapter 23

Hadley sat at a table in Sam's as men gathered for the evening's meeting. His face was still swollen, his gum sore from the tooth that bastard McCaid had knocked out a couple of days earlier. He licked his lips, anticipating tonight. The room was nearly full when his father arrived with a neighboring rancher. Hadley made a face and nodded at them, standing to greet his father.

"What the hell happened, son?" John Baker asked, shock and anger mixing in his voice.

"McCaid."

"What do you mean? McCaid did this to you? Why?"

"I tried to stop him, Dad. I tried. I overheard him talking to his foreman that he intends to buy the land adjoining his—twenty thousand acres. He'll take up all our water sources. I told him what a devastating impact that would have on the rest of the ranchers in the area."

"What did he say?" the man next to John asked, his temper rising.

"He laughed. That son of a bitch laughed. I told him I was coming to town to warn you." Hadley pointed to his face. "That's when he did this—" He smiled, baring his missing tooth.

The man looked at John. "You gonna let that sheep-lovin' bastard treat your family like that, John? You gonna take that?"

John's brows lowered. The meeting was starting, the sheriff standing by the bar, banging an empty glass down to get everyone's attention. "No, I'm not."

Luc stood in the darkened kitchen at Sam's Saloon, listening. He'd sneaked into the kitchen after Sam's crew had cleaned up from lunch. Whenever the sheriff held these meetings, Sam's dinner business was canceled and the staff sent home until later, when the bar reopened.

Luc had been following Malcolm to these meetings since that first night that Audrey was gone. Her brother always stood at the back, arms folded, silently observing the meeting. Luc couldn't tell if he stood with—or against—the ranchers. The meeting tonight scared Luc. The room was loud. The sheriff had a hard time keeping the men talking in turns. He'd never seen a mob before, but he'd read stories about them in newspapers and sometimes in his dime novels. When a mob moved, it crushed everything before it. One thing was for sure clear.

Audrey was in trouble.

As the meeting came to a close and folks were filing out, the sheriff drew Deputy Fred over near where Luc hid, and what he overheard let him know they were all in trouble.

"Audrey was supposed to keep McCaid out there. But she didn't. He came in twice. Send a couple men after those two boys of hers. Rough 'em up, kill 'em. I don't care what you do to them. I want her to know what the price is for not doin' what she was supposed to do."

Audrey felt ready to jump out of her skin. She'd made breakfast and gotten the noon meal started. Her bag was packed, but the morning was half over before Julian brought the wagon around to collect them.

"Where are you goin', missy?" Jenkins asked.

"Home. We're going home, Jenkins."

"We're going to Defiance to collect her household goods. She'll be back." Julian clarified her statement. Except that her household consisted of a brother, seven children, and Amy. There was no way he would bring them all back out here.

A rider came down the lane, moving fast. Audrey frowned as a bad feeling settled in the pit of her stomach. It remained even when she saw the rider was Sager. He tied his horse to the corral fence near a trough and sent a look around the camp. Audrey stepped outside the cook tent and waved to him. He nodded and came straight over to her. She didn't know Sager very well. He'd been gone the entire time she'd grown up with his brother, Logan. But she could tell something was wrong.

"Hello, Sager. How are you?" she greeted him.

He nodded at her, touching the brim of his hat, sparing only the briefest of glances for Julian. "I've been better. Do you want to tell me what the hell's going on, Audrey?" Sager asked, arms folded, legs braced. "Like why you left your children and came out here with McCaid?"

"I had no choice."

"What children?" Julian asked her. Before she could

answer, she saw realization dawn in his face. "The town's children."

"You could have come to Rachel and me, Audrey. I know Logan's gone, but you still have the protection of the Taggerts."

Audrey put a hand to her face but couldn't still her body's shaking. She felt blessed and cursed, in nearly equal parts. "I had no choice—there wasn't time to get word out to you. Sheriff Kemp threatened the children. Coming out here was the only way I could keep them safe."

"And you, McCaid! Audrey has the protection of my family. She's no plaything for you to amuse yourself with. You never even mentioned she was here when you visited us at the Crippled Horse." Sager cursed.

Julian stepped in front of Audrey. "Some protection you gave her. She came to me bruised and battered."

"When were you at the Crippled Horse?" Audrey asked Julian. And then she knew. *Last week.* "Julian! Franklin and Jenkins said you were out checking the fences. God, I was supposed to keep you here! We have to leave now! We have to get to town."

Julian looked. "I saw the sheriff last week, Audrey. He didn't act as if anything were unusual. He even offered to buy me out."

"I just came from Defiance, Audrey. The kids are fine," Sager assured her. "At least, they were last night. I left before they were up this morning."

Julian looked at Sager. "Get a fresh horse and catch up to us."

They parked the wagon in front of Audrey's house. The street was quiet for a late afternoon. Usually the kids were out playing by now. Perhaps Maddie had kept them inside for extra schoolwork. Audrey went around to the side of Maddie's house and knocked on the kitchen door. No answer. "Maddie?" she called, as she opened the door and peered into the quiet interior. "Maddie?" she called again, getting no answer.

Maybe Leah knew where the kids were. It was possible she had taken them up to the river for a cooling swim and a bit of fishing. She crossed back over to Leah's and was just about to knock when Julian called her name.

Malcolm was jogging down the street toward her. For the second time that day, Audrey felt her stomach drop to her feet. She gripped Amy's hand and hurried to meet her brother. His face was drawn. She looked beyond him. Jim, Sally, and Maddie stood outside the store, looking down the street toward them. "Malcolm— what is it?"

He sent a dark look to Julian and Sager, then lifted Amy and took Audrey's arm, hurrying them up to the general store. "The kids are gone."

Audrey stopped walking. "What do you mean 'gone'? Malcolm, you're scaring me."

Julian slipped a strong arm around her waist. He'd been silent and angry the whole ride in. His lending her his support now gave her a jolt of strength while she listened to Malcolm explain.

"I went to work early this morning. They were still dozing. I knew Leah was coming over, so I left them." Her brother's eyes were anguished. "They were gone when Leah came over, not an hour later. She thought they already went to Maddie's. By the time Maddie came looking for them, they'd had a couple hours' head start. We've been looking for them since."

"It's happening, Julian." She turned in his arms, grabbing fistfuls of his vest. "The sheriff's got them. I know it."

"It's all right, Audrey. Sager and I will find them. Let's get up to the store and see what the others know. Malcolm—take the wagon to the livery and get three horses. You're coming with us. We better have someone with us those kids know when we catch up to them."

At the general store, Sally and Maddie each gave her a bolstering hug. "Where's Leah?" Audrey asked, realizing her friend was missing.

"She went to the river to see if they'd gone that-a-way," Jim answered her. "But I don't think they did. Or if they did, they didn't stay there. They took some things from the store."

Audrey shut her eyes, washed with shame, knowing she was to blame for this new trend in their behavior. "What did they take?" she asked.

"Three canteens, a satchel, some beef jerky. And a compass."

Oh God. They were running. Where to? From what? Audrey moved a shaky hand across her brow. It was now late afternoon. Night would be here soon. Her children were in danger.

"That's good. That's real good," Julian said, glancing at Audrey. "It means the sheriff doesn't have them." He and Sager exchanged a look, one word unspoken between them. *Yet.*

A half hour later, Julian, Sager, and Malcolm rode a path circling the town, starting with the south quadrant. It was the consensus that the kids were heading toward Hell's Gulch. They wouldn't have wanted to be seen, so they would have kept well away from the road. Seven young kids, unschooled in the finer points of covering their tracks, were bound to leave clear signs, and Sager was an expert tracker. It was just a matter of picking up the trail, then following it.

A couple of sweeping passes showed exactly where they went south. They moved in a straight line that paralleled the road. Though the kids had several hours on them, they were on foot. The men had a hard ride if they wanted to catch up to them before nightfall. Two hours later, Sager stopped. He dismounted and studied the ground. The grass was knee-high here, excellent grazing land. Here and there it thinned out, giving way to a sandy stretch. It was just such a patch of ground Sager now studied. Julian came closer, still mounted.

"We got trouble."

"What kind of trouble?"

"The kids aren't alone."

"How many?"

"Two, on horses."

Julian frowned, and looked out across the rolling hills of wheatgrass. Night was still a few hours away. This time of year, the evenings were long, the light would be good for quite a while tonight. But after that, darkness came fast.

"Are the men with the kids, or following them?"

"Here, they are following. Who knows if they caught up to them." Sager looked up at Julian.

They moved on. They had to be getting closer. The kids on foot couldn't walk more than fifteen or twenty miles in a day. Had the riders picked them up? What was their intent with the children?

He looked over at her brother, wondering at his mettle. Having led men into battle, Julian knew what he could expect from them. They were headed for trouble, and Julian's gut warned Malcolm was a weak link. He should have left him home with the women. Now he would have to protect him and face the mess up ahead.

An hour later, Sager again dismounted. His face was hard when he looked up at Julian. "They caught them." He stood and walked around. "Still looks like just the two horses. There was a scuffle. Several kids and two men. Had a hard time wrangling them in. I think the kids are still on foot, but the horses are with the kids now."

The sun had turned orange and hung low in the sky. The breeze that had been at their backs all afternoon became a wind, making it impossible to hear anything up ahead of them. Of course, it also provided them cover. The open rangeland had no trees; there was nothing to hide them other than the coming darkness and the wind's roar.

The grass was a little lower here, only ankle-high now. He couldn't see a damned thing in the distance. A few miles ahead was a creek in a thick stand of cottonwoods. They probably stopped there to water the horses and make camp for the night.

Something moved up ahead, dark against the sun-bleached grasses. Probably a coyote starting its evening hunt. No, not a coyote. It moved on two legs—it was one of the kids! It had seen them. It started to run to one side but changed its mind and ran in the other direction. It looked back at them and must have noticed that there was nowhere to run, no shelter to be had. The kid dropped where it stood, huddling in a small ball, hands and feet and head tucked in like an armadillo but without the benefit of armor. Julian galloped toward it. Stopping just ten feet from it, he sprang from his saddle, dropping his horse's reins over his head. He crouched in the dirt and scooped the kid into his arms.

One. They had found one. The kid shook in his

arms, still tucked tightly in a ball. A malodorous warmth wet Julian's thigh. The kid had leaked. It was a she, he decided, seeing the scruffy dress she wore.

"Honey, we won't hurt you. Audrey sent us to find you. You're safe now." He stood up with the ball in his arms, hoping the leak had ended. She covered her face with her two grubby hands, but at the mention of Audrey, she looked up at him through a small gap between two fingers.

"That's Dulcie." Hearing Malcolm's voice, she pushed away from Julian and reached her arms out to her foster brother. Malcolm looked away. "She pissed herself," he growled.

Dulcie drew her hands down, and stared vacantly at nothing, limp but not leaning into Julian. Julian glanced at Sager, wondering what the hell he should do.

"Dulcie," Malcolm ordered as he stared down at them, "where are the others?"

The little girl never blinked, never indicated she knew the answer or even heard him. Julian pulled her up against his chest, feeling a cavity open in his ribs, a hole big enough to put her in. He patted her back, keeping a hand under her wet bottom.

Malcolm cursed and dismounted, coming at them fast. "Damn it, Dulcie! Don't you go silent on me! Where are the others?" he roared.

Dulcie did make a sound then, a small squeak as she buried her face in Julian's neck and nearly strangled him with her little arms.

Julian held up a hand, blocking Malcolm. "Easy there, boy. That's not helping."

"They can't be far," Sager commented. "There's a creek ahead. If that one got away, others may have as well.

We need to split up. Who knows where they might be, if they weren't able to stay together?"

Julian mounted his horse with little Dulcie clinging to him like a monkey. "Dulcie," he spoke to the top of her matted hair, "we have some hard riding. You just hold on. I won't let the bad guys get you, okay?"

She nodded. Sager went round to the east, Malcolm to the southwest, and Julian continued from the north.

About a half mile closer to the creek, when the light had truly begun to fail, Julian spotted another child, running straight toward him. "Dulcie, who's that boy coming this way?"

Dulcie turned just her head, peering forward though the sweep of her dark hair. She straightened and brushed the hair from her face. She made as if to jump off Julian's lap, but he caught her. He dismounted and set her on the ground. The wind was ripping at them now, loud enough to cover any noise they made. Dulcie ran forward, plowing into the boy's embrace. Julian approached them, perhaps faster than he should have, for the boy shoved the little girl behind him and confronted him.

"Easy, boy. Audrey sent me. Sager and Malcolm are looking for the others. What's your name?"

"Joey." He wiped his cheeks with his hand, glaring at Julian a minute longer. He looked around at Dulcie for confirmation. She nodded at him. Julian knelt down, knowing he was intimidating towering over the children. Dulcie went back to her spot on his neck. "Tell me what's going on."

"You got to go help them, mister. It's bad. It's real bad. They got Luc and Kurt. They're hurtin' 'em. Please. Please."

"Where are they?" Julian asked.

Joey looked back. His shoulders heaved with a sob.

He pointed toward the creek. "There." The creek was still a half mile away.

Julian lifted Dulcie and Joey onto his horse, then mounted behind them on the horse's rump. "Joey, do you know how to ride by yourself?"

"Yessir."

"When I stop, I want you to stay here with Dulcie. If I don't return in an hour, I want you to turn around and ride back to town. Not to Hell's Gulch. Go back to town. You got that, son?"

"Yessir."

"You watch out for Dulcie. Dulcie, you do what Joey tells you, okay, sweetheart?"

Dulcie nodded.

They had reached the spot. Julian didn't want the kids any closer than they had to be. And this far away from the creek, there sure as hell was no cover, no trees, no bushes for them to hide behind. At least Joey could ride. If they had to get out fast, they could.

Julian dismounted and took his rifle out of its scabbard. He looked the kids over, seeing how small they appeared on his big bay gelding. "Do you know how to get back to town, if you have to?"

Joey nodded. "I been watching landmarks. I can find it. But we're waiting on you."

Julian shouldered his rifle and walked toward the creek and the stand of cottonwoods at its perimeter.

Chapter 24

Long before he could see into the clearing, Julian heard a sound that cut through the wind, sliced through time and spun him back to his worst memory. Leather slapping flesh. A cold sweat chilled his skin.

Thwack!

He broke into a jog, hurrying the final few yards to the edge of the shrubs and trees bordering the creek. There the nightmare became reality. The two older boys were stripped to the waist, hands tied and stretched over their heads by ropes looped over a branch.

He saw the two men who had been threatening Audrey at the ranch. Zeke was laughing and drinking long draughts from a whiskey bottle while Howie whipped the boys. First one, then the other. It was so like that other time, when Julian was lashed to a tree, watching his tormentors lay open the flesh of his cousin, waiting for the time they would turn on him.

Julian stepped into the brush, casting a look about for the other children. They'd found only two of the kids—four counting the boys being whipped. Had Sager or Malcolm found the others? Had they gotten free?

Though the men would be easy to pick off with his rifle, he couldn't risk a gunfire exchange when he didn't know where the three other kids were. The wind stirred up the leaves, kicking up a roar in the treetops that sounded like fast-moving water. Julian moved carefully through the brush, not wanting to give himself away before he was ready to be seen.

Thwack!

The scars on Julian's back ached like fresh wounds. He pushed his way into a skeletal old cottonwood and found a child crouching within its bare branches. Kneeling silently behind the kid—another girl—Julian covered her mouth even as he turned her to face him. Her eyes went wide with fear. He could feel her scream against his palm. He shook his head, hoping she would recognize him from town. When she quieted down, he leaned close and whispered, "Be still now. I don't want them to see us. Audrey sent me. Joey and Dulcie are beyond the woods with my horse. Do you think you can go quietly to them?"

The little girl nodded. Julian helped her out of the sharp branches, setting her in the right direction and watching to make sure she cleared the brush unnoticed.

Thwack!

Julian stood and walked into the clearing. Zeke paused with the bottle midway to his mouth. Julian caught Howie's wrist, stopping him before he could hit either of the boys again. He yanked the strop from his fist and hit Howie with it, slapping his face, over and over, then tossed it aside and slammed his fist into the bastard's nose, laying him out.

Zeke broke the bottom of the whiskey bottle against a rock and came toward Julian, wielding the razor-like surface as he would a knife. Julian caught a movement out of the corner of his eye and turned to see Sager do just what he'd hoped he would—cut the boys free.

Zeke lunged, Julian moved to the side. Zeke slashed backward with his arm. Julian caught his arm and bent it up to scrape the underside of his chin with the teeth of the jagged side of the bottle. Zeke cursed and jumped back, blood running down his chin.

Howie came to his feet. Julian pictured him cornering Audrey, touching her, and was glad the bastard wasn't finished. Howie charged toward Julian at the same time Zeke lunged forward. Julian yanked Howie's outstretched hand, spinning him around so that he took the cutting slash of Zeke's bottle. Zeke recoiled in horror. Julian took hold of Howie's shoulder and chin and gave a sharp twist. He let Howie's body fall from his grip as he focused his attention on Zeke.

Zeke, thinking better of making a stand, turned to flee and stopped short when he saw Sager blocking his way, his hand hovering over his still-holstered Colt. Zeke tossed the jagged bottle away and pulled a knife from the cuff of his boot. Julian smiled, glad to give Zeke the fight he was looking for. Zeke came toward Julian, slicing at the air. For all the whiskey he'd imbibed, he was fast and agile. His forward thrust sent Julian backward, into the brush. Zeke slashed out once more, and Julian swiped his legs out from under him, landing a kick in Zeke's ribs before he could roll to his feet again. Julian held his position with his back to the woods, wanting to keep Zeke between him and Sager. Where was Malcolm? With the kids, he hoped.

Zeke was on his feet again. He threw a fistful of dirt into Julian's face. The grit burned his eyes, blinding him temporarily. Zeke lunged forward again and Julian felt the knife slice into his upper arm. Zeke laughed and leapt forward, certain of his victory. Julian caught his wrist between both hands. Zeke pulled at Julian's grip to free his knife hand. Julian tripped on a cottonwood root and went over backward, bringing Zeke down with him. They rolled in a death embrace, Julian on top, then Zeke, the knife still between them. Julian's eyes were tearing, clearing the dirt away. He could see the two boys standing next to Sager. He shoved Zeke's hand forward, into the dirt, and laid a fist hard into his jaw. In the brief second that Zeke was incapacitated, Julian yanked the knife out of the ground and shoved it into Zeke's ribs, ending the fight with a sharp upward thrust.

He pushed Zeke's body from him and came to his feet, wiping his forearm across his face to clear the grit. He met Sager's hard look, battle fury still raging in his blood. He took several calming breaths, then looked at the boys. He turned and went to the creek. Kneeling at its edge, he washed the gore from his hands. He filled his hands with water and sloshed his face. Gradually he began to hear the world around them, the wind roaring in the trees, the creek's mild gurgling.

He straightened and went to Sager and the boys. "What about the others? Did you find them?"

"Malcolm got them. He's with them over by your horse."

Julian nodded. He shoved a hand through his hair as he drew a ragged breath. "Come to the fire, boys. I want to look at you." They quietly followed him to the small fire the outlaws had started. Their backs were red and sore looking, but there was no blood. Julian was thankful that it was just a strop Howie had used. It must have been too short and flat to slice the skin, unlike the bullwhip that had been used on him.

The boys faced him. "You're gonna be sore awhile," Julian predicted. "I'm sorry we didn't get here sooner."

Sager retrieved their shirts and handed them to the boys. "McCaid, you're bleeding." He pointed to his arm. "Better let me look at that. Audrey won't like that we bring you home with a lame arm."

"It's fine. Leave it be."

"No. It needs to be bound. Get your shirt off so that I can wrap it up."

Julian looked at the boys, then back at Sager. His friend had seen his scars long ago, but Julian didn't know how the boys would react. He took his vest off and dropped it on the ground. He pulled his suspenders off his shoulders, unbuttoned his cuffs and the top few buttons of the shirt, then drew it over his head. He took a knife out of its sheath at his waist and cut a strip of cloth from the bottom of his shirt, which he handed to Sager. The wound on his arm was not terribly deep, but bled profusely.

He sat on a log so that Sager could tie the material around his arm. His back to the boys, he heard their combined gasps. Kurt cussed. And then two cold hands touched the ridges crisscrossing his skin. "What happened, Mr. McCaid?" Luc asked, looking around to see his face.

Julian frowned. "I wasn't much older than you two. I tried to help someone. I wanted to help him leave a bad situation, but his owners didn't take a liking to that. They whipped us."

The boys had come around in front of Julian, and now stood staring at him with pity and worry. Luc still had a hand on his shoulder.

"The boy I tried to help died from wounds he received

that night." Julian hated telling the story, hated the cost his cousin paid for Julian's choices.

"His owners?" Luc asked. "He was a slave?"

"He was. He was also my cousin."

"Are you black, Mr. McCaid?" Kurt asked.

"He's white, you idiot," Luc answered. "He's as white as you or me."

"My grandmother's great-grandmother was a black woman. Some places that makes me black, some that makes me white."

Sager glanced up, giving them a hard look. "Boys, a man's past is just that—his past. He's got no control over who his parents are." Sager finished the makeshift bandage and faced the two kids. "You'll come to judge a man by his actions and the quality of his word. What you learned here, about McCaid, it ain't for sharing. It's his story to tell or not, as he sees fit."

The boys nodded. "Yessir."

"Where'd you get that scar?" Luc asked, pointing to a jagged mark just under Julian's right collarbone.

"A bayonet, in the war."

Kurt cussed again. "And that one?" he asked, pointing to a long scar that crossed Julian's chest diagonally, right over his heart. Julian looked at his chest. Every scar he bore came from those bastards whose family had owned his grandmother and her kin.

"A knife, also in the war." Same fight as well. Julian pulled his shirt back on and drew his vest on, though he left it unbuttoned.

Sager chuckled. "It's good that weasel tonight didn't cut your pretty face. It's the only part of you not looking dog-chewed."

Julian smiled. "I think we should feed these kids, then

head back." Sager nodded. "Boys, go get the others and bring them here. We'll use the fire already started."

"You think it wise to bring them here again?" Sager asked as the boys trotted off to get their foster siblings.

"If they don't come back here, see it again without the bad guys, it will stick in their minds, grow into something horrible that haunts them." They laid out the two dead men, setting their hats over their faces to shield the children from the harsh look of death. Sager retrieved some supplies from his pack and set about making a supper of beans and bacon, with coffee from boiled creek water.

Malcolm brought the kids into the small clearing. Julian had never seen such a lean, threadbare-looking bunch of kids. Their clothes hung limply on their thin frames. Their eyes looked huge in the failing evening light. They lined up, smallest to largest.

Julian clasped his hands behind his back, wondering what the hell to do now. Audrey needed help with these children. He wished she'd told him about them from the beginning.

"What were you kids thinking, going off like this?"

Luc, standing second in line, spoke up first. "We were heading out to your place. The sheriff's up to something powerful bad. We had to warn Audrey. It's just a four-hour wagon ride out there. We thought we could do it in a day, day and a half at most."

"I assume Malcolm was caring for you. Why didn't you go to him with your concerns?"

Luc looked at Malcolm and frowned. "Didn't think it would do any good."

Julian wondered at that cryptic remark, but chose not to pursue it. "Tell me your names."

"Kurt."

"Luc."

"Colleen."

"Joey."

"Mabel."

"Tommy. That's Dulcie. She don't talk. Not much anyway."

Sager had the bacon frying. The children were anxiously watching the food cooking. "We're going to have some supper, then head back. I imagine Audrey is beside herself with worry about you. Are you up to more travel tonight?"

They looked at each other and nodded. "Audrey's not at your place?" Kurt asked.

"No. She's back in town right now."

Julian got the kids settled by the fire. Sager had only one set of silverware, so they all shared the fork and spoon, taking turns dipping into the beans, clearing through two pounds of bacon in no time.

After they ate, Julian cleaned the pots and banked the fire while Sager and Malcolm tied Howie and Zeke to their horses. Then they saddled up for the trip home. Joey and Mabel rode with Malcolm. Kurt and Colleen rode with Sager. And Luc, Tommy, and Dulcie rode with Julian. Julian had moved his bedroll to make a seat for Dulcie on his lap so that the saddle horn wouldn't bother her. For the first half of the trip, it didn't matter. She held on to him with a relentless grip around his neck. Julian found himself patting her back now and then, and once in a while, he even murmured words he thought would soothe her.

The trip home was accomplished in silence and seemed to take half the time it took to find the children. Little Dulcie's grip slowly eased until Julian had to hold her to keep her from falling. He looped the reins over the saddle horn for a minute as he resettled the little girl on his lap, leaning her back against his chest. Tommy, sitting behind him, was softly snoring against his back. Luc was awake; Julian could feel him thinking. As if to confirm that, Luc spoke up, whispering a question that must have plagued him the night through.

"Mr. McCaid? What happened to those men who whipped you?"

Julian wasn't quick to answer. His life was no model for a child. Violence had its place, but it was never a behavior to aspire to.

"I killed them."

Audrey paced around Maddie's parlor, too restless to sit. The hour was fast approaching midnight. Leah and the Kesslers had gone home. Maddie, kind soul that she was, fixed the two of them coffee and sat up with Audrey.

"Tell me, my dear, what are you going to do when Mr. McCaid brings the children home?" Audrey had told Maddie about Julian's offer to make her his mistress. She let the curtain fall back in place. All she could see outside was darkness anyway.

"I don't know, Maddie. I don't know what to do."

"What are your feelings for him?"

A warmth crept up Audrey's neck, making her glad for the room's dim light; she hoped her friend hadn't noticed. Maddie set her coffee down.

"Audrey," she sighed, "I'm going to give you some advice. Mind you, this is not the advice I would give Leah. You two girls are very different. I think you're stronger than she is. And you are a more practical girl." She paused and gave Audrey an assessing look.

"I've been thinking about your situation. It occurs to me, if a man were to come along who had a moderate temper, an honest soul, and a reasonable means of supporting himself and you—a man who would let you keep the kids, maybe even take others in—if such a man were to come along tomorrow and ask you to marry him, you would accept. No matter his age. No matter his looks. No matter his profession. I know you would. It would have nothing to do with love. Nothing even to do with friendship. You are mercenary in your practicality. It's why you're in this situation. You did what you had to do."

Audrey gave her a warning look. "That doesn't mean I would sell my body, Maddie. I've been at his ranch a month and we haven't—we didn't—I'm still as I was."

Maddie held up a hand. "Just hear me out, child. Let's say you marry this stranger and make a life with him. Perhaps he's a thoughtful spouse. Perhaps he thinks of making you happy, but perhaps not. Perhaps he uses you, consumes you, taking and never giving. Perhaps you lie in your marriage bed, growing bitter and sad, night after night, year after year."

Audrey sat next to Maddie on the sofa, regarding her friend in a new light. Maddie had always been her neighbor, the kind, middle-aged lady who lived alone. Now she wondered at Maddie's life, wondered what brought her to open a boardinghouse by herself in a town like Defiance. "Did that happen to you?"

"I've been married to three men, honey. The first and last died; the middle I divorced." She pressed her lips into a thin line as she regarded Audrey. "Contrary to what you read, contrary to what Sally Kessler would tell you, there's nothing sacred about what happens between a man and a woman. It is just a physical act, like eating or smiling.

"It can be nice; it can be boring. It can be awful. Or it can be extraordinary. Wouldn't it be wonderful if you could taste extraordinary? If you could know, before you settle for your stranger, as we both know you'll do, what the best of a man felt like?"

"Are you suggesting I accept McCaid's offer?"

"Why not? You certainly would benefit from it. And we know you're a practical girl. Honey, let me tell you, if a man like that offered me a summer of passion, well, I think I'd pay him for the pleasure."

"Maddie!" Audrey was shocked. Maddie had been friendly with her parents and with Leah's mother; it was strange to think of her hungering for a man. "It doesn't matter anymore. He made that offer before he knew about the children. I doubt he will feel the same way now."

"I saw the look he gave you at Jim's. He's going to feel the same way. More so, now that he knows your secret. And he went after your kids. He didn't have to do that. He wouldn't have done that if he wasn't a man worth having. He would have let Sager and Malcolm go alone."

Audrey slumped against the sofa back, considering the shocking advice her very staid neighbor had just given her. "What's the advice you would give Leah?"

"Leah is more fragile than you. She's never trusted any man. She would not survive a casual relationship. Nor would she pick just any man for a husband."

Audrey considered that, compared it to her own situation. She wasn't sure she was as strong as Maddie thought. If she gave herself to Julian, his leaving would destroy her.

Chapter 25

Audrey leaned wearily against the window jamb, trying to reassure herself that the kids were fine. They had to be. Julian and Sager were capable men. But she'd made the kids afraid of Julian, and they didn't know Sager. At least Malcolm would be there to put them at ease. They would find the kids and bring them home safely, she reassured herself, until her mind began to cycle through its crushing destructive thinking. What if the children had not stayed together? What if they encountered a mountain lion? What if they got hopelessly lost and the men couldn't find them?

What if the sheriff had sent men after them?

Audrey pushed away from the wall and started another loop around the room. Maddie was dozing on the sofa, snoring genteelly. A sound outside drew Audrey to the window.

"Maddie! They're back!" Audrey ran through the front door and down the steps. Five horses were stopped between her home and Maddie's, two with bodies strapped to them. Hysteria clawed at her, melting rational thought. Oh, dear God. What had happened?

Sager and Malcolm dismounted and began lifting children down. Mabel, Colleen, and Joey ran to her. She gave them fierce hugs, bending close to look into their faces. They looked tired and happy and relieved. Not hurt. Then Kurt stood there, looking at her. Something was wrong. Luc came and stood there too. Sager lifted Tommy down, his sleeping form slack against his shoulder.

Maddie hurried into the street, holding a lantern high. Julian dismounted, holding Dulcie in his arms. Something about the way he held her made fear catch in Audrey's chest. What had happened out there?

Julian handed her to Audrey. "She was scared. She leaked."

"Julian, what happened?"

"Here, I'll take her." Maddie set her lantern down in the drive, away from the horses. "Malcolm, help me get them settled." Maddie took Dulcie, and Malcolm took Tommy. They ushered the others ahead of them, leaving the older boys with Julian, Sager, and Audrey.

Audrey didn't like the silence surrounding the boys. They were never still, never quiet, especially not on a night like this. Audrey opened her arms and the boys stepped into her embrace. She wrapped her arms around their shoulders, pressing kisses against their foreheads. "Tell me what happened." There were two dead men. Something had happened.

Kurt spoke first. "We were coming out to find you."

"Why?"

"I heard what the sheriff's planning. It ain't good." Luc looked from Audrey to McCaid. "He's sending men out to slaughter your sheep and burn your buildings. We had to warn you. And he ordered some men to come for Kurt and me."

"We had to leave, and we had to bring the others in case the sheriff's men went after them too," Kurt added, looking at Audrey. "We didn't know what else to do."

Audrey waited for the rest of the story, the part where someone explained the dead men. She looked at Julian and Sager. The hard expressions on their faces did little to settle her nerves.

"We were about to camp for the night, when they found us." Luc pointed to the bodies tied to their horses.

"They chased us with knives. We made the others run or hide or just get away. But those two, they tied us up and took a strop to us, trying to get the others to come out of hiding."

Audrey shut her eyes, but was unable to block the images storming her mind. "How bad is it?"

Luc shrugged. "I got worse from my old man." He rubbed his wrists. "I just didn't like being tied up."

"Go inside, boys," she quietly ordered. "I'll put some salve on your injuries."

Audrey looked from Julian to Sager and back again. "I can't thank you two enough. If you hadn't ridden after them, hadn't found them—" Audrey's eyes blurred as moisture filled them. She looked at the dead men. "Who were they?"

"Howie and Zeke," Julian answered.

Audrey wrapped her arms around her waist, feeling hollow. This was her fault. She should have let Howie do what he wanted to. Warm arms surrounded her, pulling her against a hard chest as her sobs took hold. She was vaguely aware of Sager leading three of the horses toward Maddie's stable.

"Ah, sweetheart. It will be all right. The boys will heal in no time. Tonight was more than they bargained for, it's true. This is a tough place to raise children. I wish—I wish I had known about them. I wish you had trusted me."

"I wish I had known I could trust you." She resisted the urge to cry herself out in his arms. She couldn't break down now. She had to see to the kids. Her gaze snagged on Julian's torn sleeve and all the blood staining the material. "You're hurt." Audrey pulled free to look at his wound.

He reluctantly let her out of his arms. "Just a scratch. Sager took care of it. I'm going to deal with those two." He nodded toward the bodies. "I'll see you in the morning—we need to talk."

Julian took up the reins from the outlaws' horses and followed Sager to Maddie's stable as a new and troubling thought came to him. Was Amy Lynn Audrey's daughter or another of her foster children? He sincerely hoped it was the latter, for then her first introduction to intimacy with a man might not have been violent—if indeed she'd ever been with a man. *"I didn't know him,"* she'd told him in response to his question about whether she loved Amy's father. Had that meant Amy wasn't her own child?

"Mr. McCaid?"

Julian looked up, surprised to see Luc still up. He had washed his hands and face and now wore fresh clothes. "It's late, Luc. You should be in bed."

"Yessir. I just had something to ask you."

"What's that?"

"Will you take care of Audrey? Me and Kurt, well, we can't . . ." He nodded toward their small shack. "And Malcolm isn't . . ."

Julian straightened and looked at the boy. What was it about Audrey that engendered such protective behavior from the males around her—all except her brother, apparently? Julian looked at Sager, then back at Luc, who still awaited his answer.

"Yes, I will, son." *Whether or not she'll let me.*

Luc nodded. "Good night, then."

Julian stared into the darkness outside the small stable long after the boy left. How the hell was he going to protect Audrey? She was the most independent, mule-headed woman he'd ever encountered. He'd already offered his protection and been turned down—several times. He sent Sager a look; his friend only grinned. Julian swallowed an oath and went back to the work at hand, rubbing the horses down and setting out oats and water.

"You could marry her," Sager offered helpfully.

"No, I can't."

"Why not?"

"You know why not."

"Change your plans."

Julian did curse then. "Leave it alone, Sager."

"And let my friend make the worst mistake of his life? Hell, Julian, you're a maverick. You created your world, you don't have to be a victim of it. You have an empire and enough money to run a small country. Who do you think is going to come after you and threaten that?"

"The world is what it is, Sager. It's bad enough being part Cherokee. If any of my business partners found out that I've got black blood, they would no longer do business with me. My empire, as you call it, would collapse."

"Then build it again. Find business associates who aren't bigots."

"And what if slavery is reinstated? What if a few years from now the government decides it shouldn't have been abolished?"

Sager straightened and gave him a hard look over the side of the stall. "It ain't coming back, Julian. It's done."

Julian sighed. Sager had spent most of his life thinking he was part white, part Shoshone. He, of all people, should understand what Julian had to deal with. That he didn't was frustrating. Perhaps the difference was in their self-perceptions. In the war, Sager's experience in the West made him an excellent scout. Indian blood or no, he was admitted into the ranks of the white troops. Had anyone known Julian's grandmother was a slave, Julian would only have been allowed to serve in the ranks of the Negro soldiers. His situation was complicated. He was white enough to be white. He didn't need to try to pass for white—he was white.

But he was also black.

Sager came out of a stall and tossed the rag he'd been using into a bucket. "I'm gonna say this, my friend, and then I will never again discuss this with you. If you love Audrey and you leave her to go make your life with another woman, your thoughts will plague you. You'll lie awake at night, wondering where she is, if she's safe, if she's healthy, who she's with. You'll hear she's happy and it will gut you to know she's happy while you're miserable. You'll hear she's suffering, and you'll know there's nothing you can do for her. All because you made a decision, based on dumb-ass reasoning, that once made can't be changed."

"My happiness is immaterial, Sager. I have to put the welfare of my children before anything else."

Sager walked out of the stables, toward the horses patiently holding the dead men. "For a smart man, Julian, you're dumb as hell."

Julian followed him. "I don't love her."

"I fought loving Rachel. I fought it kicking and

screaming, but the truth was I loved her on first sight when I saw her standing there facing that rabid wolf. You're outflanked, Julian. Sometimes, you just have to surrender."

They led the outlaws' horses around the corner and up the street to the sheriff's. It was well into the wee hours of the morning now. Even Sam's had closed. The town had an eerie quiet about it, lying dormant in the blue-gray haze cast by the moonlight. Outside the sheriff's, they untied the first body and set it down on the boardwalk, leaning it against the jailhouse. They put the second body next to it. Rigor mortis had set in, locking the two corpses into the position they had been in draped over their horses, their arms outstretched, their bodies leaning forward slightly.

Sager tilted his head, looking at them critically. "That don't look right." He tried to reposition them, but they were too stiff.

"Leave them. Go back to Maddie's. I don't want you here for this."

"Bullshit. I'm coming with you."

"You've got a family now, Sager. You don't need this trouble."

"I got you for a friend. That's nothing but trouble. Let's get this done with."

Julian went inside the jail. The door creaked. He halted, waiting for one of the sheriff's henchmen to appear. No one did. The sheriff and his boys usually drank pretty freely at Sam's each night. They were probably out cold. Julian moved through the dark interior to the hallway that led to the stairs up to the sheriff's apartment. Sager stayed below, making sure no one else followed him.

The stairs opened immediately into the sheriff's

large, one-room apartment. The place was a pigsty and smelled much worse. Clothes and liquor bottles littered the floor. Dishes were stacked on the table and dry sink. A couple of men slept on the carpet next to the sofa. One man slept on the sofa, his snores joining with those coming from someone on the bed. Julian made his way to the man stretched across the rumpled bed. He was still fully clothed, still wearing his boots. Julian eased the silver star off his vest and tossed it in an overflowing spittoon, wondering how long it would take Kemp to discover it. Then he knelt on the bed and took a fistful of Kemp's hair and pressed his knife to his throat. He grinned down into the sheriff's face, waiting for him to focus, knowing his smile wasn't a nice one.

As soon as Kemp did awaken, he jerked forward, trying to sit up, nicking himself against Julian's knife. "Bet that hurt." Julian winced and sucked a sharp breath between his teeth. "This knife is too damned sharp."

"What the hell do you want?" the sheriff growled.

"I came to tell you I left a surprise for you downstairs. And I wanted to personally assure you that if you ever send your boys after Audrey or her kids again, or you try to harm her yourself, I will kill your boys and then I will kill you. If you doubt me, just ask Howie and Zeke." He moved back, letting the sheriff up just enough to land a solid right hook against his jaw, laying him out flat.

The drunk on the sofa and the men on the floor never roused.

Julian made his way downstairs. Sager silently followed him to the door. Outside, they took up the reins to the outlaws' horses. "What are you going to do with the horses?" Sager asked.

"Kemp can't claim them without claiming the boys

who rode them." Julian grinned at Sager. "You should take one. I'll give the other to Audrey."

"Done."

Audrey did not sleep well that night. She was too exhausted to relax and could only doze between bouts of wakefulness. She was back in her bed, with Amy beside her. The kids were all safely in their bunks, Malcolm included. Everything was back to normal.

And everything was completely different.

She knew a decision awaited her in the morning; she just didn't know what it would be. Should she try to make a go of it in Cheyenne? That option was fraught with unknowns. Could she do it if Leah didn't come too? Would Malcolm go or stay here? And what of Julian's last offer? Was it still on the table? Would he rescind it tomorrow when they spoke, now that he knew about the kids?

Her thoughts were worse when she did doze off. Maddie's crazy suggestion took root as her mind played with that option. She relived her encounters with Julian. She felt his mouth on hers, his arms banded about her, holding her naked body against his, skin to skin. She felt her fingers sift through his silky brown hair. His scent filled her nostrils, permeated her soul. In one dream, he set her on a table as he had done when he came here. He spread her thighs. He touched her.

There.

The shock of it woke her up. Dawn lightened the sky. Audrey was glad the last twenty-four hours were done. This was a new day, a new chance. She rose, sponge-bathed, then dressed and set water boiling. She intended to make sure every one of her children had a bath today.

Then she would trim their hair, scrub the little cabin, and
do laundry. Days like this were best spent lost in work.
What was coming was coming, like a wall of water down
the mountainside, straight toward her.

She wondered where she would be when the washout
came to a stop.

Leah saw her open front door and came over bearing eggs and day-old bread perfect for battered toast.
"What happened?" she asked. "I heard the kids last
night. Is everything all right? Are they okay? Are you?"

Audrey filled her in. Leah shut her eyes but could
not suppress the shiver that rippled through her. "I bet
the kids will be starving. My bread's cooling. I can help
you get breakfast going, if you want, before I have to
make my deliveries."

The smell of coffee and battered bread frying roused
the household. They quickly went through the loaves of
bread Leah brought—she had to bring another over.
Kurt and Luc were unusually reserved. Audrey would
have thought after their adventure, they would be talking about it, seeding the tall tales that would come of it.
Malcolm was quiet—sullen even. Why? She'd only been
gone a month, but something was different between
them. Something had changed.

After breakfast, Leah left to make her daily bread deliveries. Malcolm went to work. And Audrey set to work
bathing the kids. She had to change the water two times
before she filled the tub a last time for the two older boys.
She took the others outside and one by one, trimmed
their hair. Water was heating in the laundry cauldron outside. While she waited for Kurt and Luc, she stripped the
linens from all the mattresses and gave them a thorough
washing. She was hanging the sheets on the double laun-

dry lines when the boys came out, examining each other's wounds from last night's whipping.

"How bad is it?" Kurt asked Luc, presenting him his back. "I had to sleep on my side."

"It don't look so good. You got lines here, and here. You got six of 'em or so. How about me?" Luc turned his back to Kurt.

"I dunno. It looks bad too. Hurts, huh? Looks like five or six stripes. It ain't nothing like what McCaid's got on his back. We didn't even bleed. I bet he almost died."

Audrey stepped away from the sheets she was hanging and looked at them. "What happened to Mr. McCaid?"

Kurt and Luc shot a look at each other. "It's something you'd need to talk to him about. Happened a long time ago—not last night. He just got the cut on his arm last night."

Audrey frowned. She'd seen Julian twice without his shirt, but she'd never seen his back. What had happened to him?

"Come along, you two. I want to cut your hair, and I have some ointment for your backs. Then you've got to get up to the store to make restitution to Jim and Sally. We agreed last night that two days of hard labor would set the matter to rights."

It was late in the morning when she saw Sager lead two horses down Maddie's long driveway. Her gut twisted. The decision was coming, she could feel it. He tied the horses at the next yard up. She gripped her hands, trying to still her panic.

"How are the boys?" he asked, his amber eyes watching her.

"I think they will be fine. They are sore, but the strop never broke the skin. They were comparing their injuries this morning." She smiled.

Sager sighed and looked directly at her. "I'm not gonna mince words with you, Audrey. You're in love with Julian, aren't you?" She nodded. "Did he tell you he's making plans to become engaged?" Again she nodded. "Did he—did he mistreat you?"

Audrey frowned. "Do you think I would love someone who mistreated me?"

Sager blew out a breath of air and made a face. He wished Rachel were here to handle this discussion; his wife was much better dealing with sensitive issues than he was, especially when it came to women. "Your situation is complicated. I agree with McCaid that you aren't safe here. The sheriff's in a bad spot, and he ain't gonna leave quietly. I'd like you and the kids to come out and stay with my dad at the Circle Bar. I know it would make Logan feel better."

Audrey watched Sager as he made this offer. It was given with all the best of intentions. She truly was blessed to have people who cared about her. Perhaps Julian was right when he said friends could help friends without expecting remuneration. "That's very generous of you, Sager. Truly it is. But I'm afraid I just couldn't. Your father wouldn't be happy with all of us descending on his home."

"My father's lonely and would love the noise and mayhem." Sager grinned.

Audrey crossed her arms. His offer to put her large family up with his father was beyond generous. She was frustrated having to accept help from friends, yet desperate enough to take the help and risk destroying the friendships. "I can't, Sager. I can't do it. I think I may try to make a go of it in Cheyenne or Denver."

Sager nodded. "If that's what you decide, send word

to Rachel and me. We'll go with you and make sure you're settled."

"Thank you, Sager. You and Rachel are better friends than I deserve. I will send word to you about what I decide to do."

Sager returned her smile, but his eyes looked sad. "Do that. It's important you know you got choices, Audrey."

Julian appeared shortly afterward. Her nerves had tightened like a bowstring as she waited for him.

"Juli!" Amy Lynn ran to greet him. Audrey watched in surprised wonder as a smile lit his face, and he swooped her into his arms.

"Hello, infant. You look happy this morning!"

Her arms circled his neck. "I'm happy to see you!"

He kissed her temple, then set her on her feet so she could go play with the other children. When he straightened, Dulcie was there, standing silently before him. Audrey watched him kneel down and smile at her. To Audrey's amazement, Dulcie walked straight into his arms and hugged him tightly. He leaned back and swept her shiny brown hair from her face.

"How are you this morning, sweet?" Dulcie smiled and nodded. "That's good. You are very brave. Braver than I am, I think."

Dulcie's eyes widened, and she shook her head. "You saved Kurt and Luc," she argued. Audrey was stunned to hear her speak to Julian. "I just ran. I ran and ran, Mr. McCaid."

Julian tucked a lock of her hair behind her ear. "Ah, but you see, it took courage to do that, Dulcie. You were going to run all the way here to get help, weren't you?" She nodded. "That's courage. You were alone at night, a long way from home. You were afraid, but you went for help anyway."

Dulcie rarely spoke. Occasionally, she would talk to Audrey. Sometimes even to Luc. But only infrequently to the other kids, even the girls. And never to Malcolm. Yet here she was, speaking to Julian and embracing him as well. Audrey sniffled quietly and blinked her eyes to dry them.

Dulcie went back to be near the other children, leaving Audrey alone with McCaid. She met his look. His eyes were warm and dark and studying her. His straight hair spilled over one brow. She looked away. She couldn't do it. She couldn't seduce him. If she lost any more of her heart to him, she would not be able to live once he left.

"Hi." Julian's deep voice called her attention back to him as he came to his feet.

She tried unsuccessfully to smile. "Hi."

"Did you sleep well?"

"No. Did you?"

"No." The wind whispered through the sheets behind Audrey. The decision she had to make crowded her, pressing in close. "We need to talk."

She nodded. It was all she could manage.

"I asked Maddie to watch the kids. I think she's up front. Will you walk with me?"

They moved around to the front of the house. Maddie waved to them. Audrey thought she caught an unnecessary waggle of Maddie's eyebrows, but it happened so quickly she couldn't be sure. They walked away from town, toward the road that led east. Julian put his hands behind him. The silence sharpened Audrey's nerves.

"Julian—I want to thank you for helping yesterday. I'm sorry you were hurt."

He stopped and looked at her. She wondered at the words his eyes spoke that his mouth never voiced. He turned and started walking again.

"Audrey, you aren't safe in Defiance. Kemp thinks he owns you, thinks you're one of his hoodlums he can push around. I know Sager's offered to bring you up to the Circle Bar. That's one option. And I know you were thinking you could make a start in another town. That's another option." He looked at her.

"I'd like to offer you a third option. I'm not exactly known for my philanthropy, but I have done some good deeds, here and there. I opened a mill in a town in Virginia that was nearly destroyed in the war. The wool from Hell's Gulch goes to that mill. And I bought that plantation after the war and gave a good part of the land to its former slaves. The rest I gave to my grandmother." He stopped and looked at her.

"I'd like to do something to help you and the kids. I'd like to make Hell's Gulch an orphanage. The carpenters are still out there. We could build a school. We could finish the attic. There would be plenty of space to house these children and any others needing a home."

We. What did he mean by that? "Will you be staying here?"

He shook his head. "I can't. I have businesses to run."

"And a woman waiting to be your fiancée."

"And that." He continued, barely a heartbeat later. "I could build a foundation around what you're doing; there is nothing improper about the help I'm offering. And you wouldn't need to worry about feeding or housing the kids. You would have an open account at Jim's. I'll hire a cook to take over your work with the men and a housekeeper to help you with chores. We could teach the kids the things they would need to know to run a ranch, to be wives of ranchers."

We again. Audrey's heart lurched.

"Please, don't tell me I can't do this," he urged. "I

know you don't like accepting help. This isn't charity, Audrey. This is me doing my civic duty. This is me helping your children. Please, let me do this."

Audrey was helpless to stop the tears from spilling down her cheeks. He did not touch her, but she felt his soul wrap around her. "Yes. Yes, Julian. I would like that. I do accept."

He nodded, once, then looked away briefly before his eyes swung back to her. "I didn't mean to make you cry."

Audrey gave a watery laugh and swiped at the tears. "I've never met anyone like you, Julian McCaid."

"Never?" He grinned.

She shook her head. "Never."

"When will you be able to leave?" he asked.

"Not for two days. The boys are working at Jim's to make restitution for the supplies they stole. They have to clean and reorganize the storeroom, dust the front, wash all the windows, and do anything else that Jim and Sally can fit in. I would prefer if we waited until they completed their duties."

Chapter 26

Luc wrung out his mop as he cast a look around the sparkling store. He tossed the wash water outside in the weeds and hung up the mop. Jim was putting the ladder away that Kurt had used to wash the windows. The evening was hot, the sun still blazing. Luc was hungry. Since Audrey had come back, there was always food cooking at their house. He knew there would be a good supper at home tonight. Maybe stew. Maybe roast chicken and corn bread.

"Well, boys. I reckon you've done enough work to pay me back," Jim said as he and Kurt came into the front of the store. A strange mechanical sound cut off the rest of his conversation. His eyes widened as he looked at them; then he hurried into his tiny telegraph office and shut the glass door.

Luc looked at Kurt as the Morse code began to signal at the desk. They watched Jim signal back, then start writing the message down. "What's it saying?"

"Be quiet." Kurt cut him off. "I'm trying to listen." Silence. "I can't quite make it out. I can't do it. I can only read it. Shit. I can't translate it by listening to it." He glanced at Luc. "Jim don't look happy, though."

"No, he don't," Luc agreed.

The signal finished. Jim folded the note and put it in an envelope. He sat at his telegraph desk, staring at the envelope a minute, then looked at them through the glass door. He opened the door and sighed. "You boys better get home. Take this to Mr. McCaid on your way."

Luc took the envelope and the two boys left, stepping from the hot store into the hotter evening sun.

Kurt leaned over and looked at the envelope. "Can you see anything? Can you see what it says?"

Luc pressed the envelope to the page folded within. He couldn't make out any of the words. "No. Nothing."

"Here, let me look." Kurt took the envelope and held it up to the sunlight.

"What have you got there?" Malcolm asked as he joined them on the road that led home.

Kurt jumped. He whipped the envelope behind him. Luc closed ranks and took the envelope to hide behind him. Malcolm grabbed for it, but the boys jumped out of the way.

"It ain't for you. It's for Mr. McCaid," Kurt announced.

"You sure you two didn't steal something else from Jim?"

"No, we didn't. It's a telegram. See?" Luc held it up, and Malcolm did snatch it then. Both boys jumped him, but he still opened the envelope and yanked the missive free. The boys stopped fighting him, curious now that they might get to know what the communication said.

Malcolm read it and cursed.

"What does it say?" Kurt asked.

"Avenger to arrive in two weeks. JG."

"*Avenger?*" Luc asked. "You sure it said Avenger?" He and Kurt exchanged a look.

"What's the Avenger?" Malcolm asked, frowning. He stuffed the note back into its envelope.

"It can't be." Kurt shook his head. "He ain't real. He's just a character in those stories."

"What's the Avenger?" Malcolm asked again, more insistently.

"He's this guy that's in our dime novels," Luc explained. "He cleans up corrupt towns. He's bad news. The outlaws all die, those he don't send running clear outta town."

"He's the fastest man with a Colt this side of the Mississippi. He's ambi-dex-trous so he shoots good with both hands. No one can outdraw him." Kurt pulled two imaginary Colts out of pretend holsters on his hips and pointed them at Malcolm. "Like that, but quicker." He repeated the motion, faster this time.

"No, it's like this." Luc faced Kurt and drew his imaginary weapons with lightning speed. Then he spun the Colts around his index fingers and slapped them back into their holsters.

"You two are idiots. There is no such thing as an Avenger."

Kurt shrugged. "They sure got a lot of stories about him. That's a heap of stuff to make up, if it ain't true."

"It must be code for something." Malcolm frowned as he looked down the road at Maddie's Boardinghouse. "Maybe there's someone like that Avenger character coming to town. What's McCaid doing mixed up with that, though? You two better get home and clean up. Audrey's got supper ready and she's waiting on you. I'll take this to McCaid."

"No, Malcolm," Luc firmly declined. "Jim told us to

deliver it. If you want to do it, that's fine, but we're coming with you. We got a job to do and we aim to see it done."

They marched in silence up to Maddie's kitchen porch. Malcolm pounded on the open door, startling the two people sitting at the table.

"Good heavens, boys! What's got you so fired up?" Maddie glared as she looked from one face to the other curiously.

"Hi, Maddie. I got a telegram to give to Mr. McCaid."

"Well, come on in and give it to him." She nodded toward her guest at the table.

Malcolm left the boys at the threshold and stepped inside. He stopped at the table. He held the envelope longer than necessary, giving Julian a dark look. Julian didn't rise, either to his feet or to the bait. He arched a brow at the angry young man as he took the telegram from him.

Julian flicked the envelope's torn lip, giving the boy an assessing glance before pulling the short note out and reading it. There was no change in his expression as he folded it and put it back into the envelope.

"Thank you, Malcolm." He set it aside and spread his napkin in his lap, dismissing Audrey's brother.

"Wait a minute, McCaid. I ain't finished with you," Malcolm stopped him. "Audrey says you're moving her and the kids out to your place tomorrow. I don't like it."

McCaid looked around him at the two younger boys hovering on the porch. "You boys better run on home. I'm going to have a talk with Malcolm."

"Yessir," they mumbled in unison and hurried off the kitchen stoop.

Julian leaned back in his seat. "What is it you don't like, Malcolm?"

"I don't like you makin' a whore out of my sister."

Julian stared at him for a long moment. He thought about answering that comment with his fists. Grinding his teeth, he folded his napkin and came to his feet.

"Maddie, please excuse me." He faced Audrey's angry brother. "Outside. Now."

They went through the door and down the stairs, Julian counting each stride he made, taking calming breaths. In the drive, they faced each other. He hadn't completely talked himself out of a punch or two, but when he looked into the boy's eyes, he saw a child, afraid and alone. He sighed.

"Your sister is not—and never will be—a whore, Malcolm. I'd advise you to keep a civil tongue in your mouth when you discuss her." He looked over the boy's shoulder to Audrey's shack in the row of shanties.

"I'm taking your sister and the kids out of here because they deserve a better environment. At Hell's Gulch, the kids will be away from the sheriff's corrupting influence, and they can learn about ranching. I'm giving your sister an opportunity, Malcolm. Those kids are her life. You can come too. I'll pay you what Jim's paying you. Wouldn't hurt you to learn about ranching."

"Sheep ranching." Malcolm turned and spit off into the dirt. "No, thanks, McCaid." He spun on his heel and headed down the drive, shoving his hands in his pockets as he walked away.

Julian went back inside and sat at his place. He looked at the cold food on his plate and sighed.

"Malcolm may not understand now, Mr. McCaid, but he'll come to see it differently in time. It is a good thing you're doing for that little gal and her brood."

Julian lifted his gaze to his hostess. "Maddie, I think you should call me 'Julian.' All my friends do."

"Julian it is." She smiled and refilled his water glass. She nodded toward the envelope on the table next to him. "Bad news?"

Julian frowned. The envelope had been opened. He expected the news would be all over town soon enough— as Jace no doubt intended.

"The deputy U.S. marshal in Cheyenne has hired a friend of mine to clean up Defiance." Julian looked at Maddie. "I hate to see him take on a job like this." Maybe it was a blessing. If Jace was as good as his reputation, he'd put an end to the sheriff and his gang. Then Audrey and the children would be even safer. "Jace Gage makes a living dealing with thugs like Kemp. Things could get pretty rough around here." Julian met Maddie's gaze. "If you'd like to come out to the ranch for a while, I know Audrey would welcome having you out there."

Maddie studied him. "Your friend's a gunfighter, is he?"

"He's much more than just a gunfighter."

"Well, Julian, I've got a contract to provide rooms to the overnight stage passengers. I can't go. Besides, I need to be here for Leah."

"She can come out. I would like Malcolm to come, too. I'm worried about him."

"I'll tell you what," Maddie said as she handed him the bread basket, "if things get too bad here, I'll bring them all out."

The next day dawned gray and cool. Julian and Malcolm covered the wagon's cargo with a tarp and tied it down, leaving a space in the back for the children. Maddie hurried up the street toward them, bearing a basket so heavy she had to hold it with two hands. She set it on the wagon floor and pushed it under the front bench. Tightening her shawl across her chest, she turned to Audrey.

"I brought you some lunch. I'm sure you'll need to stop and feed these pups once before you get to the ranch."

Audrey tried to smile. "Thanks, Maddie. We'll miss you."

"Now, no long faces. You won't be so far away that I can't come out to visit. And you'll stop by when you're in town." She hugged Audrey, then stood with an arm around Leah. "We'll be fine here."

Julian moved to Audrey's side. "It's time." His eyes revealed nothing of his thoughts, but a muscle worked at the corner of his jaw. This was her last chance to change her mind. How she wished she could see into the future to know for certain whether this was the right thing to do. He helped her onto the front bench as Malcolm lifted the younger ones into the wagon bed.

Audrey studied the faces of the people she loved, tension twisting her stomach at the monumental step she was taking this morning. Sally and Malcolm looked disapproving. Jim's face was carefully blank. Leah remained silent and thin lipped, Wolf at her feet. Maddie sported a reassuring grin. In the wagon bed, her foster kids were rowdy and anxious to be on their way. Julian lifted the reins, and the wagon lurched into motion. Audrey waved. The breeze blew against her face. It was an ending. And a beginning.

But of what?

She and Julian spoke little during the ride out. The kids made noise enough to cover their silence. Their excitement was infectious. Kurt hounded Amy Lynn with questions about Hell's Gulch, but her responses only fueled his curiosity. She didn't have the words to describe the ranch, so she gave an affirmative answer to each question. Luc had to ask her about the sleeping giants and woolly elephants living at Hell's Gulch before Kurt realized what was happening.

Audrey laughed and exchanged a look with Julian, but he wasn't smiling. His eyes held a complicated mixture of emotions. Hope and need. Relief and fear. She pulled her gaze away and watched the slowly rolling landscape.

When they loaded everyone back into the wagon after their lunch stop, Luc hung back, troubled. "Mr. McCaid? You said a few weeks ago that it was too dangerous out at your place for us. What changed? What's different between then and now?"

Audrey looked at Julian, curious how he would answer. He met Luc's eyes unflinchingly. "I didn't understand your circumstances at the time. But given your recent misadventure, I don't think you're safe in town anymore. Out at the Gulch, you'll at least be away from the sheriff. However, until Kemp stops riling up the area ranchers, I am going to have firm rules about what you can do, where you can go at the ranch."

A short while later, they turned off the road and onto the long drive into the heart of the ranch. The kids were so excited they were standing up. Julian drove past the cookhouse and over the hill to the main house. They exclaimed in awe at the size of his home. He pulled up outside the carriage house and set the brake.

The children leapt off the wagon and ran to the front and then to the back, trying to see all there was to see of the house. Julian called the boys over and set them to unloading the luggage. Soon a procession of children followed Audrey up the steps and into the house. Julian walked at the end of the line, behind little Amy

Lynn. Dulcie stopped at the top step and faced him, silent as ever. Amy went around her and scurried inside.

Julian put a foot on the step below Dulcie and leaned close. "You will be safe here. I promise you that." She studied him, neither accepting nor refuting his promise, then turned and went to the door.

Audrey came back outside as Dulcie went inside. Julian moved toward her, his gaze holding hers as he did so. She'd said little since they left town. He wondered how she was handling this change. "I'll take the wagon up to Jenkins—unless you need help here?"

"We'll be fine. I thought I would put the girls in one room and the boys in another. Do you have a preference for which room you want?"

One with you in it. "No. Make whatever arrangements suit you." Julian climbed back into the wagon and turned it around. Outside the cookhouse, he found Jenkins in a heated argument with a stranger. As he set the brake, he called the two men over. Jenkins came first and introduced the newcomer as "Giles, the new cookie."

Franklin joined them then. Julian had Giles start unloading the wagon while he told the other two about the new residents at the Gulch. Jenkins's new assignment was to keep an eye on the kids—the older boys especially—to keep them out of trouble and make sure they didn't wander too far afield while trouble was expected.

"Boss, you left Miss Audrey at the house?" Franklin asked, and blanched at Julian's affirmative nod. "Jenkins, give Cookie a hand. I gotta get over there." He started off at a quick pace.

Julian followed. "What's the matter?"

Franklin sent him a worried look. "I also hired a—ah—a housekeeper for you."

Julian grabbed his sleeve and stopped him. "Why's that a problem?"

Franklin made a face. "She's from Defiance." He looked at Julian. "From Sam's."

Julian shut his eyes and cursed. "What the hell possessed you to do such a damned fool thing, Franklin?" Audrey would take one look at the girl and think he was opening up a new business out here. He cursed again. She would demand to be taken back to town. And he couldn't blame her.

"Bertie's changed. She's quit that life. She needed a job, boss. She needed a way to make a change. I already laid it out clear to the boys she ain't here to amuse them."

Franklin's defensiveness about the girl was an interesting matter Julian would have to give some thought to. But not now. They turned as one and hurried to the house, hoping to mitigate Audrey's reaction to having a former whore as a housekeeper. They went straight for the back door and hurried into the kitchen. Audrey and Bertie stood at the back hallway that led to the service rooms.

"Julian, what's wrong?" Audrey asked.

"Uh—" He looked from her to Bertie and back.

"Have you met Bertie?" Audrey asked.

Julian felt his face grow warm. How the hell should he answer that? By the grace of God, he hadn't used Bertie's services. But to say he hadn't met her would be a lie. He kept still. Audrey didn't look upset. The woman was endlessly confounding.

"Bertie." He nodded toward the girl.

"Julian, you really are acting oddly." Audrey frowned at him. "Is everything all right? It is okay, isn't it, that Bertie take the housekeeping job? Jim mentioned it to her and Franklin hired her. You must know anyone Jim and Franklin recommend will be dependable."

Julian looked at Franklin, whose eyes were wide and innocent. He cleared his throat. "Well, since Jim sent her out, I guess we can give her a try." That didn't sound quite right. "I mean—yes. It's fine. You could use the help."

"Thank you, Mr. McCaid," Bertie spoke up. "I'll work hard, you'll see."

Julian slowly released the breath he'd been holding. "Franklin, let's go take a look at those sheep you've quarantined."

"Yessir!" The two men exchanged a look.

Audrey laughed after they were gone. "Men!"

Bertie gave her a worried look. "Are you sure you're okay with this, Miss Sheridan?"

"Call me 'Audrey,' please. Of course it's fine. I could certainly use the help. I've never had a house this size to take care of before. And I'm glad you could get away from Sam's."

The kids had been given the afternoon off from their studies so that they could unpack and make their beds. When those simple chores were finished, they were allowed to go exploring. Not five minutes after they left the house they hurried back to get Audrey.

"Audrey! You gotta come with us. Mr. McCaid's got a shower!"

The boys dragged her outside and around to the back of the outhouse. She hadn't seen the bathing rooms since they were being constructed and was surprised at the finished product. Julian had had two roofless rooms built against the wide back wall of the three-seater outhouse. The first room was a changing area with hooks for clothes and shelves that would provide a convenient place to put a wash station so that men could clean up before coming to the house for meals. The second room was the actual shower alcove. Both rooms were open to the sky and were screened on three sides by high wooden walls. One set of swinging doors provided privacy for the changing area and another set enclosed the shower bay.

Bricks paved the floors of the two rooms, helping with drainage from the bathing area. A small windmill pumped water up to a tank on top of the outhouse roof, where the blazing summer sun could heat it through the day. Wash water from the shower was channeled away from the small enclosure to a lawn area at the back of the house. Every feature had been carefully considered.

Audrey was surprised at the extravagant details Julian had put into the construction of his house, even down to the service rooms behind the kitchen. He'd had a room built specifically for doing laundry and bathing. It was a large space with its own stove so hot water would not have to be carried from the kitchen. And the laundry tubs boasted a wringer so that the washing was a little less of a chore.

"Can we take showers here?" Kurt wanted to know.

"Maybe we wouldn't hate getting clean as much. It looks like fun!" Luc added.

"If Mr. McCaid says you may, then I have no problem with it." She smiled at the two boys. "It would certainly be nice having the two of you clean more often."

Audrey was upstairs putting linens away two afternoons later when she heard Bertie scream. There was fear in that scream. Terrible scenarios ran through her mind, varying from rattlesnakes in a cupboard to hatchet-bearing Sioux invading their house. Quickly she scooped up Amy and ran downstairs to the kitchen.

Chapter 27

Audrey slammed into the kitchen and stopped just inside the hall door. A man she had never seen before was standing at the stove. Bertie stood a couple of feet in front of Audrey, the business end of a broom held in her white-knuckled grip. The stranger was tall and whipcord lean. His worn hat was caught by a leather thong about his throat and hung off his back. Just above the leather was a scar that ran across his Adam's apple and looked like a rope burn. It made her wonder how many times the stranger had cheated death and how many more times he would try.

He was dressed in tan homespun. His hair was a sun-bleached brown. His hands and face were tanned except for a faint half-moon shape at the top half of his forehead, where his hat had shielded his skin from the sun. He wore a scarf about his throat that might once have been blue, but was so faded and dusty it looked dark beige. Even his vest was a dusty shade of dirt. He wore a double bandolier crossed over his chest. A gun belt with twin holsters hung low about his hips with a long, wicked-looking knife sheathed just to one side of its buckle. The only color about the man was in his crystalline-blue eyes.

As she watched, his left hand slowly lowered a lid on one of the pots Bertie had cooking for supper while the other hand, palm out, slowly, slowly moved upward in a classic gesture of peace. "I didn't mean to scare you ladies." His voice was quiet and raspy, his words spoken carefully. "I was looking for McCaid, but my stomach got the better of me. Sure smells fine, what you're cookin' here."

"I stepped in the hallway for just a minute and when I came back, there he was," Bertie complained. "Quiet as you please he sneaked in."

"Who are you?" Audrey asked. The kids piled in behind her. She tried unsuccessfully to shoo them back through the door, but Luc and Kurt stepped into the room and stood next to her, making that a futile effort.

"Name's Jace Gage."

"He's the Avenger!" Kurt said, staring at the gun-fighter.

Audrey looked at the two older boys. "What Avenger?"

"He's come to deal with the sheriff. That's what he does. He runs bad guys out of good towns," Luc provided.

"He looks just like they described him in them stories, don't he Luc?" Kurt said in a hushed whisper to Luc.

"Are you this 'Avenger'?" Audrey asked.

The man frowned, his hands still in the air, palms forward. "I do have business with the sheriff, ma'am, but that's between me and him."

"Boys, go find Mr. McCaid." Audrey took hold of the situation. "Bertie, put the broom down." She handed

Amy to Colleen, telling her to take the others back to the library to finish their studies. "You will be staying for supper, won't you, Mr. Gage?" Audrey asked, wondering how Julian would react to this man.

Strong, white teeth flashed in his tanned face. "I would be obliged, ma'am. A man can grow mighty tired of his own trail cookin'."

"Good." Audrey nodded. "Then you'll kindly remove your guns. I don't like weapons in this house." She held out her hand to him, expecting instant compliance.

His eyes cooled from warm blue to steely resolve. "With all due respect, I can't do that, ma'am."

"You have no enemies here, sir."

"I have enemies everywhere."

"Then perhaps I don't want you in my house." Audrey held her ground, becoming more frightened by this man the longer they spoke.

"I won't stay long, once I've seen McCaid and, hopefully"—his gaze drifted to the stove—"have a bite to eat."

Audrey felt her lips thin in irritation. She set her hands on her hips and was about to explain how things worked in her home when the back door banged open, admitting Julian and the boys.

"Jace!" Julian laughed and came forward, hand extended. "The boys said you were in here scaring the women." The two men smiled at each other. "I see you've met Audrey and Bertie, our housekeeper. These boys are Kurt and Luc, two of the eight orphans Audrey's taken in." Julian sent her a strange look, as if he'd just discovered something about her. She watched the blood rise in his face.

"Julian—are you feeling well?" she asked, suddenly worried.

His nostrils flared. "I'm fine. Really, really fine." He flashed her a smile, but it didn't reach his eyes. He clapped a hand on Jace's back and started propelling him from the room. "Jace looks like a chewed-up sidewinder, and well, he is. But he's also civil enough to know how to behave in a lady's home. I'll just show him where he can lock up his weapons. Then he can clean up. Call us when dinner's ready!"

The boys started to follow the men until Audrey stopped them. "Go finish your schoolwork. Give the men time to visit."

"Aw, Audrey—"

She folded her arms and arched a brow. They made a face and went off to the library, leaving her alone with Bertie. The two women shared a look. Bertie's grin broke the tension.

"If my customers had ever, even once, looked like him, well, I wouldn't now be standin' here at your stove."

"Bertie!" Audrey felt a heat slowly move up her skin, warming her neck and chin.

"And did you catch that look Mr. McCaid sent you? I better feed the kids in here tonight. You and the men should eat in the dining room."

"That's not necessary."

Bertie gave Audrey an admonishing glance. "Honey, if there's one thing I do know, it's men. Yours won't be able to keep his hands off you when he sees his friend making eyes at you."

The heat in Audrey's skin deepened. She opened her mouth to argue, but no words came out. She'd be a liar if she denied that's what she wanted. Ever since Maddie suggested she accept Julian's offer, she'd had a hard time thinking of anything else.

"You go make yourself pretty. I'll have the girls set both tables." Bertie pushed Audrey toward the door. "And whatever else you do tonight, make sure you give that Jace Gage a few of your smiles."

Audrey watched the burgundy liquid swirl about her wineglass as Julian refilled it. She felt strangely adult tonight, eating here in the dining room with these two men, away from the children. She wore her blue gingham dress tonight and had taken care with her hair, fashioning it in twin braids she wound around the crown of her head. She didn't have a special dress for the evening; Julian had seen every piece of clothing she owned. Still, he seemed pleased by her appearance. She learned, as she listened to the men, a bit about their time together during the war. McCaid had been Sager and Jace's lieutenant. An unholy threesome, if ever there was one, Audrey thought. The bushwhackers they fought at the Kansas-Missouri border never stood a chance.

Audrey sipped her wine, enjoying the way its taste complemented the flavor of the roast Bertie had prepared. She was not used to drinking spirits and felt a little fuzzy-headed. Her gaze drifted back to Julian, admiring the way his long fingers held his fork, watching as his mouth closed on a new bite of meat. He caught her looking at him and, for a moment, quit chewing as something darkened in his face. Audrey didn't look away. She couldn't. The room had grown dim during the course of their meal. Perhaps it was just a trick of the failing light, but Julian's eyes did look smoky. The wine must be stealing her better judgment, she thought. Ordinarily she wouldn't let her gaze linger so openly. She forced herself to focus on her meal.

Jace broke off a piece of bread and buttered it. "Tell me, Audrey, how many kids do you have here?"

Audrey glanced at him. She had not yet summoned the courage to smile at him. It was a difficult thing to do with Julian's dark eyes absorbing her every move. "I have eight children now."

"Eight." He shook his head. "And you're still a kid. Are you even out of adolescence yourself?" His eyes held hers as a smile slowly warmed his face.

Audrey met his honeyed gaze, feeling feminine and attractive being the center of so much male attention. He'd bathed and shaved and wore one of Julian's white cotton shirts. His voice was a strange sultry whisper, like a man unused to speaking. She wondered how he had been hurt. Had it happened during the war?

"How does a woman mark the end of her adolescence?" he asked with a frown as he tilted his head in consideration.

That question took Audrey by surprise—she had to give it a bit of thought. "Why, I suppose we get longer dresses," she laughed, testing Bertie's advice as she smiled into his eyes. "How does a man mark the end of his adolescence; for that matter?"

Julian choked. "Christ. Can we talk about something else?"

As if on cue; the children spilled into the room. The girls, in their nightclothes, came to stand between Jace and Julian. "Good night, Avenger," Mabel said, her eyes wide as she touched Jace's shoulder.

He looked a bit unsure of himself, but he gave the girls a bolstering smile. "Look, kids, I'm not the Avenger."

Colleen frowned. "The marshal in Cheyenne didn't send you to save Defiance?"

"What about Malcolm and Leah and Maddie and Mr. and Mrs. Kessler? What will happen to them? You gotta save the town. You just gotta, Avenger!" Mabel said earnestly.

Jace looked from Mabel to Colleen, to each of the children's faces. "I can't promise anything, you understand, but I will do what I can. I'm no Avenger, though. You can call me Jace."

"All right, Jace. We will. Good night." Mabel and Colleen gave him a kiss on the cheek. Dulcie stood back. She did meet his eyes in an assessing gaze that Audrey knew took courage to do. Amy had no such qualms. She lifted her arms to be picked up. She kissed him, then hugged him tightly. Audrey watched Jace's strong arms engulf the littlest of her children as his eyes squeezed shut. When the girls bid Julian good night, the boys crowded Jace, each getting a turn to shake his hand.

Audrey stood up, and so did the men. "I'll put the kids in bed. Bertie will bring coffee out to the front porch. I'll join you when I'm finished."

Julian and Jace made their way out front after a short detour to the den to fetch a decanter of brandy and a couple of glasses. Julian filled the glasses and handed one to Jace, then settled against the porch railing.

"It's good to see you're settling down, McCaid. Audrey's a nice girl."

Julian sipped his brandy. He didn't answer Jace, didn't want to answer him.

"When are you getting married?" Jace asked.

Julian silently groaned. Jace was like a dog with a bone. Best nip it in the bud. "Audrey and I are not getting married. I will be offering for a young lady back East when I return home."

Jace met his look, his eyes narrowing as he came to his feet. "So Audrey's not taken?"

He knew Jace was just fishing, but he took the bait anyway. "She's taken."

"You can't keep two women."

"You stay the hell away from her." They stood now, face-to-face. Julian was taller than Jace, but didn't particularly feel his height gave him an edge.

Jace shook his head. "You're an idiot. I saw how the two of you looked at each other. You're as crazy about her as she is for you. Any fool with eyes can see that. That's love, Julian. You leave her, she'll shatter. I know. I loved like that once, and you saw me after it ended.

"Half the men alive never know a love like that even once in their lives. It sure as hell never comes twice. You throw it away, McCaid, you'll never see it again." He finished off his brandy, then spun on his heel and yanked open the door.

"Where are you going?" Julian called after him.

"To get my guns," he answered without looking back. "I got some hell to raise."

Audrey joined Julian on the porch a short while later. "Where's Jace?" she asked.

"Heading to Defiance." Julian refilled his glass. His mood rode him hard. She smiled at him, and his anger deepened. It was lust. That's all he felt for her. Hell, one time, one fucking time between her legs, he would be over her. She would be, then, like any other woman he had bedded.

And his children wouldn't be in jeopardy.

He glared at her as his spirit warred with itself. The good part of his soul wanted to warn her, tell her to run, but the dark side owned him tonight. He held his hand out to her. She took it without hesitation. He drew her across the distance separating them, close to him, close enough that he lifted her hand to his mouth and kissed her slim fingers. He touched his other hand to her cheek, feeling the fine bones there, like a china doll beneath his hand.

Fragile.

He pulled her in for a kiss, his hand at the back of her head. "You are mine," he growled against her mouth.

She shook her head. "No, McCaid." He could feel her breath on his lips. "I am no more yours than you are mine."

He kissed her then, wanting to stop the words, stop his mind from thinking, stop his heart from feeling. She was soft beneath his onslaught, but he didn't let up. He took her face in both of his hands, his thumbs at the hinges of her jaw, opening her for the thrust of his tongue. She met his invasion, greeting his tongue with the sweet touch of hers as she caressed one side of it, then the other. A shiver rippled down his spine.

Her arms circled his neck, breaking his hold briefly. He moved his hands back to her face, in a fever to touch her soft skin. He broke from the kiss to taste her chin, the soft places of her throat. He wrapped his arms around her, lifted her up against his chest, tight against his heart.

"Tell me 'no.'" *Please, God.* "Tell me 'no,' Audrey."

She shook her head. He felt her lips graze his chin

as they traveled to his ear. "I'm not saying no, McCaid." Her whispered words poured like liquid torture through his soul.

He pressed his face against her hair and held still. Very, very still. In the kitchen, before dinner, all the puzzle pieces he hadn't been able to assemble about her had fallen into place. She hadn't corrected his orphan count; Amy was not her natural daughter but another of her foster children.

Audrey had never been with a man before. "I can't do this to you." But, God help him, he wanted to. He set her down and pulled away from her. Her lips were still moist from his kisses. As he watched, she licked them, clearing them of his essence. He shivered again, his body suffering withdrawal from her touch.

Grabbing the neck of the brandy bottle, he walked down the front steps. He tilted the bottle and took a long draw from it as he slammed through the front gate and moved toward the main part of camp.

Audrey watched him walk away. She wrapped her arms about herself, small comfort that it was. Holding him was like holding an angry bear: impossible to do. She more than wanted him; she loved him. And she had only this summer to show him that he loved her too.

The door opened as Bertie came out with the coffee tray. "Where did they go?"

Audrey shook her head, venturing a look at her new friend.

"Did he hurt you?" she asked as she set the tray down.

A breath left Audrey's chest, more sob than exhalation. "He left. How is it that I feel what I do and he feels nothing?"

"Honey, I seen him look at you. Trust me, it ain't 'nothing' that he's feeling."

"What do I do?"

Bertie studied Audrey, her lips pursed, her brow furrowed. "You're in love with him?" Audrey nodded. "Even though you know he's not the staying kind?"

"I know." Audrey nodded again. "I do know that. I don't care."

"Then keep doing what you're doing. You will get to him." She grinned at Audrey. "I bet he's close to breaking."

Audrey was unable to settle down that evening. She went to the library and read for a bit, hoping Julian would return, but her attention kept wandering from the travelogue in front of her. Deciding a soak in the tub might calm her nerves enough to let her sleep, she went to the washroom to heat some water.

When it was ready, she selected rose oil from among the fine soaps, lotions, and other luxuries Julian purchased at Jim's store and poured a few drops into the tub. She sank into the warm water. Slowly her tension seeped away in the quiet of the candlelit room. She washed her hair and scrubbed her body, then lingered until the water began to cool. Reluctantly, she left the tub. After setting the room back to rights, she headed for her bedroom.

She had just reached the upper landing on the stairs when the front door opened and closed, admitting McCaid. She had not meant to see him again tonight, but caught halfway between him and her room, she had no chance of escaping his notice.

He crossed the entranceway to extinguish the lamp

on the table when he looked up and saw her. He paused, then doused the lamp. He slowly came up the steps, out of the darkness into the dim ring of light from the upper hallway. Audrey wondered if he was drunk. She didn't think he was; his steps were steady, his gaze unwavering. She became intensely aware that only the meager covering of her wrap stood between her and Julian's heated gaze.

A few steps from her, he leaned forward and opened the robe at her ankles. Her feet were bare. Cool air whispered around her lower leg. He took another step, his hand rising against the naked skin of her calf. Another step, his hand was behind her knee. A ragged breath whispered past her lips. The final step between brought his hand up the back of her thigh to cup her buttock, baring one entire leg, pale in the shadowy light of the stairway.

Audrey took hold of the banister.

Julian lifted his other hand and touched his knuckles to her neck. She was having a difficult time forming a coherent thought while his hand stroked her bottom.

He leaned down and kissed the base of her throat. "Have you changed your mind?" His voice was hoarse.

She shook her head. He cursed. He took hold of her face, staring down into her eyes. "I am no tame campfire to warm your hands at, Audrey. I am a raging forest fire. I burn for you. I will consume you."

Audrey put her hands to his face, holding him as he held her. "I know what you are, Julian. I am not afraid."

And then his lips took hers, open and hungry. He bent and lifted her into his arms, the kiss unbroken as he carried her up the final steps to her room. He quietly pushed the door closed with his boot, then set her on her feet. Backing her up against the wall, he pinned her against the cold plaster.

"Don't play games with me," Julian growled. "I am not stopping. I cannot stop, do you understand?" Blood pooled in his groin, throbbing. This was a mistake. He shouldn't do this to her. His body wasn't listening. His hips rocked against her. She squirmed—to get away, he thought. When he pulled back to give her room to leave, her robe opened to her waist, revealing upthrust breasts, nipples puckered. His cock grew harder. He cursed. She dragged her hands over those mounds, to retrieve the cover of her robe, he assumed, but she cupped herself and made no move to leave. Watching her was agony—he couldn't do it without shaming himself. He grabbed her hands and held them against the wall, holding them by her wrists on either side of her face as he dragged a calming breath into his lungs. This position was another mistake. It only lifted her breasts closer to him.

"Ah, God, Audrey," he growled against her temple, leaning forward and breathing in her scent. Roses. She'd used the oil he bought in town.

"I cannot think a thought without you in it. I crave the sound of your voice, the smell of your skin." His hips rocked against her again, but he was too tall. He only felt the soft flesh of her stomach. He wedged a thigh between her legs, spreading them, making her ride his thigh. He moved his leg to put pressure on the sensitive flesh at the apex of her legs. He slowly drew his hands away from her wrists, down her arms to her chest, closing them on the hot, pale flesh of her breasts. Her nipples burned his palms. He ached to taste her. His breathing became as shallow as hers. He took her nipples between his thumbs and forefingers, gently rolling them back and forth even as his leg pressed her feminine flesh. He looked into her eyes and saw they had gone black with passion.

"Audrey, tell me to leave. Tell me to go right now." She shook her head. He felt her dig her hands into his hair, felt her pull him toward her. He opened his mouth, devouring her lips. His hands moved up her chest, her neck, to cradle her jaw, holding her for his possession. She yielded beneath him, surrendering, opening to the hungry stroke of his tongue. Her eyes were not closed, and Julian stared into their pale depths as he shoved his tongue into her mouth, seeking and finding her tongue. Oh, the exquisite torture, the feel of her soft, hot mouth tightening on his tongue as she suckled him. He groaned against her mouth, his hips rocking of their own volition.

He broke the kiss to run his lips down her throat. And when he bent to her breasts, her robe fell away completely, revealing her pale legs spread over his denim-clad thigh. He rubbed against her sensitive flesh and her back arched. He drew his hand down her chest, over her breast, down her waist, over her hip to her thigh. He massaged the hard muscles of her leg, then slowly moved upward, inward, moving his hand to the dark intimate curls hiding her secret flesh.

Audrey felt him touch that part of her that sent all conscious thought flying. The pad of his thumb rubbed her in a sweet, soft circle. He was watching her, breathing with her, his mouth open. Something was happening to her. She couldn't stand on her own and his leg wasn't enough support. She shook her head. She grabbed on to his shoulders. Her hips bucked against his hand.

"Ah, Christ," he groaned. He pulled his leg away and

Audrey moaned a protest. He went to his knees in front of her. He separated the folds of her heated flesh, and then his mouth was there, his breath hot on her inner skin. And his tongue, dear God, his tongue licked and stroked, wet and smooth with molten heat. His head was dark against her skin. He looked up at her, watching her with his big, coffee-brown eyes, his nose buried in her dusky curls. Hot liquid desire unfurled in her belly like a snake unwinding. Her hands pressed against the wall behind her. She could find no purchase, nothing to hold on to. She closed her eyes, unable to bear watching her hips grind against his mouth.

And then he pulled away, kissing her as he bent and lifted her into his arms. His tongue possessed her mouth. Her breasts were pressed against the warm leather of his vest, the texture exquisite against her sensitive nipples. He set her on the bed and removed his boots. His vest quickly followed. He shrugged out of his suspenders, unbuttoned his shirt, then ripped it over his head. He unfastened his pants and pulled them and his underdrawers down over his lean hips.

Audrey stared at the upthrusting male part of him. He was a large man, and so it stood to reason that that part of him would be large as well, but his was enormous. He kicked free of his pants and knelt on the bed, spreading her legs. He moved down over her, cradling the hard length of his manhood on top of the sensitized folds of her flesh. He braced his weight on his elbows, his hands cupping her shoulders. His dark hair fell forward, shadowing his eyes. He watched her as he slowly began to move his hips against hers. It felt delicious. Her body knew what to do—her hips began moving against his, against the hard column of his flesh.

He arched over her to suckle a breast. He moved slightly between her thighs, positioning himself at her opening. Audrey's heart beat hard, a pulsing, drumming beat. He hesitated, watching her, his eyes intense. His nostrils flared. He pushed into her. Just a bit, spreading her. Stretching her.

Julian watched her face, trying to gauge her pleasure or discomfort. She was so goddamned tight. He'd never taken a virgin before, never been with an innocent. The thought that he was her first filled him with an unfathomable joy. This couldn't be comfortable for her, but she watched him with unrelenting trust. He pushed farther in, then slowly withdrew, all the way out, before pushing forward again. He hadn't gone in very far, but he was blocked. He couldn't go in any deeper; her virgin's barrier stopped him. He pulled out and pushed in again, wanting her to be at ease with the motion, the sensation, the pressure. He was going to have to break that barrier and had no idea if it would be a minor discomfort to her or a major one.

He pulled out again, pressing his throbbing cock against the bedcover while he kissed his way between her breasts, over her ribs, and down her flat belly. His chin encountered her soft, feminine curls. He moved lower to run his tongue along the inner folds protecting her opening. He mouthed her clitoris, gently suckling her swollen flesh. He put two fingers into her opening. She was wet, ready for him. He continued working her until she writhed against him, until he felt her soft inner walls convulse around his fingers. He moved between her thighs again, entering her, thrusting up to the wall that stopped him before. Now she was bucking against him, absorbing him. He pulled back, then thrust forward, breaking into the hot core of her.

And there he stopped. He could feel the sweat on his skin, see the same sheen on hers. Still she watched him, believing in him, believing in his control. His arms shook with restraint that was quickly fading. He couldn't stop. He began pumping his cock into her hot channel, loving the feel of her, wanting to feel her release. He touched the center of her desire, working that sensitive nub until he felt her orgasm lift her away, tightening her flesh against him. He shoved himself deep into her, deeper than he ever thought possible. She arched against him, pressing her head into the mattress. He folded his arms under her, hugging her to his chest as he pulled out of her and thrust between their bodies, feeling his ejaculation wet their bellies.

He lifted his weight onto his elbows. His breathing was still ragged. Warily, he watched her. He had just been a ravening beast, taking her with a violence that shocked even himself. And he could feel himself hardening against her once again. She smiled at him as her small hands moved up his arms to cup his face. She pulled him to her, chin to chin, nose to nose, lips to lips, and kissed him with a smile on her mouth.

Julian felt something twist in his chest. He did not love her. He could not love her. He squeezed his eyes shut, wishing his heart was ruled by his mind. He rolled off her body and off the bed. He walked naked to the bowl and pitcher and had just dampened a cloth to clean his seed off them when he heard her gasp.

He silently cursed.

He'd forgotten about his back. He stood immobile, locked in place. He heard her get off the bed and pad over to stand behind him. He held himself rigid, waiting for her questions, waiting for her revulsion when she heard his answers. The time to reveal himself would have been long before what had just happened between them, when she still had a choice about lying with him.

He felt her warm hands on his back, whispering over his numb scars that he knew looked like hell. He had seen them once as he stood in front of a mirror and studied them with a hand mirror. Pink and puckered, even then, even years after he'd been whipped.

Her hands stilled, and he felt her face pressed against his back as she breathed against his wrecked skin. His shoulders slumped as he exhaled. He turned and faced her. There was sorrow in her eyes. Not revulsion. Not morbid interest. She didn't speak. Nor did he. He pulled her into his arms, feeling a little less damaged.

Chapter 28

It was the end of the next day before Audrey could speak privately with Julian. Supper was over. The girls were helping Bertie wash up. The boys were seeing to their evening rounds of chores. Audrey stood inside several lines of sheets, taking the linens down. A gentle breeze made the heavy lines sway. When she looked up, Julian was there, dark among the white sheets. Her breath caught, then started up again—too rapidly. His head was bare. His brown hair was loose, almost touching his collar; she should give him a haircut. He wore his leather vest over a beige shirt. His denims were faded over his thighs from hard use.

He must be headed for the shower, for a towel was draped over one shoulder. She knew he liked to bathe at this time of day, when his work was done and the water was warm. He stopped only when he was a foot from her. "Hi."

Audrey dropped a folded sheet into her basket. Her mind flashed through images of their night together, of him moving over her, loving her.

"Hi." She looked up at him. His eyes were hypnotic,

heated. He touched his fingertips to her cheek. Audrey took hold of his wrist, pulling his hand to her lips. She shut her eyes and kissed his palm. And then she was in his arms, a hand in her hair as he braced her for his kiss. She wrapped her arms about his neck. She lifted her body against his, welcomed his tongue into her mouth. When the kiss ended, his lips brushed her cheek, her brow, her temple. He drew her close in a tight embrace. Audrey pressed her face into his chest, feeling his heart hammering against her face until he leaned back to look at her.

"Did I hurt you last night, Audrey? Were you well today?" He swept a lock of her hair behind an ear.

Audrey looked up into his brown eyes, wondering how to answer him. Last night he'd completed her body. And he'd carved a canyon in her soul. She shook her head. "Once was not enough, Julian."

A smile slowly made its way across his mouth. "We can remedy that."

Julian left his room and walked to Audrey's open balcony door. She stood in a shaft of bright moonlight, her hands clasped in front of her, a long, white cotton nightgown covering her from head to foot, much like the one she'd worn the night he'd first kissed her. Julian entered her room. He moved forward from the shadows so that he wouldn't block what little light there was. The moonlight made her golden brown hair look silvery, her light green eyes even paler. She was ethereal. He reached a hand to her face, fearful some magic had turned her to marble.

She was warm and velvety soft beneath his touch. He ran the backs of his fingers down her neck, indulging his senses in the luxury of the caress. Her hands moved to his chest. His belly contracted at her light stroke. He stood unmoving beneath her questing hands, watching her learn the feel of him. Her hands moved down from his shoulders, her palms sweeping over his nipples.

Anticipating their encounter, he'd been uncomfortably hard before he even entered her room. Standing still beneath her soft strokes was almost more than he could bear. She leaned in and buried her face in the dark hairs of his chest. Julian shut his eyes and gritted his teeth.

He could withstand this. He was man enough. Her mouth closed on one of his nipples. A jolt of desire shot through his loins. He dug his hands into her unbound hair, gripping her head, holding her against himself, then pulling away to take her lips with his own. Her mouth opened against his, offering him her tongue. God, he wanted her. He thrust into her mouth, hungry. Insatiable.

His control was spinning away from him.

He'd hoped tonight would be a slow discovery of each other. He broke away from her. She moaned a protest. He smiled. His breathing was labored, his heart hammering. His hands shook as he unfastened the buttons of her nightgown. He spread the material open, watching her reaction as he touched the soft skin of her chest, trailing his fingers down to the valley between her breasts and lower until they reached the end of the nightgown's opening.

He pushed the nightgown over her shoulders, trapping her arms against her sides as he bared her breasts. Her breathing was as labored as his. By the light of the moon, he could see the skin of her neck and upper chest was darker than that of her breasts. Sun kissed.

He ran his knuckles down from her collarbone to the tops of her breasts, then opened his hands and cupped their heavy weight. Her lips parted on a sharp intake of air. He bent and lifted a mound to his mouth, using his tongue and lips to excite her nipple.

"Julian—"

"Hmmm?" he groaned against her skin.

"Please let me hold you."

He kissed his way up to her neck, then pushed her nightgown all the way off her body, letting it drop in a pool at her feet. He stepped back, looking at her, impatient to end this torment. She reached between their bodies and touched a hand to the bulge in his pants. His dick tightened another notch. He trapped her hand against himself. "Do you see what you do to me? I have only to look at you and I'm like this."

He unfastened his pants and pushed them and his drawers off his hips, releasing his cock. Her slim hands encircled him, running up the hard length of his arousal. The sensation was exquisite. He pulled her hands away from him, bringing them up to circle his neck as he wrapped his arms around her. She felt fragile in his arms. He ran a hand down her back, feeling the indentation of her waist, the curve of her hip. He caressed the soft flesh of her buttock. Bringing his hand around to the front of her thigh, he touched the curls at the juncture of her thighs. He slipped his fingers into the folds of her womanhood, finding the spot he searched for, caressing her. When her arms tightened around his neck, he lifted her and took her to the bed. Unable to wait longer, he knelt between her legs and eased himself into her.

Audrey felt him enter her, stretch her. He was holding himself back. She wanted more of him. She pushed up against him, impaling herself. He withdrew, slowly, slowly, pulling the long length of him from her only to slip back in. Her soul knew the rhythm. He stretched out over her, bracing his weight on his elbows as he pumped into her. The pleasure was intense. It exploded within her. She bucked beneath him. She cried out her ecstasy against his mouth. Before the passion of the moment left her, he pulled free of her, shooting his hot seed upon her belly.

Tonight she was ready for this. She handed him a small cloth and felt him wipe his secretion from her stomach. He set the cloth aside and pulled her into his arms. Audrey snuggled closer, threading her leg between his, her arm around his side. Her face against his chest, she felt more than heard the strong beat of his heart. She wished this would never end. She wished she had the right to lie in his arms every night and wake there every morning.

Maddie had given her bad advice, she realized. No man could compare to Julian. Good enough would never be enough now.

Audrey swept the back porch, absently thinking about Julian and regretting that it was only the afternoon yet— she had hours left to go before their time together that night. She'd never been so happy as in the last couple of weeks. There was a difference in Julian too. He was more relaxed around the children. He'd crated up the inappropriate books from the library and stored them in his den. But since that left only dry histories and travelogues, he let the kids corral him into telling them bedtime stories. They had been enjoying a continuing series of stories he made up about the adventures of a brother and sister sadly orphaned during the war. He added wonderful twists and startling events in the saga, keeping the children captivated.

The porch step creaked, and Audrey looked up to see the object of her daydreams coming toward her. She smiled at him, but her words of welcome died on her lips as she caught the look in his eyes.

"Julian, what is it?" She set the broom aside and reached for him, frightened.

"I have news from town. Bad news, I'm afraid." He studied her face. "Your friend Leah was attacked. She's all right—Jace got there in time. But he was forced to marry her, said it was the only way he could protect her from the sheriff and his men."

Audrey's legs went boneless. She sat heavily in a chair. Julian crouched in front of her, holding her hands. "This is not good news," she said. "Are you sure she's okay?"

"His note said she was."

"I have to go see her!"

"No. You're not going to town. You'll just put yourself and Leah and Jace in danger."

"Julian, they are not a match. She hates violence. And she's afraid of men."

He nodded. "He said it was a marriage in name only and only until he's run the sheriff and his gang out of town. She's rather stubborn, like someone else I know. She wouldn't come out here."

Audrey frowned. "I can't understand this."

"Write her a letter. We'll send it with the next wagon that goes in for supplies. Ask her to come out. Maybe if you invite her, she'll change her mind."

* * *

Audrey considered Leah's situation as she hung laundry several days later. Julian sent her note into town the next day, but Leah's return letter did little to alleviate her worry. She said she and Jace had married, temporarily. For now he was living in her home, protecting her.

Julian walked past Audrey's laundry lines, drawing her back to the present. He moved at a fast pace, leading a slow and reluctant shaggy dog behind him. Curious, she followed him. He skirted the area where the kids were playing. The other children barely noted him, but Dulcie fell into step with him. She had to jog to keep up with him. As Audrey watched, she reached over and touched his arm to slow him down.

"Mr. McCaid, you're walking too fast for him." Her willingness to talk to Julian always amazed Audrey. Julian made an irritated face and scooped the white and black furry creature up, barely breaking his stride. The dog wiggled in his arms, disliking being held.

"What's his name, Mr. McCaid?"

"He has no name."

"Where are you going with him?"

"Dulcie, this is not a matter for you."

"Mr. McCaid, what are you doing?" she asked again, her voice deepening, mimicking a tone Audrey sometimes used for ill-behaved children.

Julian paused to look at Dulcie. "He's a bad sheepdog, honey. He's no good at confronting coyotes or wolves or mountain lions. He's afraid of everything. I've got no use for him."

"He can learn." She put a hand out to touch the mutt's soft fur.

"No, he can't. A dog is either brave or he's not. And this one's not. I have to put him down."

"I'm not very brave. You wouldn't put me down, would you?"

He gave a frustrated sigh, clearly finished with this discussion. "Of course not. You're a little girl. But this is supposed to be a working dog. If he can't earn his keep, I don't want him."

"I could teach him."

Julian regarded her, then gave a slow shake of his head. "You would have to learn all kinds of commands, which you would have to speak to him out loud. It's hard work, too hard for a little girl. Too hard for you."

"I can do it."

Julian put the fur ball down, watched him walk over and sniff Dulcie. She knelt down and opened her arms to him. He wagged his cropped tail and nuzzled her face.

"Please, Mr. McCaid, please let me try. You will see. He will be very obedient. And I will be brave enough for the both of us."

"A pet is a significant responsibility." Julian folded his arms. "You have to see that he is fed and exercised. Regardless of what the weather is or how tired you are, you have to take care of him every day."

She nodded. Her eyes were shimmering. The mutt licked her face. "I can do it."

Julian frowned. "Go ask Audrey. She may not want the beast in the house."

Dulcie looked over at Audrey, a plea in her eyes. "Audrey? May I have Willie? Mr. McCaid will have to kill him if we don't save him. Please, Audrey? Please say we can keep him."

Julian looked over his shoulder at her. Audrey smiled at Dulcie. "'Willie,' is it? Yes, I think that's fine."

Dulcie's smile was blinding. It warmed her face and

sparkled in her eyes. She hugged the mutt, then came to her feet and squeezed Julian's hand.

"He may not be a good sheepdog, Mr. McCaid, but he'll be a good house dog. You'll see." Taking the lead rope, she skipped off toward the other children, who crowded around her and Willie.

Audrey closed the distance between them. "She talks to you so easily. It's good to hear her speak."

"It is."

"You weren't really going to put him down, were you?" Audrey asked, watching him earnestly.

Julian made a face as he shrugged. "She lives too much in her head." He watched the children. "He's one of my smarter dogs. I thought he could be put to better use guarding this flock than the four-legged one he was set to."

Audrey took hold of his folded arms and stretched up on tippytoes to kiss his cheek. "You are the kindest man I've ever known."

Chapter 29

"Audrey! It's here! Audrey, come see!" Mabel's excited call drew Audrey and Bertie to the front porch. A supply wagon was stopped in front of the house. Most of its goods had been unloaded, except for those needed at the house and a couple of large crates.

"What is it?" Audrey asked.

"Your sewing machine," Kurt said. He and Luc had been at the cookhouse when the wagon and outriders came in. He opened the back gate as the wagon driver came around to help the boys lift the heavy crates down. Bertie looked like an excited child as they waited for the machine to be fully revealed to them. A crowbar quickly freed the machinery, to many oohs and aahs as the children gathered close to get a good look.

Mabel touched the machine's shiny black coat and looked up at Audrey with wide eyes. "It's beautiful, Audrey."

Audrey had forgotten Julian ordered the sewing machine. So much had happened between then and now.

"Where do you want it, miss?" the wagon driver asked.

"Upstairs, I guess. In my room. I'll show you where."

She led the way inside and up the stairs, indicating where the machine should be set up in her room. They brought up the special desk first. Kurt and Luc moved backward up the stairs as Julian's man directed the two boys and carried the other end. Once settled, they made another trip downstairs to retrieve the machine and sewing supplies.

The front of the desk was elaborately carved oak in a pattern of flowers and vines with black iron drawer pulls. Audrey crossed her arms over her ribs, remembering her first kiss with Julian was over the topic of this machine. This machine was her freedom. With it, and the skill to run it, she could go anywhere. Julian had said this was her home, but it wasn't her only option. She could go anywhere.

He had set her free.

The children crowded around the machine, pressing forward to get a good look at it. Luc and Kurt backed the kids away, opening a channel for Audrey to go to the machine. She didn't move. Her feet were anchored to the floor. The distance between her and the machine elongated and swam in her eyes. Her chest felt rigid, breathing became difficult. Someone spoke to her—she didn't know who. She couldn't differentiate voices.

She didn't want her freedom. She didn't want to be rid of Julian. Hot tears spilled down her cheeks as she stared at the black machine. Her hands gripped the material at her sides.

A woman wrapped an arm about her shoulders. Bertie. Audrey heard her soothing tone, but could not understand her words. It was the end. It was over. She was done. Bertie smoothed a lock of hair from Audrey's face. Audrey didn't blink, couldn't rip her eyes from the machine.

"Go find Mr. McCaid. Quickly, boys," Bertie told the older boys. More soothing words followed the order. Audrey's breath came in tiny gasps as if her corset was too tight. Her head was humming, blocking words.

And then Julian was there. He spoke to her. She couldn't answer, words were locked away with her breath in some unreachable part of her body. He moved to stand in front of her, blocking the machine with his big body. He cupped her face and bent to look into her eyes.

"Audrey? What's wrong?" His voice broke through her shock. Tears spilled down her cheeks, pooling against his hands. He wiped at them with his thumbs, spreading the moisture before he set his hands on her shoulders and straightened.

"Bertie, take the children downstairs. I need to speak to Audrey." The door closed, leaving them alone. Julian wrapped his arms around her and drew her against his warm body. She stood stiffly, incapable of unlocking her body without her soul disintegrating.

Julian held her, rocked her, gave her rigid body a different rhythm to feel than the one burning inside her. His hands rubbed her back. After a bit, he lifted her in his arms and carried her to the bed, where he sat with her on his lap.

Audrey slowly opened her arms and lifted them around his neck. She would be lost without him. She would be nothing. She pressed her face against his throat, breathing his scent, feeling his heartbeat against her lips.

"Do you want to tell me what happened?" he asked quietly, his words whispering against her cheek.

"The sewing machine—"

Julian looked at the machine. "Do you not like it?

Though it appears complicated, we can figure it out. I'm sure it came with instructions."

"It isn't the sewing machine, Julian."

"But you just said—"

"You don't understand."

He shook his head. "Help me to understand."

"It's an end. Of us."

Again he shook his head. "There is no end to us. I will always take care of you. You have this house and this ranch."

"But not you."

"No, not me."

Audrey drew a long breath into her lungs, held it, then slowly released it. Everything had an ending. Everything. She would leave this place when he was gone. She couldn't stay here, couldn't be here in rooms he had been in, rooms he had loved her in. She would take the black machine and go to Cheyenne.

She would start her own life. Without him.

She moved off his lap and came to her feet. He stood as well, watching her warily. "Shall I help you learn how the sewing machine works?" he asked.

Audrey looked from him to the black machine. She wiped at the moisture on her cheeks and resolutely nodded.

Julian felt the silence that night as soon as he stepped into Audrey's room. She was sitting bolt upright in her bed, her nightgown buttoned all the way up to her neck. She did not greet him. He crossed the room and sat on the edge of her bed, waiting for her to speak.

She gave him a hollow smile. "I'm not pregnant."

Whatever he'd been expecting her to say, it wasn't

that. Of course, her announcement made perfect sense. They'd spent nearly every night together for the past month. It was certainly time for her courses. That news would have thrilled him two months ago, when he'd set out to seduce her. Now it left him oddly empty. Part of him wished his precautions had not been so effective. At least then the future would be decided for him, for them.

"I see," he answered at last. "Are you in pain? Can I get you a cup of tea? A hot bath?"

"I'm fine. It's just something that has to pass."

Julian looked at the crisp white sheet covering her stomach. "How long does it run?" *How long must I be without you?*

"Five days, usually. I'm very regular."

Five days. An eternity. He took hold of her hand. "May I still sleep with you? I will just hold you." *Please.*

"Of course, if you'd rather be alone, I understand."

"I'd like you to stay. I've gotten used to sleeping with you."

Julian walked around the bed and stretched out, fully clothed, on top of the sheet. He pulled Audrey into his arms. She fit against his body as if she were his other half, created for him alone. He kissed her forehead. "If you need anything, you've only to ask. I'll fetch it for you."

She smiled. "I'm not sick, Julian, only —inconvenienced."

He nodded. "Good night, then." It was an amazing thing to feel her body relax, her breathing even out. He slept not at all.

It was a pattern they repeated for two more nights. Julian could barely remember what he did during the daylight hours, for his day began at night when they were together. He lay on his side, watching her sleep, keenly aware of how fast their time together was passing. In the beginning, he'd thought if he could just hold her, touch her every minute of every night left to them, it would be enough to spread across the rest of his life.

He was wrong. It would never be enough.

The thought of leaving her caused him physical pain. He didn't want to sleep, didn't want to waste a moment of their time together. He considered and rejected several alternatives, including one fantasy where he stayed here at the ranch in this unrealistic but idyllic existence.

Julian felt a small hand tap his back at the same time he heard Mabel's loud whisper. "Mr. McCaid? Why are you in Audrey's bed?" He must have dozed. He hadn't heard her come into the room. He rolled over to look at the little girl. "Did you have a bad dream too?" she asked.

His whole life had become a bad dream. "Yes." He reached over and scooped her up, then rolled back to settle her beneath the sheet between him and Audrey.

"What was your nightmare?" Mabel asked. "Audrey says it can't hold you in its power if you talk about it."

His nightmare was too vivid. And still looming. "Audrey's a very smart woman." He looked at her to see if she'd awakened.

She was watching them, a hint of a smile on her lips. "What was your dream, sweetheart?" she asked Mabel as she brushed a lock of hair from her face. The little girl looked at her but didn't answer. "Your father?" Mabel nodded. Julian watched this exchange, feeling a disturbing mixture of curiosity and dread as he waited for an explanation.

Audrey looked at him. With a sigh, she told the story in a crisp, matter-of-fact way. "Her father hit her mother until she died. Then he dropped Mabel off at our house and went west to the gold fields. Now and then, she thinks about it, and it gives her terrible nightmares."

Julian felt gut-punched. All the time he'd spent worrying about his unborn children, this little girl had been living in hell. He touched her torso, his large hand spanning her little chest. Her heart hammered against his palm with the rapid beat of a frightened bird. He felt fiercely protective of Mabel, of Audrey's entire brood.

"You are safe now, sweet," he whispered to her. "He cannot harm you. He will never harm you again."

She looked up at him. "I wish you were my father, Mr. McCaid."

Julian closed his eyes. He leaned over and kissed her forehead. "Sleep now. I'll take you back to your bed in a bit." She shut her eyes and within minutes her breathing was even, her face relaxed.

Audrey put her hand on Julian's. In that moment, Julian felt complete. Warmth swirled within his entire being. He could start here, start with this family. His life could have meaning beyond the superficial intent he'd given it. His children wouldn't have a pedigree, but they would be loved. He was powerful enough; he could make them, all of them—these orphans and his own flesh and blood—safe.

At dusk the next evening, Julian looked up to see Audrey come out onto the balcony. The kids were preparing for bed. He and Audrey had a few minutes alone. He smiled and held a hand out to her. Drawing her into his arms, he turned her back to him so that they both faced the brilliant colors of the sunset as he settled his hands about her waist. She covered his arms with hers and leaned against him.

It was a moment like no other he'd experienced.

He knew, suddenly, that all the days he had lived had brought him to this point, to this sunset. To this woman. He turned her in his arms, wanting to see her face in the pink twilight. He couldn't describe how he felt. Everything was different—it was *more* somehow. The sunset wasn't pretty; it was stunning. He wasn't happy; he was ecstatic. He grinned down at her, embarrassed at the euphoria he was feeling.

It had to be love.

Love.

He touched his fingers to her cheek, caressing the dimple that showed when she smiled. *I love you.* His heart began a violent beat. Would she believe him? How could she when he'd made it clear he only wanted sex from her, that she had no permanent place in his life?

He could court her. He could show her, more every day, how he felt. Then he would tell her. And ask her to marry him.

"It's frightening when you look at me like that, Julian."

He leaned forward and brushed his mouth against hers, the touch more caress than kiss. "Do you know how beautiful you are, Audrey?" His heart had found its mate. He kissed her, gently, nose to nose, chin to chin. His body quickened at the sweet touch of her tongue against his. He'd seduced her. He knew every inch of her body. He knew her scent. He knew how to make her smile. But he had no idea where her heart lay. He would sweep her off her feet, woo her until she admitted to feeling what he felt.

An idea occurred to him, a brilliant start to his plan. "I need to go check on a few things. I'll be back in time to tell the kids the next installment of the story." He reluctantly left her arms and crossed his room to the stairs.

"Where are you going, Mr. McCaid?" Colleen asked as he started down the steps. Julian looked up to see Colleen and Mabel standing in the doorway of their room.

"I have an errand to run."

"An errand? Out here?" Mabel asked.

"Yes."

"But we're ready for bed. Aren't you going to continue the story?" Colleen added.

"Of course. I won't be long."

"What errand are you doing?" Mabel asked.

Julian sent a quick look to Audrey's room. Her door was still closed. "It's a surprise for Audrey."

The girls quickly hurried over. "We love surprises! What is it?"

Julian felt foolish telling them, but there was nothing for it if he wanted to get out and back in a decent amount of time. "I'm going to pick her a bouquet. I saw some flowers by the river a while back. I thought I'd check to see what was still there."

Colleen clapped her hands. "Oh! Can't we come too? We're very good at picking flowers!"

"Audrey wouldn't like you running about in your nightclothes."

"Please, Mr. McCaid!" Mabel begged.

He made a face. "Well, all right, then. Tell the others where we're going. I don't want them to worry. But Audrey is not to know. It's a surprise for her."

The girls spun around and hurried to their room. Before Julian knew it, all four girls were running down the front stairs and all four boys were close on their heels.

"What's goin' on?" Luc asked.

"It's a secret," Colleen answered.

Julian could tell the boys didn't like being left out of the adventure. "We're going to pick flowers for Audrey."

"Flowers?" Kurt echoed, looking as if he wanted to spit.

"Yes. Flowers." Julian gave him a hard look. "And it's a secret. Audrey is not to know."

"Can we come too?" Joey asked.

"Boys don't pick flowers, stupid." Kurt laid down the law.

"Mr. McCaid is," Mabel argued.

"Where are you going for them?" Luc wanted to know.

"Over by the river."

Luc nodded. "That's a bad patch. Lots of snakes over that way. I guess we could go and scare the snakes out so the girls would be safe."

"Yeah!" Kurt and Tommy agreed.

Julian looked at the mob of children. This had become an ordeal. He'd just wanted to sneak away for a quick bouquet, but the excitement on their faces made it impossible for him to ignore them. "Well then, let's get on our way."

They walked through the hallway and into the kitchen. All laughter and chatter died when they saw Audrey. She must have come down the back stairs while they were still arguing. Julian groaned inwardly at their lack of subtlety.

"I was wondering where the children were." Audrey looked from one excited face to another and frowned. "What's going on?"

Julian drew himself to his full height, tucking his hands behind him. "Going on? I don't have any idea what you're talking about. We were just running an errand."

"An errand? Out here?" Audrey asked. Mabel giggled. Julian arched an eyebrow at her, instantly silencing her.

"Yes," he answered Audrey.

"With the children?"

"Yes."

"But they're in their nightclothes."

He looked at the eight children, dressed in their nightclothes, the boys in shirts and pants, the girls in nightgowns, the white cotton stark against their black boots. Their faces were clean, their hair combed, the girls sporting neat braids for bed. "So they are."

Audrey crossed her arms. "Julian, they shouldn't be running about like this before bed. It's hard enough to get them to settle down."

"Would it hurt this once?" Julian asked, the hint of a grin in his eyes.

"Well—"

"Great!" Kurt spoke up, hearing the hesitation in her voice. "Everybody out!"

The kids ran outside, a wave of white. Julian did grin then. "We won't be long." He lifted Amy onto his shoulders, then led his expedition over the hill toward camp. Willie ran after them, barking with the excitement of having all the kids in motion at once. When they were out of sight of the house, they veered toward the river. He had no idea what he would find, but hoped some flowers still bloomed.

He was in luck. Pale lupines, petite scarlet flowers, and yellow daisies dotted the field. The girls quickly set about the work of picking flowers. Kurt and Luc found a couple of long sticks and walked ahead of them, whacking at the ground and making a terrible ruckus to chase the snakes away. Colleen had Amy fold her nightgown into a pouch to hold the flowers the kids collected.

Julian looked across the field, seeing the purples, reds, and yellows of the flowers, and the larger white spots of the children. They were like little human flowers. Alive and busy and perfect. Strange he'd ever been afraid of them. Amy let part of her nightgown drop as she put her hand in his and smiled up at him.

"Flowers are pretty, Juli."

He swallowed hard. He could only nod, stunned by the realization he not only loved Audrey, but he loved her orphans too. He helped Amy right her hem to hold the flowers in, then got busy plucking flowers himself. In very little time, with so many helpers, her makeshift pouch was full.

He swept Amy up into his arms, holding her so that the flowers wouldn't spill, then led his expedition back toward the house. He sent the boys ahead to have Audrey hide in the library while he and the girls arranged the flowers in her room. When they were done, several glasses filled with purple, yellow, and rose-colored flowers graced every flat surface in her room. Julian looked around with pride. It wasn't a couple dozen roses from a florist's hothouse, but it was a gift a man could be proud of.

A thundering on the stairs alerted him to the boys' imminent return. He ushered the girls out of the room and closed the door. Tommy and Joey were leading a blindfolded Audrey up the steps. Outside her room, they took the kerchief off. She looked suspiciously from face to face. Julian leaned against the banister, his arms folded in front of him.

"It's a surprise. In your room," Kurt explained.

"You wouldn't let them put spiders in there, would you?" she asked Julian. He only smiled. She sighed and opened her door, then gasped as she saw what they had done. She went to the closest glass and breathed the flowers' sweet fragrance. When she turned and looked at Julian and the kids, there were tears in her eyes.

"It's beautiful." She laughed and kissed the girls, who danced around her, then did the same for the boys.

"Aren't you going to kiss Mr. McCaid? It was his idea," Mabel said.

Julian hadn't moved from his place at the banister. He lifted an eyebrow as her gaze came to him. She smiled as she neared him. He smiled back at her. She was more beautiful than the whole roomful of flowers. She stopped next to him. He could sense her hesitation. The children waited, watching and silent.

She took hold of his folded arms. "Thank you too, Julian." He leaned forward so that she could reach his cheek. When she didn't immediately pull away, he wrapped an arm about her and pulled her against his chest. He closed his eyes and kissed her temple.

"You're welcome." God, he loved her. He'd traveled, like a lost soul, for half his lifetime just to find the arms of this woman. He couldn't wait to tell her. Soon.

Soon she would believe him.

Chapter 30

"Why did you do it, Julian?" Audrey asked much later that night, lying naked beneath him.

"Well, it's awkward to admit." His eyes swept over her face as he slowly grinned down at her. "I had an argument with my Self. My Self said you were more beautiful than any flower alive. But I'm more logical than my Self. I argued that there are many fine-looking flowers in the world. We agreed, my Self and I, that the only way to resolve the issue was to fill your room with flowers and see who was right."

Audrey combed her fingers through the lock of hair that slipped so easily down his forehead. "And who was right?"

He looked at the petals scattered across the pillow around her, the humor slipping from his face. "I'm sorry to say, I lost the argument. My Self had the right of it. No flower alive can compare to you."

"I'm glad that's resolved." She smiled into his somber gaze. "I should hate for you to be divided against yourself."

* * *

Audrey folded her legs beneath her and sipped her coffee. She enjoyed this time of the day. She and Julian sometimes just sat together and watched the setting sun paint the summer sky. Other times he brought out a chessboard or they played cards. On this evening, they read the latest stack of newspapers the supply wagon had brought in.

She looked at the paper folded on her lap. There had been some discussion of an actress's reappearance at Ford's Theatre in Washington, D.C., marking the conclusion of her mourning period following her husband's death. The reviewer felt Mme. Delacroix had delivered a substandard performance, but did note that Washington's elite had turned out for her latest appearance and seemed quite taken with her.

"Sometimes I wonder what it would be like to visit our nation's capital. These papers make it sound so exciting," she said as she set the paper aside.

Julian reached over and linked his fingers with hers. "I have a house in Fairfax. There's plenty of room for all of us. Say the word, I'll take you there. With the train in Cheyenne, we could be there within two weeks. We could go to the theatre." He grinned at her. "We could attend a ball."

Audrey laughed. Julian lived in a strangely unreal world. "Mistresses aren't allowed to attend such fine functions with their lovers."

When Julian didn't respond, she caught him gazing intently at the newspaper she'd just put down. He released her hand and took up the paper, frowning. She watched him read a short article, then gaze at nothing as he stared vacantly into space. After a minute, he stood up and glanced at her, his dark eyes stormy. He excused himself, saying he had some correspondence to see to.

He never came to her room that night. It wasn't until the next morning when Audrey had a chance to discover what he'd read that had so changed their evening.

Several articles were on the page that lay faceup on his desk. The one that stood out, however, sent chills down her spine: HEIRESS TO BANKING FORTUNE ACCEPTS PROPOSAL. Beneath that headline read a short clip about the millionaire banker's daughter accepting the suit of a steel tycoon's son. The marriage was set only a month hence.

Audrey sat heavily in Julian's desk chair. She knew, by some instinct, this heiress had been one of the women he'd intended to court. He moved in circles so far out of her realm, she could barely grasp the magnitude of their social differences. One thing was clear: he was losing his chosen mate as he wiled away the summer here.

She'd known all along their time would end. She'd had weeks and weeks to come to terms with that truth. She just hadn't done it yet. She had to let him go, now, before the price became too dear for his generosity to her. If he left now, he could be there in plenty of time to stop the marriage. Somehow she had to convince him to go.

The question plagued her throughout the day. That evening, she sat on the bench at the foot of her bed, brushing her hair so she could put it into a braid for the night, still without a resolution. She heard him leave his room by the balcony door and come toward hers. As was his custom, he entered without knocking and took a seat in the wing chair he'd moved into her room. He liked to watch her prepare for bed. Why he let her braid her hair, she never knew. Most nights he ended up undoing it.

Stalling, she took her time weaving a tight braid. When she finished, she looked at him. Only a single candle burned in the room. His features were cast in shadow. His chin rested on his hand, held between his thumb and index finger. He was in as pensive a mood as she was.

She went to kneel at his feet, praying she somehow would find the words she needed to set him free. "Julian, when I stole your change purse, I never intended to steal your life." That was more abrupt than she desired, but better to be forthcoming than evasive with what she had to say.

Tension whispered across his features. "You've stolen nothing except my—"

She lurched forward, quickly pressing her fingers to his mouth, stopping the words she knew he would regret, words that would cement him to her. "I've enjoyed our time together, but you need to get back to your life, and I need to start mine."

She rose to her feet and stepped away, giving him her back so he wouldn't see from her expression how hollow her words were. This was what had to be. "I've gotten quite good with the sewing machine. And now that I've finished your curtains, I'm ready to head to Cheyenne." She shuttered her features and faced him. He stood right behind her. She hadn't heard him move. The desperate drumming of her heart had masked the sound.

"This is your home, Audrey," he quietly answered.

She clasped her hands together, her fingers pressing into the bones of her hands. "No, Julian. This is your home."

"I gave it to you." His tone was tight, like a drawn bowstring.

"I can't stay here."

"Why?"

"I have to make my own way in the world. Please understand."

"I don't understand. I told you I would provide for you."

"Until when? When your wife wonders why you are supporting a woman and her children in Wyoming? Until you tire of an unending debt?"

"Until forever."

"I can't do it."

He frowned, his endless brown eyes wounded. She looked away. "You aren't thinking clearly," he said. "Consider the children."

"I am thinking of them. What does it teach them to have me accept your charity? That it's acceptable to not do for yourself if you can find a benefactor? That is not a lesson I want the girls to learn. In Cheyenne, the boys can take jobs. The girls can help me. We can earn our way—legitimately."

He shook his head. "That's an unnecessarily hard life you would consign them to. You rob them of their childhood."

"It's reality. Our reality." This wasn't working. She thought he'd be pleased to be given an excuse to break things off with her, not try so hard to dissuade her. God help her, she had to cut deeper. "There's another reason."

His eyes narrowed. "At last, we get to the point of this discussion."

She drew a shaky breath. This had to be convincing, but every word sliced her as it came up from her heart and out her mouth. "Our time is coming to an end, and I don't want to be alone. You've introduced me to the world of sex, and I find I quite like it."

His face went pale. "Is that what you think we share at night? Some empty exchange of carnal pleasures?"

"Isn't it?"

"Will you spread your legs for any man now?"

"No." She laughed. Where she found the strength to do so, she didn't know. "Of course not. You're a hard man to replace, Julian. Though I have no doubt, between my sewing and my bedroom skills, I will find what I'm looking for."

His eyes flared. "Maybe I'm not ready to release you." He moved forward. She backed away, frightened by the anger in his expression. Her knees hit the edge of the bed.

"All these nights, I've been so focused on being courteous, taking care to please you, when sex would have been good enough. You should have been clearer about what you wanted long ago. Bend over the bed."

Audrey swallowed her fear. "Why?"

"Because we're going to have sex."

She looked at his bitter eyes, wondering how she had ever thought them soft or loving. He gripped her shoulders and turned her around, bending her over the mattress.

"Lift your nightgown," he ordered.

She slowly did as he commanded, feeling the cool air on her legs. He held a hand on her shoulder, pushing her forward into the bed as he unfastened his pants. Then his knees separated hers and he entered her.

Audrey gasped, shocked. They'd never used this position. He penetrated her deeply. She could feel so much of him as he moved in her. The sensation was exquisite. She gripped the bedcover as her body's response grew. She pushed back against his thrusts, seeking more. He took hold of her hips, controlling her, keeping her still as he possessed her. The restriction heightened her senses, yet the climax he usually brought her hovered just out of reach.

"Please—" a whispered plea broke from her lips. "Please, Julian, I need . . . I can't . . ."

He groaned, but released his hold on her as he leaned over her body. "Touch yourself."

She pushed against him, absorbing the shivers of pleasure spiraling through her body. "How?"

"Like this." He took her hand, directing her fingers to her clitoris, moving them slowly firmly over her sensitive skin. He took hold of her hips again, pulling his cock from her slick warmth, then pushing in again. She gasped even as her sweet inner muscles grabbed at him. "Yes. God, yes. Like that."

He thrust himself deeper. She bucked against him, her small muscles seizing him in an intense orgasm. He pumped harder, faster, grinding his teeth against the extreme pleasure. His hands tightened on her hips, holding her firmly against himself as he groaned with his release. Hot liquid seared into her.

He pulled free of her and adjusted his pants, then leaned over her. "That, Audrey Sheridan, was just sex." She straightened and faced him. Her nightgown dropped into place, shielding her. He was breathing hard. His nostrils flared as he shook his head. "Perhaps you were right. If that's all you're after, you'll have to find a replacement for me. I want none of it."

She crossed her arms to keep herself from reaching for him. Even now, with him furious with her, she knew if she touched him, he would open to her. She knew he hadn't intended to give her release in that coupling, but he'd relented, bringing her with him. He wasn't capable of just having sex with her. She could almost believe he cared about her. But it wouldn't last. Whatever he felt for her couldn't withstand the test of time.

"You stayed in me."

"I did," he said between clenched teeth. "Do you think any man who's only after a quick romp will care if he plants his babe in your belly?"

She lifted her chin and met his gaze. "I want you to leave. Now." A minute passed. A muscle worked at the edges of his jaw. At last he turned on his heel and left her room. She climbed into her bed and drew the sheet up over her folded knees, listening to him pace in his room. After a while, she heard him go downstairs, then leave the house.

Lowering her head to her knees, she wondered whether her mother's broken heart had felt like this before she died.

Chapter 31

Audrey lay awake until dawn colored the sky. She felt gutted, as if her heart had been stored away in one jar and her soul in another, leaving her empty. She climbed out of bed, washed, then dressed. Empty was better than feeling, she reasoned. She'd done what she had to do. She set him free.

She started on breakfast. The kids came down in two batches, first the boys, then the girls. Without prodding from her, they went about their morning chores, the girls collecting eggs and milking the cow, the boys feeding the various animals.

Soon they were all seated at the table. Audrey reached for the hands of the children on either side of her, preparing to say grace.

"Where's Mr. McCaid?" Colleen asked.

"I don't know," Audrey answered, her stomach clenching.

"He's never missed breakfast before. Shouldn't we wait for him?" Joey asked.

"Not today. He mentioned he was eating with the

men this morning," Bertie said as she brought the basket of biscuits to the table and took her place.

Julian did join them for supper. His face looked carved from stone. No humor softened the hard planes of his face. No joy sparkled in his eyes. She felt the weight of his gaze often through the meal, hard and assessing. She barely touched her food.

"If you're not going to eat that potato, Audrey, can I have it?" Kurt asked, eyeing her plate. She looked at the empty serving platter, then around at the children. Somehow, the entire meal had progressed without her being aware of it. Most of the kids still chatted among themselves, but Luc and Bertie watched her curiously. She pushed her plate toward Kurt.

"You feeling okay, Audrey?" Luc asked.

She forced an easy smile. "Of course. Just tired today."

He looked from her to Julian, unconvinced.

After supper, she helped Bertie with the dishes. The kids went off to do their last round of chores for the evening. Julian secluded himself in his den. This existence was untenable. She was going to have to push the issue by setting a date for their departure.

When the kids were washed and ready for bed later that evening, she found them gathered in the front hallway, outside Julian's den. In the short time they'd lived together, it was unlike him not to participate in getting them settled at night. They felt the difference in him. In her.

"Come along, now. It's time to be in bed."

"But it's nighttime," Tommy complained.

"Yes, which means it's bedtime."

"And story time," Mabel clarified.

Julian's last installment of the saga had the two orphaned siblings encountering a nearly blind tinware salesman who offered them a bunk in his wagon in exchange for their ability to see for him and drive the wagon. The children were fascinated by the tale. She looked from one expectant face to another. "Not tonight. Mr. McCaid has work to do and we mustn't disturb him."

The children grumbled as they left the hallway and climbed the stairs. Luc hung back. Of all her kids, he was the most observant and the least easily fooled.

"What's going on, Audrey?" he asked.

"I don't know yet."

"Why is Mr. McCaid angry?"

Audrey drew a shaky breath. Nothing less than absolute truth would convince Luc. "He's missing important things in his life back East. I told him to go home, and it made him angry."

"Maybe he likes it here."

She sighed. "Luc, he is a successful businessman with critical decisions awaiting his attention at home. He can't stay here. He shouldn't stay here."

"You can't tell him what to do."

"No. You're right." Which was why she had to take the children and go.

That night, she sat on the long bench outside her room, listening to the crickets and the wind, trying to find an answer, find the strength to finish what she had begun. As if sensing her presence, Julian joined her on the balcony. An awkward silence stretched between them. Audrey came to her feet and started for her room, preferring a place where she could be miserable alone.

"The children missed you tonight," she said, pausing outside her door.

"I missed them."

"Why didn't you come tell them another part of the story?"

"What would be the point? You're just going to take them from me. They'll have to get used to doing without me sooner or later."

She did look at him then. The wind tossed his untrimmed hair, blowing his straight locks this way and that around his face. "I was under the impression you didn't like children."

"A man can change, Audrey."

She retreated to her room, trying to interpret that remark.

The next day was little better. Julian was again absent from breakfast. She got the kids started on their schoolwork for the day, then took advantage of the free time to go find him.

He wasn't at the bunkhouse or the cookhouse. She found him at the main corral, having just ridden in with Franklin. He dismounted and handed the reins to his foreman. He took one look at her, then started toward the barn at a fast pace with barely a nod of acknowledgment. Audrey hurried after him.

"We need to talk, Julian." When he didn't slow down and didn't answer, she tossed out a barb. "I thought it would be safer to have this discussion out here, in public."

He turned around so fast she almost barreled into his chest. "Don't think you're safe out here. Or anywhere, Audrey Sheridan. You've chosen to not be safe ever again."

"I want to leave."

"No." He turned and started walking again.

"You can't keep me prisoner here."

"You aren't leaving. No one's leaving."

"Why? Will you please stop and talk to me?"

He did, abruptly. "Jace sent word the sheriff's organizing his men and some ranchers. Something's coming in fast. It's not safe for you to go to town or start for Cheyenne. So no one's leaving until this thing breaks or blows over." His eyes blazed. "You'll have to be my prisoner a while longer."

When he continued on his way, she didn't follow.

A cold dread wormed its way through her nerves as she considered the implications of Jace's warning. She'd lived through one attack on the ranch, but suspected it was nothing compared to what the sheriff was now planning. Luc had told her what he'd overheard at the meeting he'd witnessed before their disastrous attempt to escape the sheriff and come warn her.

She hurried back to the house, considering what preparations she should make. The ranch was terribly vulnerable. Only a series of wire fences and Julian's armed patrols stood between her family and the sheriff's men.

At the house, she found a couple of Julian's men moving cured meat from the smokehouse down to the root cellar. Bertie told her they'd already brought over what supplies they could from the keeping house. It was as if they prepared for a siege. A short while later, some other men delivered three rifles, a Colt and gun belt, and a crate of ammunition to Julian's den.

She tried to maintain a normal demeanor as she helped the kids through their lessons, but they weren't fooled. They'd heard all the activity in the house. Audrey looked from one anxious face to the next. She sighed.

"I'm afraid the trouble Luc overheard in town may be headed this way."

Amy moved closer to her.

"Don't worry, Audrey. Luc and me ain't lettin' anything happen to you," Kurt assured her.

"Aren't," she corrected.

"And the Avenger's working the case. Nothing gets through him," Luc added.

She sent the children out to play, knowing they were brimming with curiosity. At the door, however, Colleen stopped the girls. Audrey caught the look she sent Mabel and Dulcie. As one, they turned back.

"What can we do to help?"

Audrey met Colleen's determined gaze, struck by her oldest foster daughter's flash of maturity. "Bertie's going to cut bandage strips from the bolt of cotton we used to make your nightclothes. You could give her a hand with that."

A short while later, everything was as ready as it could be. There was just the waiting. Julian left word he was eating with the men that night. After supper, she sent the boys out to bathe at the shower while she saw to baths for the girls. She hoped a good washing would help settle their nerves enough so that she could get them to bed.

When the baths were finished and the kids put to bed, she took a stack of towels to the outdoor shower to replenish the ones the boys had used. She rounded the corner of the outhouse, surprised to hear the shower in use. It hadn't occurred to her Julian might have finished with Franklin and his preparations. Well, there was nothing for it. Unless Julian had stopped by the house to grab a fresh towel, the boys had probably left none dry for him.

The louvered doors to the changing room were open. Julian's clothes were strewn about the ground, haphazardly discarded. His hat hung on a peg on one of the walls of the changing area. His vest and shirt were thrown in one pile, his boots, pants, socks, and drawers in another. Audrey swallowed and looked up.

The bathing doors were not closed either.

Julian stood naked beneath the stream of water, one hand fisted around the pull chain, one hand braced against the wall, his head bowed. Water splashed off his shoulders, splattering into the bricks where he stood barefooted. In the full light of the summer evening, Audrey could see the raised, wide, white furrows criss-crossing his back like a messy web carved into his skin. She set the towels on a nearby shelf. She knew she should leave, should allow him his privacy.

She didn't move.

Still unaware of her, he leaned forward to let the water pour over his neck, and the muscles of his back and arms contracted, cabling against the shock of what looked like icy water. The boys probably used up all the warm water. Audrey forced her eyes past his scarred back to his lean hips, his pale buttocks, his long, hard thighs. She must have made a noise because his head shot up. He looked at her over his shoulder, through the water, then released the pull chain and came toward her.

She was helpless to keep her gaze from stroking his naked body. It was probably the last time she would ever see him nude. Her eyes dipped over the dark hairs furring his chest, pausing to observe the water droplets catching the brilliant evening sun and sparkling against his skin. She looked at his flat belly, at the nearly imperceptible line that demarcated the darker skin above his waist from the paler skin below it. Her gaze lowered until it came to the thick nest of black hair at the joining of his legs, his purplish manhood hanging in a relaxed state.

Watching him, Audrey felt a frisson of desire rip across her soul. She held out a fresh towel to him. He took the towel from her, no smile of greeting warming his face. He dragged it over his hair and mopped the wet skin of his chest and armpits, then draped it around his neck. Reaching a hand out, he let his fingers whisper against her cheek. His touch was chilling—the water had indeed been cold. A shiver rippled across her skin.

They would be lost to each other soon, he to the life waiting for him in his important world, she to work as a seamstress in Cheyenne. She was infinitely better off now than she had been when the summer began. Yet without Julian she would just be a ghost of herself. She closed her eyes, shielding herself from his observant gaze, preventing him from digging around in her mind as he searched out answers better left hidden.

She reached up and cupped his hand, holding it so that she could press a kiss against his palm. He reached for her then, his lips pressing against hers, his mouth open, the kiss unconsummated. She breathed his breath, felt his essence, waited, as he waited, for some sign, a clue about how to proceed. Her surrender. Or his. She leaned into him, all too aware of his hard body, hoping he couldn't hear the sob working its way up through her chest.

"Audrey, come to me tonight. Let me show you the difference between sex and love."

She glanced up at him and was lost. He swept her into his arms, lifting her to her toes, dragging her up against his heart. Their mouths collided. She clung to him, grasping his hair. Her tongue fought with his as his mouth twisted against hers.

He ended the kiss a long moment later. "I know the difference, Audrey Sheridan," he said against her mouth, "because I love you. And, by God, you should know the difference too."

No. Not love. She didn't belong in his world, and he couldn't stay in hers. She belonged in her shack in Defiance, not in one of his many houses, attending the theatre, hosting his important social events. This was exactly what she had feared would happen. He would give up his life for hers, or drag her into his and hate her for being what she was—a backwoods yokel.

She broke away, feeling like a porcelain figurine whose glaze was starting to crack and chip. Only the belief that in time, if he stayed with her, he would come to regret his decision gave her the strength to leave him. "We're through, Julian. I thought I made that clear to you."

"I'm not deaf. I heard your words. But I'm not blind either. I see your soul in your eyes, and I think your eyes, at least, don't lie. They never have."

Audrey forced herself to leave the alcove. He was right. She couldn't hide the truth from him. But truth or not, it didn't make it right.

The wind whipped about the house, searing past the eaves with a strange screaming sound, rattling the balcony door to Julian's room. He opened the door to let the wind into his room as he debated going to Audrey. He'd doubted she would come to him, but they needed to settle this thing between them.

The sound grew louder, only it didn't ease with the ebb and flow of a normal wind. It was coming closer. When Willie began to growl in the girls' room, he knew it wasn't wind.

He heard a gunshot even as he grabbed for his gun belt. He shoved his feet into his boots, glad he still wore his trousers. He didn't have time to don a shirt. He hurried from his room, taking the steps three at a time.

Audrey came out of her room as he hit the landing. They shared a glance, their last, perhaps.

"Stay here, Audrey. Get one of the rifles in my office and guard the house. Have Bertie take the other. Keep everyone safe and inside until it's over," he ordered, then was gone.

Outside, the ground was alive with running sheep. In the darkness, it was impossible to distinguish who were his men and who weren't. Lambs were being trampled by the terrified flock. Men on horseback were shooting into the white, fleeing masses. One man, over by the barn, plucked lambs out of the flock and bashed them against the barn.

Julian couldn't risk opening fire on them from the house—he didn't want to draw the trouble to Audrey or the children. At least while the bastards were shooting the sheep, they weren't attacking his men. He shoved his way into the charging, bleating flock, trying to cross the current to get to the barn where he could take up a defensive position.

Taking aim at the man battering lambs, Julian picked him off with a clean shot to the head just as he straightened with another little victim in his hands. Julian moved around the corner of the barn and found a man dragging himself toward the barn's open doors. Julian made sure no one was lying in ambush from inside, then crossed to the wounded man. A dark wetness spread across his back. He'd flopped facedown on the dirt. Julian rolled him over, hoping he was one of the bad guys, not one of his own men.

Audrey's brother stared up at him. Julian cursed as he took hold of the boy's face, trying to get Malcolm to focus on him. "Tell me, goddammit, tell me you're not part of this!"

"Came . . . to help . . . brought Jace."

Julian holstered his Colt and hoisted the boy across his shoulder, then made his way back to the house. He doubted there was anything that could be done for Malcolm, but it was far better that he die with his sister near him than bleeding out in the dirt, alone.

Burdened as he was, Julian's balance was off. The sheep almost knocked him down twice. He made it to the back porch and banged through the kitchen door. Bertie was there, at the stove. As gently as he could, he laid Malcolm out on the table.

"Get Audrey," he ordered her. He gripped Malcolm's hand. Gunfire grew loud and active outside. He bent over the boy's chest, his hands cupping Malcolm's face.

"Wait, boy, wait for her," Julian begged, a litany of urgent words spilling from his mouth. "Please, just wait. Please, God. Don't go. Don't you goddamn dare go." Malcolm's skin felt cold beneath his hand.

And then Audrey was there. "Malcolm! Oh, Malcolm! What happened?" Her hands were frantically working him over, looking for the wound. She couldn't find any, but when she pulled away, the front of her robe was stained from blood draining down the side of the table. Julian pressed Malcolm's hand into hers as he became aware of an orange light illuminating the room.

The carriage house was on fire.

Julian moved aside, surrendering his spot to Audrey. He dragged Bertie out of the kitchen, to his den. He picked up a rifle and loaded a dozen cartridges in it, then handed it to her. He took up the other two and loaded them. He slung one over his shoulder and left the other for Audrey.

"Do you know how to work one of these?"

"You bet I do, Mr. McCaid." Bertie took the rifle and

dropped a handful of extra cartridges into her apron pocket.

"Kill any bastard who comes in the door." He squeezed her shoulder. "You keep them safe, Bertie." He checked the lock on the front door, then went back into the kitchen. Audrey was sobbing over her brother's body. The sound filled his brain, blocking out all other thoughts. He wiped the heel of his hand against his cheek, mixing his tears with Malcolm's blood as he stepped back into the chaos outside.

A man rode by with a torch, his face covered in a black hood. Julian raised his Colt and blew him off his horse. He found three more with torches. Their hoods hid their identity but flagged them as the enemy. He made his way into the heart of the camp. The flock had begun to spill outside the confines of Hell's Gulch land, straight into the waiting guns of a dozen raiders. Julian and several of his men whom he'd been training for a night such as this went forward to meet them. But they weren't needed; one by one, the enemy dropped. A sniper.

Jace!

Before Julian was halfway to the gate, the sheriff's remaining men took off, heading back toward town. What was left of his flock leapt over the bodies, human and woolly, and ran into the black night.

Audrey looked up as a knock sounded at the back door. A man she didn't know poked his head around the door. He had soot stains on his cheeks and hands. He took his hat off, turning it restlessly in his hands, spreading black dust across the brim as he hovered at the doorway. He looked from her to her brother to the children whose weeping filled the room.

"I'm sorry to intrude, Miss Audrey, but I came to get you. You gotta come with me. Jenkins was shot!"

Audrey looked at Malcolm's still form. She couldn't leave him. Not yet.

"He's hurt bad, miss. He needs you."

Audrey pushed up from the table, but Bertie wrapped an arm around her waist. "Don't go. It ain't safe."

"The killing's stopped," the man assured them. "The men have all run off. It's done. Miss Audrey, come quickly. Come now."

The gunfire had indeed stopped. Men were throwing buckets of water on the burning carriage house. They wouldn't be able to do that if the ranch was still under attack. With Jenkins hurt, there was no one to tend the wounded men. She had to go.

"I have to, Bertie. Stay with the kids and let Julian know where I am." She followed the man outside.

Franklin caught up to Julian. "Boss, I saw Hadley among the sheriff's men. Clear as day 'cause he weren't wearing no hood like them others."

Julian considered all the things that had happened with Hadley. He must have been in on the sheriff's little operation from the beginning. He'd worked Audrey. He was probably the one responsible for that first sheep slaughter the night he injured himself. God. He and Audrey had babied the bastard, sheltered him among them. A wolf among sheep.

"Who's left? Who did we lose?"

"I know fer sure we lost at least four. Several more are injured. Cookie and Jenkins are settin' up a hospital in the tent. No count on the toll to the flock."

"How many of the bastards did we get?"

"No idea yet. I got some men going after the flock. Gotta stop them before they run themselves to death. Soon as I can, I'll get collecting bodies."

Julian looked around his once peaceful ranch. Hundreds of sheep were down, not all of them dead. The scent of mud and blood, smoke from the gunfire and his burning carriage house combined to sear his nostrils, sending him back to nights like this in war, ugly times he'd thought long behind him.

"Get a detail together to deal with this mess. Save the sheep you can, kill those you can't. We'll take the skins and do what we can with the meat."

"Yessir."

"And, Franklin, get a wagon ready. We'll load the bastards in it and take them to Defiance. See who claims their hell-bound souls."

Julian headed toward the brightly lit cook tent serving as a makeshift hospital. Several pallets were laid out with men on them, being tended by Giles and Jenkins.

Tiredly, Julian crossed the slaughterhouse floor of his ranch, returning to Audrey. He stepped into the kitchen, taking in the room's setting in a glance. The children were sitting on the benches around the table where Malcolm still lay, now dead. Cloths had been wedged around his torso, soaking up his draining blood. He was sick of this night. Bertie sat with Amy on her lap and an arm around Colleen.

"Where's Audrey?" he asked.

"She went to help Jenkins."

"When?" Julian asked, his voice quiet and calm.

"Not five minutes ago."

"Alone?"

"No. One of your men came for her. Said Jenkins had been hurt."

Julian cursed and ran out the back door, hurrying to the corral where the enemies' horses, still saddled, were being gathered. He took up the reins of one and led him out into the night, carefully picking his way among the wounded sheep. Where would the sheriff's men have taken Audrey? Clearly not through camp to the front gate. They would have gone where the fewest of Julian's men were.

Julian mounted and set his heels to the sides of his horse, now charging through the bloodied pastures into the dark night. He followed the trail road that wound its way through the back acres of his property. Across a creek, the narrow road split to the southwest and the north. He turned toward the north, figuring they would try to get back to town where there were more men.

Julian heard the wagon before he saw it, moving at breakneck speed. The night was dark. He could just make out the three people sitting on the front bench. A shimmering light on the horizon caught his attention. Riders were coming in, a couple with torches. *Shit.* He leaned forward, over his horse's neck, intent on getting Audrey away before her abductors' reinforcements joined them.

He was almost to the rear edge of the wagon bed. Urging his horse forward, he jumped from his horse to the wagon. Balancing precariously, he hurried forward. The driver felt him board the wagon. He cast a look over his shoulder, and Julian saw his face. Hadley!

The bastard turned the wagon sharply, hoping to make Julian lose his footing—he almost succeeded. Julian grabbed the back of the bench seat as the wagon bed tilted. Audrey was holding on tightly to the wildly careening wagon. The man next to her raised a Colt. Before he could take aim at Julian, Audrey grabbed his hand, distracting him. Julian grabbed his shoulder and neck and gave a sharp twist, then shoved his corpse from the wagon. Next was Hadley. Julian wrapped an arm around Hadley's neck, squeezing tighter and tighter until the boy had to release the reins and focus on their fight.

"Take the reins, Audrey!" Julian ordered.

She struggled to grab them. Hadley was thrashing about reflexively, fighting for air, fighting to be freed of Julian's grip. She finally got the reins in hand and drew back on the team.

"Julian—he killed Malcolm!" Audrey said as the team slowed to a stop.

Hadley was insane. Why hadn't Julian seen it before? "That true?" Julian asked the man who struggled and writhed within his grip.

"He was going to warn you!" Hadley choked. "He was supposed to be one of us!"

"Well, he wasn't, was he?" Julian straightened, drawing Hadley up with him. A hard right cross sent him flying from the wagon. Looking up, Julian could see the riders with the torches had come much closer now. He climbed into the front bench and took the reins from Audrey. Turning the wagon around, he headed back toward the ranch where the orange flames of the burning carriage house glowed like a beacon.

"Hold on, Audrey. We've got incoming riders. I want to get you back to the house before I deal with them!"

He snapped the reins and the edgy horses broke into a fast run. He shouted at them, pushing them harder as he sent a quick look over his shoulder. They weren't moving fast enough. The men were close. Too close. They would never make it home in time. Gunfire sounded behind them. Julian cursed.

"Audrey! Quick! Get down on the floor and stay there

until I tell you!" He grabbed the back of her robe and helped her down to huddle on the floorboards as another bullet whizzed past them. Julian drew his Colt and aimed at one of the torch carriers, reaching his mark.

In moments, they were surrounded. Two men moved ahead of the horses. Grabbing their bridles, they forced them to slowly stop. Two more men yanked Julian from the bench, tossing him to the ground before the wagon had fully stopped. They kicked at his sides, his head. Julian hooked his foot around one of them and knocked him to the ground. He rolled over on top of the man, wrapping his hands about his neck in a chokehold. The other man yanked at Julian's hair, trying to pull him off the now-still man. Julian shrugged free of him. His head buzzed. His ribs hurt. His nose felt broken. Though he was now surrounded, no one was fighting him. He became aware of the reprieve as the silence carved its way into his consciousness. He struggled to his feet, turning in a slow circle to look at the wide ring of men surrounding him, some on horses, some on foot.

"Jesus! Look at his back!" One of them cursed.

From her vantage point beneath the wagon bench, Audrey watched Julian standing among the men like a wounded buffalo in a circle of wolves. She tried to identify the men, but the hoods they wore made that impossible.

"Think we got us a deserter, boys?" one man scoffed. "The army take the lash to you, McCaid? You a runner? You're lucky they didn't shoot you dead. Maybe you should start running now."

"I'm no deserter." Julian's voice was deep and calm. Audrey counted ten men. She became aware of something hard and long digging into her side under the bench. She moved slightly, quietly, trying to push it from under her. A rifle!

"I seen stripes like that on a nigger," a man said. "Maybe he's a white nigger."

"There ain't no such thing."

"Sure there is. I had me one in New Orleans once."

"That what you are, boy?" another asked.

"What I am, *boy*," Julian quietly answered, "is more man than you will ever be."

Audrey had never asked what had happened to him. The scars were horrendous. And she knew he was sensitive about them, for he didn't like his back touched. It hurt her to have him standing exposed for these men to revile.

One of the men prodded his horse into a slow walk. The others followed, moving in a widening circular direction around Julian and the handful of men standing inside the circle with him, one of whom had a whip.

Julian kept his senses trained on the one with the whip, anticipating the coming violence. He didn't have to wait long. He heard the singing of the lash as it sliced through the air to land in a cutting touch against his back, shredding and leaving faster than it took Julian to feel the sting. Still he didn't move.

He thought back to that time, sixteen years ago, on a summer night like this one, when he and his cousin were making their way through the stinking, snake-infested swamp separating the plantation from the river.

That night, there had been only three men. And despite the fact that it was legal for men to own other men, to treat them with less care than they gave their hunting dogs, Julian's young mind believed in human benevolence. It was not an error he would make tonight, not with Audrey still hidden in the wagon only a few steps away.

The lash sung out again, to Julian's left. His hand met its descent, and he used the force of the lash's arc to coil it around his forearm. He yanked on the leather, uprooting the startled man who still gripped the other end of the whip. A quick right hook knocked the hooded bastard off his feet. He landed hard on the ground, unconscious. Julian recoiled the whip and lashed out at another of the men standing, then another before they could react to the first man being struck down. Horses screamed and reared, fearing the lash and unseating a few of their riders.

Out of the corner of his eye, Julian saw a man raise his pistol and take aim at him. A rifle erupted behind Julian. The man fell from his horse. Julian turned to see who had helped him. Audrey! He cursed. Why hadn't she stayed hidden? In the silence following the gunfire, Julian heard Audrey cock the rifle again as two men drew their weapons.

"That's enough," Audrey calmly ordered. Julian didn't dare turn to look at her again; he couldn't risk taking his eyes off the men. God, they would shoot her. "I've got plenty more bullets in this gun, gentlemen. You might be able to kill Mr. McCaid. And you might be able to kill me, but I can guarantee I'll take a few of you with me." Another pause. "Who wants to die first?"

Julian heard a rider approaching from the enemy's side. A body was draped across his saddle. The man wore no hood. Julian heard Audrey's gasp about the same time he recognized Hadley hanging limply across the man's lap.

"Hold up, men. This has gone too far. Hadley's hurt.

Fred, Joe, you others, stand down. Now." *Fred? Deputy Fred?* Julian wondered.

"Good evening, Mr. Baker."

Julian heard Audrey's voice behind him. He took a step back toward her, then another, aiming for the break in the circle where she stood.

"Put Hadley in the wagon bed, Mr. Baker," Julian ordered. "I'm sending him down to the marshal in Cheyenne."

"He ain't goin' to no marshal, Mr. McMaid. He didn't mean to be involved in all this tonight. Hell, he was workin' for you until you beat him up."

"Oh, he's going, all right. He killed Malcolm Sheridan."

"My boy wouldn't have done that. Not Hadley."

"He told us himself, Mr. Baker," Audrey interjected. "And tonight he tried to kidnap me." Some of the men looked at her then, Julian included. She was a sight, dressed in her bloodied robe, her feet bare.

"You boys ready to call it a night?" Jace calmly asked in that haunting voice of his. He sat astride his horse at the far edge of the light cast by the torch. "Or do I need to kill a few of you? I've shot my share tonight, but I wouldn't feel bad taking a few more."

"Goddamn, it's the Avenger!" Two of the men spun their horses and headed off into the night.

Julian wondered how long Jace had been there, and why he now revealed himself. He did little without conscious intent. Judging from the way a few of the men had jumped when Jace first spoke, none of them had heard his approach. Julian tossed the whip into the bed of the wagon, away from the reach of the men. Audrey handed him the rifle, which he trained on the group.

"I'm done." Mr. Baker spit off to one side of his horse.

"This didn't go like we planned. The sheriff said to cut some fences, burn McCaid's barns, run his herd off. Now my boy's hurt. Men are dead. This ain't right. It's gone too far."

"Shut up, Baker. You're in it as deep as we are," the man Audrey shot said as he mounted his horse, his right arm hanging limply at his side.

"Baker," Julian said, cutting into their bickering, "put your boy in the wagon bed. I meant what I said. I'm turning him in."

"No. He'll be the scapegoat for this whole night. You can't have him."

"Do it," one of the hooded men ordered. "Give him over, Baker. I don't want the marshal coming up here for him, asking questions."

"No—" Baker continued to argue, until a bullet from one of the hooded men's guns silenced him. He and his son slid off the saddle. Then, without further discussion, the remaining men turned and rode back toward town.

Julian felt the tension in the knotted muscles of his back as he bent down to lift Hadley. The boy lay at an odd angle, his neck broken. Julian hoisted him into the wagon, then lifted his father in as well. Jace picked up the unconscious man who'd whipped Julian and dumped him into the wagon. He tied Mr. Baker's horse to the back of the wagon.

Julian climbed up into the bench. He didn't want to linger here, so far from the main buildings of his ranch, but one look at Audrey's face stopped him. Moonlight glittered along the wet tracks on her cheeks. He un-cocked the rifle and set it under the bench, then pulled her into his arms. She wrapped her arms around his waist. He closed his eyes against the panic he was only now beginning to let himself feel. She'd put herself in unspeakable danger. Why hadn't she stayed hidden?

"Hush, sweet. It's over. It's done." It had been so much worse than he'd feared it would be.

Jace exchanged a look with Julian. "I'm sorry about Malcolm, Audrey. He came to get me in town, told me what these men were doing," Jace said. "We got to the ranch just before the first group. We split up—he went to warn you at the house. I should have stayed with him. I didn't know about the Baker kid."

Audrey drew a ragged breath against Julian's chest. Malcolm had brought Jace, and Jace very likely saved Julian's life tonight.

She pulled free of Julian's fortifying hold and reached for Jace's hand. "Thank you, Jace."

"He was brave, Audrey. He loved you," Jace rasped.

Audrey nodded, swiping at the tears on her cheeks.

"We better get back." Julian took the reins in one hand and wrapped his other arm around Audrey. She curled into his strength and tried to shut all thoughts out of her mind, but couldn't get fear to leave her alone. She'd lost Malcolm, and she was soon to lose Julian.

Her world had gone to hell.

As they drove back onto the main area of the ranch, Audrey looked at the devastation that lay about her. Dead sheep were everywhere. Wounded sheep limped and bleated and bled. Some thrashed about on the ground, unable to stand, more dead than alive. Men moved among them, cutting the throats of those whose wounds were too great to heal.

Audrey glanced at Julian. His face was hard, expressionless. He drew up outside the kitchen door to the house and set the brake, then jumped out of the seat and reached up to help her down. Blood seeped from open wounds on his left forearm. She knew his back bled—she'd seen it when he stood among those men. They'd gotten one effective lash in before he stopped them, but he had shredded his arm to do that.

She didn't immediately release his shoulders. "Julian, come inside—let me tend your cuts."

"No. I have things I need to see to out here."

Jace dismounted and tied his horse to the back of the wagon next to the Baker horse. He walked over to them. "Don't be stubborn, McCaid. Let your woman patch you up. I'll take these turds over to the others. You can come out when you're not bleeding."

"Jace—you'll stay the night with us, won't you?" Audrey asked.

"I can't. I gotta head out to Meeker's Pass. The silver's coming in tomorrow." The two men exchanged a look.

"Do you need me?" Julian asked.

Jace shook his head. "No. Just thought I'd tell you." He climbed up to the wagon bench. He sat still a moment, then looked down at Julian. "If something happens to me, promise me you'll take care of Leah."

Julian reached a hand up and shook with Jace. "You've got my word on it."

Jace flicked the reins and set the wagon in motion.

Grim-faced, Julian turned Audrey toward the house. Inside, Bertie and all eight children were still seated around the table. Malcolm, thank God, was no longer there. The table and floor had been washed clean of his blood.

Bertie hurried over to them, giving Audrey an impatient hug. She drew back and gripped her arms, then her face, studying her. "Are you hurt, Audrey? I shouldn't have let you go."

Fresh tears spilled from Audrey's eyes. "I thought it was

over. I didn't know he was one of them." She looked at Bertie. "A friend of mine was the one who killed Malcolm."

"Come sit down." Bertie led her toward the table. "I'll make you a cup of hot coffee."

"I can't—Julian's bleeding. I need to see to his cuts."

Julian felt a cold sweat chill his skin as he became the focus of the room. He held out his arm for Bertie's inspection, hoping to distract her and everyone else from the cuts on his back.

Colleen poured out two bowls of water, one cold and one hot. She was returning from gathering fresh linens when she saw Julian's back. "Mr. McCaid! What did they do to you?"

A herd of children rushed to see what she was seeing. He cringed. "It's nothing. A scratch."

"The man who came for me was one of the sheriff's men," Audrey started to explain what had happened. "My friend, Hadley—the one who killed Malcolm—was waiting for me. Mr. McCaid caught up to us. They fought. Other men came." Audrey looked at Bertie. "One had a whip."

Julian held his shoulders rigidly straight, weathering their examination. He was naked to their discovery of his secret, the part of himself he hid from the world.

Audrey brought a stool over near the table and ordered him to sit. Dulcie stood before him. Her hazel eyes were wide with hurt. His hurt. *Shit.* He wished he'd sent the children to bed before this. With a sigh, he sat on the stool and opened his arms to her. "Come," he ordered. "Sit with me while Audrey patches me up, okay?"

She blinked a tear away and nodded. He drew her up to sit on his thigh, holding her with his right hand. Bertie fetched him a snifter of brandy. He downed the glass and handed it back to her for a refill; then Audrey began to clean up the long slices on his left forearm and wrist.

"What happened to your back, Mr. McCaid?" Dulcie asked, her whispered question carrying across the room.

"You don't ask a man about his past, Dulcie," Luc answered for him. "If he wants to talk about it, it's his choice. But it ain't right to ask him."

Hearing Sager's words come out of Luc's mouth, Julian felt his heart tighten. These children listened. They learned. He mattered to them, and they to him. Spreading his hand against Dulcie's small back, he pulled her close and kissed the top of her head, breathing in the sweet scent of her hair.

"My story begins long ago, before I was born." He wished he could see Audrey, see her reaction to his words. "My grandfather was a full-blooded Cherokee. Many of the men in his village were forward thinkers. They saw the impact the white men had on the tribe's traditional ways. Some of it was good, some bad, but the changes had come to stay. They began to buy land, build successful farms, and carve a place for themselves among the white men. My grandfather was one of those men.

"He worked hard. His farm thrived. One day he decided it was time to invest in some horses. He had plans to breed a strong freight team to get his produce to market. So he went to the county seat, where auctions of all types of goods were conducted, including slaves." Julian looked at the children, who watched him with such rapt attention. Perhaps they thought it another of the fairy tales he told them. But this was a true story.

"On his way to the area where the horse auctions were, he passed a slave auction. There was a woman on the platform who was, he said, more beautiful than any he'd ever seen. She had pale white skin, long curly brown hair, and enormous brown eyes. She was an octoroon slave and was being sold. My grandfather never made it to the horse auction. He bought the woman instead.

"Theirs was a stormy relationship, but eventually he freed her, and then married her." He looked at the children. "I am their grandson."

"What's an octoroon?" Joey asked.

"It's a person who's one-eighth Negro," Julian explained. "I grew up with stories of my grandmother's search for her brother and his children. The summer I turned fourteen, my uncles found her brother's only surviving grandson at a plantation near where my grandmother had lived. His owners would not sell him to my grandfather."

Julian's lips thinned. He wondered what Audrey's reaction was. "While my parents were away getting my brother settled at West Point, my uncles went to find our cousin. I knew where they were headed. They wouldn't let me join them, but I stowed away on their ship. When they docked, I followed them to the plantation.

"By the time I got there, they had been turned away, empty-handed. I hid until night, then went to the slaves' quarters. The first few I met were afraid of me, looking white as I do. But when I told them who I was, they remembered my grandmother. They took me to my cousin. His name was Jeremy. He was tall, like me, though dark-skinned. He had eyes so similar to mine.

"I convinced him to run away. We headed out that night, but went too far to the south when we should have gone east." Julian shook his head, knowing what that tactical miscalculation cost them. "Jeremy's owners caught up with us. They beat us both, then strung us up and whipped us. Jeremy never recovered. When he died, his owners claimed to own me. They put me in the fields, doing Jeremy's work. My back festered. By the time my father and uncles found me, I was nearly dead." Julian paused, wondering for the first time what his parents had gone through when they discovered him missing.

Dulcie's eyes were wide and dark, her face pale. Her small hand was gently rubbing the back of his neck, as if to soothe him. "That's a sad story, Mr. McCaid," she said, breaking the silence.

"Quiet, Dulcie. He's not finished," Luc admonished.

Julian almost smiled, recognizing the bloodlust in Luc's eyes. "No, it's not the end. My wounds healed. Time passed. I grew into a man and went to college. When the war came, I joined the Union army. Eventually, my unit was sent to the western border where bushwhackers were ravaging the towns. That's where I met Jace and Sager. My cousin's owners were among those bushwhackers. We skirmished one night—"

"That's when they stabbed you," Kurt broke in, anxious he get to the details.

Dulcie touched the jagged scar on his chest. "They did this?"

"Yes."

She looked up at him. "Did you run?"

"No. I killed them. When the war ended, I made some business investments and earned some money. I bought their plantation and gave it to my grandmother. No one there will ever be hurt again. It is over."

Dulcie hugged him. "I'm glad it's over, Mr. McCaid. I don't like bad men." She kissed his cheek, then slipped off his lap.

Audrey was wrapping a couple of bandages about his chest to hold the one at his back in place. He watched her face. He was worried about her, worried about how she took his revelation. Her face was blank. She did not meet his eyes. She'd been through so much tonight. And now this news. She'd given her innocence to the grandson of a slave.

It was the early hours of the morning when Julian went to Audrey's room. He carried a candle so that he could check on her, assure himself she was sleeping. He stood by her bedside and brushed a lock of hair from her face. Her eyes were swollen. She mumbled something and stirred restlessly in her sleep.

Julian's soul troubled him. He'd wreaked so much havoc and destruction in her life. He'd separated her from her brother, seduced her, forced decisions upon her she wasn't ready to make. Even now she might be carrying his child. God, he prayed it was so. It was his only hope.

She'd said nothing to him after he'd explained his scars. There was nothing to say. Except for Jace and Sager, and of course the boys, he'd never told another living soul the truth. He'd lied about his back since he'd incurred the injuries. Mostly blaming his father. An abusive father was the only truth white people could accept without shunning him.

He blew out his candle and set it on the bedside table, then sat in the wing chair, his elbows on his knees, his head in his hands. Tomorrow she would look at him with revulsion. He should have told her who and what he was before he'd taken her choices away from her.

Chapter 32

In the light of day, Julian's small ranch looked like a Chicago slaughterhouse. His men doctored the sheep they could save, butchered the ones they couldn't, and burned what they couldn't get to. In all, Julian lost 325 sheep, three sheep dogs, five men, and Malcolm. The toll was much higher for the sheriff's men.

Hammers banged through the entire day after the massacre as the carpenters built six pine coffins from lumber meant for the schoolhouse. Audrey and Bertie washed Malcolm and dressed him in an outfit one of Julian's men volunteered. Audrey had been withdrawn and unfocused, weeping often throughout the day. Julian didn't know what to do to help her other than get the children out of her way. He took them to find a site for a cemetery.

They spent hours, walking around the ranch in ever-widening circles, looking at the land from different vantage points. When they climbed the bluff of a hill to the west of the house, Dulcie decided it was the perfect place. And so it was. Julian had his men dig six graves. They built six headstones out of planks of wood and seared them with the names of the fallen men and the date they died.

By the end of that day, the slaughtered sheep had been disposed of, the blood rinsed away or turned over into the dirt. The wagon full of the sheriff's dead men had been taken to town. A tense truce of sorts had been put in place between Hell's Gulch and Defiance. Julian's men, now having experienced an attack of the magnitude he'd been expecting, knew better what was needed from them. Only two men had quit, following the fight. The others, Rebel and Yank alike, stood together to protect their livelihoods.

In the middle of the second day after the massacre, Maddie, Jim, and Sally came out for the funeral. They brought the makings of a feast, which Bertie heated up while the funeral service took place. Their visitors planned to stay the night and return to town tomorrow. To make room for them, the children had been temporarily relocated to the attic on pallets made from spare blankets.

All six men were put in the ground in the same long ceremony, Malcolm being the last. The assembled mourners stood on either side of the graves, forming a horseshoe, open at the end where Franklin stood presiding over the ceremony. Julian's foreman, being the most religious of those on the ranch, volunteered to do a Bible reading and a sermon of sorts. Franklin focused his speech on the honor of dying a hero's death, as the six they buried had done.

Audrey was crying now, softly. Julian longed to go to her, hold her, comfort her, but each time he'd tried in the last thirty-six hours, she had turned away from him. She hated him now, and he couldn't blame her. When the ceremony was over, Maddie ushered the children down the hill. Audrey turned to Sally, finally letting her sorrow take hold of her. Both women sobbed in each other's arms. Julian stood off to the side, unnoticed, unneeded.

Jim clapped a hand to his shoulder. "Let her be. Let her mourn."

Julian drew a ragged breath. "I can't walk away, Jim."

"Sometimes you have to." He turned Julian toward the house and walked next to him, in silence.

Julian's men had been invited to the house to partake in the feast the women made. They filed by and murmured their condolences to him—Sally and Audrey hadn't yet returned. Julian barely listened. He felt nothing but a gradual numbness that started at his gut and threatened to swallow him whole. Deciding he wasn't fit for human company, he took himself off to the front porch. Willie settled at his feet. He rubbed the soft fur at the sheepdog's ears, then sat back and waited for the day to end.

After a while, Maddie came out and brought him a plate and a cup of punch. He sipped the punch, then set it on the table and looked at his plate. He knew Maddie and Sally had worked hard to make the feast. He simply had no appetite. He felt like a human void, a dark hole where no conversation, no emotion could exist, only black, hopeless sorrow. Silence surrounded him, and he stayed within its hold.

"You'll be leaving soon, won't you?" Maddie asked as she sat next to him.

"Yes."

"I'll be sorry to see you go."

He looked at her then. Her eyes were red and swollen. She'd known Malcolm since the Sheridans first came to town. She'd seen Audrey and her brother and the kids grow. He looked away.

"You didn't kill Malcolm, Julian."

"I brought Audrey out here. I might as well have killed him."

"Julian, we aren't God. We don't get to know why things happen. I do believe Audrey is better for having known you."

A muscle worked at the sides of Julian's jaw. "Nope, you're wrong there too." He set his plate down next to his cup and walked off the porch, his hands shoved in his pockets.

A week later, Audrey and the children had settled back into a routine, though still a somewhat subdued one. Julian had resumed his stories to the kids at night, needing the time with them as much as they seemed to enjoy having him near them. He and Audrey rarely spoke. She had retreated to someplace inside herself.

He saw her pass by his den on her way upstairs with a cup of tea and hurried to the door to call her back. "Audrey, could I have a word with you?"

She stopped and looked at him. No emotion showed on her face. She nodded and followed him back inside his den. He shut the door, then moved away from her before his yearning to hold her displaced his better intentions. She'd made it clear how she felt about him. He had to be a man and accept it.

At his desk, he turned and faced her. He withdrew his pocket watch and checked the date. "A month ago, you said your menstrual cycle was regular. If it is, then in four days you will know whether you are expecting my child." He looked at her. "In five days I will ask you to tell me if you are indeed pregnant."

The teacup rattled in her hand. She set it down and folded her arms as she watched him warily.

"If you are not expecting, we will pack the children up and I will take all of you to Cheyenne or Denver or wherever it is that you would like to go. With the sewing machine."

"And if I am with child?"

"Then we will marry."

Audrey couldn't believe her ears. He hadn't come to her since the night they argued. It had to be unlikely she would conceive after one unintentional encounter. Her arms tightened over her stomach. She was torn between wishing she was pregnant so that she could stay with Julian forever and wishing she had the strength to face the alternative. His proposal, if that was what it could be called, was delivered without any emotion whatsoever. He did not want to marry her.

And who could blame him? He had the pick of debutants from the upper echelon of Washington society. She was merely a convenient backwoods woman he had bedded.

No matter what, she wouldn't let him do it. He deserved better. He deserved the life he wanted. "Then we shall speak again in five days," she finally answered him.

The house was silent and dark. Julian quietly made his way upstairs to his room. He took off his vest and threw it across the foot of his bed, then sank down on the edge of his mattress. His every movement felt heavy, as if he moved through water. He took his boots off, then went to the washbowl and pitcher to clean his hands and face and brush his teeth.

None of it made him feel any better. Without Audrey, nothing would ever make him feel better. He'd said he would take her anywhere she wanted to go. And he would. But he would stay there too, make sure she was safe and, if not happy, at least not suffering.

He stretched across his bed and stared up at the ceiling. It was the night of the third day. Tomorrow her menses should commence. He would have his answer in two days.

Audrey felt no cramps, no swelling, no discomfort in the days since her discussion with Julian. On the fifth day, her bleeding had still not begun. She was jittery at breakfast, feeling as if he watched her too closely. After he had gone out with Franklin and the kids had started their studies, she pulled Bertie aside.

"What is the matter with you, Audrey? You look as uptight as a cat tied in a sack."

Audrey wrung her hands together. "My courses are late."

Bertie patted her shoulder. "Well, now, don't you fret. You've had a stressful month, with the attack and losing Malcolm and all. It's natural that your body is acting funny."

"You don't think I—I'm pregnant?" Some of the women, besides Amy's mother, had become pregnant at Sam's. Surely Bertie would know what the symptoms were.

"I ain't no doctor. I sure wouldn't like to guess if you were or weren't."

"What are some of the symptoms? How would I know if I was?"

"Have you been vomiting?"

"No."

"Dizzy?"

"No."

"Extra hungry or peeing a lot?"

"No."

"Then I bet you're not pregnant. Just give it a few days and you'll know."

Audrey wanted to scream. She didn't have a few days.

"Honey," Bertie continued, "if you are, it won't be the end of the world. Who will notice one more child?" She smiled. "You're here among people who love you. We'll get through this together."

At supper that night, Audrey's nerves sizzled until she felt dizzy. She no sooner sat at the table than she had to pee, even though she'd just been to the outhouse. She was starving, but she ate too fast and then felt ill. She sighed heavily. This was foolishness. She'd just talked herself into all the symptoms Bertie had mentioned this morning. She wasn't pregnant. It was just stress. No one got pregnant after one time.

Did they?

"Are you still hungry, Audrey? Shall I carve more chicken?" Julian asked from the other end of the table, his eyes watchful.

"Yes. No!" She looked around the table. "Perhaps the kids would like some more?"

When the meal was over, the kids went out to do their chores. Audrey started to help Bertie with the supper dishes.

"Audrey, I'd like a word with you in the den, please,"

Julian quietly requested as he stood by the hall-way door.

"I'll be along as soon as I finish in here."

"You go on, Audrey." Bertie shooed her away. "See what the man wants. I'll do these."

Audrey looked at Julian as he held the door for her. More than anything in the world, she wished she could step into his arms and bury her face in his chest, have him hold her as he'd done so many times in the past. She followed him down the hallway and into his den. He closed the door behind her. She did feel like vomiting now. She must have caught a stomach disorder.

He came to stand in front of her. Not a foot separated them, but it seemed unbearably far from him. She couldn't read his expression. She felt disconnected from him. If she said she was pregnant, those words would bind him to her forever. She would rob him of the life he was entitled to. And if she said she was not, she would lose him forever. Neither choice was one she desired.

He broke the silence. "It's been five days."

"I'm not pregnant, Julian." He shut his eyes and bit his lip. She dropped her gaze, unable to witness his relief.

"Then we will begin packing. You will take everything you think will be of help to you in the new home we find for you. I don't want the children to do without."

"Julian, it's easier if you just put the kids and me on a wagon and send us on our way."

"I will see you to your new situation, Audrey. We will find a building whose size is adequate for you and the children to live in a portion of it and have your shop in the public area. And I will be hiring a staff of seamstresses for you to employ. I will not have you hunting for a situation. And I will not leave you to deal with this alone."

"No." She shook her head. The fool man. She was setting him free. Couldn't he see that?

"Yes. Denver is not the place to turn to picking pockets if your seamstress plan doesn't pan out. And in Cheyenne, they'll just shoot you and save the trial expense. I won't leave you to that."

"You're making that up." She glared at him.

"I'm not making up the fact that I intend to see you happy and settled. Now, do you want to tell the children, or shall I?"

This wasn't good. If this move took too long, and she was indeed pregnant, then he would see the evidence and still force her to marry him. The sooner she gave in and accepted his help, the sooner he could be on his way back to his real life.

"I will tell them."

She gathered the children together that night in the girls' room. Julian was not in the house; for that she was thankful. She had no idea how the children would take the news.

"What's the matter, Audrey?" Luc asked. "Why are we having a family meeting?"

Audrey looked at the faces of her children. They'd grown healthy and happy here. Their cheeks had color. Their eyes were bright. She was grateful for their stay. "We will be leaving Hell's Gulch in a few days."

"Why?" Kurt asked. "I thought this was going to be our home."

"We have imposed on Mr. McCaid long enough. We need to leave him to his life now."

"I thought he was going to be our father," Mabel said, her eyes watering.

"I thought so too," Tommy agreed.

"Where are we going?" Luc asked.

"We're going to look at Cheyenne. If that town doesn't need a seamstress, then we'll go on down to Denver."

"What's Mr. McCaid going to do?" Luc continued.

"He is coming with us to see us settled, then he will go back home. He has important things to do, such as finding a wife and running his businesses. We've taken up too much of his time."

Luc gave her a hard look, then spun on his heel and left the room. Joey and Dulcie exchanged a look. Mabel started crying. Amy climbed up on Colleen's lap. Kurt, Tommy, and Joey silently filed out the door.

Audrey sat unmoving, wondering how that had gone.

That night, after Audrey went to bed and once Mr. McCaid quit pacing in his room, Luc and Kurt woke the other boys, and they returned to the girls' room for a second meeting. They slipped inside quietly and shut the door. Luc woke Colleen and drew her over to the other bed, away from Amy. Amy sometimes cried when she woke up, and they couldn't risk being caught out of bed.

Dulcie and Mabel sat up, confused at seeing the boys in their room. All seven children sat on their bed.

"What do you think about what Audrey said?" Luc opened the conversation. He'd watched the sheriff hold his meetings with the ranchers. He knew how to run a meeting. Start off with the issue at hand, then let others speak, then tell them how it was going to be.

"I don't want to go," Colleen said.

"I don't want to leave Willie," Dulcie said. That shocked the others. For a minute, they simply looked at her, then Luc nodded.

"We gotta do something. There's gotta be some way of stopping this," Kurt said in an urgent whisper that had Luc shushing him.

"Maybe we could get Jenkins to help," Colleen said.

"How could he help?" Luc scoffed.

Mabel smiled. "He could have wagon problems."

"That would only delay our going, not let us stay here for good." Luc shook his head.

"Well, maybe a delay would be good enough." Kurt grinned. "We could take the time to work on getting Audrey to change her mind."

"Maybe you should talk to Mr. McCaid, Luc. He listens to you," Joey suggested.

"Let's see if we can get Audrey to change her mind first."

"We could all get sick," Tommy offered. "My whole school closed down when we got the measles."

"What's the measles?" Mabel asked. "I don't think I want to get sick."

"Not really sick, pretend sick. You get a spotty rash and you itch and cough and you get a fever and you hurt all over. It lasts for weeks," Tommy explained.

Kurt and Luc looked at each other. "That's brilliant. If we each get sick, say in a couple days of each other, it'll be more than a month before we could leave. And by then, maybe Audrey and Mr. McCaid won't be fighting anymore."

"I don't think they were fighting," Joey said. "She don't got any bruises."

"Some people fight differently," Luc explained. "Sometimes they fight with words. Real quiet words."

"How can we fake a rash?" Colleen asked.

"We could rub sand on our skin. And we could wrap ourselves in blankets until we get hot, then call Audrey to check on us."

With that, a plan was hatched. The boys returned to their room feeling very much better. The spotty fever would begin tomorrow, with Colleen.

Chapter 33

Audrey worriedly watched Colleen at breakfast the next morning. She looked flushed and had begun a dry cough. She sat too far away for Audrey to be able to touch her forehead. "Colleen, are you getting sick?"

Colleen cleared her throat and looked at Audrey. "I don't think so. Why?"

Audrey shook her head. "I was just worrying about your cough."

"I'll give her some hot honeyed tea. That'll fix her right up," Bertie offered.

A few minutes later, tea in hand, Colleen and the other children settled in for their morning schoolwork. Audrey fretted about her, but Colleen assured her she was fine. As soon as she left with Amy, Kurt handed her a small pouch of sand. She dabbed some on her fingers and rubbed her face with it, then hid the pouch.

Luc grinned at her. "Take your cup and put it to your face. That'll really prove you got the spotty fever."

Colleen did as he suggested, holding the hot cup as close as she could to her face. In a short while, Audrey returned to check their work and help with questions.

She took one look at Colleen and ordered her off to bed. She sent a worried glance over the other children, searching for any sign they were becoming ill. Just last summer, when Rachel and Sager were getting married, the children had a round of chicken pox. It went through all seven children—Tommy hadn't arrived yet. That was one of the hardest months she'd yet endured as a mother. Hopefully this was just a short-lived cold Colleen had.

At supper that night, Julian noticed Colleen's absence. "She got the spotty fever," Mabel told him around a mouthful of peas.

"Spotty fever?" He looked at Audrey.

"She has a rash and a fever."

"Chicken pox?"

"No, she had that last year," Audrey told him. "This is different."

"Measles, then?"

"I hope not. That brings a high temperature, doesn't it?"

"It does. My sisters were very sick with it one year," Julian commented. "I've had it myself, but don't remember the experience."

After supper, Audrey and Julian visited Colleen in her room, keeping her company while she ate soup. Poor thing. Her throat was so sore, she could barely swallow.

Julian felt her forehead. She was warm, though maybe not feverish. The rash looked odd. It was just on her cheeks. He remembered his sisters getting the measles the summer before his life had gone to hell. Colleen's rash was mostly on her face, but Julian thought his sisters had rashes from their hairlines down to their chests. And they were much more feverish. But perhaps this wasn't the measles. Or perhaps she had a mild case of it.

Without a doctor's diagnosis, it would be impossible to know for sure.

Within the next four days, five children were sick in bed. Audrey and Bertie ran themselves ragged caring for them. Julian had quarantined the girls' room. Tommy and Joey were sick, as were Colleen, Mabel, and Dulcie. Amy was put to bed with Luc. Kurt slept in Tommy and Joey's bed.

Julian was bringing up a tray of hot soups and a soothing salve Audrey had concocted to rub on their chests to help them breathe better when he found Audrey leaning with her head against the jamb of the girls' room, her hand on the closed door. He quickly set his tray down and hurried to her side.

"Julian—" Her voice broke on a sob as she looked up at him, her face showing her fatigue and fear.

He swung her up into his arms and carried her to her room. "You've had enough. I'm putting you to bed too."

"I can't. I have to stay with the children."

"I'll stay with them. You aren't alone in this, Audrey Sheridan." He set her gently on her bed.

Tears collected in her eyes. "I am alone, Julian."

"You don't have to be. You choose to be."

She touched his cheek, studying his eyes. He kissed her hand, then leaned forward and kissed her cheek. "Please rest tonight. I will be with the children."

"I haven't done any packing. We're supposed to be getting ready for the move."

"The move can wait." *Forever.* "I don't want you getting sick. I'm going to feed the kids, and then I'll come back and check on you."

Audrey sniffled and rolled to her side, too tired to undress. She was always weeping lately. She missed her brother. She missed Julian. And the children were so sick. Her monthly time would never start if this stress kept up.

Julian sat with the sick kids while they coughed and whimpered through their broth. He looked at the lot of them, thinking something just wasn't as it should be. And then he figured out what bothered him. They were all sitting up. His sisters had to be held while broth was spooned into their mouths. These kids were . . . perky.

He excused himself and went downstairs to round up Kurt and Luc for bed, preoccupied with what he'd just discovered. Amy had to be taken to the outhouse—she was too young yet to go by herself. She scampered ahead of him and saw to her business while he waited at the door. When she finished, she straightened her clothes as they went around to the wash station. Halfway back to the house, she bent and collected a handful of dirt and sand and began briskly scrubbing it against her cheeks.

"Amy Lynn, what are you doing?"

"I'm getting the spotty fever!" She grinned up at him.

Reality blasted in on him with the force of a wooden beam. He picked her up and stormed back to the house. Inside, he set her down and told her to go get Luc. Luc came alone into his den.

"I would like to have a word with you and all the children. You will please bring them down here."

"They're sick, Mr. McCaid. I don't think I should get them out of bed."

Julian looked grim. "I think, if you don't get them out of bed, you will discover an aspect of my personality you have not yet encountered."

"Yessir."

Not a minute later, all eight children were lined up in his office. He paced in front of them, anger warring with curiosity. He made another pass by them, looking each one in the eye. "One of you will please tell me what the hell is going on."

"It was my idea, sir. Not theirs," Luc spoke up.

"We all thought of it together, Luc," Kurt clarified.

"There's no point in all of us getting a whipping," Luc growled at Kurt.

"I can take a whipping as well as you," Kurt responded.

Julian spoke up before the boys could come to blows. "There's not going to be any whippings given out. At least, not until I get to the bottom of this. Now, what is it you all thought of together?" Julian came to a stop in front of the older boys.

"Audrey told us we were moving."

"And we didn't want to go."

"We thought if we could get sick, good and sick, then maybe you two would quit fighting and we could stay."

"This is the best home we ever had, sir."

Julian felt that confession like a fist in his gut. "Did Audrey tell you we were fighting?"

"No. She said you had important stuff to do and we were keeping you from it."

"Stuff like running your businesses and finding a wife."

"Why couldn't Audrey be your wife? Then you could be our dad."

That brought Julian up short. He'd done everything in his power to show Audrey how he felt. Hadn't he? He'd told her he loved her. He even offered marriage, if she were pregnant. He shut his eyes, hearing that pronouncement. God, what a damned fool he'd been. Who would accept a proposal like that? Had she declined because of the graceless way he delivered his offer and not because of who—what—he was?

His heart began a painful beating. Did he still have

a chance with her? He looked down the line of the children. "Is that how you all feel?"

As one, they nodded. Except Luc. "Luc?" Julian prompted.

He sniffed and wiped the back of his hand against his nose. "I had me a pa once." He shook his head. "I reckon I don't ever want another." Kurt slammed his elbow into Luc's side. "But, maybe, if you was to be our pa, well, maybe that would be okay. I guess."

Julian crossed his arms and glared at the kids. His heart was hammering so fast, it made thinking difficult. "Well then, you'd best be off to bed. Colleen, please help Amy Lynn wash the spotty fever off her cheeks. I will think up a suitable punishment for the lot of you. In the future, you will speak to me directly when you have a problem and not pull this type of shenanigans. I expect to see you all at the breakfast table, clean and healthy. Good night."

The kids filed out of his office, but in the hallway, they let out a loud whoop! Julian popped his head outside his office. "You've exhausted Audrey with your playacting this week. You will get yourselves settled quietly. Now."

"Yessir!" they called as they hurried away.

Julian sat in the wing chair in Audrey's room and watched her sleep. She still wore her dress, but he'd pulled a blanket over her. For the first time in weeks, maybe even in his lifetime, he felt happy. He knew who he was and what he wanted. This turn in his life wasn't where he'd expected to find himself. It was far better. If the kids wanted him in their lives, he knew he could convince Audrey.

"Julian?" she whispered from her bed as she leaned up on her elbows to look at him.

"Yes."

"What are you doing?" she asked sleepily.

He drew a fortifying breath. "I love you."

She sat up, regarding him. "But it isn't enough, is it?"

"It's enough. It's everything." He moved to sit on the edge of her bed. "Marry me, Audrey. Make me whole again. I can't bear to face life without you." He didn't touch her. He didn't want to overwhelm her.

"You really do love me?"

A pained huff of breath broke from him. "With every fiber of my being. I even love your eight misbegotten orphans too. I cannot live without the lot of you in my life."

Audrey covered her face and started crying. "I don't know what's wrong with me. I can't seem to quit crying. Julian, I love you so much it hurts." She hiccuped. "I've tried all this month to set you free. And you just wouldn't go."

He wrapped his arms around her and held her tight. "I thought you were ashamed of me. Because of what I am."

She drew back and looked at him. "How could I be ashamed of you? You are beautiful. And kind. And generous. I was ashamed of me. I'm no society girl. I will embarrass you, I'm sure."

"Never, heart of mine." He kissed her then. Sweetly. He breathed her essence. "God, I've missed you this month. You wouldn't let me comfort you over Malcolm. I could do nothing but watch you suffer."

She looked up into his eyes, wishing the moonlight was brighter so she could see his expression more clearly. "Julian, I think I might be pregnant. My courses haven't begun."

He stilled. She drew a ragged breath.

His hand went to her stomach, feeling the flat plane of her belly. "If you aren't, Audrey Sheridan, you soon will be." He drew her to her feet. "Why don't you change into your nightgown? You need to rest. Tomorrow's your wedding day."

"My wedding day?"

"Yes. I'm not living another day without making you mine."

"You'll stay with me tonight?"

"Always, my love."

Audrey changed, then climbed back into bed. It was sheer heaven feeling the bed dip as Julian settled next to her. He wrapped his arms around her and drew her back against his body.

"There's one other thing, Audrey."

"Mmm-hmm?" she mumbled, fading fast.

"The kids are all better now. They were faking a 'spotty fever' so that they wouldn't have to leave. I guess they've voted me in as their dad, if that's okay with you."

"They're bad kids, Julian."

"No, my love." He kissed her cheek. "They're perfect." Brilliant, in fact. He set his large hand against her belly, hoping against hope she was indeed expecting.

Chapter 34

Audrey sat next to Julian the next morning as he drove the wagon into town. The day had a dreamlike feel to it, as if she were observing something happening to someone else. She sat close to Julian, unable to bear being near him without touching him. She was so excited; she wasn't sure whether she'd stopped grinning the whole trip in. He smiled down at her and wrapped an arm about her shoulders.

Julian drew up outside Jim's store, pulling behind another wagon. He jumped down, then lifted Audrey down, pausing for a minute to grin at her before helping the kids down. The children ran into the store and the adults quickly followed.

"Julian!" Jim hollered as he hurried from the counter to greet him. "You came back!" he said, shock evident on his face as he pumped Julian's hand in a robust handshake.

"I never left."

Hearing the commotion, Sally hurried from the back room. "Oh, thank God!" she whispered fiercely as she came forward to give Audrey a quick hug. The door behind them opened and banged close, admitting Sager, Rachel, Jacob, and Maddie.

"Audrey!" Rachel exclaimed, coming over to hug Audrey. "I haven't seen you for too long! I was sorry to hear about your brother. How are you doing?"

"Thank you, Rachel. I miss him terribly. But I have good news—Julian and I are getting married today!"

Rachel squealed and hugged Audrey.

Julian shook hands with Sager, noticing immediately that something wasn't right with his friend. "What's wrong?" he asked.

Sager made a face. "It's Jace."

"What's wrong with Jace?" He looked from Sager to Jim.

"I had to send for Sager, Julian. We thought you'd left. No one could stop him. He's gone berserk."

"What do you mean?" Julian asked. The room grew silent. Audrey stood with the women, but turned to focus on the conversation the men were having.

"Leah left him," Jim started.

"He's been unable to find her."

"I went to see if I could pick up her trail." Sager shook his head. "She's not coming back."

Audrey reached for Sally's hand. "She did this before, when the sheriff killed her father. She was gone for a month then." She looked at the worried faces of her friends. "Leah did come back then. She'll come back from this."

"It's too late. Jace has gone crazy. No one in town will help him—they're all afraid of him, after how he handled the sheriff," Jim said.

Julian frowned. "What's he doing?"

"He's tearing down the shanties with his bare hands. He's out of his mind."

Sager exchanged a look with Julian. They'd both

seen what happened to him after his wife's betrayal during the war.

Julian sighed and turned to Audrey. She smiled at him. "Go. He needs you."

He kissed her cheek and left with Sager. They had only to step outside and turn down the street to see the havoc Jace was creating along the row of shanties where Audrey and Leah had lived. The house closest to the store was just a rubble heap. The second house was in an imminent state of collapse, the roof bowing down over the front half of the house.

They walked around the far side of the house and found Jace gripping one end of a long piece of siding with his hands, a boot braced against the wall as he tugged at the wood. Red marks stained the board when he repositioned his hands to get a different grip. Julian looked at Sager.

"Hi, Jace. What are you doing?" Julian asked casually, at a loss as to how he could reach his friend. He thought he'd try a normal, calm approach first.

Jace did not respond.

"Jace, what's goin' on? What are you doing?" Sager asked, coming up and touching Jace's shoulder. Jace shrugged him off. Sager put a hand on Jace's shoulder and another on his arm and pulled him away from the house. "Come on, it's enough now."

Jace turned and planted a fist in Sager's jaw. "Leave me the fuck alone." He turned back to the piece of siding, which he now had half off. "She did," he muttered. Julian wasn't certain he'd heard that correctly.

Sager had a hand on his jaw. He'd expected the blow and had been able to deflect the worst of the punch. He angled his jaw back and forth as Julian came up behind Jace and pulled him away from the house. Jace landed an elbow in Julian's ribs and turned to face his friends, fists clenched.

There was something unfocused about his eyes, something akin to madness, Julian thought. Jace lurched forward, and Julian and Sager jumped him, slamming him back against the splintering siding, restraining his legs with theirs, pinning his fists above his head.

"What the hell's wrong with you?" Julian asked.

Jace's face was tense, his eyes dark. His breathing was shallow and irregular. "Get off me!" he fumed through clenched teeth, still struggling to be freed. Neither friend let go of him.

"Not yet. Not till you're calmer," Julian declared.

"Jesus, look at his hands."

The remnants of his leather gloves hung in shredded tatters from his fingers and palms. Bright red blood flowed freely from his torn skin, splinters spiking through the swelling flesh.

"That's it. You've done enough. Let's get you cleaned up." Julian pulled him from the wall but did not release him. He and Sager walked on either side of Jace, holding his arms folded behind him as they headed for the public water pump a little ways down the street.

Audrey, Rachel, and Maddie hurried toward them to see what they could do to help; Sally stayed with the kids at the store. As the men passed the women, Julian sent Maddie for some hot water, salt, bowls to soak his hands in, scissors, tweezers, and bandages. She hurried off to gather those things. Audrey went ahead to prime the pump. Julian and Sager pushed him to sit on the low rock wall surrounding the waterworks. He complied without resistance now. The men stood back and let the women take over getting him cleaned up.

Audrey was stunned. Jace looked nothing like the man she'd seen in her kitchen several weeks ago. His shoulders hung limp, his hair was dusty and matted with dirt, blood, and construction debris. His eyes were bloodshot and unfocused. His cheeks were gaunt, his hands shredded. Blood was splattered over his clothes, dried on his face. Dirt was caked into his clothes, as if he'd lived the last year in the same outfit. A weeks' growth of beard added to his unkempt appearance.

Audrey brushed a chunk of his once golden-bronze hair away from his face. "What happened, Jace?" she whispered. He didn't respond, didn't even look at her, just stared listlessly into space.

Rachel set to work cutting off the glove of his left hand so that she could soak his hand in the warm salt water Maddie brought over. She handed the scissors to Audrey, who repeated the procedure with his right hand. The salt water on his raw skin should have elicited some reaction, but he gave no indication he felt anything.

Watching, Julian wondered if he would ever be able to handle a pistol again. "Where are your guns, Jace?"

"I took them off."

Audrey looked at him, thinking of the ordeal it had been to get him to remove his guns when he'd visited Hell's Gulch.

"Where are they?" Sager asked.

He shrugged. "I dunno."

Rachel bent over his hand, trying to clean out all the foreign objects he'd gotten embedded in his skin. Audrey dampened a cloth and washed the blood and dirt from his face.

He looked at her. "She wanted a church."

Audrey smiled. Leah had always wished they had a church in town. For a while, a traveling preacher used to provide Sunday service at least one week a month. Audrey wondered what happened to him. It had been years since he'd come through.

Jace stared at the line of tiny houses behind her. "I'm tearing down those shacks. Gonna build her a big white church." A muscle at the corner of his jaw flexed. "Then maybe she'll come home."

Audrey and Rachel exchanged a look. "With a bell," Rachel added. "It needs a bell so that we can ring it and call her back."

He looked at Rachel and nodded. "A bell."

"There's a thunderstorm threatening. I think we should take him inside," Audrey said to Maddie, feeling the chill in the air as the storm blew in.

"I've got water heating for a bath," she answered. "I'll fetch a change of clothes from his packs while you two get him cleaned up."

"Whoaa—he's a grown man. He doesn't need help in the bath," Julian grumbled as he lifted Jace by the armpits and hoisted him to his feet.

"Look at his hands, Julian. He can't bathe himself." Audrey gave Julian an admonishing glance. "It's not as if we haven't seen a nude man before."

The women each tucked one of Jace's arms around their shoulders and turned him toward Maddie's house, supporting him with an arm around his waist.

As he watched them go, Julian's brows lowered. "Sonofabitch."

Sager laughed and pounded him on the back. "Jace is in no shape to be thinking what you're thinking. Let's go get the kids. I bet Sally's worn out by now." They started down the street toward the general store. "What are you doing in town today anyway, all of you in your fancy duds? Did I hear Audrey say something about a wedding?"

Julian sighed. "Audrey and I were going to get married today."

"Well, I'll be damned," Sager said in shock. "You did come to your senses. Rachel said you would." He clapped his hands, then rubbed them together. "This calls for a celebration!"

Two hours later, with a feast on hold in the kitchen and Jace bathed, shaved, and standing in fresh clothes, Audrey and Julian exchanged their vows in Maddie's front parlor.

Julian was struck by every detail about Audrey as he stood before her, about to kiss his wife for the first time. She wore her prettiest dress—a beautiful sage-green wool dress with a scoop neck that showed her soft skin from her throat all the way down to the tops of her breasts. He leaned toward her, his eyes open, wishing he could run his hand from her cheek down that soft expanse of skin. She smiled as she met his kiss, her face coloring. He grinned—his wife was a mind reader.

The children swarmed them then. Audrey kissed their cheeks and hugged each of them. Julian picked up Amy so that she wouldn't be trampled and turned to his friends. The women hurried back to the feast that was ready to be served up. Sager shook his hand, grinning like a man who believed in love. And then came Jace.

Julian shook hands with him at the wrist, a less painful proposition for Jace's bandaged hands. "I'm sorry—" Julian began, but Jace stopped him.

"I'm happy for you, my friend. I was afraid you'd screw this up." Jace's smile did not reach his eyes. What the hell had happened between him and Leah? Before Julian could dwell too long on those concerns, Jim brought over some choice cigars and poured celebratory whiskies for all the men as they awaited supper.

It was an eternity later before Julian and Audrey lay in their marriage bed in one of Maddie's boarding rooms. The bed wasn't as large as those Julian had grown accustomed to, and his feet hung off the end of it. But Audrey was naked and snuggled up next to him—he couldn't remember ever being happier.

"We never talked about what our life would be like once we were married," he said as he absently stroked his thumb over her skin.

"No, we didn't." She brushed his hair away from his forehead and leaned over to kiss the faint cleft in his jaw.

"I'd like to stay in town and help Sager and Jace build that church."

"Mmm-hmm."

"Then, perhaps, we could go to Virginia. You mentioned you wanted to go to the States sometime. We could spend the holidays with my family."

She pulled back, her eyes aglow with happiness. "All of us?"

"Of course all of us. How could we enjoy the holidays without the children? We're a family, Audrey McCaid." He put his hand on her belly. "All eleven of us."

She squealed with delight and straddled him, pressing kisses to his cheeks and lips and nose. He had a hard time remembering what he was trying to say to her.

"After that, I usually go to the Caribbean to check up on our family shipping interests there. Have you ever been to the ocean?"

Audrey pushed up from his chest, her hands on his shoulders, her hips rocking against his hardening cock. God, this was torture. She shook her head, her eyes wide.

"Then, perhaps, we could come back here and spend the summer."

"All of us, together?"

He growled and rolled her over, embedding himself in her slick warmth. "Always, my love."